The *OREGON REBELLION*

E.G. Ross

PREMIERE EDITIONS INTERNATIONAL, INC.
CORVALLIS, OREGON

OTHER TECHNO-THRILLER NOVELS BY E. G. ROSS:
Engels Extension
Project BTB

AUDIO CASSETTE NOVELLAS BY E. G. ROSS:
Before the Beginning: Lost in the Caves
Before the Beginning: The Revelation

DAILY INTERNET NEWSLETTER EDITED BY E. G. ROSS:
www.ObjectiveAmerican.com

PREMIERE EDITIONS INTERNATIONAL, INC.
2397 NW Kings Blvd. #311, Corvallis, OR 97330
(541) 752-4239 – *FAX (541) 752-4463*
– *email: publish@premiere-editions.com*

Visit our Internet web site: *www.premiere-editions.com*

EDITORS: Irene L. Gresick
                  Beatrice Stauss

DESIGNERS: Karen Freeman
                  René Redelsperger

ISBN: 1-891519-17-4
Library of Congress Control Number: 2001087148
Printed in the United States of America

Defiance, not obedience, is the American's answer to overbearing authority.

— Ayn Rand

Acknowledgments

As always, to my wife, Susan A. Peterson, for her untiring reflection, insight, and encouragement; to Irene Gresick and her staff at Premiere Editions International for their excellent work and confidence; to Jeff Lewis and Orrin Stoddard of Lewis Systems for their loyalty and support; and to my many fine, anonymous contacts in the defense and technology communities for their tips, explanations, and corrections.

Prologue

What's going on?" the sergeant yelled into the dented, dirt-crusted radio. "Talk to me!"

There was a short pause and a click. Then the young soldier's voice hissed in an urgent, rushing whisper, peppered with digital breakup, barely comprehensible, "Sir, they're . . . the match to the butt of the nuke . . . at the *capital* . . . Sir, what do I . . . can't squat here like a—"

"Take it easy, soldier," the sergeant soothed. "We're on your trail. Stay *cool, son,* or you'll bust us open like a rotten pumpkin!"

"Yes, sir!"

Face deeply lined with the strain of responsibility, the sergeant turned to his corporal. "I think he got that. I hope. Okay, listen up. In one minute you and I push in with Alpha, right behind our wonder boy. Set the others to flank. We'll be rollin' our smokes on the run."

The corporal frowned, "Sir, if I understood what I just heard, shouldn't we try to notify the capital to evacuate?"

The sergeant snorted and spat to one side. "The civvies wouldn't know how to scramble or where to ramble. Now get moving!"

"Yes, sir!"

The corporal slid down the slight rise and slogged over the marshy ground. A chilling trickle of sweat ran down his spine as he muttered to himself, "How the hell could this be happening? How did it come to this? How did things get away from everyone so *fast*?"

PART ONE:

"We the People"

Chapter 1

"The GIRA Disease"

State Senate President J.B. Washington loosened his maroon tie. Sweat stung his eyes. He was a big, tall man with a burly red beard and thick-fingered hands. He fished out a crumpled handkerchief and wiped his face. The air conditioning in the senate chambers was out again. The janitorial union's strike had seen to that. The temperature of the early August morning was edging past ninety. The forecast called for a high near 105, exceptionally warm for Salem, Oregon.

J.B. leaned back in his black, high-backed leather chair and let his imagination wander. Let's see, he thought as he closed his eyes, where would I rather be? Ah, yes. Silver Falls would be nice about now. He visualized walking the trail that wound under the hundred-foot waterfall in the hills 30 miles east of Salem. He'd been there many times. He could almost feel the cool back-spray on his face and see the lush collection of sword ferns, vine maple, and trillium lining the rock of the huge, bowl-shaped basin into which the water plunged. He remembered the icy tingle on his skin when, as a kid, he used to swim in the deep pool under the falls. An angry shout brought him back to reality. He sighed, reluctantly opened his eyes, and looked around the room.

Tempers were riding the heat. For nine sweltering weeks J.B. and his honorable colleagues had argued. And argued.

And argued some more. It was mind-numbing. The whole political fracas was about a single item: what to do about the lingering Oregon recession. Unemployment in June had topped an unheard of 18%. The state's residents were screaming. They wanted relief and they wanted it now.

Of course, the other states and the federal government were mired in their own economic *and* foreign problems. The malaise was nationwide. Uncle Sam not only had no financial help to offer Oregon, but had recently implemented a stiff 10% national sales surtax. It was hitting most of the states hard, but Oregon especially so. Oregon was a proud state with a tough, independent pioneer tradition. This new federal burden seemed callous. What was it his wife, Julie, had called it? "An indifferent elbow to the jaw." That was about it, J.B. thought. He ground sweat out of his eyes with his thumb knuckles and sighed heavily.

Not that the feds would budge on Oregon's account. They had a ready excuse, of course. The U.S. Constitution didn't permit discriminatory taxation. If the rest of the nation had to suffer the new tax, well, too bad that Oregon's economy was among the least able to handle it.

J.B. swore inaudibly, "We're like a house cat trying to swallow a deer."

He reached under his desk and pulled a Coke out of the small fridge. He cracked it open with a practiced movement. It was his latest vice. He took a long swig while secretly wishing for a cigarette instead. Six months ago he'd assured Julie that he'd quit for good. But lately he'd been sneaking in three or four a day. He felt guilty, but consoled himself by giving silent credit to her political observations at breakfast that morning. She'd nailed it. If Oregon was to recover soon from its first and worst recession of the 21st century, it was going to have to nurse *itself* back to health. But with exactly what medicine? After all, these were not exactly the days of Dubya Bush, when trimming taxes and red tape was still considered smart and popular policy.

He squinted across the haze of the chamber, watching his

colleagues sweat and bicker. Bless Julie's helpful heart, but diagnosis was only half the answer. These doctors of democracy weren't stupid. Probably too good-willed by half. In J.B.'s opinion, it was Oregon's long history of well-meant self-burdening that had led to its present problems. GIRA—Good Intentions Run Amok.

How far back did it go? He searched his memory. Oh, yes, 1844. Fifteen years before statehood, under the hand of the Provisional Government, Oregon had started regular levies "to cure its defects." The taxes had built up over the decades— falling only temporarily—and always for some noble purpose or another. Like crows following carrion, more regulations tended to accompany the taxation. The old government guaranteed obedience to its levies by a simple expedient—it refused to protect citizens who wouldn't pay. If someone stole your land or cattle, well, too bad; no help from the government. Even back then, the levies were professedly noble. After all, as in most states, there was never an end to what some politician or pressure group thought was "in the public good" and deserved tax support. Yep, J.B. thought, our motives have always been pure-hearted and high-minded. It's always been the best altruism Oregon tax money could buy.

Now? Well, he mused, it was adding up. As simple as that. With years of noble goals and virtuous tax-spending piled on a scale, the weight of the accumulated costs had grown outlandish. Worse, voters were using a lot of "or else" language. He shuddered. It was hard to believe, but two legislators had been attacked and beaten by mobs in their home towns. It was unheard of in easy-going Oregon. Five years ago, he could not have imagined it would come to this. Not in his craziest, most catastrophist daydreams.

Yet there it was. The GIRA disease. Decades of infection was tough to fight. Of course, Oregon politics had always been tumultuous. He chuckled to himself, recalling that it took several votes to *get* statehood. There'd even been a movement to make Oregon an independent republic. And not a few citizens wanted to become part of Great Britain's empire. Bickering and brawling were part and parcel of Oregon history. He grinned. Actually, politics could be thought of as the unofficial state sport. Certainly more people followed politics than followed the Blazers, Beavers, and Ducks combined.

He looked out at his fellow senators and his grin slowly faded. He sipped his Coke and grimaced. Truth was, he saw nothing promising on the legislative field this morning—and J.B. could see quite a lot. Or so the pundits said. "The political sight of an eagle," the *Oregonian*'s editors had complimented him once. He felt another stab of guilt. If they only knew how much of his foresight over the years had been through his wife Julie's eyes. He might have eagle wings, but she was the one with the eagle eyes. He gave her far too little public credit. He'd have to work on that.

He scratched an itch deep in his beard and watched young Jim "Ben" Colby, the senator from Springfield, rise to speak. Colby was pot-bellied, balding, with a wide, good-natured youthful face. The freshman senator waited for three of his elderly colleagues to stop barking at each other. J.B. tolerated their rudeness for a few moments, then banged his gavel with a crack like a shotgun.

"The Honorable Senator Colby of Springfield has the floor gentlemen," he said sternly. "You grumpy old bears can claw each other again later. Give your paws a rest."

The three legislators looked at one another blankly for a moment, caught off guard. They'd fought many times, only to part the day arm-in-arm for the nearest golf course or bar. They plopped down heavily in their padded chairs. Two of them poured ice water.

"Much appreciated, Mr. President," Colby said, nodding toward J.B.

Turning in the direction of the quarrelers, most of whom were twenty years his senior, Colby bowed humbly and said, "I know blood boils these fine days of summer, gentlemen. I don't like getting scalded by it. This is especially so when, unmarried to an old fashioned woman, I have to wash and iron my own shirts and haven't the foggiest notion how to get rid of the stains of senate strife. "

The laughter was light, like a breeze across a grain field. The senators poured ice water or popped open soft drinks and settled back to listen to their colleague. Colby had proven to be a diplomatic, amusing thinker. He was also an excellent orator, although of an older and more flowery school. A bass singer in a barbershop quartet, his rich voice could hold an auditorium without a microphone. The combination of his appearance and personality had earned him the nickname "Ben," for Benjamin Franklin. Colby had sense enough not to discourage the comparison. It was hard for a new senator to make his mark. It didn't hurt to be compared to one of the U.S.'s great Founding Fathers.

"Go ahead, Ben," J.B. urged. He, too, was ready for a bit of entertainment. It would ease everyone's frustration and perhaps generate some ideas. *Somebody* better grab some answers, he thought, or the voters were going to start warming the tar and plucking the chickens.

Colby braced his thumbs in his vest, cleared his throat, and looked over the room.

"Esteemed senators," he began, "has it occurred to any of us that the practical answer to this state's predicament might lie *outside* its borders?"

Several men frowned. Colby raised his eyebrows. "No? I see not. Well, let me back up a stride or two. The average citizen of this great state now pays 20% of his income to the coffers of Oregon. He shook his head sadly. "That is simply too much, and we all know it. The voters are breathing down our well-starched collars."

A few senators snorted. This was news to no one.

"It's a bramble patch," Colby said with more force, "and we've all assumed that it would take this side of forever to find our way out. Up until last night, I agreed. It seemed that the mistakes that took many decades to make could not be unmade quickly. The onerous burdens that this honorable body, in its eagerness to help its own dear citizens — yes, often at their request and demand — cannot be tossed away in a morning, nor indeed in a summer of many mornings. Or so I had once thought."

He paused to sip water. Several senators smiled knowingly. They were waiting for the punchline to one of Colby's infamously overextended jokes.

"Promises have been made, gentlemen; promises to the fixed-income elderly, to the sadly unemployed, to the strapped schools, to those who wish their highways and bridges to be capable of carrying their families to work and play. These obligations and hundreds of others cost money; the money comes from taxes; the taxes cannot be reduced with a single slice of our legislative knife. It may not be fair; it may not be kind; it may ignore the longer term destructive ramifications. But that's how it is. It's a quandary of epic proportions.

"Despite this, the citizens of our state want their loads lightened, *somehow*. The *how* is the horror. Cut, and they squawk that we're shredding their safety net. Don't cut, and they scream that taxes and regulations are killing them. Both are correct, yet it's either one or the other. Or is it? Last night, in the dark of solitude, a different answer came to me. It was blindingly convincing."

The legislators shifted and frowned. This didn't sound like a joke after all. Worse, it was grinding them back to their former state of grumpiness.

Colby instantly realized it and slammed his fist onto his desktop to break their mood. Practically roaring, he said, "Despite the magnitude and meanness of the public mood, and indeed, of our own, all problems have answers! Reason *can* prevail if we've the will and courage to engage it, ladies and gentlemen! We've tinkered and toiled; puttered and pried; doddled and drawn out half-solutions here and crimped compromises there. Out of this we've delayed implementing a true solution. Yes, we must cut taxes. Yes, we must return more services to the more efficient private sector. This, the whole world knows. It's been the planetary trend since the late 1970s. Over time, many formerly hopeless lands of Eastern Europe, Asia, sections of African and most of Latin America, all did it.

They all rapidly prospered. They learned it from us, once the freest of major nations."

"But we're hog-tied for time!" someone shouted with genuine anguish.

Colby turned and pointed at him, nodding vigorously. "Exactly, my truthful friend! Exactly. It will take far too much of the temporal commodity to make sweeping transitions, even though we all know it is the long-term path to prosperity. Better men than I have proven it. I also agree, Honorable Senators of Oregon, others had what we do not: time. They did not have to implement their tax cuts and privatizations—and the ensuing deprivations of the public sector—in the midst of the worst recession since the Great Depression!"

"Well, hell—then we're back where we started, Ben," another man yelled from the opposite side of the aisle. "What's the joke?"

Colby glowered and shook his head. He spoke in a low voice at first, gradually raising the volume. "There is none, sir. No joke. I am not here to provide amusement today. But there *is* an answer to our monumental dilemma. Ladies and gentlemen, I propose a truly radical solution. I propose that we do something untried in a century and a half. I suggest something daring, bold, brazen, and outrageous."

People sat up straighter. Despite the heat, they found goosebumps rising on their arms and legs.

"If my plan doesn't work," Colby continued, his voice exuding a confidence none of them had heard before, "then we shall be no worse off than now." At least I hope not, he thought. He surveyed the huge chamber. "But if it does work, good people, my idea will let us cut the burden of taxation by two-thirds in a *single day!*"

Jaws dropped. A few of his colleagues began to snicker. Ben was known as a careful gradualist, not a radical. This had to be a joke, after all.

Colby did not smile, but rolled on, his sonorous voice almost shaking the chamber.

"Fellow senators," he said, "while the taxes of this state

take 20% of our citizens' money each year, let us not forget another, more impressive fact. The taxes of the nation, of the federal government, now take another 40%. In total, we now bear burdens almost as great as the sad old European socialist states." He took a deep breath, rose to his full height, and said, "Therefore, my esteemed colleagues, I propose that we rid Oregonians of the federal tax."

More than a few senators felt an almost mystical fear at that moment. The look on Colby's face had grown unearthly. They did not recognize him. He looked suddenly towering, unstoppable, and irresistible. It was like watching a ghost of the Founders—or the Oregon Pioneers—step into their midst.

"I propose," he thundered, "that we reject both the benefits and burdens of membership in these United States. I propose that the great state of Oregon secede from the Union *now!*"

After a stunned silence, one man started clapping. Another joined him. Then another. Hesitant hands slowly built into full applause joined by whistles and shouts and foot-stomping. The reaction rose and rose, building into waves of a pounding, roaring crescendo that went on for an impossible, heady twenty minutes.

In one of those rare moments of American progress, the waters of reason and emotion had combined into a gargantuan surge, bursting the dam of politics and creating a flood that history would not and could not ignore.

What it might wash away, no man could say.

Chapter 2

"Varmints Are Rising"

W hat fool's play has my cousin tried now?" U.S. President Sam Washington demanded of Secretary of State Craig Goldstein. They sat together, along with the president's wife, Annette, 3,000 miles away at the White House, wading through the routine work of a Saturday morning, pumped by hot buttered cinnamon rolls and steaming black coffee—Full City brand, imported from Oregon at the president's insistence. At the moment, Washington was going over his daily news summary provided by the White House staff. Looking remarkably like his cousin, J.B., Sam Washington rubbed his temples with two meaty index fingers. He had a headache and it was affecting his mood. He had nearly reached the bottom of the first section of the summary when an odd, two-line item caught his eye.

"Oregon says it's *seceding*?" He looked inquiringly at Goldstein. "What is this bull?"

Annette Washington, thin, tanned, and athletic, tore off a piece of roll with her teeth, waved one slender hand admonishingly, and said, "Watch your nouns, dear. We're having breakfast."

"All right, then. What is this bovine blandishment?"

Annette smiled in spite of her intentions. Her husband had always been a man with a few rough edges.

"I heard it on the radio in the car this morning," she said. "Didn't pay much attention. Probably some wired-up reporter with too much time and too few facts."

"Hmmph," the president said, swallowing coffee. "Don't remind me of the Wire problem. The Senate's threatening to hold up the World Trade Organization modifications unless I get my rear in gear and sign a ban on the device. And if I thought it would solve anything, I would."

He caught his wife's eye. Both shivered, remembering the hair-raising consequences that "the device" had created during the Engels Extension crisis—also known as World War Three. Washington tried to recall the scientific explanation he'd heard. Far more addictive than heroin, the Wire used a type of technology distantly derived from work funded by NASA and the FOM Institute for Atomic and Molecular Physics in Amsterdam in the late 1990s. It came out of a field of science called "entropic depletion ordering." Very crudely stated, an electric current fed through a headset caused a type of resonance which set entropic forces in motion on the cellular level in the brain. These forces led to a self-organizing cascade effect, culminating in a concentration of chemicals that stimulated the brain's pleasure centers. Once perfected, the Wire had proven to be cheap, easy to make, and so far, perfectly legal. The Wire had swept the world and then the nation many times faster than any previous addiction mode.

China was particularly adept at satisfying the American public's demand for the device. Traffic in Chinese Wires was already in the hundreds of millions. That's where the politics got sticky. To ban it would violate the World Trade Organization's free-trade rules. It was, after all, a legal product. Personally, Sam Washington wanted to modify the rules to allow the ban. The Senate wanted the ban first. Yet if *either* happened, China, which was now America's number one trading partner, threatened to impose punitive tariffs on *any* good or service imported from the U.S. Meanwhile, the sharks of Europe, Japan, and South America were hoping that China would do exactly that. A big tariff on U.S. goods would shift trade their way. In this worldwide recession, they'd love to take over even a significant percentage of American trade with China. With a $25 trillion annual gross domestic product, the U.S. market was still gigantic, even during the current economic downturn.

The president burned his tongue on his coffee. He swore, "Some days it doesn't pay to fall out of bed."

"Aw, it's just summer," Craig Goldstein said, trying to mollify the mood. Balding and gray, thin-shouldered, wearing small gold-rimmed glasses, he said, "It's dog days. Boredom sets in and all kinds of things make the news. After awhile, it's more fun to invent things."

"Are we talking about the president or the press?" Annette asked sweetly.

Her husband ignored her. "Maybe April Fool's Day has been moved and nobody told me," he groused, trying to force a grin. He placed his huge left palm over his eyes and winced. Anything that resembled smiling seemed to accent the headache. He caught his wife's eye and pursed his lips. Of course, if he hadn't had three double VO whiskies and stayed up half the night bouncing around the bed with the First Lady—

Seeming to read his mind, she winked. He felt himself blushing. She smiled serenely, got up, brushed crumbs from her dress, pecked him on the cheek, and said over her shoulder as she left, "Late for an appointment with my staff. Try some Anacin, sweety."

"Uh-huh. I will, if it gets worse."

"See you tonight?"

"Dinner at home?"

"Hope so."

He watched her hips sway out of sight, then sighed, and stared back down at the secession news item. If it was a joke, why had the staff included it in his briefing? It made no sense. By his orders, his briefing was supposed to be steel-serious. On the other hand, whatever was going on, it gave him a good excuse to touch bases with his favorite cousin.

"Phone, get me J.B.," he ordered the White House computer, whose smart terminals were literally everywhere in these hyper-digital days.

"Dialing," the machine said softly. Many White House occupants kept their computers' voices turned off, but the president liked the sound of this particularly sultry cyber-gal. The synthetic voice reminded him of Annette's when she was ready to— Well, never mind, he told himself. Focus on the situation at hand like a good boy.

In his bathroom across the country in Oregon, J.B. Washington, the president's cousin, barked his usual answer at his own wall phone, "Sound only. What?"

The ultra-thin, organic polymer video screen remained dark. Video wall phones had become common in homes in recent years. Cheap, too. With the exponential growth in data bandwidth and processing power, the once-dreamlike devices were within reach of most of the middle class. J.B. had yet to embrace them with enthusiasm, but Julie loved 'em. As did his two daughters, Newt and Ginger. Right now he looked like a possum after a meeting with a truck. He didn't need to advertise the fact on video. When no one answered immediately, he spat toothpaste into the basin and said irritably, "Yeah, this is J.B. Who is it?"

"One moment for the president," said a computer voice. Presidential calls were never put through directly. Among several others things, the White House computer would first set up a filter on the line to watch for screechers. Screechers were a new sonic terror-weapon, downloadable off the Internet, that used calculated dissonance to produce anything from headaches to brain damage, although the latter was rare. The White House filter—provided by the NSA's research basement—could detect the nanosecond start of a screecher and squelch it before it could do harm.

J.B. scowled. After a late nighter with both houses of the Oregon legislature and the governor, he was tired and short-tempered, and not particularly eager to talk to anyone. As news of the secession story had spread, the night had been followed by an early morning of steadily increasing news media interview demands. He hadn't come home and tumbled into bed until six and it wasn't eleven yet.

"This is your guvmint cousin," Sam's voice said suddenly. "I hear you varmints are raising a confederate flag out there. How come nobody invited me to the rebel party?"

"Hi, Sam," J.B. replied. "Heard the news, eh?"

"A blurb on my morning summary. Says your senate has decided to—"

"That's old."

"Beg pardon?"

"Old news. Not just our senate, Sam. The house also voted to secede. And the governor signed the joint bill. It's official. We're gone."

The president stared at his phone screen, wishing he had J.B. on video. He did better when he could read people's expressions. His cousin was in the technological Bronze Age.

"C'mon, J.B.," Sam said. "Clue me in. This is another of Oregon's annual first-in-the-nation whimsies, isn't it? Like picking a state grub or the official motto for moss." He snapped his fingers. "No, wait, I've got it. It's a promo for tourism. Come visit the only state that's *not* a state. Hey, I like it. Maybe I'll move back."

J.B.'s answer came unexpectedly flat and straight, like a thrown discus.

"Mr. president," he said, dropping all familial informality, "I guess Governor Corcoran didn't call you yet."

"I'm not surprised. With the new surtax I signed, I don't think I'm his biggest fan."

"Well, I might as well lay it out. As chief of the Oregon Senate, I'm telling you that we're absolutely for real, Sam. Oregon has left the Union. It's too damned expensive to belong. The taxes alone are like a cement sack on our backs. They're sinking us in this muck of a recession."

"J.B., I've got Secretary of State Goldstein in the room with me. Why don't you run it by again now that I've got a witness, okay? Your little secession joke flew over my head like a pigeon with a hawk on its tail. I don't get it."

"Nothing to get."

"J.B., this is a crummy way to double-jerk a punchline. I haven't had enough coffee for fancy leg-pulling this morning."

"No punchline, Sam. But there is a *bottom* line. We're fed up out here. We're leaving the party. We're vamoosing the caboose. We're exiting the stadium. How many ways can I say it to get you to understand?"

The president nodded sagely, winking at Goldstein. "Right, J.B. Yeah, okay, sure. Gotcha. Say hello to Julie and your fellow rebels. I'll have the White House band play Dixie for you."

"Phone off," he said. He turned to Goldstein, smiling broadly. His headache only hurt a little now.

"Well?" Goldstein asked, reaching for another roll.

"I'm an idiot," Sam said, taking a careful sip of coffee. "You don't know my cousin."

"Can't say I do. Just what I've read. But he didn't sound like he was kidding to me."

"Don't *you* fall for it, too."

"Fall?"

"Yeah. J.B. just tried to set my hook."

"Pardon?"

Sam Washington laughed fondly. "See, ever since we were kids, J.B. was an *el primo* practical joker. Not even the wizards at West Point or M.I.T. or Cal Tech produced sneakier guys. J.B. could come up with the darnedest stuff this side of a tornado. Real, big screen productions. We used to call him The Hollywood Man. He could sucker people five ways to Tuesday and back again and have 'em begging for more. I remember when he set up a false telephone and e-mail exchange deal that had an entire sorority's ears burning with not-so-sweet nothings from their various boyfriends. Took months to restore honey to that hive."

Goldstein shrugged and said, "I can imagine. Well, it sounds like you spotted the lure in time."

He held his coffee up in a mock toast.

"But Craig, the thing I can't figure out is how J.B. got the bait on a line this *size*. It's big enough to hold an orca."

Goldstein said nothing. This sounded like a long-standing family thing; better to stay out of it.

"Ah, well," the president said, chuckling and pouring fresh, dark coffee from the table decanter, "he's a clever one. Only way to avoid being sucked in by The Hollywood Man is to forget about him. No nibbles and J.B. will reel in and try his luck in another part of the pond."

The president resumed scanning his morning news summary, still chuckling. There was nothing quite like a jolt from old J.B., he thought. What a great relative.

Chapter 3

"Slapstick"

Well," Oregon's craggy former governor and current president huffed, "it seems like everyone's a trifle amused. *Too* amused!" Alf "Corky" Corcoran smacked his palm against the desktop. "It's been two days since we declared our independence, but the whole country thinks it's the funniest thing since slapstick!"

Despite the heat, he lit a cigar. A sweet cherry wood aroma filled the room. He took a puff and blew smoke at the ceiling.

"If this rebellion is going to work, we can't have the rest of the nation guffawing its brains out. Looks bad. This is supposed to be a real revolution, not a comedy special! I went along with the idea thinking it would work toward the best interests of the state. Toward our *serious* interests."

J.B. Washington cleared his throat.

President Corcoran glanced at him, but held the floor. He leaned back in his chair and unexpectedly smiled, deep wrinkles creasing his tanned, cowboy-gaunt face.

"Well," he said, "it's purely coincidental that I personally paid fifty gees a year to the feds and didn't get a thing for it."

His anger partially released, he sucked on his cigar and glared in turn at his friend, J.B., at House Speaker Bard Candor—a short, stocky man with thinning salt-and-pepper hair and an unruly brown moustache—and at Ben Colby. At the moment they were the only ones in his office.

"It's all fairly evident," Candor said, interjecting himself in his crackling, pushy, and slightly condescending ex-radio commentator's voice.

"Huh? What is?" Corcoran demanded, narrowing his eyes.

"Don't you see? What you've described as your own interest is much like what other people in the state are currently experiencing."

"You've lost me, Bard."

"Well," Candor said, raising his nose, giving the impression that he was looking down at the bigger man, "I know I'd rather stick all my federal taxes into a fund for my kids, or into an IRA, or two-dozen other things."

"So? Where's the news in that? If they've got half a brain and a pan to keep it in, *everyone* feels that way. It's just that fewer can afford it."

"Yes, of course. However," Candor continued, raising an instructive index finger, "the fact that almost the entire legislature unexpectedly jumped at this secession idea indicates that the sentiments are, indeed, widespread. Even seminal. No more *outsiders* ruling Oregon. Oregon for Oregonians. That's the crux of it. Why even I was astonished at the depth of the feeling. The polls back me up. And believe me, little shocks this old reporter anymore. No sireeee!"

Humble, as usual, J.B. thought.

Corcoran was thinking that he'd be a happier man if he didn't have to deal with Candor. Something about him tended to grate on a guy. The President of the Republic of Oregon considered making a lewd pantomime toward the speaker of the House, but refrained. He also refrained from mentioning that in Candor's younger days, he had been among the state's prime apologists for increased taxes, state and federal. Always in the name of fiscal responsibility and "shared duties for the privilege of living in a great land." Or some such rationalization. After acquiring a family, though, and gaining a reputation as a tough, if rather annoying state representative, Candor's views had miraculously morphed. Now he was anti-tax, anti-regulation, anti-federal government, and anti-other-states. Behind his back, House members had taken to calling him "Auntie Bard." Candor knew about it, but said nothing, choosing to nurture his resentment in other ways. Big ways, he told himself, big ways.

"Excuse me, but aren't we perhaps pouting over a cracked wine jug?"

Everyone turned to look at Ben Colby.

"This unseriousness by the national government and media might be a good thing, you know."

President Corcoran rolled his cigar between his bony thumb and forefinger and asked, "How so, Ben? I'm afraid my creaky computer ain't processing."

"Oh, your computer is fine, sir," Colby said jovially. "But after all, this is an option which few people have considered since the War for Southern Independence, what most of us call the Civil War. No one's had much reason to think through the full ramifications of secession. Let's face it; there are few modern precedents."

"Correction, there are *none*," Candor interjected, nodding knowingly.

"All right, none," Colby said, shrugging. "At least no exact ones. There have been some instances of cities seceding from counties here and there."

"Well, all I can say is that it better not come to a Confederacy style physical facedown with the feds anytime soon," Corcoran growled, the lines of his always gaunt face growing deeper. "We aren't prepared for it. How would tiny Oregon stand up to the Pentagon? For that matter, how would we stand up to the FBI? I can tell you this: we sure wouldn't get any help from our neighboring states' national guards. They think liberal Oregon has finally dived off Loony Tunes Tower. The governor of California won't even take my phone calls. And he's not exactly to the right of Ronald Reagan."

He slammed the cigar into his ashtray, as if to dare anyone to contradict him. Corcoran wasn't known as a gentleman. A lanky six-six and eerily resembling the Father of Oregon, John McLoughlin, he was a presence in any gathering.

"All that might be to our advantage," Colby said. "Indirectly, of course. In the tradition defined and explicated by the great B.H. Liddell Hart."

J.B. fished out and lit a cigarette. Like the other men in the room, he was beginning to wonder if they'd leapt before they'd looked. He wasn't ready to give up the idea. None of them was. The rewards, if they could get away with even a portion of this rebellion, even for two or three years, were enormous. They were talking economic salvation. End-of-depression stuff. As Ben Colby had said, using one of his disarming consonant-switched phrases, all of Oregon's dire economic problems could be solved in "one swell foop." A fine-tuned ear in the broadcast media had picked up the silly phrase and passed it on. Now the entire American press, chortling over their keyboards and microphones, was privately calling Oregon's secession the "Foop Rebellion." J.B. thought it sounded suspiciously like "Poop Rebellion," not precisely a phrase to encourage high-mindedness. In their actual stories, of course, the media were politely calling it "The Oregon Rebellion."

Well, it wasn't that well known, especially in today's short-on-history schools, but King George III's minions had laughed derisively at the American rebellion, too.

At first.

It took persistence and courage to be taken seriously. It also took a lot of blood and treasure. Persistence, they probably had. Blood and treasure, maybe. Courage— well, that was another matter. The founders of Oregon had certainly had plenty. They'd eventually ripped away control of their land from the Hudson Bay Company of England. Had they not had the courage to do that—a move whose success was in great doubt at the time—would there even have been a state of Oregon? Would their descendants in the 21st century manage to muster the courage to take Oregon to its next stage of political evolution? J.B. Washington couldn't honestly say. He hoped the rebellious pioneer spirit still smoldered. Whether it did, no one really knew.

Colby stood, hitched his pants, adjusted one wide red suspender, wiped his bald head with a folded handkerchief, and began pacing the room.

"Gentlemen, there are several things which we need time to do," he said. "The humor about our position is an excellent cover, a diversion. It's first-rate currency, funds to buy breathing space. However, it will not be the last diversion and the account will soon run dry."

"You can say that again," Corcoran muttered.

"When the feds start to believe us, when actual confrontations begin, which they will," Colby emphasized, glancing at his new president, who nodded darkly, "then we'll have to be prepared. It's imperative that we ready our forces. All of them. Otherwise everything will collapse like a rotten beaver dam. As I was the instigator of this action, I have taken the liberty of making a list of things we urgently need to do."

"Well, at least *somebody* this side of the border has thought ahead," Corcoran said. "If we're gonna do it, let's quit talking about it and get on with it."

"Exactly," J.B. said eagerly. "Let's stop whining and throw some tea in King Sam's harbor."

"Precisely what I was thinking," Candor said pompously.

The others ignored him. He had a habit of trying to take credit after the fact.

"Well, I *was*," he snapped peevishly.

No one met his eyes—which is why they didn't notice the undiluted hatred of the glance he turned on them.

Bard Candor's hatred was complex and secret. Unlike many men, who put their differences on the table, did their best to work them out, and then moved on, Candor was a grudge feeder. He forgot no slight. Some of his more astute colleagues sensed this condition, knew there were hot, barely controlled emotions swirling inside Candor, torrents that might someday burst out and do who-knew-what damage. But he was a prickly fellow who did not encourage personal advice. Strategic political advice, yes. He was open to that, but not to the personal stuff.

In a sense, it didn't seem to matter. While Candor was not loved, he was respected. He'd achieved and retained the House speakership on the basis of sheer intellectual prowess and determination. Blessed with a cunning intelligence, an almost perfect memory, and prodigious energy, he also possessed a shrewd intuition about the needs and weaknesses of others. This combination made him formidable. Abrasive arrogance aside, he was a man to reckon with in the state of Oregon.

However, had any of his House fellows been able to look deeper, they'd have been flabbergasted. The seething currents in the psyche of Bard Candor were made up of far more than the grudges acquired in his broadcast or political careers. They went back, way back, to his days as a ten-year-old kid in Coos Bay, Oregon . . .

One event in particular stood out. It was what some psychiatrists called indelibly formative. For several weeks his mother had done the unthinkable: she had "taken up" with a dark-skinned drifter. Black, Hispanic, Oriental—no one really knew his background. Nor, back then, did it matter. In a nearly all-white population not known for its tolerance of outsiders—especially darker-skinned ones—this was a scandal. The ridicule Bard suffered at school was almost unbearable. Yet, had things been slightly different, he could have managed it. That he couldn't do so was ultimately due to the fact that his mother was an astonishingly poor judge of character. Where Bard was astute, she was dense. Where he was cautious, she was gullible. Where he had questions and doubts, she jumped in with only her mind closed shut. The truth of it was, his mother's new man was a charming user and would never be anything more. He did not like Bard. He did not like the penetrating, angry eyes of the ten-year-old—or his tart tongue. Even in those early years, Bard had not hesitated to express his opinions brashly. As long as he did this in his mother's presence, not much happened. Both his mother and the drifter just laughed at his puckishness.

But whenever the drifter was alone with Bard while his mother was at work, he delighted in tormenting the young genius. He made fun of his gawky looks, his bookishness, his lack of a girlfriend, anything that would irritate and embarrass Bard. When Bard seemed to become immune to the verbal taunts, the drifter gradually escalated to physical violence. It started with ear-cuffing and painful finger-jabs in the ribs and kept getting worse. One of his favorite tricks was to confront Bard in the bathroom and threaten to "turn the little white boy into a girl."

Then one day he just disappeared. Neither Bard nor his mother ever heard from him again. Bard hoped the man had been killed somehow. A favorite daydream was to watch him being eaten alive by sharks in the bay. Fact was, the man had grown bored and moved on down Highway 101 into Northern California. He didn't know, and wouldn't have cared, that he'd left behind a scarred and bitter boy who forever after would be afraid of anyone who was not obviously discernible as white. As he grew older, Bard realized that not all non-whites were like that drifter; in fact, very few were. But by then, it didn't make any difference. It was too late. He had brooded on his personal hatred until it had become inextricably entwined with racial hatred.

Through the years he had quietly nursed the neurosis. He kept his views mostly to himself, sharing his thoughts with only a few carefully chosen people. If his colleagues or the media were to find out about this sickness growing inside him, Bard knew it would be the end of his political career. While predominantly white, Oregon was now a more mixed-race state, known for its tolerance. An unabashed racist would never make it in politics. Those days were long gone.

The days were gone, but the pressure inside Candor kept building. Always in the back of his mind lurked the resolution, "Somehow, someday, I'll get even with *them*." Now, finally, if his political intuition was correct, that time was approaching. The goal was clear. It was all that counted. He would find the means. For once and for all he would erase the grinning, tormenting face of the drifter from his far too perfect memory.

Chapter 4

"But It's *My* Gun!"

L et's see your weapon, son," Sergeant Larry Rigg said to the young man. Rigg stood about six feet-two with crewcut brown hair and a muscular, compact build.

Probably no more than sixteen, the youth held out his 30.06 hunting rifle. It was an old model.

"Relax," Rigg said. "You're not at attention. What's your name young fellow?"

"Stan Crothers, sir." Skinny and tall, he shifted nervously from foot to foot. One of his shoes was untied.

Rigg examined the gun, noting that despite its age, it was maintained.

"Well, let's see what you can do with it, Stan," he said, detaching the cheap snap-on scope and handing the bare rifle back. Answering the unspoken question on Crothers' face, he said, "Unless you're picked for sniper duty, this eyepiece is going to do nothing but hang you up in the brush. Stick it in your pack and don't drag it out unless I tell you to."

"Yes, sir," Crothers said. He took the scope and carefully wrapped it in a piece of sweatshirt cloth and placed it in the faded blue canvas athletic bag that served as his pack.

Rigg nodded. "There's a lot to be said for deer hunting experience, Stan. But there's a lot it won't teach you—like the fact that deer don't turn and chase you with guns of their own."

Crothers gulped, his Adam's apple moving prominently. Rigg suppressed a smile.

"Now," he said, "see that old milk jug on the far right?" He pointed to a spot a hundred feet up the isolated, boulder-strewn canyon in the Coburg Hills northeast of Eugene. "Can you hit it without using the fancy peeper?"

"I reckon."

"We don't take your word for anything in this outfit. Let's see you do it."

Crothers stepped forward and away from Rigg and the others, raised his gun, sighted quickly, squeezed the trigger. Almost simultaneously with the crack of the rifle, the milk jug jumped, followed a fraction of a second later by the whine of a bullet careening off rock.

"Again," the sergeant said, "this time the tin can to the left, the one twenty yards on."

Crothers barely seemed to aim. The can jolted and disappeared behind an old log.

Rigg pointed out three more targets in rapid succession, each farther up the ravine than the last. Crothers never missed. Twice he didn't even appear to aim. One of the people watching let out a low whistle. Crothers seemed unaware of the amazed reaction.

"Who taught you that?" Rigg asked casually.

"My gramps, sir. Gave me my first gun, a twenty-two single shot, when I was goin' on seven. Started me huntin' gray digger squirrels and birds. Worked up from there. Always kept Mom's freezer full. Hardly ever used the scope, actually," he said sheepishly. "Just played with it. Kinda useless, really. Wiggles around on those snap mounts. Can see just about as good without it."

"How's that?" Rigg asked, cocking his head skeptically.

"Uh, well. I got something the eye doc calls five vision, whatever that is."

After a moment, Rigg asked, "Five? Wait a minute. You mean *twenty/five*?"

Crothers shrugged. "Maybe. All I know is I see okay."

Rigg shook his head and said, "Son, you don't see 'okay.' Twenty/five vision means you can see at twenty feet what most of us can only see at five."

Crothers thought it over a moment, then said, "Oh. I thought everybody could see this good. You mean they can't?"

"Son, don't you realize that not one man in a million can see that well?"

"Well, heck," Crothers said, apparently embarrassed, shifting from foot to foot.

"Yeah, heck," Rigg said. He grinned inside and turned away, hopping onto a massive fir tree stump.

He waited a few seconds then raised his voice to include all fifty of the men and women before him.

"Listen up," he said. "I'm assuming you're here because you want to be. If that's not the case, if any of you are here because somebody told you to do it, or thought it would be a good way to lose a hungry mouth, or to get rid of a mud-dragging husband, I want you to leave. You're not militia material. I don't want you. I don't need you. Not unless you think it's a good idea, on your own judgment and on its own merits. Have you got that?"

He looked up and down the ragged group of individuals. They ranged in age from kids who couldn't be over thirteen to two men who had to be crossing the bridge to eighty. There were seven women. Everyone, except for two late teenagers, a boy and girl who looked to be brother and sister, had his own gun. They were mostly cheap rifles—a lot of 30-30s and 30.06s, several .22s, even an ancient Enfield fifty-caliber. There were pistols, including .357s, .45s, .38s, .40s, and nine-mils. There were a few mini-15s, the outlawed semi-auto version of the military's old M-16. Two kids had arrived with new pump-gun Crossman air rifles capable of putting out more power than a typical .22. Several individuals had brought knives and machetes. There were some exchanged glances, but nobody else left.

"Okay," Rigg said, "The first thing to realize is that this is not the U.S. Army or the Marines or anything else official. Not in the old sense, anyway. It's not even the Oregon National Guard, though I'm told they're on our side, for now. Or what used to be called the Guard. This outfit right here, the one you aim to join, is something completely different. It's something with a lot more history. It's probably different than what most of you have heard. What you've heard from the big media has probably been wrong. This outfit is an independent militia. I stress the word 'independent.'"

A couple of the old-timers nodded. Most everyone else looked blank.

"For those of you who don't know American history," Rigg continued, "especially you youngsters who went through some of our more retarded schools, independent militias are volunteer organizations. Not paid by Uncle Sam. Paid by themselves. They are dedicated to the defense of a certain way of life. In this neck of the woods, they're dedicated to a *free* way of life. They're dedicated to a kind of living where government doesn't have its nose halfway in your door and part way up your ass, get me?"

Mumbles of agreement and several snickers criss-crossed the small crowd. They had answered Rigg's ads in the *Springfield News* and *The Register-Guard*. The ads had made the same point, but in fewer and kinder words.

Rigg shifted to his other leg as he stood on the stump, hands on hips.

"Militias helped found this country and helped protect it as late as World War II. That's when the boys from Tillamook, Florence, Coos Bay, and elsewhere trained to fight the Japanese. There was even a back-up militia called the Oregon State Defense Force that existed officially until fairly recently, although it never did any fighting. But today, here in the 21st century, we are under the direction of the President of the Republic of Oregon. As long as he doesn't wimp out on us," he added, smiling ruefully. "If he does, we might have something to say about it."

Several people laughed nervously. Nobody wanted that to happen. But politicians did not have the best of reputations for integrity. Most Oregonians weren't sure that their Esteemed Elected would carry through with the rebellion. They hoped so. They wanted to think that Oregonians, one and all, were something special, more trustworthy than average. But while the polls showed that 65% of residents backed the idea of the rebellion, a solid majority also doubted the resolve of their leaders. There was a lot to be proven on the field of future battle.

A light drizzle started to fall out of the heavy, lead-gray clouds. Only a moment before, it seemed, half the sky had been blue. Two of the Three Sisters mountains had been briefly visible above the forested hills 40 miles east. Glistening blindingly as the sun touched their ten-thousand-foot, snow-capped peaks, the Sisters were among the taller and more glorious of Oregon's Cascade Range. Rigg had scaled one of them as a teen. He recalled the experience as almost religious. Oregon's beauty could grab a guy that way. It was as if the environment reflected the face of God. On the other hand, things could sometimes show an opposite face, turning hellishly disagreeable. Well, it was a small price to pay for living here, he thought, as a chilly breeze picked up from the west. No one seemed to notice. Oregon's sudden shifts of weather were second-nature to them all. Rigg cleared his throat to speak.

"Now, as most of you know, my name is Larry Rigg. You can call me Sarge. Not Rigg. Not Larry. Not Mr. Rigg and definitely not Mr. Larry. Not Hey You. Not Buddy. Not anything but Sarge or Sergeant Rigg. Or Sir. When you sign the contract to join this militia, if you do, I'm your boss when you're on tour. The contract, which you've had a chance to read, spells out the organization's rules and obligations. This is a *disciplined* group, not some night-flight vigilante club. Got that? What I'm saying is, if you're here thinking you'll get to kill your favorite Mexican, black, Jew, neo-Nazi, China Red, or that funny neighbor you think might be banging your wife or daughter, think again. If I smell that gunk, you won't last five seconds."

One man, a tall, middle-aged fellow with a bald head and a black mole on the bridge of his nose, cursed under his breath, threw a mean glance at Rigg, slung his rifle over his shoulder, and trudged off and away, muttering to himself.

"Anymore of you?" Rigg demanded. "Better leave now. Later, there won't be time for charity. Not from me."

No one left, but someone in the back yelled, "Don't mind him, Sarge. That was Buford McConnell. All he wants to do is shoot him some fat-assed nigg— uh, African-Americans."

Rigg nodded, glancing at two tall blacks in the crowd, who shook their heads and smiled slightly. He was glad McConnell had weeded himself out early. Grudgers, especially racist ones, were unreliable soldiers in this day and age. In anyone's army.

"All right, now," he said evenly. "Here's the lay of my land. As long as you meet the terms of the contract, you're in. You break the terms, you're out. That simple. No exceptions. And there's no jury of appeal. I'm all you've got, so try to make me happy."

He paused, trying to meet as many eyes as possible. Rigg was rugged, muscular, and exuded confidence. He'd always been that way. Over the years, he'd learned that it took a strong-willed individual to challenge him and he was counting on it staying like that.

"I'm not kidding," Rigg snapped, glaring at the direction from which a bitter laugh had come. "Think hard about it. This is a dedicated organization. We have a mission to defend the new nation of Oregon. If that doesn't scare you, then sign the contracts and pass 'em forward. After that, gather 'round for our first training session. School starts in five minutes. Bear in mind that once you sign up, there's no turning back. You'll be expected to devote a minimum of three weekends a month from here on out for at least two years. Longer, if the president so orders. If you try to desert, I'll track you down and shoot you. I'm authorized to do it, and I *will* do it. Two years is a lot of missed barbecues. Those of you who've got jobs to hold down and have to keep bread on the table, of course I understand that. The contract provides for it. The rest of you, I expect you to be spending a lot of hours here during the week, too. It's especially true for anyone aiming to pull weight as a platoon leader, and that could be any of you."

After five minutes, 45 people had signed the contracts. One of the women and three of the men had second thoughts. They silently gathered their materials and walked away.

"Okay," Rigg said, "our first order of business is to reinforce the nature of our basic purpose." He cleared his throat, spat into the dirt at the foot of the stump, and said, "A militia must foremost know its mission. From the newspaper ad you saw, you know what it is in general. If not, you probably wouldn't have shown up.

"Our second order of business will be a briefing on weapons safety. One other thing before we get started on that. By direct order of President Corcoran, we do *not* use U.S. military jargon, at least not for now. I concur in this policy and I want you guys with military background to make a special note of it. It'll be hard for you to break the habit, but I want it done. We'll keep our language simple and clear. No more acronyms or made-up words than we can help. For example, you don't say 'egress' or 'disinfiltrate,' you say 'get out' or 'pull back' or 'leave.' You don't say 'roger,' you say 'yes.' You don't say 'that's a negative,' you say 'no.' Got it? There are a few exceptions, like numbers, which we'll catch later, especially for communications people who might have to deal with regular units that can't chuck the habit. I know this'll take some practice. But since most of you are already non-military, it'll make it possible to get everything rolling faster. That brings us back to our present mission."

He spat again, this time onto the stump, then ground the spittle into the damp wood with his boot.

"You'll note that we're officially called the Springfield Independent Militia. We have one main purpose: to help defend the sta— excuse me, the *nation* of Oregon against destruction of its new independence and the increased liberty it represents. I know, I know. Right now most of the rest of the country, most of our neighbors over in the U.S., are laughing up their sleeves at us. Believe me, that *will* change. We'll eventually face physical opposition. And that means opposition from Uncle

Sam's federal boys. When they come, they won't be carrying toy guns. It might also mean we'll quite likely have to face invaders from other states or even other nations. It could mean facing your own neighbors or relatives, should they turn traitor. This is no high-rez video game, people. A lot of you could go belly-up and buttless."

A few people paled, but then looked at their tougher companions, swallowed, and set their jaws.

"For the most part, we'll be on our own," Rigg said. "Corcoran is commander-in-chief of the Oregon guard units, ground and air. For now, at least, they'll be handling any big confrontations. Hopefully there won't be any for awhile. It appears the U.S. of A. is having its usual trouble getting its backside in motion. Meanwhile, our specific missions—like most of the other militias that have formed or will form around the state—will be primarily small stuff."

"What's that mean, Sarge?" someone yelled.

"Well, my own specialties, for example, are border security, ambush, and reconnaissance. We will operate mainly in Lane County, but that's a big territory. It goes all the way from the Pacific Ocean to the summit of the Cascade Mountains; bigger'n many states back east. On occasion we'll link up with other militias. At times we could be under the direction of various Oregon federal units."

He raised his eyes, glancing at the sodden sky, and added, "How much of this will occur, or how often, I can't tell you. Nobody really knows. That's how it is in war. It will depend on what the enemy does. Maybe not much of anything will happen to our militia. We may luck out, but don't count on it. We will assume that confrontations will occur and that they will be deadly. I intend to see that we are skilled enough to match that assumption—and then some."

He paused and coughed, clearing his throat again. He hadn't talked this much or this loud since a college speech course ten years earlier in which he'd analyzed the U.S. Supreme Court decision that led to George W. Bush's winning the 2000 presidential election.

"Now, at the end of the day, I'll be handing out a booklet to each of you. It lists provisions such as food, clothing, ammo, and so on. You must somehow obtain these things yourselves by next weekend. Other equipment, I'll be providing as I get my hands on it. I'm told there are at least a few things that'll be trickling down to us from the Oregon federal level. Any problems, let me know; maybe I can help you out. Okay, let's get down to it. The newspaper ad asked you all to bring guns and a minimal amount of ammunition. That's because this weekend we'll be covering the basics of the aforementioned course in gun safety. To handle the primary instruction, I'd like to point to my second-in-command, Karl Hochman. He is a firearms expert. He knows his stuff, so listen when he talks."

Hochman, who had been laying out various guns and ammo on a series of tarps on the ground, stood briefly and nodded. White-blonde, he was massive; nearly six-seven, broad-shouldered, perhaps 270 pounds. His blue eyes were deep-set and unreadable. He didn't smile.

"You can call him Corporal," Rigg said, as Hochman went back to what he was doing. "The rest of you are privates."

"Uh, Sarge?" an unshaven, fortyish man asked.

"Yes, private?"

"I, uh, don't think I'll be needing this part of the training. You can just let me skip it."

Rigg looked intently at him for a moment, then asked slowly, "How do you figure that, private?"

"Well, now, I've been a member of the National Rifle Association for years. I know all this junk."

"Same here," a burly man in a green plaid shirt next to him said, stepping forward. "I'm a cop in Eugene. They grilled us on this twenty years ago. No need for you to be changin' my diapers, is there?"

Both men grinned and winked at each other, then looked insolently at Rigg.

Rigg nodded slightly toward Hochman, then smiled broadly at the men. "I see. Well, it sounds like an interesting point of view. And you boys would be who?"

"Jim Hanston. With a T," one said.

"Billy Crenshaw. With a 'sh,' as in 'shucks,'" the other one said, smirking. "Drinkin' buddies. Jes' like that." He held up crossed fingers, then made a slurping sound.

Rigg nodded, holding his exaggerated smile. He flipped through the stack of contracts still in his left hand.

"Ah, yes. Hanston and Crenshaw."

He pulled out two sheets and set the other 43 aside. He carefully held up and tore the Hanston and Crenshaw agreements in half, then in quarters, then in eighths, then sixteenths. He held the pieces eye level in one fist, opened his hand, let them fall, dropping his smile. A breeze scattered the pieces into the brush and rocks.

"Now, hey!" Hanston growled, taking a step forward, "what the—?"

"You're history," Rigg said flatly. "Take your gear and beat it."

Neither man obeyed. Both glared at Rigg. None of the other militia members said a word, but several edged away from Hanston and Crenshaw.

"I said leave," Rigg said, raising his voice only slightly.

Hanston started to raise his rifle. A deep voice from behind him said, "Put it down or die."

Hanston's head whipped around. Corporal Hochman had an M-16 raised and sighted at him.

"But it's *my* gun!" Hanston whined.

Hochman fired a burst of three rounds over the man's head. Several people hit the ground. A girl screamed. Hanston and Crenshaw dropped their rifles and ran.

"As I believe I mentioned," Rigg said after a few seconds, "this will be a well-disciplined outfit."

Chapter 5

"Gotchum Don't Getcha"

"Well, it's now or never," Ben Colby said to J.B. Washington. "As they say in physics, from here it all runs downhill."

"I thought they said that in solid waste engineering," J.B. said, looking warily at the door of the U.S. federal building's Portland IRS office.

"In some circumstances, it's hard to tell the difference."

"Here goes," J.B. said, unconsciously lowering his head as he pushed through the double glass doors.

"May I help you?" a worn-looking, languid woman clerk said after several moments, not looking up.

J.B. said, "Yes, you may. You can get me the head of this organization."

The clerk adjusted her glasses, which immediately slid back down. She smiled thinly. "I'm afraid Mr. Gotchum doesn't see just any—"

"I'm J.B. Washington, head of the Oregon senate. I have an emergency legislative restraining order to serve on Mr. Gotchum."

The clerk's eyes widened. "Just a moment," she said. She straightened an overly tight skirt and walked rapidly down a corridor, glancing over her shoulder several times.

"Too bad her attitude doesn't match her figure, " J.B. said.

"Amen, " Colby replied.

In a few minutes, a reedy, ascetic-looking man with brushed-back red hair appeared. He touched the side of his black-rimmed, round-lensed glasses and said, "Yes? I am Frank Gotchum. What's all this about?"

J.B. handed him the order and said, "I'm serving you and your offices in Oregon this mandate of restraint. To put it simply, sir, this is the IRS's official notice to cease doing business in the Republic of Oregon. In fact, it orders you to close your offices at once."

Gotchum looked startled, then laughed and said, "You're from the Cancer Society, right?"

"Pardon me?" Washington asked, shaking his head and glancing at Colby. Colby spread his hands in a don't-ask-me-what's-going-on gesture.

"You know," Gotchum explained, "like that mock jail thing they do?"

"Huh? Jail thing? What in the world are you talking about anyway?"

"Oh, come now. I'm not unfamiliar with charitable organization techniques."

"I guess I am," J.B. said.

"I'm referring to where they put people in this little fake paper jail and they have to raise so much money for the Cancer Society before they can get out. You know?"

Ben Colby rolled his eyes.

"No, sir," J.B. said, "it's nothing like that. Please, look at the order. This is the real thing."

Gotchum continued to grin. He nodded knowingly at the receptionist, who smiled uncertainly. Gotchum pulled out his wallet and opened it.

"Uh-huh," he said, "well, look fellas, I like your drama, but I really can't leave work. Higher public duties, you know. People to torture and all that, heh, heh. So just tell me how much of a donation you want, and I'll—"

J.B. put his big right hand on Gotchum's shoulder and squeezed.

"Ow!" Gotchum yelped, jumping back.

"We aren't playing around," J.B. said. "We're not from the Cancer Society. We're not from Easter Seals. We're not from the Old Ladies' Tea-Sucking Society. Now try to focus your little bean brain on what we're saying."

"But, I don't—"

"Mr. Gotchum, close this place down or we'll do it for you! *Now!*"

But Gotchum was used to people shouting at him. He merely looked over the top of his glasses, noted Washington's face more carefully, then said, "My God, you *are* J.B. Washington, aren't you?"

"Yeah, I already said that. Now, please—"

Gotchum grabbed Washington's hand and shook it vigorously, exclaiming, "Well! You led the fight last year to get the voucher system passed so my kid didn't have to go to that awful school in our old neighborhood. Man, that's the best thing that ever happened to my little Alvin! He was a regular peanuthead before that. Couldn't even add. We used the voucher to switch him into Montessori classes and—"

"Er, uh, yeah, that's great," J.B. said, confused and momentarily disarmed. "Now if you'll please examine the restraining order—"

"What? Oh, sure, sure!" Gotchum replied, waving the order in the air. "Hah, hah! Part of the big secession scam, huh? Hey, you know, I think it's fabulous!"

"You do?" Colby asked, looking at Gotchum like the man needed heavy medication.

"Sure! Great publicity stunt. Great way to get people to visit the state. Something extraordinary to write into the old fifth-wheeler log, eh? Why, I myself am planning to take the family to—"

"I don't know if you've noticed, but you're not getting anywhere," Colby whispered into J.B.'s ear. "I believe it's time to call in the cavalry."

"Mr. Gotchum," J.B. interrupted, "please examine the order. It permits us to close you down by force if you don't indicate immediate cooperation."

"Eh? Force? What do you mean, 'force'?" the IRS agent asked, cocking his head at the highly familiar word. He squinted for a few moments at the restraining order, then seemed to finally get the drift. "Hey, wait a holy minute! You guys can't *really* mean — "

"Yes, I'm afraid so."

"But I thought — that is, our regional director said he was told that it was all a joke, some kind of P.R. deal."

J.B. leaned into the man's face.

"It's not," he growled.

Gotchum compressed his lips, again looked down at the served papers, frowned angrily, then backed up in little decisive steps, waving to the receptionist.

"Shirley, call security, quick!" he shouted. "Get these state clowns out of my offices. We've got a case of federal trespass on our hands!"

The receptionist got the call through, but at the same moment, Ben Colby spoke into his personal phone and issued his own orders. When an IRS security man reached the lobby, he was immediately detained by one of fifty armed Republic of Oregon Policemen (ROP), formerly state highway patrolmen. The rest of the ROPs spread through the IRS offices and, at gunpoint, ordered people out of the building. Everyone was told to go home. Employees were informed that they would be allowed, under controlled conditions, to retrieve personal possessions over the next two days.

Gotchum tried to threaten. "You'll never get away with this," he squeaked in a voice suddenly as brittle as sun-baked newspaper. "You'll be sent to prison and, and, and catch *AIDS*! This is Uncle Sam you're abusing, Mister!"

"No, sir," Colby said. "Uncle Sam's the abuser, whom we are disabusing of his mistaken status. If you like, you may think of it as Oregon's answer to involuntary fiscal sodomy."

"Huh?"

J.B. pointed to the troopers. "Look, you little wallet squeezer, *this* is the federal government now — the federal government of the sovereign Republic of Oregon. You and your people, if you live here, may remain as citizens of the new republic. But you will not be allowed to act as henchmen for the foreign government of the United States."

"Why, you unpatriotic son of a—!" Gotchum started to scream, trying to tear away from a huge ROP cop. "How ungrateful. After all America has done for you!"

"What about all it has *taken* from us?" Colby interjected.

"What? Hey, that's the system, man! You can't just willy-nilly trash it!"

"No? We can, and we are," Colby said, reaching the end of his own patience. "If you try to continue your illegal actions, if you in any way attempt to maintain or reestablish foreign tax intervention in our sovereign domestic affairs, you will be summarily jailed. Now go home, Mr. Gotchum, and think it over. Who knows, Oregon may even have a use for you, although I'm hard-pressed at the moment to say where or how."

Gotchum tried to dive for a desk telephone, but Washington doubted he knew whom he intended to call or what he'd say. The man was out of control.

"Soak his heels," J.B. said to the police officer. "This guy's got a case of federal fungus."

The officer took the struggling, sputtering Gotchum away, handling the taxman as easily as if he were a declawed housecat.

There were no further physical incidents. It took less than an hour to clear the IRS offices of scores of employees. When it was done, Washington and Colby sped off to meet with the ex-governor and current president.

"What about the other federal buildings around the sta— er, country, Corky?" he asked. "Everything okay, there, too?"

"Yours was the last," Corcoran said. "I understand the FBI and ATF people put up armed resistance down in Salem and Eugene. Five people were shot, two of them ours. Nobody was killed, though. But the timing was good. We shook their rugs in under an hour. Guess I'll have something serious to thank the Lord for in church this Sunday."

"Didn't know you went."

"I'm thinking of starting up again."

"Er, Corky, are you sure you don't want *me* to call the White House? Sam is my cousin, you know. Maybe it's best if someone closer to him breaks this latest news."

"I'm the commander-in-chief. The responsibility is mine. Keep the family goodwill in reserve, though. We've barely stepped into the woods. I imagine there'll be critters layin' for us. A cousin in the bushes might not hurt."

"I don't know how much goodwill we'll be able to count on from Sam."

"I know. But there's nothing wrong with hoping, is there?"

"Oh, by the way, Corky. Got a surprise call from Grieve McDouglas at my house last night. On the sly, he said. Wants to chat with you at your convenience. Said not to call him at the Pentagon. Left a private number."

J.B. handed the president a slip of paper with a phone number jotted on it and said, "Wouldn't tell me what it was about, but said you'd understand."

Corcoran took the paper and said, "Odd. I'll check it out. Grieve and I go way back. Ah, he probably wants to catch up on old war stories. Haven't talked with him since he got out of the hospital, you know."

"I'm not that close to him, but I've met him twice. Had a good time. Easy guy to like. Sam introduced us when I visited back East after Big Three."

"Good man. Knows the psychology of strategy better than anyone I've ever met."

"As I say, sir, I don't know him that well."

Chapter 6

"These Idiots *Mean* It!"

And so, we stand, an independent nation, the Republic of Oregon. The main message I wish all our former brother states to hear is this: we harbor you no ill-will; our quarrel is with your federal authorities only.

"We therefore invite the 49 remaining states to continue normal business with a newly sovereign, freshly freed Oregon. As before, our borders are open to trade; as before, our hearts are open to each and every part of America. In fact, the only change is that we of the Republic of Oregon are no longer controlled by Washington, D.C. As a result, no one doing business in Oregon will be subject to the heavy U.S. income tax.

"We extend the same trade invitation and the same no-U.S.-tax status to those foreign nations with whom we have had long-standing relations, including, but not limited to, Japan, Korea, Singapore, China, Taiwan, and many other trading partners. We are evaluating trade with nations that were on boycott lists of the U.S. government. We expect to make a few changes."

He raised an eyebrow and smiled lopsidedly.

"Finally, we ask all nations to officially recognize the birth of our new country. We invite all to establish embassies in our capital city, Salem. We are starting fresh. I have personally notified Bjron Jannesson, Secretary General of the new United

Nations in Geneva, that Oregon will apply for U.N. membership. Secretary Janneson has informed me by phone that Oregon's membership will be seriously considered. He has extended his personal best wishes. We hope all states and nations will follow his example, extending their best to this new, *sovereign* Republic of Oregon. Thank you, and good night."

President Corcoran looked into the cameras for a few seconds, waited for the signal that he was off-air, then exhaled loudly, jerked his microphone off his coat, and pulled a fresh cigar out of the humidifier on his desk.

"Nice job," J.B. said from his position behind the television crews. Bard Candor, next to him, said nothing.

"Not bad," Ben Colby added.

A stunned *CNN* cameraman whispered to a companion, "I think these idiots mean it!"

CNN, Fox News, and the *BBC* were the only international, old-line networks to cover Corcoran's speech. However, most Oregon TV and cable systems had sent reporters and/or cameramen to his office, as did a half-dozen Internet services. The newspapers and radio stations were also well represented. The electronic media unplugged, folded, rolled, and packed equipment. In a scramble and flutter that reminded Corcoran of chickens getting a feeding call, they moved out, heading to set up in a basement press room to fire questions at Corcoran within the hour. The governor had refused to be grilled immediately after his talk. He wanted time to meet with his advisors, who were now, in effect, his new cabinet.

Turning to J.B. Washington, Corcoran said from within a cloud of cigar smoke, "Don't tell me it wasn't bad. Thank Ben Colby for those words. I never could master the written word. Thankfully, I can make it sound okay. At least I don't honk like a goose with twisted ankles. By the way, J.B., your cousin wouldn't talk to me."

Corcoran looked accusingly at his cigar, which appeared to have gone out. He tried and threw a defective plastic cigar lighter aside, then pulled out a pack of wooden Diamond matches. He got the cigar going and gazed at J.B., waiting for an answer to the implied question.

"That'll change, sir," J.B. said, shrugging one shoulder. "If these network reports don't do it, word will filter up to Sam from the FBI, ATF, DEA, IRS, Forest Service, and all the other feds we dismantled and kicked out. Gotta figure he already knows. If not, somebody'll tweak his ears pretty quick. Count on it. The feds are inefficient as spastic gophers in many areas, but they can move like snakes when their nests are threatened."

"The longer they refrain from that, the better," Colby said from off to one side. "If they send force against us, I'd like more time to get ready. I'm not sure it's wise to push contact with the White House. In fact, I thought you'd absolutely decided not to."

"After that speech? Only a couple hours after poking the fed nests? Got to assume Sam knows," Corcoran said, puffing smoke at the ceiling. "Got to."

"Perhaps," Colby said. He cleared his throat. "But my point isn't tactical; it's strategic. As long as we can keep the fight against *individual* agencies, the feds will remain at least somewhat divided. Division creates confusion and confusion is a disadvantage for them; an advantage for us. Once the scope of this rebellion finally sinks in at the White House level, we face a unified front. That's when our job grows magnitudes bigger. Let's take the time to pick up media sympathy. Like the Balts did against Gorby back in '90."

Corcoran narrowed his eyes, then nodded and said, "Maybe I'm too eager to know where we stand with the big boys back east. Okay. I'll try to rein in my Paleolithic confrontational impulses."

Almost in unison, the other men in the room let out a theatrical, if unintentional sigh.

He got their point. Corcoran had a reputation for never refusing fights, even politically pointless ones. It was a weakness and he knew it. He looked like Oregon's father, John McLoughlin, but he felt more like the fiery first territorial governor, Gen. Joseph Lane—minus his pro-slavery impulses. Well, Lane had earned his reputation with Uncle Sam in the Mexican war. Maybe it would take a war to make the U.S. take Corcoran seriously, too. Even in Oregon, his reputation was uncertain. Some pundits said he'd been lucky to have won the governorship at all. The vote had been closer than the hair on a gnat's ass. From one perspective, Corcoran's temper was a liability. A diplomat, he was not. On the other hand, he was smart enough to know that it also lent passion to his overall leadership. Corcoran kept a sign on his desk that visitors saw before anything else: "If your butt is cold, I CAN build a fire under it." Yeah, General Lane probably would have liked that, he thought.

"By the way," he asked Colby, "how's the militia call? Is this commander-in-chief, slash, defense secretary, going to have any men to work with? Or do I get a bunch of pot-bangers flushin' brush?"

Corcoran was a former Army officer and had led troops in the New Panama, Montenegrin, and Second Cuban Revolution campaigns. His interest in his fledgling military was far more than political. Or rather, given the old maxim that war was ultimately an extension of somebody's stupid politics, it was a big *portion* of the political.

"It's faring well," Colby said cautiously. He was acting in several positions himself, including national security advisor and deputy defense secretary. His extensive knowledge of military strategy had impressed Corcoran. He'd always been better at tactics, himself. Colby provided a broader dimension. Impromptu briefings such as this were getting to be common. And with his near-perfect memory, Ben Colby was the one to give them.

"About 10,000 people have signed up with some 250 or so independent outfits," he said.

"That many already?" Corcoran asked, arching both eyebrows and sitting straighter.

"Yes, sir. However, it will take months to get them in decent shape. Most, anyway. The sizes of the units vary widely. Some have fewer than ten men. Others as many as several hundred."

"Huh," Corcoran grunted in surprise. "You're implying that some are ready to go? *Now?*"

"A few, for extremely limited missions. There were 12 pre-existing militias, you know."

"No. Never paid much attention to 'em."

Colby grinned. "Hardly anyone did, except themselves. The oldest is called the Hochman Independent Reserve Troops, HIRT, or *Hurters*, as they like to call themselves. It was started down in Lane County several years ago by Erik Hochman. His younger brother helps run another outfit in the same area. It musters in Springfield under a guy named Rigg. Erik might be a man for your national security staff, maybe even defense secretary. I'm told he's a creative thinker; good at using minimal force for maximum gain."

Corcoran nodded. "Stick the word at him. See what he says. I'll want to talk to him, of course."

"Yes, sir. Wrapping up the militia business, all except three or four pre-existing units were rag-tag; not much more than glorified shoot-clubs or paintball wargame enthusiasts."

"Easy," J.B. warned. "Don't belittle paintball. I do it on weekends now and then. You can learn more about brush tactics than you might think."

Colby looked skeptical. His efficient fat-storage system did not lend itself to extensive physical adventure.

"Whatever the theoretical virtues of paintball," Colby continued, "our front line is going to be the guardsmen. They are, of course, now Republic of Oregon regular army troops. Regulars is what they prefer to call themselves. They're referring to the militias as the irregulars. I'm not sure that's wise. Dissension at this early — "

"Oh, don't sweat it," Corcoran said, shaking his head. "It's just a form of pride. The competition between the two factions will make 'em both better. Morale-booster. What's the hard inventory?"

"Weapons, you mean?"

"More than paintball guns, I hope."

"Yes, well, it sits with the Regulars. They include the old

41st, the air guard, assorted other units. We've got a respectable variety of equipment. More than I'd hoped."

J.B. wondered about the last remark. He was starting to get the idea that Colby pre-planned a lot more than he ever let on to others.

"Details, Ben, details," Corcoran prodded impatiently.

Colby ticked things off on his fingers. "The inventory ranges from small boats, a dozen upgraded F-22 Raptors, two dozen old close air support CAS F-16s — the ones with the larger wings — about fifty Rutan CAS ARES mini-jets, a few old F-15Ms and F-18 SuperHornets, seven or eight Harriers, several types of copters, two AWACS left over from the Colombian drug wars, lots of SuperStinger missiles, several kinds of smart mines, plenty of GPS guided artillery and JDAM kit bombs, and so on. Even have a few David tactical lasers second-hand from the Israelis and one of the Air Force's seven Boeing 747-mounted ABL anti-missile battle lasers. Don't know how we got hold of those."

"What does 'and so on' mean?" Corcoran asked.

Colby coughed and said, "Well, sir, I didn't know how detailed you — "

"Ben, in this setting, knock off the 'sir' stuff, okay? Gets in my way. I've been 'Corky' to you for years."

"Er, well — Okay, Corky."

"What else? Snap it up. I gotta go shmooze reporters in a couple of minutes."

"We have troop transports, light tank and hypervelocity TOW units, PERN Dragon missiles, machine guns of all sizes, other odds and ends. Bottom line is I'm saying we have a decent mix. It's better than most states would have, except some of the biggies like California, New York, or Texas. Oh, almost forgot. Oregon was also one of just two states issued an inventory of special operations test devices by SORDAT."

"Uh, that would be?" J.B. asked.

"SORDAT's a kind of a special operations forces' skunk works outfit. Most people have never heard of it."

Corcoran shrugged, exchanging glances with J.B.

"Anyway," Colby went on, "that particular arsenal includes a few suits of full-body carbon/ceramic armor; ultrawideband walkie-talkies; mini-stealth RPVs for reconnaissance
or bombing—really small stuff, some the size of bumblebees—
various deception devices; and other jingles and jangles that
appear exceptionally suitable for small-scale actions. Not a lot
of it, mind you. But enough for a few critical operations. Also,
I'm not sure the U.S. really knows how much we've got. The
big stuff, like the ABL, certainly. But accounting of smaller arms
and supplies for several years running has been poor at the
Pentagon. It all kind of fell into disarray during the latter part
of the 20th century. But now, I'm rather glad. Their disarray
will keep them more cautious than they otherwise might be.
It'll force them to use up a lot of time guessing and second-
guessing us. I'd say we're almost as prepared as the Serbs were
back in the 90s—and you remember how long it took Uncle
Sam to move against them."

"Could be worse," J.B. said.

Corcoran pursed his lips.

"We even possess a few dozen PAC-4 and -5 missiles from
Big Three with Russia," Colby added. "They comprise a limited, but significant deterrent against ballistic missiles and satellites. Might need some dusting off, though."

"Well," Corcoran said, striking a match and putting it to
a fresh cigar, "it sounds like enough to make Uncle Sam stop
and think. That's something. What we've got is no Pentagon
arsenal, but if we threw it intelligently into a full-bore conflict,
there'd be a ghastly number of body bags heading home in
both directions. However, I doubt Sam Washington will be
nuking us, no matter how tight the screws get turned."

The president's cousin nodded slowly. Corcoran noted
that it was not necessarily with a lot of confidence. J.B. look
tired. Well, who wasn't? The U.S. president might be able to
lounge around, but not the Oregon president. Or any of his
close advisors.

"As you all know," Colby inserted into the silence, "ballistic missiles can carry many things besides nuclear weapons.

Medium and short range ones fired from neighboring states or offshore could, for example, be significant anti-personnel weapons. Syria showed that with its Scud arsenal back in the '06 conflict with Israel. With upgraded guidance, they could take out bridges across the Columbia. The capitol could be hit. I think we should watch out for an RSC whopper, too."

"Huh?" J.B. asked.

"Reconnaissance Strike Complexes," Colby explained. "A concept developed by the old Soviets under Nikolai Ogarkov. It means simultaneously hitting all the enemy's most important targets, including political, military, economic. A body-blow designed to stun hard enough for more conventional forces to move in and consolidate a victory at minimal cost. A highly effective surprise attack, if done properly. It's blitzkrieg, raised by a factor of ten."

"Ogarkov, shmarkov," Corcoran retorted. "It's the old U.S. run-and-gun plan to defend Western Europe—proven in the Gulf War against Iraq, again in Bosnia, again in Kosovo and Montenegro, and—"

"Point taken."

The governor gave up on his cigar, glared at it, then jammed it into a metal wastebasket. He selected and fired up a third one, then looked piercingly at Colby.

"Ben, as my national security advisor, tell me straight. Can we *count* on the guardsmen? They were, after all, first and foremost sworn to protect the U.S. Constitution. But we're not the U.S. anymore."

"I think they're solidly with us. Most of them have lived here all or most of their lives. They know the story. They know we've got right on our side. Remember, they've seen their folks and their friends bent to breaking under the fed tax load. However, in order to mortar up any cracks of doubt, I've written material for special persuasion lectures; it's being presented this week."

"You mean indoctrination?" Candor scoffed sarcastically, finally speaking up.

Colby said patiently, unruffled, "Bard, I mean *persuasion.*

Indoctrination presumes acceptance without full understanding. My presentation outlines the freedoms we are protecting and how they were lost or made impossible by the feds. It should conceptually solidify what a lot of the regulars already feel. Dedication to explicit principles powerfully shores up gut feelings. It's an old tenet of not just political, but also of military education."

"Well, call me grumpy, but I worry about treason," Corcoran said. "This is a new nation; not much time to fill the reservoir of patriotism. Bound to be mold-brains who liked the temperature of the water the way it was and resent it changing. I'm especially worried about the hurt that a high-placed turncoat could do us. You can stunt a tree the worst if you damage it young. What are we doing to make sure that doesn't happen?"

"For one thing, as in any other army, they'll be watching each other. Remember that the guardsmen have signed new loyalty oaths to the Republic of Oregon. They've forsworn their previous allegiance to the U.S.."

"Yeah, but—"

"They'll be watching for any punches pulled, Corky. Beyond that, we'll rely on internal intelligence. Procedures for that already existed and are adaptable. The ROP is offering some good suggestions. I think the guardsmen, the Regulars, will be fine."

"And the militias?" Candor asked. "Sounds like a fairly disorganized group to me. Practically primed to turn against us when we don't expect it."

"No, I don't think so," Colby said, shaking his head and calmly meeting Candor's hostile gaze. "Remember, the militia are all volunteers. That's important. We gave the same option to the regulars. In the whole state, we only had about fifty people or so refuse the transfer from a U.S. to an Oregon commander-in-chief."

"That makes me feel better than anything you've said so far," Corcoran said, glancing at Candor, as if daring him to deny it. He relit his third cigar, which had, dutifully, sputtered out. He scowled at it.

He turned to Washington.

"J.B., as my new secretary of state," he said, "I want you to triply underscore the free trade bit to the American states and other nations. If we're going to pull Oregon out of its economic hole, I'd like to count on more than shrugging the federal tax. We need new blood, new capital, new money coming in from other places. We need investment; all we can get. New people, too. I think we should consider completely unrestricted immigration for awhile."

Candor grunted and let out a low whistle. The combination sounded like an asthmatic pig. He said, "There's a lot of provincialism in this state, Corky. I recommend saving that bomb for later, until other things cool down, until we know we're solid and won't be forcefully reabsorbed."

"Hmmph," Corcoran said. "What difference does that make, Bard?"

"Well, it's just that immigrants' reliability is extremely questionable."

Corcoran cut him off by slamming his hand on his desk top and glaring.

"Can it, Bard!" Corcoran said. "Let's not go there. Immigrants will be here because they want to be. That's why immigrants have historically been the most avid patriots. They *think* about what freedom means. I may not know much, but I know what makes a patriot. Oregon needs their kind. Anyway, Bard, I thought your radio commentaries used to brag about how tolerant the Oregon people were. What was it you used to call Oregon, 'the Mecca of Understanding'? What happened to that generous outlook?"

"Well, I, uh— yes, of course. But in a *crisis*, there's something to be said for a more, er, homogenous culture, one unencumbered by the— well, by the historic and ethnic differences that can disrupt a smoothly driven social order."

"You're saying that you don't like anyone who doesn't look like you, Bard?" Corcoran asked quietly. "Is that what you're trying to say?"

"That's not what I meant and you know it!"

"I'm not sure I do. What *do* you mean, then?"

"It's just that, culturally, the inertia of divergent backgrounds can be chaotic, strategically speaking."

"Can the bull, Bard. I want open immigration and if you can't hack it, well, you can emigrate right out of this administration any time."

Candor turned red and shut up.

"See to it, J.B.," Corcoran ordered Washington.

J.B. leaned forward, elbows on knees and said, "I've taken the liberty of swearing in Sparky Katz, our old tourist bureau chief, as commerce secretary. She's already e-mailing and faxing out detailed projections of the improved business climate here. They're going worldwide. They include invitations to outside businessmen to visit Oregon. I'll expand that to include anyone else, businessman or not. She's putting up a great new web page, too."

"Fine. But make it clear that we're not running a welfare wagon. I don't want the free-lunch loafers from our neighbors or overseas swamping us."

The governor looked out the window at the heat waves rising off the white concrete pavement bordering the capitol park lawns.

"Personally, I think it'll take a bushel of sweet-talk to get anyone to come here," he said. "Oregon's got a long, bad, anti-business rep to overcome. Since the Tom McCall era, it's been hanging over us. We haven't exactly had a knack for making outsiders feel officially welcome."

Candor started to voice a protest, then stifled it. His fascination with the late Governor McCall legend was well known — although McCall had been no racist and would've blanched had he known who some of his admirers were these days.

Corcoran sighed, shook his head, and took a third try at lighting cigar number three.

"Sorry if I'm sounding negative, fellas," he said. "I feel like somebody's added twenty pounds of lead to my pockets, and I've barely started flapping my wings."

"No one said it would be easy," J.B. said.

"No, well," Corcoran added, standing and stretching, "to further exasperate Ben with my habitual bad metaphors, I've got to go out and feed the wolves some sirloin tips."

He grinned grimly, clamped the cigar between his teeth, and strode off to the news conference.

None of the men in the room, except one, had any desire to fill Corcoran's shoes.

Several hours later, Corcoran rolled over and gently kissed Sparky Katz on her lips. The two had been lovers for the better part of a year. It had been four years since his wife had died in a freak fall and Katz was the first woman for whom he'd felt any romantic interest. They had kept their get-togethers secret, usually meeting at her small studio house in West Salem. Katz came from a fairly wealthy family, and she herself had invested wisely in real estate and maintained three residences. Her hobby was oil painting and she used this place to work. Its north-facing atrium had perfect light, she said.

It's certainly perfect for her, he thought, looking at her smooth skin and dark, dramatic eyebrows and hair.

She saw the look, smiled, and touched his gaunt face, running one finger along a deep line on his right jaw.

"Hey, prez," she teased, "like that free trade deal?"

"Wasn't free," he said, reaching for a cigar on her nightstand. "I had to work for it. That's what you get, carrying on with a man 30 years older than you."

"I'm not complaining."

"You never do. I'm just saying that I wouldn't blame you."

She shook her head and smiled ruefully. They'd been down this dead-end trail before. Why'd he keep bringing it up?

"You're perfect for me, Corky," she said, snuggling closer and watching him try to get the cigar going. "Body and soul."

He smiled at her through the smoke and replied, "If you say so. But I don't like how complicated this is suddenly getting. Bedding a gal in the tourist bureau was one thing. But now that you're heading into the job of Commerce Secretary, it's going to raise a few eyebrows if word gets out."

Katz frowned, leaned up on one elbow, and said, "Then let's uncomplicate it. Let's get engaged and make it public. Nothing to hide, nothing to fear, right?"

Corcoran gave her a shocked look and asked, "Woman, did you just propose to me? Is that what 21st century gals do?"

"The braver ones," Katz said, slapping him lightly on the chest. "So what do you think? Let's open this romance and let the world spit and sputter!"

Corcoran grinned, took several puffs of his cigar, then said seriously, "I don't think I'm ready for that, Sparky. The age difference—"

"Is negligible in these days of life-extension and high-tech medicine. You are in better shape than half the 30-year-olds I know, Corky."

"And how many is that?" Corcoran prodded.

"Enough to know. Besides, I love you. Do you love me?" she asked, suddenly grabbing a handful of chest hairs and tugging. "You've never said."

"Ow! Hey, woman, you're treading dangerously—"

She tugged again, harder, and demanded, "Do you?"

"Yeah I do," he said quietly. "I do. But still—"

She touched his lips with one finger, smiled, and said, "Okay. That's enough for now. I'll wait for the rest."

"You know, after this rebellion—"

"Sure, Corky, okay. Put that tobacco weed away and give me a back rub."

He nodded, relieved. He stubbed out his cigar and said, "You got it. Roll over, beautiful. Let me show you why experience counts."

"I never doubted it."

"You should."

"Now you're contradicting yourself," she said, turning over on her stomach.

"Hey, politicians are supposed to be good at that, right?"

"Yes, sir, Mr. President, sir. Love it when you get all illogical on me."

Then he started rubbing her back. She groaned.

Half an hour later, they stood quietly together in front of the west, upstairs window, sipping a local merlot and watching the sun descend behind the blue-green hills of the Oregon Coast Range 20 miles distant. Tendrils of gold, rose, and violet streaked along a lazy band of low, wispy clouds. A huge flock of Canada geese circled up into the air, twisting and flowing like a school of a thousand airborne fish. The sun crossed momentarily between the lower edge of the clouds and the top of the hills. The nearby buildings caught the slanting rays and turned a brilliant bronze. The effect lingered for a few seconds until the sun slid away, then the sky flushed deep red, almost purple.

She sighed and hugged him closer with her free arm. He look down at her and smiled.

Chapter 7

"Peeled Off By A Low Branch"

U.S. President Sam Washington thought he should be steamed. He figured the feeling would come, eventually. But it was hard to be steamed when he was flabbergasted. He felt as he had once as a kid when a horse he was riding peeled him off by ducking under a low branch, nearly knocking him out. He'd known what had happened, but couldn't quite believe it at the time.

He absently hit the "fade" button of the remote control for the 100-inch video wall monitor. The image of a gray-haired *CNN* correspondent quickly disappeared. Sam slumped back in his chair and let out a long, "Sheeeeez!"

Alone, he'd watched Corcoran's speech and follow-up news conference. He finally—if not fully—saw that his cousin J.B. had not after all been pulling his leg. Even a state senate president couldn't get a governor to load *this* big a punchline into a legislative practical joke. Governors didn't do that, not for anyone. Declaring the official state moss was one thing. Declaring independence was a ball game from another planet.

Sam found it tough to get a grip on it. Oh, sure, he'd heard what Corcoran had said. The U.S. president's exceptional auditory memory could probably come close to recalling every seditious word. But the idea of a state suddenly seceding, in *this* day and age, refused to sink all the way down to the emotional level. Or maybe it had — numbing his emotive center like a flashbulb stunning the retina.

He considered calling his cousin direct, but decided it would be pointless and embarrassing. After all, J.B. had tried to set him straight.

"Well," he declared to the empty room, "I can't just twiddle my thumbs and sit on it."

He dialed his secretary, Ella Paxson. He didn't have to dial her, but did it out of habit, to keep an important ruse in good practice. Ella's high-tech transceiver earphone, which everyone presumed was a simple hearing aid, was tuned to a hidden microphone system in the president's office. No one knew this except the two of them. Ella was not merely a secretary, but a back-up witness. She heard everything anyone said to the U.S. head of state. It was an unconventional arrangement, but it made him comfortable. Given Ella's efficiency, the system eliminated the chief-of-staff position.

Unlike his predecessors, Sam Washington didn't tape his meetings. He felt it would discourage honest conversation and inhibit good, heated discussions, the kind that forged wiser decisions. Yet he wanted a record of *some* sort. Ella had not just superior, but perfect recall of the spoken word. His was good, but hers was better. She was his recorder.

Other than his wife Annette, Ella was Washington's most frequent and trusted advisor. He didn't want one who didn't know the score. An uninformed advisor could be a fountain of distractions, always drawing the chief executive off course.

"Yes, sir?" her courteous middle-aged voice answered.

"Ella, get together the core group. I want everyone in the Oval in two hours. No, make it two-and-a-half. I've got to grab a bite first. Include Tom Rosco in the meeting. He'll have to be there to prepare a response for the media. I guess you know what about."

"The secession."

"Yeah, exactly," Washington said, massaging his temples. His headache of a few days earlier had mysteriously returned. He was prone to migraines. Not serious, but annoying.

"Anything else, sir?"

"Have the cook send over to the Oval Office a roast beef and mustard sandwich with nachos and hot sauce on the side. Aspirin, too. And a couple antacids while you're at it."

"For the hot sauce and mustard, or for the rebellion?" Her voice danced.

"Both, probably," the president said grouchily.

"Certainly."

He was at his Oval Office desk, wiping beer foam from his red mustache, when the core group began wandering in. The core group was basically his National Security Council, which in this administration included most of the cabinet and a couple members of Congress.

The first to arrive, as usual, was Tom Rosco, his young press secretary, whose office was just down the hall. The lanky Rosco smiled mischievously, grabbed coffee from a mobile sidebar, and asked, "So, when does the Union emancipate your home state, suh?"

"Enough of the 'suh' stuff. Leave that to Sunderleaf. It comes naturally to him. And don't remind me of my Oregon heritage," Sam said glumly. "It's hard enough already. Bring me a cup of that java brew, will you, Tom?"

He pushed his beer aside, burping. Acid unpleasantly scorched the back of his throat. This was not turning out to be a good week.

"Sure," the younger man said cheerfully, pouring a fresh cup of coffee and setting it in front of Sam Washington.

The president and Rosco seldom used formality. Other than Ella, Tom Rosco was the person in his administration with whom the president was most relaxed. The press secretary had fallen into the job when his predecessor, Donald Ray, had been forced to resign after failing to fully recover from a nasty traffic accident. Sam and Tom had developed a rare, almost father-son rapport. Rosco was casually outspoken and never expected his boss to take offense. The president seldom did. The young man's directness and generational difference was an asset, not to be discouraged by pointless bristling.

"Heard a good one the other day," Rosco said.

"Oh, yeah?"

"There's a new kind of soup on the market in honor of philandering presidents. Know what it consists of?"

"Haven't a clue."

"A weenie in a lot of hot water."

Sam Washington chuckled and said, "Yeah, I can think of a couple predecessors who'd fit that one."

The two men traded several more jokes and then, all in a row, the rest of the core group began to arrive.

First was Jeanne Allison, National Security chief. She was followed by the new Joint Chief's head, General Glenn "Spaceman" Young. Almost on their heels were the moody young Bill Brighton of the CIA, Secretary of State Craig Goldstein, and the aging Secretary of Defense, Grieve McDouglas. Trailing them were the taciturn Vice-President Kurt Leininger and ever-homespun House Speaker Baker Sunderleaf. Several aides and lesser officials also came in. Ella Paxson entered last, efficiently carrying a secretary's yellow palm computer, which was as much for show as function. She carefully closed the door behind her, as though fearing to awaken someone outside.

From his desk, President Sam Washington looked over the group, thinking back. Except for McDouglas, who had been ill, all had seen him through the scary, touch-and-go days of Big Three, the Third World War—sometimes called the Engels Extension incident, mainly by arcane historians. Although both nukes and biological weapons had been involved, by a near miracle none had detonated on U.S. territory. Nor had the Big Three proven to be the planetary Armageddon that many experts had predicted. When it came right down to it, it hadn't been a war anyone had expected. From first warning to last shot, it had been over in weeks and much of it was fought completely out of sight of the world's public.

Waiting for the group to get coffee and settle into seats, he reflected that no one should have been surprised by that war. Not really. *Many* major conflicts had been significantly different than their predecessors. In each, the attacked nation or nations had been shocked. After each, the political landscape had changed, often dramatically. In the case of Big Three, the U.S. had narrowly escaped Project Engels Extension, a daring sneak attack aimed at establishing world domination by a new leader of the Russian union. World domination, the old advocates of *glasnost* had sniffed, was an outmoded goal, if it had ever existed. Nevertheless, in one bold stroke, someone had tried—and come within a mosquito's wing of winning. But with defeat had come something even less expected. Russia had lost its centuries-old empire, lock, stock, and borscht barrel. It did not even rule itself anymore. A thousand-year regime had fallen. In its place ruled a more brazen power that had unexpectedly erupted out of the ancient east. China's Shang Empire was creating a new Middle Kingdom.

"Crack of hell," Sam mouthed silently, "it's as though the Master Plotter didn't get enough kicks out of Big Three and this post-war recession. Now He has to harass me with this stupid rebellion."

He sighed and ordered himself to switch focus. He laced his fingers and stretched husky arms, one by one. For a moment, he felt sympathy for the late Mr. Gorbachev. Washington wondered if this was how it had started for Gorbachev—just a papery crack in a no-problem province that no one took seriously until it was much too late to easily solve. Sam Washington was not Mikhail Gorbachev, though. He believed in decisive, early damage control. If Oregon went, no one could say how wide the crack might become, splitting and dangerously weakening the whole of the Union. Wouldn't the Shang thugs of Beijing love that! He would not give them the satisfaction. No way.

He moved away from his desk and settled his tall, husky frame into the worn black leather chair at the head of a small conference table, which he'd kept in the Oval Office virtually from day one. It was non-traditional, but more business-like in his view. Anette thought it made the Oval Office too crowded. Well, she wasn't the president. He placed his palms flat on the surface and closed his eyes for a moment, an old self-calming trick. Conversation quieted. When he looked up at the group of trusted advisors, more than one person shivered. Their president's face had a familiar, stony cast. It was the look they had sometimes seen during Big Three. It was the face of a leader who had taken Ivan's best punches and then flattened him. This was the man who had saved the entire free world, and maybe civilization itself. And he looked downright grouchy.

CHAPTER 8

"One on One"

Sergeant Larry Rigg and Corporal Karl Hochman stood on a small bluff. In a light rain they watched two members of their independent militia run through a drill in wet, brushy evergreen terrain spread out across a wide gully. To either side of the two leaders stood some forty men and women not currently engaged in action. They, too, were observing. They were supposed to be learning about concealment in movement.

The previous week had been devoted to weapons handling and shooting drills. Considering how little experience the volunteers had brought with them, Rigg was reasonably pleased with the progress. He focused on the positive. Hochman, on the other hand, thought there was a long, long way to go. A perennial pessimist, he incessantly worried about what would happen if the militia were actually forced to defend anything. He expected heavy losses, maybe complete disintegration under fire. Objectively, the tug-of-war between the affirmative and negative mindsets of Rigg and Hochman created a training momentum and mood that was about right. When the troops got discouraged, Rigg would lift their spirits by reminding them of what they'd accomplished. When they got cocky or careless, Hochman would remind them of the consequences of their ignorance and sloppiness. Call it carrot and stick, yin and yang, good cop and bad cop. Whatever, Rigg thought. He and Karl made a pretty decent training combo.

"Hey!" Hochman yelled to a girl in black Lycra tights and a gray sweatshirt. She was gingerly kneeling on a mat of pine needles, trying to scan the brush ahead of her.

"You pop up over the top of a log like that and you're gonna have a blood-gusher for brains," Hochman said. "How many times I gotta tell you, private: if at all possible, look *around* your concealment, not over the top!"

The girl yelled back, "There *is* no around to this log, sir! It's lying flat. It goes on, like, *forever*."

"Forever, huh? Well then, it's the first tree I've ever heard about that never stopped growing. See that rootball about twenty feet to your right? Is that forever? I don't think so. It's about ten feet across; it's real; you can't miss it. It appears to be a fine place for a look-see to me."

The girl looked, scrunched her face, and yelled, "But it's so, like, *muddy*!"

Rigg stifled a smile; he pushed a damp pebble around with his boot. Hochman swore vividly and trudged in giant strides down the shale talus below the bluff. He grabbed two giant handfuls of mud from the soggy ground and flung the sticky stuff at the girl. The mud splattered her from head to toe. She squawked, dropped her gun, jumped to her feet, and tried to wipe the goo away with manicured, multicolored fingertips. Hochman wondered what in the world had attracted this one to the militia. He did not expect her to be an asset.

As the girl raised up, she was hit on the side of the head by a paintball.

"Owwww!" she cried. The blue paint ran down her neck and under her sweatshirt. She put her hands on her hips and screamed petulantly toward the direction of the offender. "Stan, you little puke, you'll die for this!"

She was answered by another paintball, this one smacking liquid across the front of her sweatshirt.

The girl yelped, "Oh! Oh, yuuuck!" and began bawling and cursing at the same time.

"Ease up," Hochman told the shooter.

Stan Crothers stood behind a rock thirty yards away. He grinned, the guilty paintgun in his hands.

"Sarge!" Hochman shouted to Rigg. "She's yours."

To himself, he mumbled, "Spare me the blubbery babes."

Rigg sighed and made his way down to the girl, put a hand on her shoulder, and began talking quietly with her.

Hochman trudged over to Crothers and said, "Nice shooting, Private. You just double-killed a federal duck."

Crothers' grin grew less certain. He said, "But jeez, Corporal, sir. I didn't mean to make her *cry*."

Hochman spat on the ground, put his hands on his hips, and said, "Crothers, for God's sake! You only temporarily altered the color of her clothes. If you can't swallow that level of damage, how are you ever gonna shoot to kill?"

Crothers looked down and muttered, "This is different. She don't get it yet, ya know? How to do all this stuff, I mean."

Hochman leaned down and pushed his huge face next to Crothers thin, chiseled features. "Of *course* she doesn't get it yet, Private! That's why we're running this exercise. You don't get it, either, do you? This is *serious*. Except for the fact that a paintball isn't lead, as far as you should be concerned, it's the real thing. All the tactics, all the tricks, all the principles—they work basically the same, except for distance modifications. If you can't keep that in mind, you're in the wrong place. You simply will not feel sorry for a buddy when she screws up in her training."

"But—"

"Don't 'but' me. What are you, a damned billy goat? Look, Crothers, if she thinks you'll whine and pine over her whenever she gets her knees or elbows dirty, it's no favor to her. Your sympathy now could get her killed later."

"Well, I—

"If she does the right thing and bad luck whacks her anyway, fine; then feel sorry for her."

"I know, Corporal, I know, but—"

"You *don't* know! If you get mopey-dopey over her this early in the game, she'll never learn. Private, when I'm talking, look me in the eye!"

Crothers raised his fallen gaze and said, "Yes, sir."

"That's better." Hochman eased his voice down a notch. "Crothers, you've got the makings of a platoon leader, maybe better. Don't let it go to your head, but you *are* learning faster than anybody I ever trained."

"Uh, well, gee. Uh, thanks." Crothers' face brightened.

"Crothers, nobody says 'gee' anymore. And a leader isn't a stinking sob sponge! You're not here to wipe cry-baby salt, or even to think about doing it. You're here to kick ass — the enemy's — and to make sure that all your buddies do, too. Do you think if that little prissy stands up and squawks to the enemy that they're gonna feel sorry for her? Do you?"

"Well, no, sir. Not exactly."

"What?"

"No, sir. Not by a long sight. They'll, uh, kill her."

"Oh, no. Worse. Lots worse."

Crothers blanched.

Hochman smiled wickedly and said, "Yeah, now you're starting to get it, Private. You want to know what the enemy's gonna say if she screws up in combat?"

"Well, er—"

"I'll tell you. They're gonna say, 'Why thank you very much, lady priss private. BANG! We love priss-kickin'!' Or maybe first they'll say, 'We're awfully pig-horny. They'll strip those little Lycra tights off her like skinnin' a frog. You can guess the rest, Private. *Then* after they've all had a few turns, that's when they'll shoot her."

"Yes, sir."

"Then they'll say to her dead body, 'Oh, by the way, thanks for revealing your whole squeakin' squad!' Because if you think she's not gonna talk, *you're* the priss. Then she's gone, and maybe half your men with her, because she was on point and blew their advance because you felt sorry for her and went easy on her when she whined today in training. Is that what you want for her or for your other buddies, huh?"

"No, sir."

"Hmmph," Hochman nodded, then spat into a bush.

"Besides," Crothers added, "I, well, I kinda like her, sir." His ears grew bright red.

"I figured," Hochman said, scowling, but softening his voice slightly. "Then you want her to be tough enough to live. Get me?"

Crothers nodded. Hochman slapped him on the back and said, "Great. Now reload your splatterer and squeeze back into some cover. We're gonna send her through to you again. The less mercy you show, the better her chances in combat, okay?"

"Yes, sir," Crothers said.

He turned and worked back into the damp brush.

Hochman spat an obscenity to himself, then slogged and climbed back to rejoin Rigg and the rest of the unit on the bluff. The girl was down on the ground again, behind the middle of the same log. They watched her crawl towards the rootball of the fallen tree, then stop, putting a finger to her lower lip for a moment, thinking. She suddenly smiled, a narrow, mischievous little grin.

"What's she doing now?" Hochman whispered skeptically to the sergeant. "Her lipstick get smeared? Going back for her make-up case?"

Rigg didn't say anything, but the skin around his eyes crinkled. In the distance, he spotted Crothers between two alder shrubs. He was lining up his paintgun on the rootball, expecting the girl to show.

The girl changed directions. She gritted her teeth and squirmed rapidly to the other end of the log. Ignoring a patch of thick mud, she slithered behind a clump of dead thistle off the narrow, broken head of the fallen fir. The thistle provided better cover than the foliage of the tree itself. Crothers, his attention fixed seventy feet to the girl's right on the rootball, had now passively broken cover; he'd let his position become one-dimensional. He hadn't done it by much, but enough to show part of one shoulder and his rosy right cheek to the girl. She pressed her lips together, carefully aimed her paintgun, took in a breath, let it half out, and then squeezed the trigger. The paintball took Crothers on the temple. The observers on the bluff heard a low grunt from him followed by, "Aw, horseballs!"

The girl whooped, pointed at him, and yelled gleefully, "Your brains are paste, paint-packer!"

The other militia members broke into cheers and applause.

"Live wire, isn't she?" Rigg said softly to his corporal. "She ever gets that spunk under control, she might do okay."

Hochman said, "Big if"—but he secretly agreed.

He shouted at Crothers, "You've paid the price for an unwarranted assumption, Private. How does it feel? Foul shot for the foul-mouthed lady. Next pair!"

Crothers and the girl climbed out of the exercise area. The boy wiped paint from his head and cheek. The girl stuck her tongue out at him and he blushed.

Hochman hissed, "Sarge, she *should* have sneaked by him to reach her objective. I oughta ream her pampered little—"

"A bit at a time, Karl," Rigg said, as the next two trainees skidded down the talus to take their turn in the brush. "Let her savor it for awhile. Besides, her shooting was on the mark."

Hochman cursed, nodded, sighed, and lit a cigarette. He was enjoying every minute of this.

Rigg called the next exercise basketball. The day's particular version was one-on-one. The object was to penetrate past an enemy trooper, or "kill" him as a secondary option, and make a goal. A goal was a stretch of ground some three-hundred yards away and fifty yards wide. It was basic, simple practice. Later, teams would go against each other. A goal was, as in basketball, two points. Killing the enemy was one point, a foul shot, but not the best choice. The analogy to a familiar sport made it easier for the novices to understand the exercise. It was especially good for the younger recruits, but those with experience could benefit from it, too. Each person went through the course eight times daily and at the end of the day scores were tallied.

After two days, young Crothers was tied for the lead with a white-stubbled, seventy-four-year old carpenter from Marcola. The old fellow was in excellent shape and better at using cover. But Crothers was the superior shot with faster reflexes. Rigg wished wistfully that all his men had Crothers' reflexes and the old guy's wiles. It could be something to shoot for, so to speak.

But, he thought, momentarily feeling more like Hochman, there *was* an immense amount of training to go through. It would take a lot of time. He wondered how much they'd have.

He had reason to wonder. That morning, he'd heard a story from a cousin who lived near Ashland, not far from the California border. Two hunters in the area claimed they'd spotted a squad of six men outfitted in what the hunters thought was U.S. Army battle dress. Too far off to positively identify, the squad had reportedly made its way north across a remote forest clearing in the Siskiyou Mountains. Rigg didn't know what to make of it. Some hunters told bigger lies than fishermen. Personally, he had until now believed it was much too early for a federal response. But Rigg knew his corporal was right about one thing. Given current skill levels, a few snips from U.S. Army scissors would make paper dolls out of most of his militia.

Chapter 9

"Best Laid Plans"

So let's go over the idea again," Sam Washington said, wiping his brow after hours of haggling. "We'll build the pressure slowly, assessing progress as we go. Cover the elements again, would you, Craig?" he asked the Secretary of State. "Let's make sure we all agree on this idea."

"Yes, sir," Goldstein said.

The president leaned back and took a sip of coffee. Sam longed for a cigarette, but was again trying to stop. On a promise to his wife, he'd quit after Big Three. Maintenance was the difficulty. He looked enviously at Grieve McDouglas, who had lit his own cigarette and appeared to be thoroughly enjoying it, with not even a touch of guilt.

McDouglas, the Secretary of Defense, lowered his black eyebrows and tapped his weed against an ashtray. Despite outward appearances, inside he was seething. He was outraged that Goldstein had been put in charge of the secession mess. McDouglas felt that sooner or later the job was going to end up being military. As it should be. Sooner was better, though, and things didn't seem to be heading that way. If a military man was quickly put in charge, things would get solved quicker and smoother. Lives and treasure would be saved. Sure, the U.S. was civilian-run and his position was civilian, just like the other members of the Cabinet. But he didn't think of himself that way. Not deep inside where no one but himself could see. He'd always believed in immersing himself in the essence of the mission of his profession. His essential mission these days was military. If he saw the evolving political picture correctly, he figured he'd get his turn only after the devil himself squirted out of a volcano. He forced himself to keep his face calm. He stopped tapping his cigarette and looked at Goldstein, whose intelligence he respected. But respecting his *judgment* was a different brand of tank.

Goldstein busily adjusted a sheaf of scribbled notes, repositioned his glasses, cleared his throat, and said, "Well, ladies and gentlemen, the plan has three prongs. They will ring with three forms of pressure: political; economic; then—God save us from family feuds—military."

He nodded at McDouglas, who gave him a blank stare. Until the enemy broke into the Oval Office and smashed the orange juice pitcher, the military would remain the boor at breakfast in this conflict, McDouglas thought. His ear to the political ground brought a highly unsettling conviction that the president and most of his people were taking this rebellion *way* too lightly. He'd have to try to talk to Sam Washington alone. This was going to require some deeply indirect, behind-the-scenes work. These meetings were too public. But that could be useful. As could Goldstein's obvious naivete.

Goldstein said, "No use being unnecessarily rough at first. Oregon must be given the opportunity to save face. Thus, we'll roll first with very gentle pressure."

Moron, McDouglas mused. Sounds like he's talking about a foam-rubber tank. Gradual escalation, of all things! I thought we dumped that after Vietnam and again after those screwball Balkan troubles!

Goldstein pontificated on, "The pressure will start at the highest non-presidential level; that is, with me, heh-heh. I'll work at it for a few weeks, and then—"

"*Weeks?*" McDouglas blurted. "Forgive me, sir," he said, leveling his tone and directing his comments to Sam Washington. "That makes *no* strategic sense. It'll give them time not only to consolidate their forces, but to hire the entire Shang army if they want to."

"Well, I appreciate your concern, Grieve," the president said, uncertain about the vehemence of McDouglas's tone, "but I'm sure Oregon isn't expecting anything to go that far. This appears to be primarily a diplomatic matter. Besides, I don't think they're either unpatriotic or wealthy enough to hire foreign help."

"*We* certainly did, as a young nation over two centuries ago! And we were a lot poorer than they are now," McDouglas pointed out. "Sam, at least let me send some Ranger recon or a DIA undercover detail in. Let me get a few of Allison's satellites reconfigured to watch Oregon's military bases. Let me put feelers into their guard units so we'll *know* what we're dealing with, instead of just guessing."

"Grieve, if I think that kind of thing is necessary," Sam said, "we'll get to it. There are other forms of toughness."

"There are *certainly* less hardware-oriented options to explore," Goldstein said, wrinkling his nose.

"But you see, sir," McDouglas said, ignoring the intrusion and speaking to his president, "you thereby compound your logistics disadvantage. Down the road that means—"

"This isn't the former imperial USSR we're dealing with," Goldstein said sullenly, forcing McDouglas's attention back to him. "Nobody from Oregon has threatened or attacked us, or any individual state. I frankly doubt that Corcoran plans military action. To the contrary, he appears to be taking a purely political and economic tack. His address to the world indicated as much."

"Ever heard the word *deception*?" McDouglas shot back.

Goldstein sighed and said, "I think we must extend him a generous measure of good will. If he sees us moving militarily at this stage, it could completely freeze any predilection he might have to bring civil closure to this terribly unfortunate misunderstanding."

"Believe me," McDouglas said, gritting his teeth, "Corcoran understands exactly what he's doing. Oregon has no intention of compromising its way out of this. Those boys have defined a mission and are bearing down on it like a cruise missile. Don't forget that I served with their president way back in the old days. I know Corcoran's mentality. He doesn't sign on for anything he doesn't think he can finish."

"Some soldiers graduate beyond their weapon-toys," Goldstein snapped. "Corcoran almost certainly has more refined motives these days."

"Craig, men like Corcoran don't change," McDouglas said. "Take it to the bank."

"Given the right circumstances, *all* men change."

"Not this guy. If you operate on that premise, he'll steal your pants, press 'em and clean 'em, and wear 'em to your funeral. Try it out. Go talk to him. See where you get."

McDouglas sat back and sealed his face to emotion while staring at Goldstein unblinkingly. Goldstein quickly looked away. McDouglas knew that if he hadn't been laid up unconscious in a hospital during Big Three, he'd never have approved of Goldstein being appointed Secretary of State. He'd have fought it and fought it hard. What was Sam *thinking*? Didn't he see what a typical State Department *worm* he'd picked?

As if sensing the thought, Goldstein looked back up at McDouglas and started to voice a sharp retort, but the president held up his hand and said, "Enough. Let's move on. Craig, it's your show—for now."

McDouglas flicked another cigarette to life and leaned back in his chair.

"Naturally," Goldstein said smoothly, quickly regaining his composure, "I'll try measured reason. If that doesn't work in due time, then I'll fork it over to you, Mr. President, to tweak the economic prong. I see this as a classic thrust-and-parry diplomatic contest, snatching opportunities as they arise, remaining flexible and agile the whole time."

"Yes, I understand," Sam said, drumming a pencil against his old-fashioned yellow legal notepad, then jotting a memo. "I've been a politician long enough to know the role of the impromptu."

"Y'all gotta rope a gator where he swims," House Speaker Baker "Bake" Sunderleaf unexpectedly drawled. "And make no mistake; Oregon's got a mess o' gators in charge."

"Amen," McDouglas said.

"What's *that* supposed to mean?" CIA chief Brighton asked, entering the fray. As usual, Sunderleaf irritated him. He didn't like his drawl and thought that his Southern metaphors clouded more than they clarified. Precision, he thought, is a foreign word to Bake. It's no wonder he irritated McDouglas. Now *there* was a precise guy. In fact, Brighton found that he had far more in common with the defense secretary than their age differences and backgrounds might indicate. Since Big Three, Brighton had toughened up. He'd listened and learned.

"On t'other hand," Sunderleaf added, ignoring the question and catching McDouglas's eye, "a good hunter don't unnecessarily rile his prey."

McDouglas blew smoke at the ceiling and rolled his eyes. He knew that Sunderleaf was a smart old dog, but he was too much of a politician. Too prone to debate and delay.

"What will you try first, Craig?" Jeanne Allison of the National Security Agency asked.

"Why I'm going to take Grieve's advice. I'm going to fly out tomorrow and talk to the governor personally," he said, throwing a thin smile in the defense chief's direction. "I believe a warm, face-to-face approach has the best chance of melting the ice. I'll look for common ground with Corky. That sort of thing. Standard fare in my department. We're trained at it."

"I take it you're going to see what it'll require to bring him back into the Union?" the Joint Chiefs head, General Glenn Young, asked.

"What? Oh, yes. Exactly, Glenn. I'm sure he wants it as much as we do. This sounds like an elaborate ploy to me; a form of psychological positioning in order to gain concessions of some sort. Of course, we'll naturally have to establish *our* position, too."

"What exactly is that?" Sunderleaf interposed. "All I'm

hearin' is pretty words."

"So will they, Bake. Pretty words, but firm words. I'll courteously refuse to acknowledge that they have left the Union. We can't appear to give up the high ground."

"Seems to me the beaver state boys have already taken it," Glenn noted.

McDouglas nodded at him, straightening his suit. It hung loosely on him since his long stay in the hospital. He thought to himself that he'd missed the entire war with Russia and now his clothes didn't fit. What a way to live.

"You know what they'll demand, Craig," Sam Washington said. "They'll demand that we lower their federal tax in a big way."

Several of the group assented.

"That's their main beef," Tom Rosco added. "I don't see that they'll give much on it, either. I've been talking to some of the Oregon reporters here in town. They say the leadership is united on that. Worse—from our point of view— Gallup, Harris, Roper, Zogby, and the other polls concur that some two-thirds of their voters *back* the secession. And it's growing."

"To be expected," McDouglas said, grinding out his cigarette and folding his arms.

"That high?" Sam asked, expressing mild surprise.

The president was determined to be firm in this matter, of course, but also wanted to make it clear that he was being prudent. Oregonians were more stubborn than many. It was his home state. He knew. Less than most Americans, they didn't like to be pushed around. It was well that everyone in his group of advisors remembered it.

"The only way to ax their tax," Brighton said, "is to do it for everyone. In the whole country. Across the board, in all 50 states. But the sentiment on the Hill is that it won't wash in the Beltway laundromat."

"Unfortunately," Goldstein glibly picked up, "that's completely correct. There is simply no Congressional consensus. Too many Big Three war bills still have to be paid and too many recession transfer payments are going out or are already committed. The annual deficit is triple what it was before the war. And unlike the Gulf War of '91 or the several smaller conflicts that have followed, our allies aren't covering much of our costs. Their troubles are even worse than ours. Big Three was an unfortunate conflict which knocked the West for an economic loop. Oregon has got to understand the big picture, not just from their provincial point of view, but from our side of the frame. That's the way it has to be. We have to be tough on that point or all the other states will demand special treatment, too. Then where would we be?"

"Back to supply-side economics and more financial freedom, perhaps?" Vice President Leininger interjected. His opposition to the current state of high taxation was frequent and unbending, but he was among the minority in the core group who felt anything could be done about it.

McDouglas chuckled bitterly and shook his head.

Actually, the president thought that McDouglas probably understood Oregon's determination better than anyone present. But he also felt that his secretary of state was showing wise judgment. Any military move would push Oregon away, not bring it back.

"Well, I, for one, tend to agree with Craig's cautious approach," Vice-President Kurt Leininger added. "But what, really, *is* the big picture here? I'm not exactly sure anymore."

He tamped fresh tobacco into his ever-present pipe. He looked at his old friend, Sam Washington.

Sam sighed. A few minutes ago, he had assumed that the consensus for action was settled. Now it seemed to be crumbling like a piece of dry corn bread. Oh well, he thought, if I had a dime for every squabble in a meeting, I'd be as rich as old Bill Gates.

Leininger puffed his pipe to life, then went on, "As I see it, we're repeating the mistakes of the Great Depression. That dark period was unnecessarily prolonged by a resort to heavier taxation and more regulatory restrictions. Not to mention tight money and trade restrictions, which we also have. As the works of Sennholz showed—and the studies of practically every competent free market theorist of the last several decades—had Roosevelt lowered taxes and cut regulation, the Depression would have been over in two years; three at the outside. In a way, I can't blame the Oregonians."

He puffed a cloud of smoke into the air over the table. Goldstein frowned at it. He tended to be a preachy non-smoker.

"Maybe," Leininger added, "they have seen the error of *our* ways. Perhaps this is their way of saying so. We didn't listen to anything less, did we? And, after all, they're a small state with not a lot of power in the halls of D.C."

Sunderleaf added, "Sometimes li'l fellows have got to jump high and shout loud to be noticed."

Sam nodded and tapped his yellow notepad with a heavy index finger.

"Okay," he said, "as an Oregonian, and a free marketer, of course I agree. But as an American, and a tactician, I can't. I'm on the hotseat. As chief Brighton implied, I have to work with Congress. Cutting taxes means cutting benefits. Try that and it means constituents screaming to their congressmen. Every senator and representative on the Hill sees unemployment and homelessness as a political death threat. Buck 'em and die. To them, it's a bronc they don't want to bust. Economically, theoretically, sure, you're probably right, Kurt. And frankly, I'm hoping that as we sink deeper, as the surtax backfires, Congress will gain some guts. Right now, though—" He spread his hands and shook his head. "It's a no go."

"But you've got war hero popularity, Sam," Leininger said, raising an eyebrow. "Why not cash in on it? You seldom have. As Reagan said, if not now, when? Make a few TV-side and national forum Internet chats to the nation on the virtues of tax cuts. There are a lot more taxpayers out there than people on the dole or in the street. Congressmen know that, too. Give 'em a *choice* of broncs."

"Don't think it hasn't occurred to me," Sam Washington said. "If it didn't take so much time, I'd do it. But a few chats won't turn things soon enough in this Oregon rebellion." The president shook his head slowly. "No, like it or not, it's the unemployed and the breadliners who are screaming the loudest and getting the big media coverage. On top of that, most of the working people are stuck in the old altruism trap. They're sympathizing too much and thinking too little. No doubt it's hurting more people in the long run. But as I peg this cribbage game, the folly's got to run its course."

"Perhaps we could rejuvenate the privatization movement, then," Allison suggested. "It's certainly doing well for the Third World. Your slogan could be something like, 'Why should they have what we can't?' Unlike the major industrial powers, the poorer nations—even old Russia lately under the Shang—are making a hell of a run with the policy. They picked up where we left off under Reagan."

"Right," Leininger said, gesturing in the air with his pipe. "Sam, the thing about privatizing is that it doesn't involve raising taxes or at least not if it's done right. That could be the ticket to break the—"

Washington cut him off, "Nope, not now. Perhaps down the road. The crowds who won't let go of their dole certainly won't want to see the agencies that *do* the doling get mowed under by the private sector. You know that's how they'd translate it, Kurt."

Leininger shrugged. He could see that there was no point pushing the issue further today. He was a man who believed in judiciously picking his battles and clearly the president had already set a course. Leininger retreated behind his pipe.

"As indicated, the next logical step would be economic," Goldstein resumed. "Sanctions, small ones at first, I presume. A full economic blockade if necessary."

"Well," Washington said. "Let's just make sure that day never comes."

"It won't. I assure you that it's simply horsetrading," Goldstein said, "although Oregon has to *think* we'll do it."

Idiotic, McDouglas thought, because it's already way beyond that.

"Not only that," Goldstein said, "I believe that they *want* us to talk them down. They took a dramatic step in order to make sure we got the message that items for sale were being spread on the table. Population-wise, Oregon's a pip-squeak. As Bake noted earlier, it's hard to be heard in Congress unless you do something spectacular."

The president stood up and said, "Well, no need to get into the third option, the military stuff, for now. I think the first two points will carry us for awhile."

"But, Mr. president—" McDouglas started.

"Grieve, there's no advantage setting plans too firmly when the rock might roll any which way."

McDouglas held the president's eye a moment, then nodded. An oddly interesting idea had come to the old defense secretary. He made a point to draw Sam aside for a private meeting later. On a hunch, he also decided to ask CIA chief Brighton to join them.

Chapter 10

"Ante Up!"

Secretary of State Craig Goldstein felt like a hearing impaired frog in a vise. His mouth gaped, his chest was tight, and he couldn't believe what his ears were trying to tell him.

"Uh, come again, Governor?"

Republic of Oregon President Alf "Corky" Corcoran barked, "You heard me, you little twit. First, I'm not a *governor* anymore. Second, Oregon is seeking a confederation with Taiwan. Taiwan is a free nation, and it has a lot to offer us — and it's interested. We're the first country in decades to treat it with full fledged respect. Considering Uncle Sam's patronizing attitude toward us, as amply expressed by your uppity little visit here, I understand exactly how those poor guys feel. Especially with the Shang wagging nukes in their faces."

"But a confederation with foreigners is not only hopelessly outdated, it's completely unconstitution — "

Corcoran steamrolled, "Your constitution, great document that it is, if any of you took it seriously, doesn't apply here. We've got our own."

"But that's a mere *state* document."

"You don't get it yet, do you, Goldstein?" Corcoran leaned forward, his face doing a reasonable impersonation of a thunderhead. "If you want the flat-down, tread-to-the-threads report, I don't see that this is any of your business. What we do with either our internal or international affairs is our call and our right. We're sovereign and our allegiances are our own. All we want you to do is what we've been saying from the start: leave us alone!"

Goldstein snorted, "You sound like the Baltics talking to the old USSR."

"Son, if it hasn't occurred to you," Corcoran said, holding his cigar up and inspecting the end, "that happens to be exactly why people secede—to be left alone."

"But that's, that's, that's positively anachronistic!" Goldstein sputtered, "In this day and age it's ignorant in the absolute ext—"

Corcoran interrupted, flipping a huge hunk of ash into a black marble tray in front of Goldstein, "Think of it as a whole state emigrating, taking its turf with it."

"But—"

"I've had enough yakkin' at an ambulatory federal fencepost. Good day, sir!"

Corcoran stood.

"But, you haven't even listened to my complete diplomatic proposals!"

Corcoran pointed his eight-inch cigar at the door and said, "You're the one with wax in his ears, buddy. I'm tired of flappin' my talk-ropes. I'm sure our friends in the news media will be glad to fill you in about the Taiwan deal—after the word is made public, of course. Meanwhile, I'd appreciate it if you'd keep it under your hat for a week or so, if that's not a major strain."

Stuttering, Goldstein let Corcoran virtually pull him out of his chair and escort him through the door. Corcoran stuck the smaller man's hat on his head. Goldstein stared at Corcoran as though he were a creature from the lower depths of Jupiter. Mumbling, the U.S. Secretary of State walked down the marble stairs and out into an Oregon thunderstorm. He jerked his coat collar tight and angrily ordered one of his escorts to retrieve the rented car. Like a cat clawing chiffon, Corcoran had shredded Goldstein's entire political persuasion plan. Well, Goldstein thought bitterly, we'll see how the big blowhard likes it when Uncle Sam gets *really* mad.

"Did he buy it?" Ben Colby asked a few minutes later in Corcoran's office.

"More like he suffered it," Corcoran purred, grinning widely. "He came in here with that down-the-nose attitude of most D.C. career politicos. Tried to lay on the syrup."

"Am I correct to assume that you force-fed him a spoonful of hot sauce instead?"

"It'll take a day or so before it runs through his gut."

Colby winced at the crudeness, but smiled. One had to take the head of the Republic of Oregon as he was.

"By the way," Colby said, "the representative from Taiwan is here."

"Good," Corcoran said. "I hear they've got a weapons industry with too few customers."

Chapter 11

"Thicker Than Blood"

Several weeks later, the situation from the White House's official point of view was worse. It could hardly have been otherwise.

"The economic blockade isn't working," Sam Washington told his core group. His words fell heavy and flat, like a plate of iron—which is how he intended them to sound.

"Er, no, sir," Goldstein said, throwing a worried glance at his boss. The president had talked to virtually no one in the past 24 hours. From their experience with him during Big Three, they all knew what that meant. Washington was contemplating a major change of direction. He'd probably already picked his path. But for awhile, he would still listen. It might not be irreversible, whatever it was.

"None of Oregon's neighbors and hardly any of the foreign nations that it's done business with have complied with our sanctions," Goldstein affirmed. He knew how pessimistic he sounded and wished he could put a happier spin on the news. "Oh, some of them *say* they've complied. Some have even pretended to do so. But our intelligence indicates that the flow of goods and services to Oregon hasn't stopped."

"This paper blockade is like trying to block light with an open window," McDouglas grumbled.

"What's it been, now? Two months?" Washington asked,

curiously taking no offense at McDouglas's tone.

"About that, yes," Goldstein answered. He was embarrassed that he'd been unable to manage either a political or economic solution in recent weeks. He'd stayed in Oregon and made a pest of himself until—well, until they finally got sick of him and kicked him out. In his eyes, he'd returned to D.C. in disgrace. Meanwhile, a lot of time had passed and things in Oregon were changing rapidly.

"I hear that while we're wallowing in a recession, they're booming," General Glenn Young said, smiling. He admired the spunkiness of the Oregonians. He glanced at the vice president, who smiled back.

"Ya'll give a 'gator room to swim, 'n' he's gonna do it," Baker Sunderleaf quipped, chomping into a piece of giant bearclaw pastry.

"Tell me, Bake," CIA's Bill Brighton asked, giving the speaker a scathing look, "Do you know any analogies *not* involving gators?"

"Sure," Baker answered serenely. "Know lotsa snake metaphors."

Brighton smiled mirthlessly. The CIA chief knew that Sunderleaf didn't trust him. Brighton was the youngest, Sunderleaf the oldest. Brighton thought it was jealousy. In fact, Sunderleaf spent almost no time thinking about Brighton. He considered him a lightweight whiz-kid, much in the mold of some of the JFK crowd. As far as Sunderleaf was concerned, Brighton's brand of bureaucrat was the cause of some of the biggest goof-ups in U.S. history—the Bay of Pigs, for instance. On the other hand, Sunderleaf had become more isolated since Big Three, occupied by a tough campaign back home. The recession was threatening his House seat for the first time in many years. As a result, Sunderleaf had failed to notice how much Brighton had grown in his job.

"Sir, the problem is obvious," Grieve McDouglas said. "I'll say it if no one else will. There's no *enforcement*. No fangs to our policy. We've left it all up to the Washington, California, Nevada, and Idaho state cops. That's like asking the rooster to insure the celibacy of the hens. That anemic Coast Guard of ours in Oregon isn't much better, either."

"Actually, they're not ours anymore," Allison observed, holding up a printout. "They went over to Oregon this morning, taking our boats and equipment with them. They were the last of the holdouts."

The president put his head in his hands momentarily.

"Wonderful," he said, rubbing his eyes. "Just wonderful."

"The next step is pretty plain," McDouglas said, shifting in his chair, sitting on the edge. He stared at the president. "Time for option three. Time for military action."

Washington toyed with a pen, head down.

"I wish I could disagree," he said after a few moments of contemplation. He looked up, eyeing each person individually. Everyone sat up a bit straighter.

"Last night I had a long talk with my cousin, J.B.," Washington said. "He gave me the bottom line. He says that under present circumstances, there's flat-out no hope of Oregon backing down. Economically, he told me Oregon is easily making it on its own now, at least in most sectors they've surveyed. He seemed pretty proud of it."

"He has a right to be," Ella Paxson said, scratching behind one ear with the eraser end of a pencil. "The San Francisco Federal Reserve economists say it's the only state that's moving ahead during this recession. Oregon went from minus 10% to a positive 5% growth rate in a few weeks. That's astounding. The fact is not lost on the state governors. Although the pros and cons are roughly divided by the Big Muddy."

"Did you see that *Wall Street Journal* story this morning?" Brighton asked. A couple people shook their heads. "It was hanging out there on page one like somebody's unzipped fly. Three counties in California and two in Idaho are making noises about petitioning to leave their states and join Oregon! So far it's just talk, of course, but—"

"But when a gator starts lookin', he's thinkin' 'bout chompin'," Sunderleaf finished, looking innocently at Brighton.

The CIA chief ignored him. Sunderleaf might not think

much of Brighton, but that didn't mean the younger man wasn't fun to tease. McDouglas chuckled inwardly. Like Sunderleaf, he used to think Brighton was a little light upstairs. If only Sunderleaf knew . . .

"The Western governors are stymied," Leininger said. "It's economics. That's why they won't help us enforce the blockade. They can't afford to. They're deathly afraid that if they anger Oregon, they could lose the trade that's keeping them from sinking any lower. They're not growing yet, of course. But they're not doing nearly as badly as they were before Oregon's boom. They know there's a connection and they don't want to sever it."

"It's like suggesting to an intensive care patient that he jerk out his glucose tubes," Young said.

"Oregon has become a new conduit for Taiwanese and other goods from the Far Eastern free nations," Allison added. "They love it. Here's Oregon, passing on a huge U.S. federal non-tax and demanding no tariffs! That's a double shot in the economic arm."

"Well, when a gator sees an extra duck on the pond—" Sunderleaf began, then stopped, catching the president's slight shake of the head.

"This morning in the *Washington Times* I read that the Conference of Eastern Governors is set to consider endorsing the opposing party," the president said, switching subjects momentarily. "They claim I've gone soft on Oregon."

Several voices automatically objected. A loyal crew, Washington thought. He held up his hand, nodded halfheartedly, and said, "I appreciate the cheers. But, folks, it doesn't *matter* if they're wrong. The East isn't experiencing the benefit of Oregon's boom. For now, it's going to the West, and mostly the far West, at that. The people here in the East are jealous. At least that's their cover story. They say I should be taking stronger action."

"They don't see why they gotta go dry while the hummingbirds in 'Fornia get to suck juice off the Oregon blossom," Sunderleaf said.

"Well, at least birds are prettier than swamp lizards," Brighton said under his breath.

"What about lowering taxes across the board," the vice president asked. "It may be the perfect moment."

"I'd be for it," Washington said, "but unfortunately it's still bad timing. It's not the kind of action the Eastern governors want. Their states are heavily dependent on Uncle Sam's largesse. They don't want to give it up just yet."

"They'd get over it, once their own economies started growing. They can see what's happening in Oregon just as well as we can."

"Yeah, but they've been hooked to the federal tit longer, and they don't want it to let go," Glenn Young said. "Still, I agree with Kurt. They'd get used to it."

"Well, there's another thing, and that's that they know I need their votes," the president said. "On the wide screen, I'm afraid they're absolutely right."

"But that's so parochial," Ella Paxson said, indignant on behalf of her long-time friend and president. "Surely it's not the only way."'

"What politics isn't parochial, Ella?" Washington asked sourly, tugging a corner of his beard.

He scanned the faces of his core group and added, "You can give it any noble name you want, but modern politics has become a primitive game. It's main point is to get your gang to top somebody else's gang and keep it there. I haven't mentioned this yet, but I got a private call this morning from New York's governor. He was speaking for the governors of 30 states, which includes only a couple of Westerners. They decided in a secret, encrypted video conference call last night that they want me to send in federal troops and the navy to secure these sanctions against Oregon."

Sunderleaf chuckled acidly and said, "They know that if one state gives up suckin', then the sow might think all the piglets are old enough to run on their own."

Washington gave a curt nod and said, "That's about how I read it, too."

"Against your own state, Sam?" Leininger asked quietly. "Would you use federal troops against your own people?"

It was a question every person in the room had considered, unspoken. Sam Washington had earned a reputation for standing by a decision. But if the decision were to endanger his friends and relatives, what then? Baker Sunderleaf, for one, had no doubts. Like many Southerners, he had learned his Civil War history well. Brother against brother, father against son, he thought.

Blood might be thicker than water, but war was thicker than blood.

Washington looked directly at Sunderleaf. He knows, Sunderleaf thought. The old house speaker did not show it, but he shuddered inside.

"Yes," Washington said, "and I'm going to."

The bare statement wasn't reassuring enough, though. He could tell by their faces that several people were unconvinced. He needed the entire group fully on his side and he needed it right now.

"Look," he elaborated. "I'm an Oregonian. But I'm a citizen of the U.S. first. For God's sake, people, I'm the *president!*" For emphasis, he smacked a heavy hand on the table. Ella dropped her pencil. Brighton spilled coffee on his shirt. McDouglas smiled inside.

"I've sworn to defend the integrity of this great country and its constitution," Washington said, his voice simultaneously hard and light, like chain armor. "Oregon is going to rip this Union apart. It's already cut itself from America's proudest processes. Maybe it doesn't mean to hurt us. Maybe it feels it has no choice. Maybe it feels it's been treated unjustly. But it has also flung mud at our outstretched hands of friendship. I wouldn't tolerate that from a neighbor. I surely won't tolerate it from my fellow Oregonians."

Washington placed his hands on the table a moment, then slowly stood to his full height. He was an impressive figure. It underscored his determination, as he knew it would.

"Ladies and gentlemen, this is no longer parochialism. It

has become something larger. Small-minded politics is the easy answer. But it's not the true one. There's a longer range consideration. History may say I'm making a cold calculation. So be it. It's a calculation which another president once had the responsibility to make. I will do no less than Lincoln. I'm talking about a consideration which bears on not just the prosperity, but the lives of this country—and more: on the foundations of the future of freedom. Good people, I tell you what I think you may know. I tell you what you may have dreamed in the dark, when the chatter of smaller politics was quiet and the sounds of deeper thoughts could be heard."

He paused, inhaled, and said, "It's quite simply this. If Oregon goes, it'll draw others in. Before we know it, we'll no longer be a nation. We'll bicker and fight and become isolated. We'll become jealous blocks of Balkanized mini-states, unable to see beyond our noses, like the weenies of Old Europe!"

A few people laughed, nervously.

"Before you know it, we won't be able to cooperate to preserve our most important government function: a common defense. You all know what *that* will mean."

Everyone shuddered.

Tom Rosco whispered the words for them: *"The Shang."*

Chapter 12

"All Bets Are On"

The end of the Third World War, like the beginning, had been a surprise. The "new" Soviets had started it, and lost. The Chinese had finished it, and won—at least in Asia and parts of Eastern Europe. Like a wave washing over an elaborate castle of sand, ten million Chinese troops with untold numbers of secretly manufactured weapons had swept apart a demoralized Russian Army. Within weeks, the Chinese had occupied almost all the land from the Pacific to the Baltic. Mother Russia became a memory. The biggest land empire in the world suffered under a non-European thumb. But while the Chinese communists were celebrating their outward glories, a single man was rising behind them—from within. Virtually no blood was shed. Publicly, the man was not an advocate of communism or of capitalism. Like much else about him, his ideology was hard to define. He was simply *The Shang.*

One moment he wasn't there at all. The next, he was China's first emperor of the nuclear age. "The Shang" was one of only three titles he liked. He also tolerated "Emperor" or "Emperor Shang."

No intelligence agency in the West had anticipated him. None knew anything about his past. There was no public record. No one knew how The Shang had achieved his position. The Chinese press printed no accounts. One day, the coa-

lition of reformed Maoists and neo-Marxists and neo-capital-
ists had ruled together in uneasy alliance, and the next day
they had dried and fluttered away, scattered by an impossibly
fast, hot wind.

However, now that he was Emperor, some details about
him were coming to light. Not many, but a few. The world's
intelligence services—mainly British, American, and Israeli—
had gathered some interesting stories. They painted a glitter-
ing picture, always in the present tense. The Shang was said to
be a strategic and political genius. His young age and his re-
puted physical and mental prowess lent credence to the report. He was barely twenty years old. He possessed an infal-
lible memory, an I.Q. off the scale, *and* needed only an hour of
sleep a day—taken in four fifteen-minute naps, unpredictably
spaced in order to foil his enemies. He was also said to be extraordinarily athletic, with snake-quick reflexes. To the disbe-
lief of the world, the Chinese press claimed that their emperor
had privately broken Olympic records in everything from sprinting to gymnastics to martial arts—but was too considerate to
enter official competition.

The details of The Shang—at least the *alleged* details did
not end there. The man was said to effortlessly create complete
loyalty. This was true even among his few surviving, former
political enemies. There were many stories similar to the one
told about an old, powerful Maoist.

The Maoist had been a high official in the defunct Chinese Communist Party. Known for his sharp, ruthless brain
and undaunted bravery, he had bitterly denounced the new
emperor. He had done so even after the disappearance of many
of his colleagues, knowing that death was his likely reward.
Yet, after a single audience with The Shang, the old warrior
had unreservedly reversed himself. He began to praise the young
ruler's wisdom, maturity, and far-sightedness.

A few, but not all such reversals could be written off to
simple side-switching survival. But U.S. intelligence services
thought that there was more to it. Exactly what, they weren't
entirely sure. There was an extra *something* about the young

ruler that no one could adequately explain. The dry, official CIA conclusion was that The Shang possessed "unusual powers of persuasion." However, there was an unofficial explanation, too. This one was heard only in quietly guarded conversations among agents assigned to watch The Shang. They noted that his talent for persuasion seemed well beyond the reach of what one could call human. The word *mutant* came up now and then. It was uttered nervously. It was the kind of nervousness felt by men who can't bring themselves to believe something, but can think of nothing else to explain it. That was the Occidental view, the view of the analysts of the West.

The Oriental view was different. The whispered word was not *mutant*, but *god*.

The Shang did not discourage Chinese press speculation that he was partially divine.

Worship cults — an ancient phenomenon in China — sprang up like weeds. People left flowers, animals, household goods, baskets of rice, even newborn sons, on the broad outer steps of The Shang's palace. The Shang accepted them all, creating a bureaucracy to handle the gifts. He ordered special nurseries and schools for the baby sons. He called them his little priests.

It was said that The Shang laughed a great deal.

At first glance, he was physically unimpressive. Tiny, wiry, four-feet-seven and only eighty-five pounds, he had black hair and odd, yellow-irised eyes. Despite his diminutive stature, he was a young man with giant ideas. He particularly liked to discuss them with his advisors while playing cards.

He did not play bridge or chess like many of the old communist leaders had. He preferred a tougher game. Counting cards and calculating chess strategy was no challenge to him. He preferred the endlessly varied effort of predicting human deception. He preferred poker.

"Do you know why the Americans are our primary adversary again?" he asked his cardmates, smiling.

"Because they are the only superpower left?" one of them asked tentatively. He instantly feared that his statement of the obvious might be fatally construed as an insult.

"No, my friend," the Emperor said, shaking his head in amusement. He threw some chips in the pot. "I see your hundred and raise you another."

The "friend" was momentarily tempted to raise back. A glance at The Shang's face changed his mind. He called, though, and laid down an impressive full house, jacks high.

The Emperor bowed his head ever so slightly.

"Well done," he said. "Unfortunately, for you, not quite well enough."

One card at a time, he exposed a small straight flush. He pulled in the pot with relish and carefully stacked his chips.

"It has nothing to do with America being a superpower," he said jovially. "Besides, they are not the only superpower. That is an outdated myth. There are others. India, Brazil, even United Southern Africa. Western Europe, if it could ever unite sensibly. Oh, is it my deal?"

Someone nodded and lit a cigarette.

The Shang lit up, too. He was a chain smoker. He eschewed the traditional Panda brand, preferring Camel filters. No one had ever dared ask why. Had they asked, he would have told them: they tasted better. He gathered the cards and shuffled, blinking away smoke. Then he held up the deck in his small hands, a thin, black eyebrow raised.

He showed the deck to the five others at the table and said, "My outlook on the Americans has everything to do with this. They perfected, almost invented, this game—on their riverboats, in their back alleys, their saloons, their hearts. *That* is why they are our number one enemy."

His advisors looked puzzled, which they often were, but The Shang was patient and cheerful, as with small children.

"An enemy weaned on this game," he explained slowly, "is more dangerous than all the chess masters of old Russia ever were. Now, my little wise ones, why might that be so?"

"The uncertainty factor?" someone ventured.

The Shang dealt two cards down and one up to everyone.

"Seven stud, one twist," he said, naming the hand. "Yes,

uncertainty is involved. But that is not a true issue here. The *essential* point is always how one turns uncertainty into an advantage. In other words, how one creates personal certainty out of general uncertainty."

His advisors nodded. The Shang was a frightening teacher, but a good one. He earned, rather than simply commanded, the respect of his students. Each of his advisors was utterly convinced that he was a far better man for basking in the mental glow of the mysterious young Shang.

Noting the ace of spades face up in front of himself, the Emperor smiled delightedly. He silently threw two ten-chips into the pot, sucked deeply on his Camel, and watched the other players. Two folded immediately. Three called, one with a jack on board. The Shang chuckled, high, almost like a young girl, then dealt another round of cards face up. Another ace turned up in front of him. The owner of the jack also matched for a pair. The Shang doubled his bet. The man to his left shook his head and turned his cards over. Two people called, including the jacks.

The Shang dealt another round of face-up cards to his last competitors. This time he got an eight of hearts.

"Possible dead man's hand," he noted, clapping in delight. "Oh, does anyone know why it's called that?"

"Yes, Emperor, I believe I do," a middle-aged, very fat player with an out-of-style Fu Manchu mustache said. "Because one of the American gunslingers, an 18th century man named Wild Bill Peacock, was shot dead while holding a hand of two aces and two eights."

The Shang nodded, "Correct, except that he was a scout and U.S. marshal and lived in the 19th century, from 1837 to 1876, and his real name was James Butler Hickok, not Peacock."

"Western names often sound alike to me," the man said sullenly, embarrassed.

The Emperor chuckled and continued to deal.

The man with the pair of jacks got another; trips showing. He grunted.

"New leader on board with a possible full house," The Shang called it. "Or is what we see all you've got?" he asked, winking and bowing slightly to the holder of the jacks, who remained impassive.

The third man—the old converted Maoist—grinned, showing three hearts on board, king high.

The three jacks bet fifty. The hearts raised fifty. The Shang frowned, pursed his lips, and reluctantly dropped chips into the pot, calling, as did the first bettor.

The next round matched the three jacks with an unimpressive six. The Maoist got a fourth heart and grinned widely. The Shang dealt himself another eight up, sighing. Aces and eights. He smiled.

The three jacks looked at the potential flush, apparently lost his bluffing nerve, and refused to bet. The flush, now sensing blood, bet a hundred. The Shang hesitated, scratched an ear, picked up a couple of fifty chips, put them back down, then threw them in, rolling his eyes hopelessly. The three jacks frowned and folded. He'd seen *that* ploy before.

"Don't forget, there's a twist. Are you certain you don't want to buy an extra card?" The Shang asked him. "No?"

The Emperor turned to the only remaining player and said, "Very well, old convert, it's just you and me."

"Indeed," the Maoist said merrily. Although the game was still new to him, he also enjoyed poker more than bridge. And these days he enjoyed The Shang. Usually.

The Emperor dealt the final regular down cards. The Maoist glanced at his, snorted, and bet two hundred. The Shang looked at his own card, then called the bet.

"Twist?" he asked the Maoist.

"No, Emperor, but thank you."

The Shang nodded, taking another peek at his three down cards. Quietly, he said, "Then I shall not take one either. We will tread in the path of equal odds—comrade."

The Maoist's face fell and he asked, "What? Are you saying that you have already beaten my flush?"

"Perhaps I only want you to think so," The Shang replied.

"As you know, checking and betting and checking and raising are allowed at my table. I will grant you the first move of courage. I check. Your bet. The limit is two-fifty, if you recall."

The Maoist grunted, nodded, shrugged, and bet another hundred.

The Shang matched it and raised two-fifty.

The Maoist narrowed his eyes, smiled at The Shang, then pushed five-hundred into the pot, matching the Shang's two-fifty limit and raising as much.

"This time, you are bluffing, Emperor," he said. The Shang is unwise, he thought, to permit checking and-betting.

Not only did The Shang call, he raised again.

That did it. The Maoist shook his head, let out an exasperated sigh, and said, "I fold."

Although not required, he turned up his hidden cards, showing a five card flush, king high.

The Emperor bowed his head, then turned over his hidden cards, too. The Maoist cursed softly. The Shang had not improved his aces and eights. He had won on a bluff after all.

The old man mock-spat on his own superior cards.

"Never trust a man who tells you his hand is dead," The Shang said, pulling in his winnings and suddenly growing unaccountably serious.

The Maoist scratched his chin and said, "So, the secession troubles of the Americans. They are too eager to tell us that their hand is dead?"

"Was I too eager?"

The Maoist held up his hands, "My Emperor, I did not mean to imply —"

"Don't be troubled, for that, too, is part of tonight's lesson. But I compliment you, as far as you have taken it. As the Americans say, for an old dog, you can learn new tricks."

"Then, are you saying, Emperor, that the Americans are actually weak, but want us to fold?" another man asked, a former general staff member. "You are saying that they bluff somehow — that this secession is fake and somehow intended to frighten us? How could that be? I can see no logic to such a ploy. Our intelligence services say otherwise, and you do not appear to be frightened."

The Shang shrugged, stubbed out his cigarette, and asked, "Is it a ploy? I have yet to decide. But I will, my little wise ones. I will. When I do, I will play the grandest of hands. And I assure you that this time I will not be holding aces and eights."

No one doubted him.

He passed the cards to his left, leaned back, crossing his arms, and lit another cigarette.

It is his eyes, thought the Maoist. Looking into them was like gazing into a well with no bottom—or across a plain with no horizon. The ex-communist suddenly felt tired and cold, like an old man caught in an unexpected winter snow. The Shang glanced away, then looked back. For a moment, his yellow-irised eyes grew sharply intense and then almost dreamy. To his amazement, the Maoist's depression faded. He began to feel strong and warm, like a strapping youth basking in an endless summer sun.

Chapter 13

"The Burner Boys"

The three men sat around a kitchen table, again. None of them liked telling lies to sneak away. But it was the only way to carry off their meetings. They'd been getting together occasionally for several weeks now, they and a very few others, discussing strategy.

"Do you think it's working?" asked the first man, the youngest of the three.

"What part?" asked the second man, the oldest.

"The whole idea, I guess. You've done this more than I."

"Not on *this* scale," said the old man, chuckling wryly. He pushed aside his hamburger, not hungry. "Insufficient information. But I think it's got a better chance than anything else, if that's what you're asking. He was fond of the young man, even though he'd never let it show in front of other people.

"You both realize," said the third man, the tall one, "that if we're found out too soon, it will be—well, it'll *all* be over for us. Careers, pensions, future prospects, our family names. It won't be understood, or forgiven. Not unless it works."

The other two nodded, glancing at each other.

"It's got to be tried," the old man said briskly. "There's no alternative."

He sipped at a glass of whiskey, savoring the burn of the alcohol as it slid down his throat.

The young man bit eagerly into a thick, juicy, double hamburger, laden with at least an inch of trimmings.

The old man involuntarily flinched, as though afraid of being splashed by whatever might squirt out of the huge sandwich. But he was amused by the appetite of the youth. He remembered when he could eat like that. Long gone, those days, even though he could stand to add a pound or two.

The tall man said, "Look, it's not a pleasant choice, that's for sure. We've been over that. But if—"

"You think it's *unpleasant*? Wait 'til you hear the latest," the young man interrupted, talking mushily through a mouthful, then swallowing. "Our men—who of course don't know their true missions—have penetrated most of their defenses. The other side's morale is not low, it's high. Extraordinarily. You'd think they were fighting to protect the American way of life or something."

"Maybe they are," said the tall man, raising his chin. "But listen, damn it! Oh, sorry for the language, sir."

"Forget it. It's all informal here."

"Yes, okay," the young man said. "It's just that equipment-wise, they have more than we thought."

A sour look crossed the tall man's face as he said, "You know, it's too bad that we have to get half our information this way. I don't like the way it dribbles in. I'd rather get it all from the top. Too bad he couldn't join in again today. That way we could set things a bit farther out."

"He doesn't have the details we need, either," the old man reminded. "I can vouch for that. You know it wouldn't work for him, not right now. He doesn't exactly have a rep for micromanaging. Besides, if wishes were horses."

"But this makes for a double deception! There could be hell to pay later. We didn't agree to this level of action."

"Unavoidable," the old man said, shrugging. "Besides, it will be understood, in hindsight. If he doesn't, who will?"

"We're saying that about a lot of things," the tall man said, skeptically, making wet marks on the table with the bottom of his glass.

The young man wiped his mouth. "Anyway, as I was saying, the other side has acted rapidly to consolidate and prepare its forces. Their militias, for instance, have come along much faster and are far more formidable than we had initially anticipated."

"My gal warned me that they might be," one of them said.

"Your gal?" the other two exclaimed, alarmed.

"Easy! Just something she read, as usual. A theoretical remark, offered in a different context. Don't worry. She's always doing that kind of thing. I didn't spill anything."

"Well, anyway," the young man said, a worried expression remaining on his face, "they may have some things we don't know about. We'll have to make sure that the top neutralizes anything like that, or else—"

The tall man wrinkled his nose, "Well, I don't know about that. It would look bad."

"I just meant that major logistical surprises could occur. Bad ones."

"Risk is part of conflict."

"Sure, of course. But even with *his* help, it could be bloodier than we thought."

The tall man stared at him, his face unreadable.

"Yeah, so?" he finally said.

"Well, I mean, for instance," the young man elaborated, "it turns out that they may have some developmental weapons, the only copies in existence. We know they were produced and haven't been able to account for them in our inventory. Those guys were a testbed for quite a few things like that."

"Where? I didn't know they had any facilities of that sort?"

"Oh, sure. It's amazing. It's buried under some volcanic butte, or something. More hush-hush than Area 51 or any of that stuff. Read the Project BTB report. I sent it with you in that stack of stuff last time. It's in there."

"Yeah, I will. Just got a lot on my mind."

"Some of the tests were doubtless in progress when they went flying."

"Went flying, eh? Huh. Well, I guess that's one way to

put it," the tall man said, pouring the second half of his second beer into a glass and waiting for the foam to settle.

"Nevertheless," the oldest of them said, "that's in the pot, as good cooks say. The seasoning will have to do the rest. Time to turn on the burner."

The tall man said, "No insult intended, but just remember, no hint to our special people that we're the guys with our hands on this particular stove. More than our fingers will be burned if they catch us."

The others compressed their lips into thin lines. But they knew he had the most to lose. They didn't blame him for reminding them to be careful.

"The Burner Boys," the young man said, laughing nervously, "I guess that's as good a nickname as any."

"Well, any last-minute thoughts?" the old man asked them. "No?"

He pushed back from the table.

"Okay," he said, "much of this is seat-of-the-pants, but you know what has to happen next."

"I only wish—" the young man began.

"What?" the tall man asked, frowning.

"That it could be done without—so much ugliness."

The old man spread his bony hands wide and said, "Out-of-context idealism. Remember, it was partly your plan, son. And a good one, even if you can't ever brag about it on the street corners."

The young man closed his eyes a moment and whispered, "God, don't I know it."

The old man nodded and said, "Okay, let's keep our confidence up, fellas. It'll work—has to. Just remember the lives and fortunes we'll save down the line."

"In strategy," the tall man said, "there's nothing that makes a few lives now more sacred than many later."

"Yeah," the younger man said. "That's the part that keeps bothering me."

Chapter 14

"The Massacre"

The news of the first conflict hit the networks while it was still dark on the West Coast.

A pre-dawn riser, J.B. Washington happened to catch the earliest report on *Fox News*. It was four in the morning and he had just finished making a breakfast of bacon, eggs, toast, and tomato slices. As usual, his wife Julie and their kids were still asleep. He set the plate of steaming food on the dining bar and flipped on the kitchen video, keeping the sound just high enough to hear easily. He salted and peppered his eggs and started buttering toast as the hourly summary began.

The rangy brunette announcer, Lyndsy Salvador, said, "*Fox News* has just learned that a few hours ago the U.S. military encountered troops from the former state of Oregon—now calling itself the Republic of Oregon. We have a report on the incident from our own Bob Lonsdorf. He is live from the scene in the mountains of southern Oregon. We caution you that some of the footage is graphic."

J.B. grunted to himself, said, "What the devil?" and punched up the TV's volume.

Lonsdorf, a short, stubby reporter with unruly, prematurely white hair, looked bedraggled and ashen. It was partly the pre-dawn light, thought J.B., partly the fact that it was raining. Those forests always looked gloomy then. But

Londsdorf's voice quavered slightly, indicating that something more than nature's lighting trick was going on.

"Thank you, Lyndsy. Here behind me," he began, standing aside and letting the camera show a background of soggy, splotchy scrub and low, grayish, oddly-shaped rocks or perhaps stumps, "you can see for yourself the aftermath of what I can only describe as the bloodiest battle this reporter has witnessed since the Arabian Wars."

As the camera panned in closer, the rocks and stumps resolved themselves. They were human bodies covered with mud and blood. Working frantically among the bodies were military personnel and medics, all with U.S. Army markings.

J.B. frowned and put down his toast untouched.

Lonsdorf answered the unheard question for millions of viewers: "About two hundred yards from me are approximately one-hundred bodies. A few of them, very few — the official word is five — are, or were, U.S. Army personnel. The others are members of a militia of the former State of Oregon. Only one word can accurately describe the outcome of this first encounter between a special contingent of U.S. Army forces and the untried defenders of a would-be new nation. That word is unmistakably *massacre*."

He took a deep breath, shook his head, and continued, "Right now, Lyndsy, the Army has sealed off the area. Only a few reporters from a hastily assembled White House media pool have been allowed in, but we are not being permitted to get any closer than this."

He gestured with one arm, looking professionally peeved.

A shadowy helicopter took off in the misty, drizzly dawn. Three or four others, blades slowly whipping, were on the ground. Far off, almost out of camera range, two others were landing, edging below tree level in the rough mountain clearing. The branches on the large firs shook and shed sheets of rainwater.

"As you can see, Lyndsy, these bodies, like the injured before them, are being evacuated as I speak," Londsdorf explained. "The Army says the victims are being flown to an unspecified location in California. We are not sure why the location is not being disclosed, but from there, we are told, kin will eventually be notified. However, and this surely underscores the ominous nature of this initial conflict between Uncle Sam and the Oregonians, one Army official told me that the surviving militia have been rounded up and are considered prisoners of war. They will undergo interrogation."

"Bob," Lyndsy Salvador broke in, "can you hear me?"

"Yes, Lyndsy, loud and clear," Lonsdorf answered, looking at the camera and touching one finger to his headset.

"Bob, can you tell our viewers if more fighting is expected? Was this an isolated battle, or the start of a larger conflict?"

"Well, all I can give you at the moment is the official word from the Army. First, no. No other Oregon troops are thought to be anywhere near. That's *according* to the U.S. Army. Second, there's the chronology of this horrible event. At about two this morning, West Coast time, in the darkest hours before dawn, U.S. forces on patrol came upon an independent militia. The Army told *Fox News* that the militia is known as the South Mountain Contingent. It was allegedly operating under direct orders of the gov — that is, of the President of the Republic of Oregon, Alf Corcoran. Indeed, I called Corcoran's office by cell phone just a few moments ago. A spokesman there — in fact, it was his assistant defense secretary, Ben Colby — confirmed that there was such a militia in the vicinity. He said that it was conducting defensive patrol night maneuvers. Colby would not comment further, however, which is unusual, because he's known to be outspoken and fairly free with reporters. While he said he was aware of a loss of lives, he seemed genuinely shocked when I mentioned that the figure was nearly 100. Corcoran's office, according to Colby, will have a statement on the matter at 4:30 am, not long from now. All I can say, Lyndsy, is that if the tone of outrage that Colby's voice carried is any indication, there's little doubt that president Corcoran is going to condemn the U.S. action."

"Uh, Bob," Salvador asked, "when the Army says it 'came upon' this militia, what specifically happened? That seems rather vague, doesn't it?"

"Well, yes, the Army was exceptionally hazy on that point. All the officers here are saying is that they responded to hostile action. Now, in lay language, that would imply that the militia fired upon the Army first and that the Army responded—overwhelmingly, I must add."

Lonsdorf sounded utterly disgusted, as though the Army had somehow been unfair in the fight, as though it shouldn't have been so successful at defending itself. As he spoke, his cameraman again panned the field of broken, bloodied militia bodies. The impression was that the inexperienced Oregon fighters had done approximately as well as a pet parakeet against a wild tomcat.

"All right, Bob, you said there were 100 Oregon fatalities. I didn't catch how many U.S. Army troops were lost."

"As I said, their spokesman claims it was five—with several more injured. But Lyndsy, I hasten to add that I've no way of confirming that. Our cameras did not actually find *any* Army bodies. Of course, they would have been the first to be evacuated and I'm told that's the case. Nor did we arrive until the overall evacuation had been underway for at least an hour. There was a delay in getting the motor pool in, so we could have missed a lot. I'm sure we did."

"And you say the Army isn't revealing to what hospital the victims are being taken?"

"Right, but I want to re-emphasize the other point. A *Fox News* camera count of the bodies showed no U.S. Army uniforms. What we saw—and that was only by long-range camera at first—were bodies with black and gray outfits. I'm told that's the battle dress favored these days by the Southern Mountain Contingent."

"Who told you that, Bob?" Salvador asked.

"Well, uh, the U.S. Army, at first. But Colby confirmed it for us."

"Bob, can you tell our *Fox News* viewers what exactly the U.S. Army was doing in Oregon in the first place? I mean, isn't it a sovereign nation now?" Salvador pressed. "Our contacts at the White House and Pentagon said just yesterday that President Sam Washington has not yet decided to move on Oregon to enforce the sanctions, isn't that right? So, I mean, this kind of comes as a surprise, doesn't it?"

"Yes, indeed. The *new* official word, Lyndsy—from a service spokesman on the ground here—is that the Army was conducting 'recon in force.' In one sense, that wears fairly thin. Based on my previous war coverage, the facts suggest to me that the U.S. Army had at least several hundred men in the area. The main method of live recon is stealth, but you can't achieve that easily with several hundred men. Not in any military manual I've ever seen."

He shrugged and gave a distinctly nonobjective sneer.

"Well, what are you saying, then, Bob—that this was a prelude to an actual invasion? A preliminary move by the United States to force Oregon back into the Union?"

"No, I'm not saying it was a prelude," Londsdorf retorted testily, "I'm saying that by the looks of what I see and hear on the scene, this was probably the first actual U.S. effort to invade Oregon. It doesn't look like there was anything preliminary about it. As I read it, it likely was a force large enough meant specifically to test the strength of the Oregon resistance—not just to reconnoiter it. Based on the results, I'd have to guess that they've learned that the resistance is minimal, in this part of the state, anyway. By that standard, the Army's probe was successful. But, Lyndsy, it's more than that. The big question hanging unanswered here—and it troubles many other reporters, not just me—is why did the U.S. Army have to wipe out so *many* men in a test of strength battle? I assure you, that's an issue the media will prod in the days and weeks ahead."

"Bob, are you able—"

"Lyndsy, excuse me. Let me quickly add that our cameras caught the Army removing several white flags scattered around the battle area."

"White flags?" Salvador asked, now sharply attentive. "Did you say white flags?"

"Yes. The consensus of the media pool here—and of course

this entails some speculation, but I stress that several of us reporters are war veterans, thus not without expertise—anyway, the consensus is that the Oregon forces several times tried, in vain, to surrender."

"But, Bob, that could only mean that—"

"Exactly, Lyndsy. Given the body count, it strongly suggests that the U.S. Army ignored the surrender pleas and simply *mowed down* the militia men in cold blood. Now, I put this question directly to an Army official, but he refused all comment, turned on his heel, and walked away. I did not earlier use the term 'massacre' without reason, Lyndsy."

At that point, Lonsdorf literally glared into the camera, his anger shining like a flare at midnight.

Within hours, virtually the entire U.S. press corps picked up and amplified his anger. Within days, so did the U.S. public. Americans believed in defense, but they did not believe in slaughter. Especially not of their own people. As far as the U.S. public was concerned—and the polls confirmed it—although those oddball Oregonians might be playing funny secession games, they were still *Americans*.

Chapter 15

"Media Massage"

ASSOCIATED INTERNET, Salem, R. of Oregon—In a bid which Secretary of Commerce Sparky Katz called "merely an extension of existing economic policy," the Republic of Oregon today released an invitation to the U.S. media.

According to Katz, the media—currently based primarily in New York, Washington, D.C., Los Angeles, and Atlanta—would do 'far better' financially if they relocated to the new Republic of Oregon.

"I simply want to emphasize that the same lower-tax status that applies to manufacturing and services would also apply to the media companies," Katz said, emphasizing that relocation "would result in an immediate savings of substantial proportions to media corporations."

"We don't want to discriminate against the media industry," she said, "because Oregon has always been a fair-minded government."

Katz cited a study by her office which indicated that *CBS, ABC, NBC, Associated Internet, Fox, Turner-Warner, AP/DOW, Murdoch International, Nokamura USA,* and other large media operations could immediately double their annual profits by emigrating to Oregon.

"Oregon, as a sovereign nation, does not require payment of U.S. taxes," Katz pointed out, "not for car makers, retailers,

or the news business."
Katz cited Oregon's no-federal-tax benefit as the main
reason for her projected jump in media profits. But Katz also
said that Oregon was growing at a "blistering" 12% annual
rate. This "feeds back positively" to every other business here,
she said.

Disputing more dour U.S. federal figures, she said that
the states of California, Idaho, Nevada, and Washington had
already pulled out of their recessions. She attributed the four
states' growth to their proximity to Oregon.

Katz also said that Oregon was on track to becoming the
West Coast's primary conduit of trade with Asian nations.
These include Taiwan, United Korea, Singapore, Japan, Ma-
laysia, New Burma, and Thailand. All those nations, and several others, have recently signed zero-tariff trade confederation and zero-restriction immigration pacts with the Republic
of Oregon.

Several network executives interviewed by *Associated
Internet* indicated that they were seriously considering the offer. Warren T. Brookersmith, CEO of the mega-media group,
Wall Street Journal General, said his corporation has been considering relocating for some time.

"The war scare deal doesn't bother us," Brookersmith said.
"We'd probably plant our operations in a small Oregon town
where the lifestyle quality is high. Besides, no one seriously
believes that President Washington is going to dust his home
state off the map."

Brookersmith denied the thrust of a question suggesting
that Oregon was trying to "buy off" the media.

"The implication is preposterous," he said. "This would
be a purely business decision. No way would the offer affect
the objectivity of our reporters."

However, Brookersmith acknowledged that a move to
Oregon "might well" make larger salaries possible for employees in "the news end of things."

Other executives contacted by *Associated Internet* indicated
similar sentiments.

CNN's chief operating officer, Jason "Bread" Turner, reportedly told his top staff to set up an experimental remote network center in Salem, Oregon's capital, by the end of next month. Mr. Turner, away on a honeymoon with his new animal-rights activist wife, could not be reached for comment.

However, officials at CNN anonymously confirmed that the company's real estate division has been leasing "respectable amounts" of office space in Salem.

Chapter 16

"Utmost Restraint"

REUTERS, Salem, R. of Oregon—On the capitol steps of the Republic of Oregon yesterday afternoon, spokesmen for the heads of several East Asian nations gathered to publicly urge the President of the United States to "exercise utmost restraint" in its dealings with the breakaway state.

Speaking for the group, President Don Wan Too of United Korea said that "any further aggression" by the U.S. against Oregon would be viewed with "great dismay" by its East Asian trading partners.

"It would be the United State's own Tiananmen Square massacre," Don said, referring to the late-eighties Chinese murder of peace demonstrators in Beijing.

Don said the trading alliance had established "deep, dynamic relations" with a "blessedly free Oregon" and did not wish to see them "fold in the withering heat of impetuous, resentful U.S. ruling circles."

"The free nations of Asia deplore the massacre of innocent Oregon militia members," Don said. "We would doubly deplore further incursions by U.S. troops. The enlightened of the world know that Oregon's secession is a genuine move toward liberty, consistent with the founding principles of the original U.S.A. itself."

Don elaborated his warning, claiming that United Korea

and other nations would "probably" boycott any American state that contributed troops to incursions against Oregon. However, any state that resists incursions, Don said, would "be treated with delight and efficacious favor."

Don expressed additional concern about a war between the U.S. and Oregon when he pointed out that over 100,000 East Asians — including 20,000 Koreans — had emigrated to Oregon in the months following its secession.

"This now poses a question of protection for our relatives and friends," Don said. "We would find it difficult to stand idly by and watch our ancestors' grandchildren be killed or injured" merely because they were "joyously enterprising in another part of their present life."

Don would not comment on reports that various nations of the East Asian Trade Association had been providing modern weapons to Oregon. *Reuters* sources have reported several times that Taiwan is supplying some avionics and other defensive electronics and optronic systems to Oregon.

The White House issued a statement within an hour of Don's remarks. Spokesman Tom Rosco said that U.S. government had "noted" Don's remarks.

However, Rosco said the U.S. would not be "intimidated by threats of sanctions." When asked by a reporter if the White House was still expecting its sanctions against Oregon to work, Rosco said, "Yes, that is the official position, because the president feels that Oregon initiated the trouble, so its moral position is entirely different than our own."

When asked to comment on some economists' claims that, in light of Oregon's phenomenal growth, the U.S. sanctions against it were having absolutely no demonstrable effect, Rosco said, "That's because they're not being enforced, yet."

Rosco would not answer questions on either the timing or nature of possible enforcement. Surprising most reporters, Rosco denied that the so-called "mountain massacre" in southern Oregon was a part of U.S. enforcement operations. Rosco said that despite almost universal criticism of the U.S. Army's role in the incident, the White House position continues to be that

"Oregon forces viciously attacked our legitimate reconnaissance patrol and we were simply defending ourselves."

Rosco was asked how a "simple defense" turned into a massacre. "That our defense was immensely effective should not be a mark against us," he said, "and I think the wives and children of our surviving forces would wholeheartedly agree."

Reuters asked Rosco about the "prisoner-of-war" status of the captured Oregon forces, about which virtually nothing has been heard. The presidential spokesman said "prisoner-of-war" was "erroneous."

When asked to explain, Rosco said, "We view them as medical detainees."

Rosco denied earlier Army statements that the "detainees" would be interrogated. "We asked them normal questions relating to their health conditions," Rosco said. "What medications are they on, whom do we notify, that sort of thing."

Rosco said the White House had already contacted next-of-kin. President Corcoran's office in Oregon confirmed to *Reuters* that notification had "quietly taken place so as to avoid painful publicity" for the families of the slain men.

So far, none of the massacre victims has been publicly identified, despite efforts by several news organizations. However, Rosco assured reporters that some of the injured would "soon be available" to interview, adding, "We have no intention of suppressing anything."

Meanwhile, President Corcoran told reporters that while Oregon "deplored" the massacre, he and his top officials had "resolved the matter privately for the time being." Corcoran refused to expand on that cryptic comment. However, he did say that Oregon would not stand for any further incursions and was preparing unspecified "new options" to defend itself.

Chapter 17

"The Real Diving Board"

Sparky Katz, Oregon Commerce Secretary, stood and shuffled her notes and looked at the other people gathered in the presidential conference hall, the Round Room. She scanned the faces of nearly two-dozen individuals and their aides, finally meeting the eyes of President Corcoran. He smiled at her. Craggy and intense, looking every inch the picture of Oregon's nominal founder, John McLoughlin, he sat at the precise middle of the giant table. Remembering the night they'd spent together earlier in the week, Katz felt an involuntary thrill. She had to consciously suppress the urge to squirm in her seat. How inconvenient, she thought. Maybe Corky was right. Maybe this was too much—at least until the rebellion crisis passed. She glanced back up at Corcoran. She saw the hint of a wink. Or maybe not. The thrill returned and she sat down abruptly, making a show of trying to find something among her papers. Until she got herself under control, she refused to look at Corcoran again.

Corcoran smiled inwardly and courteously ignored her.

The giant conference table—donated by an Oregon logging firm—was a five-foot wide band of deeply polished myrtlewood laminate. It formed a nearly complete circle, forty feet in diameter. Along the inner edge of the round table was carved an honor role of the names of great Oregon discoverers, explorers, pioneers, innovators, and leaders: Gray, Heceta, Vancouver, Lewis, Clark, Astor, McLoughlin, Priest, Whitman, Spalding, Parish, Blanchet, Lee, Demers, Meek, Gilliam, Lane, Bush, Palmer, Hill, Pennoyer, McKenzie, Skinner, Hale, Bonneville, Wyeth, Baldwin, Honeyman, Iwakoshi, Whiteaker, and dozens of others. The names were inlaid in gold leaf and protected with clear resin. One side of the table, opposite the president, was open for service staff to replace coffee decanters and snacks.

This week, he noticed, the staff was made up of smiling, courteous McDonalds' personnel. The catering—all donated by private firms for advertising value ("We serve the president!")—rotated weekly by lottery. Corcoran's office had not paid for refreshments in months. So many firms were scrambling to get on the lottery list that Corcoran wondered whether it might be time to actually sell the rights to cater the president. Katz had suggested it earlier. Well, despite Oregon's growth, it had a long way to go. Any method of saving money was welcome, as far as the president was concerned.

It was such thinking by Katz that had convinced Corcoran of her worth in his cabinet. Promoting her from simple state tourist bureau chief to Commerce Secretary of a new nation had been a stroke of genius. But whom had it been who had suggested the change? He tried to recall. Colby? J.B. Washington? Corcoran was losing details in the storm of activity.

Katz was at his right, only two chairs away. Nearly everyone was seated now, coffee, tea, and water poured, chatting among themselves. Katz cleared her throat and nodded at the president.

"Okay, first let me remind everyone that we're not here to discuss the recent massacre of our troops," Corcoran said. "I know it worries you all, but I assure you that we are taking action. Details are necessarily classified. You all understand that good strategy requires a certain amount of military secrecy. Now, Sparky, let's have your econ report."

The room quieted.

Katz cleared her throat and made herself smile. She wondered if she'd ever fully overcome her gnawing nervousness at public speaking — especially in front of her own clandestine lover, the President of the Republic of Oregon.

"As you all know," she said, "almost immediately after Oregon seceded, our President Corcoran approved a long-range economic recovery plan. Shrugging the huge fed-tax burden helped a lot. That was the real diving board for the plunge into full independence."

Three or four people clapped at the word "independence." One person whistled. Nearly everyone smiled. Almost to a person, those in the Round Room felt highly patriotic toward their new nation. It was, after all, their baby. They were the fathers and mothers of a new country.

"But we knew we had to do more than that," Katz said, her nervousness slipping away as she gained momentum. "We knew we had to do as much to shrug other burdens. Those were the burdens which we, at the old state level, had imposed on ourselves over the years. Partly this chronology was strategic. If we were ever forced back into the Union, we'd have to solve our domestic problems anyway, so —"

A chorus of "No!" and "Never!" and "Plug the Union!" interrupted her.

"This Beaver stays in his own pond!" someone in the back shouted jovially.

She took a deep breath, stealing a glance at Corcoran.

"You're doing, fine, kid," he said quietly. "These hooters are behind you. They're just showin' their good feelins'!"

Katz was only twenty-nine, the youngest member of the presidential staff. Unlike some more defensive women her age, she did not resent the term "kid." At least not when this man used it. In private, it was one of his nicknames for her, although of course no one else knew that. She was a vibrant, slender woman with auburn hair and sharp features resembling the late actress Natalie Wood. She smiled gratefully at Corcoran, looked around the room, nodded, held up a delicate hand, closed her eyes a moment, then went on.

"If anyone's learned anything in the last twenty years, it's that socialism doesn't work," she said. "Believe it or not, that was once a controversial statement on this continent. But after the horrid revelations when the Iron Curtain fell—well, everything gradually changed. Since then—and actually for a decade or so before—the key to the recovery of successful economies, worldwide, has been directly dependent on desocialization. That is, the key has been to return state-owned or super-heavily regulated enterprises to the private sector, where most of them originated and were more efficiently run."

She flipped the top page of her notes and paused to sip water, then said, "You'll recall that in the 1970s and 80s, Oregon took some solid steps in the direction of desocializing. But in the years following, in the flushness of the 1990s budget surpluses, we lost our way. We slid back. Badly—like many other states did. Where Oregon's tax burden was once 9%, it's now 20%. That is, it was 20% until a few months ago, until after the rebellion!"

"Yes!" several people shouted, drawing a grin from Katz.

"Since secession, the gross tax rate has been dropping steadily," she said.

"And it was pretty gross!" J.B. Washington interjected, drawing laughter.

"So it was," Katz responded smoothly. "But it's come down with no significant loss of services. As my calculations this morning show, Oregon's total internal tax rate is now only about 12%. Not even Ireland, which heavily de-taxed itself in the 1990s, can claim as good a rate."

Applause and "Hear! Hear!" cheers bounced back and forth around the room.

"Further, the onerous, infamous property tax, once over 5% of assessed valuation in some sectors of the state, a tax so terribly hard on fixed-income elderly and the poor, has been entirely abolished. The remaining income tax rate is going to drop further, I hope. Once our school privatization plan is in place—financing meantime having been shifted from property to income taxes—we should be able to work the total tax rate down to under 5%—perhaps to zero, although I can't promise that. We're not eliminating government entirely; just creating a minimal state. However, I have some ideas for how to keep things going on a zero tax rate, as long as—"

"You always do!" someone said.

"—as long as subscription fees to finance defense and other things are on the table," she finished. "But that's for another time a bit farther down the road."

She waved the subject away impatiently.

President Corcoran nodded at J.B. Washington and Ben Colby who had both mouthed silent "Wows!" at the mention of the possible elimination of all taxes. Neither, at the moment, saw how it could be done, but given Katz's phenomenal creativity, they weren't going to say it was impossible. In recent months, Katz had shown them that many impossible things could be done. Katz would never accept it, but Washington and Colby knew that her innovation would someday put her down in history as one of the new republic's great founders.

Katz felt no quivering of greatness. As she saw it, she was merely struggling to do her best to handle an incredibly difficult job, day by day, hour by hour—while also being deeply in love with the new republic's president. Thoughts of greatness never entered her mind. Little did she know that someday historians would call her "the Second Mother of Oregon," placing her name next to that of the state's First Mother, Tabitha Moffatt Brown.

Katz drew a deep breath, brushed a lock of unruly hair aside, and hated the fact that she was starting to sweat in an air-conditioned room. She blinked, ran a finger down the third page of her notes, and said, "I just want to underscore that we've accomplished this tax reduction by a unique program, which your president approved, with the consent of the legislature, of course. Without the vision to okay that program—"

"Which you originated," Ben Colby added. "Don't be so modest, Sparky. You deserve the bulk of the credit for creating this tax reduction policy and everybody knows it, including the president. I know, because he told me so."

Corcoran winked at his commerce secretary. This time

Katz blushed while everyone was watching her.

After their applause died, she stood up straighter and said, "Er, well, I'd better get on with it. I know many of you are aware of the specifics, but some of you perhaps are not—especially our recently-elected members of the legislature."

She nodded to three men and a woman sitting together, at the side of the room. They'd been invited, as a courtesy to their freshmen status, by the president himself. Corcoran had been around long enough to understand the importance of building political good will early. That would be as true of a new nation as of a state.

"Now the key to reducing our tax burden," Katz explained, "has not been due solely to privatization. We've also been capitalizing on out-of-state resources. Bluntly put, we've strongly linked privatization to immigration. We have been, and are, selling off our state enterprises—if you can call them enterprises—to immigrants from all over the world. Most especially, we are selling to various firms from Asia. Not to their governments, mind you; but to private companies and individuals. This has a doubly positive effect. It brings in needed capital and it keeps the financial and education status of immigration quite high. As to the former, our ex-highway department is a good example. It's now made up of five different firms owned by Hyundai, Myuta, Kawasaki, Mitsubishi, and Thaiex. Another example would be Royal Dutch Shell, which has a joint deal with Disney Enterprises. They've bought controlling shares of our state park system. I'm happy to tell you that the system is not only being refurbished, but is already running at a profit and the new firm is buying land to expand some of the parks' wilderness attractions. Of course, the motor vehicles department is virtually abolished by default. The seven firms running the highway system—including the former U.S. interstate roads—all have their own methods for keeping tabs on their customers."

"Explain that one, if you would, Sparky," the president said. "It's pretty new, at least around this neck of the woods. Besides, not everybody's district has the system yet."

"Yes, sir. I'd be glad to."

Two of the freshman legislators, both from rural areas, sat up straighter.

"Actually, the technology was pioneered in the 1980s and conceived even earlier. Instead of cumbersome license plates and taxes, the road companies issue bar-code window decals. The same kind of code you see on groceries. The road companies use an infrared scanner to read it as you cross onto and leave their freeways. That way they can tell how far you've traveled. Computers do it all automatically and calculate monthly toll charges and send you a bill. It's really just like a utility company, except instead of tabulating water or electricity, they are tabulating miles traveled."

"What about people who can't afford the tolls?" House Speaker Bard Candor suddenly demanded, his voice simultaneously surly and patronizing. It was the first time he'd said anything at recent Round Room meetings. He'd grown increasingly, unaccountably distant from the thrust of the rebellion.

"Uh, beg pardon? What do you mean?" Katz asked.

Candor hooked his thumbs in his vest and said dryly, "It's all well and good to be efficient, of course. I'm for that. But somebody's going to be swept under. Namely, the little guy. He's going to get stomped by all this new fangled capitalism."

Katz narrowed her eyes. She had never liked Candor. He rubbed her wrong. She considered him an unpredictable troublemaker. She knew that Corcoran didn't like him, either.

"Speaker Candor," she said, holding his gaze, "no one is being stomped or swept under. The elimination of the federal gas and national income tax has quadruply offset poor people's costs of using roads. Besides which, the road companies' fees are less than we'd expected. My most recent studies show that *more* of the poor are able to afford to drive than ever before. They pay lower fees than they did gas taxes, which were formerly used for road upkeep."

"With more pollution thrown in, I'll bet," Candor snorted. "Everyone knows that lower driving prices mean more driving, right?"

"Well, I don't think—"

"And that means more gas-burning, and that means more pollution," Candor rumbled on.

"Not at all," Katz countered, trying to keep her voice from rising and sounding out of control. "You're completely off base, Mr. Speaker."

"Eh?" Candor demanded, "How's that?"

He sarcastically cupped a hand to an ear.

Katz forced herself to exhale slowly and said, "You can insinuate that only morons would disagree with you if you like, but I am not stupid and neither are you. The facts are that the road firms use an ultraviolet sensor to detect exhausts from untuned cars. It's untuned cars that account for 90% of all road pollution. That's been known for decades, despite hogwash from the militant environmentalists."

"So now you're attacking those of us concerned about Oregon's environmental heritage, is that it?" Candor asked, shaking his head sadly.

"To the contrary, Bard," Katz said, unconsciously dropping his title, "the road firms notify the owners of polluting cars that they must get a tune-up or pay a higher road-use fee. They give them a month—and subsidize half the cost out of their own pockets. The result has been a 50% reduction in pollution in only four months. And it's still getting better."

Candor "harrumphed," mumbled something about "lying statistics," folded his arms across his chest, and abruptly switched subjects, saying, "Well, I can tell you that my constituents are certainly not terribly crazy about all the foreigners taking over."

Katz looked bewildered and asked, "How did we get on that subject?"

"You know exactly how we did!" Candor fumed, half rising from his seat and pointing a finger at Katz. "You're talking about selling off this blessed land of empire-builders to those little yellow bast— that is, to our *friends* from across the Pacific, right? Well, efficiency is one thing. As I said, I'm not claiming there's no place for it. But it's another thing selling our great state to the Chinks and Japs simply to get—"

President Corcoran slammed a palm against the tabletop.

"That's enough, Bard!" he said. "Shape up your language and attitude or deport yourself from these proceedings!"

"It's not racism, Mr. President," Candor said, sounding both injured and exasperated. "It's an obvious fact. What I mean is, that's how my *constituents* feel. You may not like what I as a messenger say. You may even be personally fond of the Kors and Sings and Thais. Why, I've personally known some darn nice little guys from over there. But the point I'm trying to make is that the people who had the confidence to put *me* into office resent the yellow race—and, yes, that's how they talk about them, whether we like it or not. They think the Asians are interlopers, whatever their wealth or skills. And they don't care how good they are at bowing and scraping to us and saluting to Ms. Katz's capitalist flags. Anyway, that's the way *my* people look at this so-called rejuvenation of Oregon's economy. In my district, it's the bottom line, voter-wise."

"I doubt it," Corcoran said. "But if so, Bard, then your constituents are more out of step than a centipede with nine legs missing. Besides, nobody's interloping. The Asians were invited, and you know it."

Candor directed his eyes ceilingward and shook his head, a cynical smile touching the corners of his mouth.

Corcoran rolled his cigar between two fingers and looked fiercely at Candor from under thick eyebrows, then said levelly, "I don't know what's gotten into you lately, Bard. But you've been jumping on any xenophobic bandwagon that creaks by. I don't get it. You're too smart to believe that crap, so I have to assume that you have some other motive. What is it, huh? Mind enlightening everyone in this room?"

Candor just looked at him, his eyes hooded, silent.

Corcoran sighed and made a sour face.

"Well, I won't try to guess your game," he said, "but I can tell you this, Bard ol' boy. If you want to stay on my good side, you'd better try to re-educate your constituents instead of fanning their retrogressive flames."

"I want only what's best for Oregon, Corky," Bard said, his voice suddenly calm and infinitely reasonable. "It's my native state, after all. It's my homeland. I cherish it. I want to preserve its traditions and its character."

"A home is where you choose to set roots," Corcoran said. "Since when are immigrants to Oregon inferior residents?"

"For a long time!" Candor cried, thumping an index finger on the table and making Katz jump. "Remember the old slogan, 'Don't Californicate Oregon'? Well, it's not Californians I'm worried about anymore. *Any* immigrants are a danger when they exercise too much power, when they want to change things too fast, in strange ways! At least Californians speak our language and know our general customs. My concern — and I dare say the concern of a great many otherwise silent people in this once great state — is that Oregon isn't going to be Oregon anymore. If you want me to spell it out, okay. Here it is: my people are willing to suffer slower growth — or none at all! — if it means preserving the social integrity of this state."

"Bard, we've been down that dark road," Colby interjected in his deep, mellow voice. "You're talking moldy old protectionism, which is always at the expense of the majority of citizens — who, by the way, prefer the recent changes. The majority cheers this government at every public appearance and vehemently tells pollsters that almost nine out of ten do not wish to go back to the old ways as a destitute U.S. fiefdom. Maybe your own constituents are willing to suffer again, Bard, but the bulk of the evidence demonstrates that the rest of the people aren't interested."

"Your evidence, not mine!" Candor retorted acidly, his face turning red. "Besides, as you well know, it's not just an Oregon question anymore."

"How's that?" Senate President J.B. Washington asked. Candor had danced on the edge of "undesirable foreign influences" — although not so boldly — even before the secession. But this sounded like something new. Although J.B. distrusted Candor as much as Katz and Corcoran did, but he was more patient. He didn't want to tick Candor off too much. He wanted to know what he faced in his counterpart in the House. You didn't learn much by pouring gas on a man's fire.

"There's a strong undercurrent running in my district— and other districts, too, I assure you," Candor said, looking over his shoulder at one of the freshmen legislators, who nodded back and gave a "thumbs up" sign.

Corcoran caught the exchange and frowned.

"I'm still not sure what you're getting at Bard," J.B. said, scratching his sideburns and looking confused.

"J.B., whether or not many of my colleagues acknowledge it, there is a powerful popular force that resents our loss of American condition."

"What the devil condition are you talking about?" Corcoran snapped. "I haven't noticed anybody hitching us up and tugging us off to another continent."

"Be sarcastic if you will," Candor said piously, "but I believe you know what I meant, Gov— Oh, excuse me, *Mister* President. I mean the condition of good ol', U.S.A.-type America. Red, white, blue. Apple pie. Star Spangled Banner. All the stuff that's apparently outdated in your new world order of privatized beaver dams and foreign fire sales."

"All right," Corcoran said wearily, "that's enough of this political tripe, Bard. We're here to listen to Sparky and—"

"You can't just send me to a corner!" Candor yelled. He jumped to his feet and thrust a fist into the air. "I represent a legitimate viewpoint in this state and I'm certainly not going to be brushed aside like some little kid who—"

But Corcoran had had it. He motioned to two giant security guards. Before Candor knew what was happening, they'd grabbed his arms and carried him out of the room, thrashing and squawking. Outside the room he quickly calmed himself down, shook off the guards, and marched out of the building with quick, determined steps.

Chapter 18

"Fifth Column"

***

So anyway," President Sam Washington said, "the lawyer climbs out of the tank of piranhas, nonchalantly shakes off the water, looks at the politician and the priest, and says—"

His desk buzzer sounded twice.

"Oops," he told his press secretary, Tom Rosco, "better take this."

Rosco shrugged. He'd failed to hear the endings of more jokes than he could remember.

The president touched his heat-sensitive computer screen and asked, "Yes, Ella, what is it?"

"Sir, I've got an unusual, unsolicited call that you might wish to take on line three—although I'm not sure," his secretary's voice said. "He identifies himself as Bard Candor. Says he's speaker of the house in your home state. Says it's urgent, imperative, and several other high-level adjectives. On audio only."

Washington wrinkled his nose and formed a crooked smile. "Yeah, I suppose it is. That's ol' Bard's style. Always dresses his salad with an extra shot of vinegar and pepper."

"I can brush him off if—"

"No, I'll take it, Ella. He's never called me since I've been wearing the Beltway bonnet. Who knows? Maybe it *is* something urgent."

Washington said to Rosco, "I'll zap you that punchline a little later."

"Yeah, no problem." Rosco smirked and rose to leave.

"On second thought, stick around. I'm going to put Bard's call on the speaker. You gotta hear this guy. I'll need a witness to be believed."

"Sounds intriguing." Rosco rubbed his palms together and sat down.

Washington smiled, touched the screen again to activate the line, and said, "Sam here, Bard. How're you doing?" Chuckling, he added, "You planning to jump off the secession ship or something?"

Candor stuttered, then demanded, "How did you know?"

The president caught a look on Rosco's face. He was sure the same look was on his own. He leaned forward, twice as alert, answering amicably, "Actually, Bard, I was joking. I thought you top dogs in the Oregon kennel were all pissin' on the same lamp post — mine."

Candor uttered a hollow laugh and replied, "Well, sir, that's part of why I'm calling. Frankly, many of my — uh, colleagues, embarrass me with their treatment of you. In fact, there are quite a few of us here, out of the mainstream, so to speak, who disagree with their attitude. But our thoughts are virtually suppressed. Why, I myself was bodily escorted from a presidential meeting just yesterday when I tried to speak."

And you probably deserved it, Washington thought.

"Sorry to hear that, Bard. Sounds pretty totalitarian. What's on your mind? My secretary said it was urgent."

"Oh, yes. Yes, it is." Candor lowered his voice confidingly, "Sir, you could say that I speak for a rather large, and, er, *growing* dissident faction."

"Dissident, eh? Strong word for a mainstream speaker."

"Exactly! But I don't think you're — well, fully informed, about the political ins and outs here these days. Things are taking devious and dark directions. Despite the economic and media smokescreen about high growth, there are many of us Oregonians who miss being part of the U.S. Frankly, it's downright unpatriotic not to feel that way, Sam."

Washington scratched his beard, noting both the remark and the fact that Candor had dropped "Sir" for "Sam." Whenever Candor had become informal before, back when Washington had dealt with him in Oregon, he'd been angling for something; usually something expensive.

"Don't mind my mentioning it, Bard," the president said, "but that sounds a touch odd coming from you."

"What? Oh. I suppose you're going to remind me that I helped get the secession moving?" Candor said defensively.

"You have to admit it would logically cross my mind."

"My role was overblown by the media!" Candor said, his voice strained. "In fact, they were totally wrong. The reports, I mean. Totally! They're lumping us all together. But nobody asked me a thing! Not Corky, not your cousin J.B., not that cocky young slob, Colby, or that little cun— uh, that new Commerce Secretary, Katz. I got caught in a power play out here, Sam. That's what it was. Squeezed dry. Lots of us have been!"

"Uh-huh. Well, why'd you wait so long in order to let me know, Bard?"

"Well, as I said, you don't understand the situation. Slippery as hell. Hard to move against the tide. 'Til now, I mean. So, of course, I was hoping that you could— that you might be able to— uh, that is, I felt that—"

Candor petered out. Just like him, Washington thought. Often started down the hill before checking the grade.

"You said you were hoping?" Washington prompted, toying with a pencil on his desk and shaking his head. Rosco spread his hands and widened his eyes, bewildered.

"Well," Candor said, "I was hoping that maybe we could establish some kind of understanding, Sam."

"Ah."

"I mean, a dialogue, like. Maybe a regular open line. To sort of coordinate things, just you and me."

"Toward what end, Bard?"

Candor sighed heavily, "Why, naturally, toward getting Oregon back on track! Back into the Union, of course!"

"Oh, of course."

"It's what you and I both want. Isn't that obvious?"

"I see what you mean," the president said, vividly recalling the words of some forgotten wiseman of history: *Never trust a turncoat.*

Whatever the source, Candor instantly jumped on the obviously noncommittal response, "Well, you don't sound particularly grateful!"

"Hold on, Bard. Don't misunderstand me, but this call's quite a surprise. All the time that's passed, without hearing a thing from you. It caught me off guard. But you go on. I'm listening. Go ahead."

"Well, okay," Candor said, somewhat mollified. "Let me tell you, Sam, you wouldn't like what's happening to your old stomping grounds. The Chinks are taking over!"

"The Chinks, eh?"

"The Chinks, the Japs, the Kors— you name it! It's the yellow horde in three-piece suits!"

"Really?" Washington questioned, cocking his head to one side. Rosco made circling motions with an index finger pointing at his own temple.

Candor hurried on, almost eagerly, "It's incredible, Sam! You know what I mean. All those Asian shrimps with their shiny briefcases, smiling and bowing all the time. Well, they're buying the place up. Lock, stock, and barrel. Destroying the government, too. I'm not for an excessive government, mind you. You know that. But this is going too far, Sam. Hell, they've even sold the highways and parks to the jaundiced little sneaks! And now that termite Katz says she's going to open up state and federal forest lands to homesteading. Homesteading! All our precious, unspoiled Oregon lands! She says it'll lower housing costs or some greedy nonsense like that. And if that's not enough, you oughta hear about the—"

Washington listened to the diatribe, which went on and on. Every once in awhile he made a few notes. Even in the lowest grade ore there was always a gem or two. Candor rambled for several minutes, non-stop.

When it ended, Washington said, "Okay, Bard. I appreciate the call. It's been enlightening. But one question. We're both politicians, so level with me. What do you want out of this, personally, I mean?"

Candor cleared his throat and let out a short, rough laugh, "Well, Sam. When you fellows finally move in and, you know, to overthrow Corky's regime, you're going to need somebody to run things."

"And you'd like to do it?"

Unabashedly, Candor answered, "Sam, I think I have the experience and the true interests of Oregon at heart. If that would be your decision, I'd be your man! That's all I'm saying. Nothing more, but nothing less. I've been a leader here and I know where the bodies are buried and what strings to pull. You need someone with a strong will and determination to act. Frankly, Sam, I'm the only one with the right thinking to handle reconstruction."

Washington was silent a moment, trying to keep from laughing outright at the man's utter arrogance.

He suppressed the feeling and said instead, "Well, Bard, you've given me a truckload of seed to sow. Lots to think about. It's gonna take some time. But if anything new comes up, give me a call, okay? I'll count on you to update me now and then. At this point, I need intelligence more than anything. And, Bard, when we get Oregon where it ought to be, let me just say, I won't forget your help."

Candor was not so easily satisfied. He knew a hedged promise when he heard it and blurted angrily, "Sir, I was hoping that we could work out something more specific, *today*. You see, it's urgent that my people here, my constituents, know that their leader, me, is going to stay top dog when the new order comes into existence."

"Bard, it's the best I can do. Besides, you don't want to tip your hand too early. That's bad tactics. If Corky and his crowd are as terrible as you say, they might remove you from the picture if they knew your intentions were to aim so high."

"Well, I suppose," Candor said.

"Bard, I know that you know how these things have to be handled. You've been around. So let's quietly work together awhile. You feed me your insights and we'll take things a step at a time."

"But I hoped— Oh, all right," Candor said grudgingly, like a hungry boy being told to wait 'til after supper for cookies. Washington tried to ease his hurt feelings with a minute's worth of small talk, but Candor became more sullen and withdrawn. Eventually, Washington simply claimed another appointment and disconnected.

"Velkomm to ze New Orderrrr! Hoo, boy!" Rosco offered.

Washington rubbed his eyes and nodded. "In lots of ways he's like that. Short-sighted. Pushy. Extremely impatient. But he's clever, Tom, more than he sounds. Lots of people have underestimated him over the years. When he mentioned buried bodies, he's shoveled a few of 'em under himself. Remember that you can't be a total nonentity and rise to be speaker of a state legislature."

"Some people might argue the point," Rosco said.

Washington chuckled, "No doubt. No doubt."

Three thousand miles away in Oregon, Candor sank deep into a stuffed chair in his office, glaring at the phone receiver, brooding. The more he thought about it, the more obvious it was: the president had already sold out somehow. He'd only pretended to listen. He'd brushed him off. Crudely. Insultingly.

"I'm the Speaker of the House of a whole country!" he hissed, unaware of the implied contradiction.

He straightened up, grabbed the phone, and furiously punched in the number of the new mainland Chinese embassy.

Chapter 19

"Land ho!"

There were no covered wagons. There were no horses or oxen or pushcarts. There were no miles-long lines of settlers gathering to push into virgin territories of the Old West. This was not the Oklahoma land rush or the plodding, wagon train entry into Oregon Territory. Yet it was a land rush, and its was the biggest in history.

Where once there had been wagons, there were now digital stock exchanges. Where once there had been horses and oxen, there were now fiber optic and wireless telephones and the Internet. Where once there had been lines of settlers, there were now hundreds of thousands of people talking to brokers. Where once it would have taken years to dispose of over 40,000 square *miles* of land, it was now happening in hours.

Sparky Katz smiled to herself. She, Corky, J.B., and Ben had agreed on several new strategic goals. Perhaps the most important was being implemented as she watched: empowering the people with property.

It was basically Katz's idea. Once they understood it, Colby, Corky, and J.B. had called it brilliant. Katz thought it was just a simple, practical plan. Besides, some of the former East Bloc countries had done it after Gorby had let them go. It was really an application of a real estate and legal adage that possession is nine points of the law. In this case, her reasoning was to give ownership rights to thousands and thousands of individuals. They would own almost half the land in Oregon — the half that had long been owned by one level of government or another, mostly the feds and the state.

What people *personally* owned, Katz reasoned, they would fight ten times harder to keep. Ownership would bring the new Republic of Oregon billions of dollars of sales, which would be used to further cut taxes. But equally important, ownership would create hundreds of thousands of instant, self-interested allies — the most powerful kind.

However, the plan had to work fast to succeed. If it took too long, when the feds tried to regain control they would find it easier to reverse. If done quickly, Katz reasoned, it would make things infinitely more difficult for the enemy to change.

Thus, on a Monday morning in late September, a full-page ad appeared in the *Wall Street Journal* and approximately a hundred other major metro newspapers. Internet, TV, radio, and fax commercials simultaneously broadcast the information. The ad informed the world that as of that moment, virtually all government land in the Republic of Oregon was up for sale — first come, first served. The land would be sold by electronic auction in hundred-acre parcels for whatever the market would bear to any private concern in the world.

Governments were forbidden to buy. All the land contained a perpetual deed restriction forbidding its resale to any entity of any government.

Buyers could consult detailed, high-resolution, digital maps showing the location of any land parcel and punch in bids by web browser, telephone, e-mail, or fax to any major brokerage subcontracted to distribute the deedshares.

It had taken Katz a harried, headache-inducing two weeks to set up the deal. She hadn't been able to spend a romantic moment alone with Corky, but there was no way around that. Her time was consumed dealing directly with the heads of major finance houses, such as BankAmicrosoft, Merrill-Lynch, Schwab, Greenspan-Clinton, FedEx Financial, PakMail/TWR, Datek E-bank, and so on. Given the tremendous commissions at stake, Katz had few problems securing their silence on the deal until the moment it was offered.

She turned up the sound on the *Business Information System (BISnet)* channel webcast to get an update.

" — that's the bandwidth options rundown, now, to that radical new Republic of Oregon mega-offering," the chatty announcer said, a twinkle in his eye. "Interest is nothing short of astonishing. Word is that over 80% of the deedshares were snapped up, worldwide, within the first two hours of trading today, across all major exchanges. Two hours. My, my! One source told *BISnet* that it was like letting cats loose in a mouse factory, heh-heh. Analysts expect the remainder of the deedshares to go before noon. And folks, get this: *secondary* markets have already sprung up! The mercantile exchange, OTC, GatesDAQ, and the rest are offering futures in the issues and trading is reported to be 'blistering.' Options are trading at a hectic pace, too, with almost all the action on the 'call' side, that is, betting that this new market is going nowhere but up, up, up!"

He shuffled his colored prop back-up script and continued, "Now, for an assessment of the impact on the seller, here's Laurie Grift in New York."

"Thanks, Bill," a small, washed-out blonde woman said with a crooked-toothed smile. "If the new nation of Oregon was worried about the value outsiders would place on its extensive land holdings, it needn't have been. Deedshare prices opened for a stipulated $20,000 each, but many of them have already shot over $100,000, with a few prime shares — mostly in scenic areas, such as in the John Day Valley, the Coast Range, and Crater Lake — as well as places close to urban service boundaries — topping in the millions."

"Er, Laurie," the anchor interrupted, "how do those shares actually work?"

"The shares are unique in that they are numbered, Bill. Each number corresponds to a micrometer GPS-verified location grid. Oregon set no limit on who can own how many shares, although many brokers have spontaneously set their own limits at 100 to the customer, or 10,000 acres. That supposedly avoids blocking out or angering long-time, valued clients. The limits are, however, only for today. In fact, they may not last out the afternoon. Tomorrow, it's almost certain that the shares will be traded freely in the discount markets."

"I see. Laurie, if I may, let me ask who's grabbing the biggest hunk of this land-pie? Any word on that? Who are the fat cats eating the fresh mice, eh?" he asked, winking conspiratorily at the audience.

"Word on the street is that the major buyers so far have included timber firms, oil companies, large development houses, and banks."

"Ah, *hah*!"

"You'd expect those, of course. But Bill, they aren't all 'fat cats,' as you put it. There have been thousands of individual purchasers, too. Unexpectedly large buys have come in from the war chests of various environmental organizations."

"How's that, Laurie? Did you say *environmental*?"

"Exactly, Bill. They say that they intend to operate their shares as wildlife preserves. A spokesman for Habitat for Nonhumanity, for instance, told me in these words, 'We had to get into the act, because Oregon threw everything, including endangered species sites, up for grabs.' These, and other environmental groups, such as the militant Biosphere Brigades and the Plant Protectors—the bee-bees and pee-pees, as their detractors call them—say that while they didn't get everything they wanted, they intend to negotiate with individual and perhaps corporate buyers to acquire more or different parcels. A Forest Liberation League activist said, and I quote from my notes, 'You know, maybe we should have tried to buy more things all along. We are going to get more land under our own, direct protection this way, without the political fights, than we ever could have acquired under the old system of government stewardship and Congressional patronage.' That's a quote. Word for word."

"I see. But Laurie, back to the business side of things? Surely if the environmentalists are relatively happy, that must mean the industrialists are anything but, eh? Would it be fair to say that they were edged out?"

"To the contrary, Bill, and that's the odd thing about all this. Most of the businessmen we've talked to have also been quite satisfied. The head of Behemoth Lumber, for instance, a timber conglomerate based in nearby Idaho, told us, and I quote again, 'With all this stuff up for sale, we'll be able to make deals over and over again, until the natural market forces level out all the players.' In other words, Bill, when everything's open to negotiation, everyone is talking and dealing instead of fighting in the courts and legislatures. For instance, word on the street is that a big behind-the-scenes deal has already been cut between Behemoth and the Forest Liberation League. Contrary to what many might have expected, there seem to be no victims. At least that's the initial gist from this wild day of land trading. It's quite astonishing, when you think about it."

"Thank you, Laurie, but I'll wait for the fireworks safely back here in New York," the anchor said skeptically, facing the camera again. "Meanwhile, business analysts are trying to map out the political ramifications of Oregon's move—trying to decide exactly how this is going to affect Oregon's fight with the White House. Nothing like this has happened, and, frankly, most analysts seem to be at a loss to understand the long-term consequences. But to give it a stab, here's *BISnet*'s resident prognosticator on all subjects political, Hartley Edwards. Hey, Hartley, your tie is blinding me today, heh-heh!"

A white-haired, fast-talking, wry-witted man in a dapper gray suit and bright blue bow tie came on and said, "Thank you, Bill. Anything to keep you away from a camera. Well, there's an old saying in the credit and real estate markets, 'he who holds the paper, holds the opportunity.' In other words, there's every reason to believe exactly what Oregon's Secretary of Commerce Sparky Katz said. Namely, this move will make it more difficult, and some might say next to impossible, for the U.S. feds to come rolling in again. As my grandfather used to say, 'It's one thing to walk your own fields, another to stick your nose in the badger's cave.'"

"But Hartley, isn't it a—?"

"No, it's not just an economic move, Bill," Edwards said, smoothly putting his own spin on the interruption. "That's a narrow view of a wide-open situation. We're talking about birth-of-a-nation drama here. It's grand strategy in the greatest capitalist tradition—except there is no tradition for this kind of move. Why, you ask? Because it's a *first*, at least for the last two centuries. And will it work? Only time—and a president named Washington—will reveal the cheese in that future. So far, we might add, the U.S. president is about as quiet as a devoured mouse."

"Hah-hah, well, thanks, Hartley. Now, to our market sum—"

Katz muted the sound. She took a long sip of hot coffee, closed her eyes, and smiled. It was going well. Maybe soon there'd be time to meet Corky in West Salem again.

Across the continent, in his own office, President Sam Washington sipped coffee, too. He closed his eyes, then he punched in the private numbers of his Secretary of Defense and the head of the CIA. Sam Washington had a surprise of his own for the world.

Chapter 20

"These Brave Men"

Six U.S. Army military police guards led three men into the auditorium of the Press Club in Washington D.C. The three were dressed in identical, sharply pressed dark slacks and white shirts. Their black shoes were spit-shined and reflected the bright room lights. The men were freshly shaved and their hair was trimmed neatly. All wore handcuffs and leg irons. Despite their crisp superficial appearance, the men themselves looked haggard and weak. They slumped as they walked. One had a black eye; another had a bandage over his forehead; the third had an arm in a sling and limped. All blinked painfully at the cameras, as though they hadn't been in the light much lately. No American soldiers had looked so worn since the television parading of prisoners during the Arabian Wars of several years earlier.

"It's like they've been in a hole for weeks," *Fox*'s Bob Lonsdorf hissed, elbowing a friend from *NBC*.

Their guards shoved the prisoners onto metal folding chairs set up behind a bare table topped with three microphones, one in front of each man. The men kept their eyes down.

An Army public relations officer cleared his throat into a fourth microphone standing off to one side.

"Ladies and gentlemen of the press," he said in an oily voice, "I'd like to introduce our three guests for today. They are James Donald Carnay, Peter Allan Paul, and Granvey Lupus Lopez. They are all ex-members of the South Mountain Contingent, an Oregon so-called militia. For the record, Misters Carnay, Paul, and Lopez are medical detainees, although possibly dangerous. You must bear in mind their anarchist background. That's the reason for the confining restrictions. It's for your own good."

Several reporters snorted and rolled their eyes as one of the prisoners, Lopez, muttered a very audible obscenity.

He spat toward the PR man, who jerked a leg back. The audience chuckled.

"These brave men," the PR man continued, forcing a hard smile, "are here today voluntarily, despite, er, contrary appearances. In fact, they are here at President Washington's personal request."

The latter statement got the reporters' attention. They buzzed questions to one another, directing a few at the public relations officer.

He held up a hand for silence, then said, "The detainees are here to freely answer your questions about what happened at the, er, unfortunate incident in southern Oregon. You'll recall that rebel troops attacked a peaceful U.S. reconnaissance outfit several months ago, forcing it to defend itself. One more thing before we let you at them. The president personally asked that I stress this fact. Contrary to rumors about prisoners-of-war, these men have not been available until now simply due to their injuries. Nothing more. Their injuries required a period of extended recovery before they could be considered fit for the stress of this sort of trying event. We know how tough you are. All right, Ladies and Gentlemen. They're all yours."

He turned abruptly from the microphone, nodded to a press club emcee, and took a chair at the side of the room, folding his arms across his chest and warily watching the room full of reporters.

"He doesn't look particularly trusting," one whispered sarcastically. But the words were lost in the general rush of yammering questions.

"Please! One at a time!" the emcee said. He pointed to a woman in a royal blue dress in the front row.

"I guess what's on everyone's mind," *ABC*'s Judy Roughfir said, standing, "is whether the government story about the incident is true. How do you fellows see it? Mr. Lopez?"

"I believe my earlier exclamation expressed the full range of my sentiments," Lopez replied articulately, flashing a lopsided, but bitter grin. The Army PR man fidgeted.

"Uh, could you elaborate?" Roughfir asked.

"First off, we didn't attack them. Second, they shot most of us after we tried to surrender."

The other two prisoners nodded agreement.

"Now just a minute!" the PR man started to say, rising half out of his chair. The emcee waved him down.

"Third," Carnay jumped in, speaking fast, as though afraid he wouldn't be allowed to finish, "we're not medical detainees, but prisoners-of-war. And we aren't being treated according to the Geneva Convention regs. Just look at us. A lot of these injuries happened *after* they took us into custody."

The Army PR man was on his feet now, his face red.

"Besides that," Paul said, "they told us we weren't supposed to say any of this. Told us if we didn't vomit up the government's rotten spiel, our families would be hurt and—"

"Enough of this baloney!" the Army overseer yelled, motioning to the six MPs, who quickly jerked the prisoners to their feet and hustled them away, leg irons clanking, amidst the din of outraged reporters. The PR man stomped after the prisoners, ignoring the press uproar. His face was lined with barely repressed fury.

Bob Londsdorf had not joined the noisy shouts and protests. He stroked his chin and squinted speculatively at the empty stage for a moment.

"What is it?" his pal from *NBC* asked, noticing. He'd half expected to see the feisty Londsdorf run after the prisoners.

"Something's off here."

"Huh? Meaning what?"

Londsdorf shrugged, turning and making his way out of

the room, "Meaning—well, I don't really know. It's just a feeling I have."

"Yeah," his friend said, following, "I got a feeling, too. I talk to my wife about it now and then, but she's always got a headache."

Londsdorf smiled at the old joke, but his mind was still on the three prisoners.

Chapter 21

"Mobilization"

I n the front seat of the car, Corporal B.J. Erikson kissed his wife. He brushed aside a strand of her light brown hair from her face, then held her close. He smelled a subtle, musky perfume and felt the warmth of her left breast against his chest. He remembered her frenetic, almost desperate lovemaking only three hours earlier. It was often like that before he left for duty — as though she were anticipating, trying to make up for things in advance, in case he didn't come back. Her hot tears rubbed into his cheek. After a few more seconds, he gently pushed her back and cupped her face in his large, warm hands.

"I'll be home before you know it, hon," he said.

He gently touched her pouting lower lip with a calloused forefinger.

She nodded, make-up streaking down her face. "Just you make sure."

He grinned, a boyish, cocky smile. It was a look that had first attracted her, and still did. He kissed her again quickly. He didn't want to start the good-bye thing all over. There wasn't time.

"Keep the other guys' bread sticks out of your oven, kid," he teased.

She made herself smile and nodded and said, "You know I bake only yours."

He winked, then reached down, pressing his hand gently against her lower abdomen, wondering if this time they'd be lucky. They wanted kids, but— Well, no point dwelling on that again right now. They were both twenty-four years old, married for seven months. There was plenty of time.

He got out of the car, opened the back door, and pulled out a duffel bag. She scooted over to the driver's seat and waved. He waved back, turned, and walked briskly away into the foggy night toward the big military base housing the 90th Airborne.

To his mind, it was the way he always left her.

But she felt a difference. It wasn't obvious—more like a draft from an unseen door somewhere that shouldn't be open. She pulled her coat collar tighter, even though the night wasn't particularly cold.

He heard their car pull away behind him. He picked up his stride and made himself not look back. His jaw was tight, shoulders unaccountably tense. He felt angry at being forced to leave her. He always did. But he knew it would pass. He had a job to do, like a million other servicemen. Well, at least that's what most everyone thought. His job was anything *but* like theirs.

He reached the entrance gate, was cleared, fished a cigarette out of his pocket, lit it, resumed his stride, and almost fell over a buddy squatted on the pavement in the fog.

"Jeez, Bardo!" he said, "what're ya doin? Playing with yourself in the sight of God and everyone?"

Corporal Tim Bardowski looked up and scowled, "Hi, B.J. Nah, the carry strap slipped on this stupid thing. There. That does it. Seems okay now."

He hefted the bag over a shoulder and asked, "What gives, huh? How come this halloweenie, middle-of-the-night walk? Another exercise?" he asked hopefully.

Erikson shook his head, dragging on his smoke. With the weed between his teeth he said, "Not this time. Too many cats with their backs up, I think. Know what I mean?"

Bardowski's face fell and he said, "Yeah, me too. Hopin' I

was wrong. Shoulda heard the tone of the idiot flunky who notified me."

"Yeah?"

"Yeah. Like somebody'd stuck a big, ugly fork in the wrong orifice."

"Oh, I thought he was always that way."

"He is, but this seemed like a bigger fork."

Erikson laughed and spat a piece of tobacco off the tip of his tongue. He smoked unfiltered cigarettes. Gonna use 'em, might as well taste 'em, was his motto.

"I was hoping—" Bardowski continued.

"Don't," Erikson snapped. "Think the worst, Bardo. Then you'll feel good if you're wrong."

"Yeah, I s'pose."

In the distance, they could hear an unusual amount of activity. Troop trucks growled insistently. A big C-17D troop transporter was winding up, like a giant, otherworldly beast. Men shouted back and forth. Their voices were unusually urgent—some high and strained, others low and angry. It didn't sound like a drill. It didn't have the feel.

Neither Erikson nor Bardowski could see anything through the fog. For a few moments, they wanted it that way. The mist was an emotional cushion, a transition of softness between civilian peace and—well, whatever was to come.

Erikson picked up his pace. "Hoof it, Bardo. Enough of this second-guessin.' Let's get our balls blistered and our rods rectified."

"Yeah," Bardo said, voice husky with nerves, "why not."

Erikson dragged once more on his smoke, then flipped it off into the fog. It arched away like a miniature comet, exploding fifteen-feet away in a burst of red sparks.

"Bye-bye, dinosaurs," he said. "Here come the mammals."

Chapter 22

"An Elephant Sniffing the Wind"

L arry Rigg was stretched out on his stomach. He and the Springfield Independent Militia were eighty miles from home in the middle of the night on the chilly central Oregon coast. Rigg was on watch atop a 120-foot dune. Propped on his elbows in the sand, he was hidden between two thick clumps of grass, a spiny variety with deep roots, imported decades earlier to prevent the wind-driven wandering of the great, scenic mountains of silica. Unfortunately, the bureaucrats who'd brought in the grass had failed to see how it would change the character of the terrain. In too many places, the grass now completely covered the sand, making the dunes far less scenic, a fact that had dampened Oregon's coastal tourist income.

On a personal level, the grass wasn't any better, at least not as far as Rigg was concerned. The spiky tufts easily penetrated battle clothing. He shifted slightly, groaned, and scratched a leg where he'd been poked several times. In the morning, it would look like he'd been attacked by fleas and itch something terrible.

He sighed and lifted the night vision glasses. It was an hour after midnight and he'd been on watch already for three hours. His eyes were gritty from fatigue and wind-driven sand. His bones were fed up with the cold ground. He scanned the beach below, left to right, back again. Then he did the same for the water, back and forth, simultaneously shifting his focus farther and farther out.

In the surf, he spotted a fin slicing the water. He'd heard that temperamental blue sharks were common here. Or perhaps it was an innocuous nurse shark, riding a bottom current up from California. He shook his head; he didn't really know. Like most Oregonians, his knowledge of the ocean was minimal, because 95% of the population lived well inland, as he did, on the other side of the Coast Range and, increasingly, on the other side of the Cascade Range in the booming high plains and desert country. He kept scanning the sea surface. Three brown seals played in the half-moon light, barking and yelping, impudently ignoring the shark, chasing and pushing an orphan plastic net float.

A half mile out were several fishing boats. One was significantly larger; given its draft, Rigg inexpertly thought that maybe it was too close in. He shrugged. The boat's reflections bobbed on the silvery swells. He took a closer look and thought that he saw a thin anchor line. The other vessels were moving steadily seaward, a mini-armada on the prowl. Or perhaps they were simply avoiding shoals or volcanic reefs.

He regretted that there was no one in the unit experienced in the local fishing industry. He had a buddy, Carlton Campeneau, who lived in Coos Bay, but that was too far south. Besides, Rigg didn't believe in letting people with no militia experience tag along. They got in the way and tended to mess up missions.

He scanned for another ten minutes, then his corporal thumped massively down in the sand and grass beside him.

"Anything?" Karl Hochman asked quietly.

Rigg shook his head, taking another look at the large fishing boat. It had pulled anchor and was now moving out, rapidly catching up with the other vessels.

"Why have they got us over here on this cold-assed coast, anyway? That's what I can't figure," Hochman said, bored, wanting some talk.

"You know why," Rigg answered, chuckling slightly. He

tucked the glasses into their case. "Corky wants us to get used to operating anywhere. SIM is supposed to be a versatile unit. This is versatility training."

SIM was the unit's acronym, Springfield Independent Militia, one of the few acronyms Rigg let the men use. It was less of a mouthful.

Hochman grunted, "Versatile isn't the same as omnipotent. Why not use us inland where we know our stuff? I'm a mountain boy myself. This stuff scares me. Hasn't Corky ever heard of division of labor and efficiency of skill? Must've flunked basic economics. Sad story in this new nation."

"Sure, sure," Rigg said, hardly paying attention to Hochman's complaints. Rigg pulled out the night glasses and resumed surveying the sea. Something bothered him. He watched a seagull dive-bomb the seals.

"I'm a woodsman, not a sand-scraper," Hochman chafed.

"If you hate sand, be glad we're not in Arabia."

"Well, I was there. At least it was warm. I'm freezing my biscuits off," Hochman said.

The corporal dragged hard on a cigarette, but kept the bright end shielded from the beach with the cup of a hand. Rigg glanced at him. Hochman looked at the ocean and shivered. The sergeant gently punched his arm.

"C'mon, Karl. We could be sent anywhere in Oregon, you know that. And we oughta be. I'd order it if I were Corky, too. Oregon's militia forces are thin. These exercises make us more adaptable."

Hochman snorted, "Adaptable and drowned dead, if you ask me."

"The salt air's good for your breathing," Rigg said, smirking at Hochman's cigarette. "Trying to forego that advantage?"

The big man rubbed his nose with the back of his sleeve. He'd had the sniffles ever since they'd hit the beach. He glared at the ocean and winced.

"Aw, Larry, it's just that I, uh—"

"What?"

"It's too much water in one place!" he blurted out.

Rigg looked at him, flabbergasted. He said, "Karl, I've seen you swim. Dozens of times! What's the deal?"

"Yeah, I know."

"You float like a piece of Styrofoam."

"Yeah, yeah, I know that, too."

"What're you worried about, then?"

Hochman screwed up his lips in distaste and said, "Creeks and rivers are okay, but not—" He made a sweeping gesture toward the ocean. "Not all that. It's too *big*!"

Rigg shrugged and replied, "Well, nobody's asking you to join the Navy. Besides, if you would concentrate—"

Hochman had put a hand on Rigg's shoulder to quiet him. He pointed urgently out to sea.

Rigg's eyesight was not as good as the younger man's. He pulled the night glasses up to his face again.

Beyond the farthest sandbank, but coastward of the fishing boats, most of which were now nearly two miles out, the heads of eight men had broken water. Like black fishing floats, they glistening in the moonlight. As Hochman and Rigg watched, the swimmers oriented themselves, then made fast time directly for the beach.

"My, my, my, it looks as though we've got ourselves some genuine intruders," Rigg said in a low voice. His mouth was suddenly as dry as sandpaper, although his voice remained calm, almost sarcastic.

"U.S. Navy Seals?" Hochman asked.

"Dunno. Maybe. Well, let's take 'em alive if we possibly can, Corporal."

"You got it, Sarge."

The two friends always reverted to acknowledgment of rank when action picked up, although they tended to slip back to first names after a few minutes if no one else was in earshot.

"Opportunity for a pincer configuration, I'd say," Rigg said. "You know the move."

"You mean the one we practiced for a night advance down off a hillside toward a river encampment? Mighty wide river, you ask me."

"Not askin'. Do it, Corporal."

"Yes, sir."

"It's just a bigger river and a sandier hill."

Hochman grunted, snuffed his cigarette in the sand, then squirmed backwards until he was down the rear side of the dune far enough to stand without being seen from the water. He waved in both directions, getting the attention of the nearest troops of a long line spread almost a third of a mile both north and south.

Hochman held his right arm overhead, forefinger extended, thumb pointed to ground—the SIM militia's signal for "enemy in sight." He pointed toward the beach and then extended both arms horizontally. He slowly curled them up over his head, ending with a double grasping motion. That was the code for an encircling tactic. If he had concluded the motion with a flat hand slicing across his throat, it would have indicated that the primary intention was to kill, not capture. He hoped that wouldn't happen. He agreed that the SIM needed to know who the intruders were, what they knew, what they wanted. They needed them alive.

The north man got the message right away, but the south man whirled both hands, eggbeater fashion, in front of his face, meaning that he didn't understand. Hochman swore under his breath. The "man" was the Lycra girl—Private Jamie Simpson—who'd faced off in the paintball arena against Stan Crothers, giving Hochman fits. Hochman repeated his signals, forming them a bit more slowly. Simpson extended her arm forward, palm facing Hochman. She understood now, and was more than ready.

"You better be, Jamie, you spoiled little nutcracker," Hochman muttered to himself. Actually, his confidence in her was above average these days. After "paint" day so many weeks earlier, she'd done rather well. Hochman found that he was starting to like her. Sort of. Except for Rigg, he never seemed to like anyone wholeheartedly. Could be that's why he had trouble keeping girlfriends, he thought.

He scrambled back up to join Rigg and said, "Okay, Sarge,

we're getting set. Ready in three minutes. Then it's entirely on your say-so."

"Right," Rigg said.

He paused a moment, observing the advancing swimmers, calculating their pace, where they'd probably find their feet, where they might head, then said, "I want the intruders up on the sand far enough so that they've no chance of making it back to the water before we can cut them off. Probably at least beyond that first line of low dunes."

He pointed and Hochman nodded.

"We've got people circling around the rocks closer to the water, Sarge. They'll fuzz in fast to stop any escape. What do you suppose those frogs want?"

"Got me. Recon maybe. Sabotage. Maybe they're laser-painters. Could be anything."

"The only civilization of consequence is Florence, and there's nothing up there but gas stations, cafes, galleries, real estate offices, and souvenir joints."

Rigg shook his head, "You haven't been there lately, have you? It's a nice town. But I know this. It sure ain't how tourists tend to arrive."

"Amen."

Hochman checked the load on his M-16, making sure that the gun was on burst rather than single shot.

Rigg said nothing aloud, but noticed that the ocean all of a sudden didn't seem to bother his second in command. Every soldier that ever lived had always found more to complain about when nothing was happening. It was a way of battling the persistent boredom and dampening the grinding, low level tension of waiting.

Rigg watched the men in the water for another two minutes, then took a brief moment to check his own gun. He also checked the meter on the battery-powered megaphone he'd brought, a gift from a lifeguard buddy from California. Quite a lot of SIM's equipment was makeshift, well-worn, borrowed, and jury-rigged.

Rigg rethought his plan quickly, checking for flaws. Both

152 ☆ E. G. ROSS

he and Hochman, the "generals" of the militia would keep to their vantage point, overseeing the operation. Rigg wished that his people had all been wired with the tiny ultrawideband tactical radios that were rumored to be on their way to the best militias. A product of the SORDAT special operations whiz-kids, the radios were digital and said to be completely noninterceptible, rugged, and offer tremendous promise. Some militias used cell phones, but in Oregon's vast, rough terrain, there were way too many dead spots for Rigg to consider cell phones reliable tools of communication. Well, he thought, maybe next time, voicing an ages-old cry of the under-equipped field commander.

He looked out to sea again, exchanging occasional subdued words with Hochman. It took the swimmers several minutes to haul themselves out of the surf. Two of them had dragged black waterproof containers of equipment in with them. After stripping their fins and buckling them to waistbands, all eight men trudged up through the nearest row of dunes. They settled in the southernmost of three hollows which Rigg had anticipated as their most likely initial rallying point. The insurgents were clearly unaware that they were being watched. There was, of course, no obvious reason for them to assume otherwise. The beach was deserted, apparently too chilly to attract even the most dedicated night beach roamers. Rigg heard the newcomers chuckling and talking; not loudly, but in his opinion it wasn't professional behavior. Whatever they were after, to this point they seemed to consider it a piece of cake. If they were Navy boys, they were going to be awfully embarrassed in a few moments.

One of the intruders pulled a transmitter from his belt and said something, listened, looked up the beach, then said something else, nodding his head.

"Letting mama know they're here perhaps?" Rigg asked in a low voice.

"Now why do I think mama wears red, white, and blue, and goes by the name Sam?" Hochman replied.

"Oh-oh. Sweet Jaycee," Rigg said, peering through the

night glasses, "what have we out there?"

Hochman scanned the ocean and saw it too. From a few dozen yards closer than the point where the men had first popped up, the black turret of a small, tractored vehicle appeared. As the vehicle caterpillared forward through the surf, a short, thick gun turret, slung low, became visible.

"Some kind of submersible, mini-tank. Ten tons at the most, I'd say. Looks like it's got a 20-mill shooter perched on top," Hochman noted.

"I didn't know Uncle had anything like that in his arsenal."

"Me neither," Hochman said, his voice a shade flatter. "But then, Uncle tends to keep a lot of stuff tucked away that nobody sees until it's nose-to-the-ground time."

The tank was exceptionally quiet. It made a low humming sound, not a rumble like a diesel or gas piston engine or a whine like a turbine.

"What do you think?" Hochman asked. "Electric?"

"Must be. Makes sense. Allis-Chalmers and Hyster build big forklifts for use in cold-storage warehouses. They run on batteries for hours. Water-tighten the engine and batteries, throw 'em in a cat, and you've got a clam-crawler. Didn't the Rooskies have machines like this one snooping along Swedish beaches in the Cold War?"

"Yeah, but the Red Army's long gone. Besides, they wouldn't have had a beef with us. This is an Uncle Sam jobbie if it's anything. Nobody else has got it in for us naughty, running dog, rebel anarchists."

Rigg wasn't so sure of Hochman's assessment. Despite the chill, sweat was forming along his spine. His hands wanted to shake and he gripped the night glasses tighter so they wouldn't jerk. Veteran that he was, it often happened like this. He knew he'd calm down once things got going.

He conned the water farther out.

"Don't see another one," he said. "This tends to bother me big-time."

"Yeah. I've never been too fond of charging a 20-mill lead

spitter, either."

"No, I mean, what would these guys need that kind of firepower for? Something's screwy about this, Karl. If it's a recon mission, it makes little sense. A crawler like that just slows 'em down."

"Uh-huh."

"And they're not bringing enough guys in for any kind of serious assault. You can't capture a town with one cannon."

"Sabotage?"

"Of what? Florence's antique shops?"

"Back-up protection, then?"

Rigg shook his head and said, "For a few commandos? If that's what they are, a tank would be in the way."

"You got me. But it looks like we're gonna need Big John."

"Well, our pea-shooter M-16s sure aren't going to take the hide off that armored waterbug. Okay, give it to Crothers. He's our best belly-boy. Have him make sure, Corporal. If he gives that machine time to turn on him, he's ground round. Not to mention the trouble it'll cause the rest of us."

The vehicle unexpectedly stopped at the water's edge, indecisive, its gun barrel pivoting first to one side, then the other, like an elephant sniffing the wind. One of the intruders in the dunes stood and waved to the tank.

"They're awfully confident," Hochman said.

"That's one way to put it. Another way is 'stupid.'"

The mini-tank made a slight turn, jerked, then started toward the men. Whatever its purpose, Rigg noted, it was slow, either low-geared or badly underpowered.

"Crothers has to take that waterbug out before we can catch the fish, Corporal. Step on it."

"Right, Sarge."

Hochman slid away. He was back in less than a minute. He scooted down next to Rigg to watch the fireworks.

Crothers was equipped with Big John and moving. To their left, from their vantage on the tall dune, they saw his slim figure glide among the clumps of thick grass, edging low and catlike, ever closer to the advancing tank. Crothers was angling for a position to hit it a few dozen yards from the camped swimmers. Rigg and Hochman watched him stop in the nape of two low dunes, barely rills in the sand, behind a piece of silvery driftwood. From that angle, he remained hidden from the intruders' hollow slightly farther up the beach.

"He's taking his sweet time," Hochman whispered, his voice even, despite the rising tension in his gut. "Anytime now. C'mon, son, c'mon. Don't let him get too close or you'll never get out of there! Blow that sandfish back to Neptune!"

Rigg and Hochman held their breaths as Crothers raised the special .65-caliber rifle called Big John. He waited a few seconds for the tank to chew up another five yards. The wait put the vehicle well up onto soft, dry sand. Crothers rested the massive rifle barrel on the driftwood, snuggling the pneumatically cushioned stock against his skinny shoulder. He shot twice in quick succession. Two booms like giant shotgun discharges echoed up and down the beach. The superloaded slugs slammed into the tank at well under 30-degrees. At that angle, any normal slug or shell would have glanced off, doing minimal damage at best. But these were unique.

The slugs passed through the inch-and-a-quarter armor like pins through a sheet of plastic. As they penetrated, their special spun titanium surface alloy helped heat them to incandescence. Upon contact with the tank's interior air, the slugs' copper alloy interiors exploded like rocket fuel. In a split second, a mini-firestorm cooked the driver and gunner and most of their instruments. The tank's interior turned into a horror chamber of metal and plastic slag and organic slime that had once been human. With a grind and lurch, the tank stopped, smoke and steam pouring out where the seams had been raggedly breached.

Crothers looked stupidly at the gun in his hand. He had fired scores of inexpensive mock-up bullets, fitted with the same, powerful kick. But he had never believed the real slugs would work as well as he'd been told.

He had no time to think about it. One of the eight insurgents had spotted the flashes of Big John and began firing in

Crothers' direction. Two other men joined in. Crothers auto-matically slid back, but not before being burned across his left temple by a slug. For a moment, he was stunned. He felt blood running down his cheek. But the adrenaline had kept his body retreating and he was out of the line of fire. As much as he wanted to stay and fight, getting Big John to safety was ur-gent. It was the militia's only tank-killing weapon, worth its weight in gold. Two of the intruders kept firing, more wildly now, since there was no obvious target.

The SIM militia used the action to rapidly close its pincer. Confused by the shots from Crothers closer to the water, and by the inexplicable devastation of their tank, four of the in-truders bolted. They broke toward the higher dunes, seeking better cover. Before they got more than a few feet, almost three dozen concealed militiamen fired three-burst rounds into the sand around them.

Showing shocking lack of discipline, they froze, looking crazily in all directions. Rigg raised the megaphone. His voice sounded like a god's: "This is Sergeant Larry Rigg. You are trapped by the Springfield Independent Militia of the Republic of Oregon. You are prisoners of war. Drop your weapons, move away from them, and raise your hands. I don't want to kill you, but I'll mash you like bugs if you disobey."

The encircled intruders looked at one another, then slowly let their guns fall. They moved as told, hands up. In a few minutes, after a brief firefight, the other four frogmen were routed. One was killed and another suffered a minor leg wound while tripping over a half-buried log. He and the two remain-ing uninjured men surrendered. Twenty SIM men, covered by ten others, rapidly confiscated weapons and forced the cap-tives to lie face-down in the sand. They searched them, then bound their hands with cheap plastic cuffs, the kind usually used for riot control by the Springfield cops; more borrowed gear, but workable.

Using hand signals, Rigg ordered most of the SIM troops to resume former positions, but to stay sharp. If other insur-gents had landed close by, they could be on their way to help.

He privately thought that it was more likely they'd head back to sea after hearing the boom of Big John. Big John never sounded meek or friendly. Rigg sent reconnaissance patrols along the beach in both directions. A stiff, low-howling wind picked up out of the north, stirring sand and whipping the dune grass in unpredictable eddies. The effects would mask his men's movements — but also those of any remaining intruders. That was the game; you dealt with it as it came.

He and Hochman descended from their vantage point to look over the POWs.

"What the hell?" Hochman exclaimed. "They're Japs!"

"No! Not Japanese!" one of the prisoners said, his voice contemptuous. He stepped forward and spat insolently at Hochman's feet.

Hochman smirked and said, "Spit all you want, you slimy little sea worm. Whoever you are, you're the loser."

Rigg looked the man up and down and said in a low voice, "I'm the commander of this militia. If you're not Japanese, who are you?"

The man gave Rigg a tight smile, bowed his head and said in perfect English, "Lieutenant Li Zhing. Royal Navy of the Empire of The Shang."

Chapter 23

"Oregonians are Americans!"

President Corcoran looked the man over. He was wiry, about five-seven, maybe a hundred forty pounds. Black hair, neatly swept back. A face that was all sharp angles, somewhat like the old movie actor, Lee Van Cleef, had he been Chinese. He was dressed in a dark sweater, black pants, matching shoes. It was the outfit in which he and his men had been apprehended on the beach just a few hours earlier. He stood at attention, but with a wisp of an irksome grin on his face.

"What's so funny, Lieutenant Li?" Corcoran asked, making the effort to at least keep his tone civilized for awhile.

"You destroyed The Shang's gift."

Corcoran looked at him stone-faced, holding the gaze for a full fifteen seconds.

"What gift?"

"The submersible tank, of course. It was a gift, signifying The Shang's desire to help your young republic to escape the clutches of the oppressive Americans."

"Oregonians *are* Americans," Corcoran snapped. "And don't you forget it."

"I, that is—of course, I meant the oppressive *United States* of America," Li's grin was gone, wiped away like dry snow off a windshield.

Corcoran leaned back in his chair, chewing his ever-present cigar. After nursing the huge tobacco stick's fire back from near death, he asked, "Zatso?"

"I beg your pardon?"

"Help, you say?" Corcoran's voice rumbled.

Li swallowed and nodded.

"What's in it for you guys?" Corcoran asked.

"We had heard that you were in need." He spread his hands. "One must start somewhere, so we—that is, the holy Shang—thought a suitably unusual weapon would—"

His voice faded as he looked into Corcoran's bushy-browed, deep set eyes. For some reason, they made him remember stories he'd read about Viking marauders.

"Your boss could have called," Corcoran said.

"But—"

Corcoran suddenly flicked ash into a new black ceramic tray. The tray was shaped like a sharp-toothed, leg-iron bear trap. On the side, in blood red block letters, it said: "STEP ON ME AND DIE!"

Li focused on it for a second, mouthing the words. Then he licked his lips and prayed for a glass of water.

Corcoran looked back and forth between Li and the ashtray, then said, "That's why we Americans invented telephones about a century ago—so dung-pit empires like yours could call ahead before visiting and stinking up the place."

The brutal insult got Li's attention in a hurry. His face flushed and his eyes sharpened.

"Big Daddy Shang *does* know how to use a telephone, doesn't he?" Corcoran asked. "It's not too complicated?"

Li's face turned violet and he spat, "The holy Shang knows more than any man alive!"

"Yeah, I bet. Don't they all? Just ask him, eh? Well, son, if what he wants is for real—if you're shovelin' truth and not horse manure—then I'd say he doesn't know much about diplomacy or strategy."

"The Shang is the world's greatest expert on strategy!" Li hissed, his body shaking.

For a moment, Corcoran wondered whether the little fellow might actually come across the desk at him. Corcoran raised an eyebrow and blew smoke at Li. The man stayed put. Nope, guess not, Corcoran thought.

"Invading our beaches, breaching our sovereign territory, shooting at our people," Corcoran ticked off the transgressions on his fingers, touching each with the side of his cigar. "Now maybe I'm just a dense Oregon country boy, but somehow that's not what I'd normally call a hand of friendship—no matter what color the hand or how dire the need. Try again, Lieutenant. You're not very convincing."

Li stuttered then blurted, "Your men fired first!"

Corcoran sat upright in his chair and jabbed finger at Li's chest, "Well *you* came in armed and trespassing! What did you expect? Season passes to the Blazer games? Like I said, better try again."

Corcoran leaned back, glaring at Li, chewing angrily on the cigar.

Lieutenant Li compressed his lips.

"The truth, then," he said. "Very well. We brought our men with us in order to show you how to best use the weapon."

"That's a compost heap that hasn't been aired out for a good long while."

"It's true, I swear by The Shang! Unfortunately, you destroyed our magnanimous gift without giving us a chance to explain ourselves."

"Well, you certainly have that chance now," Corcoran said quietly, "but so far you're not making much of it."

A sly look came over Li's face as he said, "You must admit, Mr. President, that a silent, water-going tank such as ours would be an asset against the Ameri— against the, er, U.S. federal troops when they attack you again."

Corcoran laughed and said, "We'll never know, will we? That contraption's nothing but a seagull nest by now."

Li nodded curtly, then smiled, cocking his head slightly, and said, "However, The Shang is gracious. He may be willing to provide another. Many others, perhaps. But of course I must be allowed to communicate with him."

"Fine."

"Eh?"

Corcoran held out his cell phone to Li. "Call your boss. Now. Tell li'l Shango Bango that I'd like to talk to him, too."

"Shango B—?" he stuttered, then composed himself and said, "But without an appointment, he wouldn't—"

"Call him," Corcoran growled.

Li started to say something, glanced at the ashtray, nodded, then gingerly took the phone with two fingers. Corcoran thought Li handled the instrument like it was a poisonous snake. Li took a deep breath, punched in numbers, spoke rapidly in Chinese, waited a few moments, spoke again, waited a few moments more, then suddenly began bowing deeply, receiver pressed to his ear. He looked like a bird trying to find seed on the ground.

Corcoran forced down a laugh and watched Li's performance through a haze of cigar smoke. Corcoran deliberately put his feet up on his desk. But deep inside, he didn't feel nearly as nonchalant as he was acting.

Li spoke for almost a minute. Then he turned as pale as cooked crab meat, making two quick affirmative sounds, bowing again vigorously. He held the receiver out to Corcoran and said, "His Imperial Shang holiness wishes to speak with you."

Corcoran pursed his lips, but made no immediate move to take the phone.

"Please, I beg you!" Li whispered, shaking the receiver. "One does not keep the Emperor waiting!"

"Maybe you folks don't keep him waiting," Corcoran said, making no effort to keep his voice down. He pulled out another cigar. He took his time sniffing, biting the end, and lighting it. Li almost peed his pants. Finally, after thirty seconds of ceremony, Corcoran casually took the receiver and said, "Howdy, there Mr. Shang! Sorry 'bout the delay. Had to get my cigar lit. Can't seem to carry on a conversation without it!"

"Ah," came the light voice, "I'm afraid it is the same with me and cigarettes. I smoke Camels, you know."

"Yeah, so I've heard. Hey, tell me, how's it hangin' over

in Confucius Land?"

Lieutenant Li fainted. Corcoran stood up and looked at the body slumped at the foot of his desk.

"Tsk, tsk, tsk," he said. "Poor little guy."

The Shang chuckled, "It's hanging well, Mr. President. Thank you for asking. I imagine that by now Lieutenant Li is gracing your rug in a highly ungainly fashion."

"That he is," Corcoran said, "that he is. Poor little guy."

"He has been known to lose consciousness under extreme political stress. His vulnerability is—ah, amusing to me. It's one reason I keep him around."

"It's pretty funny, all right. Well, you sure know your man, Emperor. He's as prone as a fish in a fryin' pan—but with considerably less sizzle."

The Shang laughed easily.

Corcoran took a moment to have Li removed from the room, then said, "Now, Mr. Shang, what was your boy doin' prowlin' around my front yard?"

"Ah, well, he is not exactly 'my boy,' President Corcoran. But the answer is simple. Lieutenant Li is a renegade."

"Oh, yeah?"

"Yes, from one of the old Maoist factions. There are several and we've had trouble purging them from the armed forces. They use a difficult to penetrate cell structure and the Communists always were a bull-headed lot, anyway. They are quite adept at perpetuating fantasies, mostly suicidal—economic and otherwise. So, what story has Li told you?"

Corcoran summarized.

"I see," the Shang replied. "As usual, imaginative. But totally false. As I'm sure you know, Mr. President, wise heads of state should not engage in this type of surreptitious diplomacy—if the lieutenant's crude efforts can even be called surreptitious. Li is a trouble maker."

"That much is obvious," Corcoran said.

"It is possible that he started out with some kind of scheme in a misguided effort to please me," The Shang went on. "But it would only have been for short-term gain for his pathetic

Maoist ambitions. Naturally, I have been watching him closely."

"Hmmm. If you've had such good tabs on him, how'd he get as far as my beach, Mr. Shang?" Corcoran asked, dropping all his folksiness and putting steel into his voice.

"Why, he has been supplying your rebel movement, of course—Mr. Corcoran."

The President of the Republic of Oregon sat still for a moment. For the first time, he had heard steel in the Emperor's voice, too. He shook his head and asked, "You'll have to run that by me again, sir. 'Fraid I've missed something here about the size of three horse barns."

"Apparently you have, Mr. President," the Shang said, lightening his tone again. "I would have told you soon enough. I've merely been waiting to see how much rope Lieutenant Li needed to hang his high ambitions. I've also wanted to see how much rope your house speaker needed in order to do the same."

Corcoran's back stiffened. Slowly he asked, "You're talking about Bard Candor?"

"None other, Mr. President. You see, this was not the first landing on your beaches. By my calculation, Lieutenant Li has successfully provided Mr. Candor's rebel army with at least a dozen weapons, each at least as useful as the tank which your little militia destroyed."

"*Army*? Where'd you get the idea that Candor has—"

"Not to mention other forms of lethal combat gear and ammunition," The Shang continued. "Don't tell me you didn't know that Mr. Candor is preparing a civil war against your new republic?"

Corcoran took a puff, let out the cigar smoke, and said quietly, "No. I didn't."

"A shame, sir. For the head of a young republic, you are paying entirely too little attention to intelligence. Candor and his disgruntled crowd of xenophobes—quite a large crowd, I understand—wish to secede along with as much of Oregon as they can take with them. By persuasion *or* by force, I'm told."

"The little ingrate," Corcoran said, grinding his teeth on his cigar.

"Aptly stated," The Shang said merrily. "But these are times of unification, of consolidation and cooperation, not of disintegration, don't you agree?"

"Depends."

"Yes, context is always paramount, is it not? What I meant, is that there are certain exceptions, of course—such as your own republic's secession from the Union. Therefore, I do not wish to see Mr. Candor succeed."

"How's that?"

"Lieutenant Li was lying, but didn't know that his lie was actually the truth."

"You're losin' me, Emperor."

"Ah, we *are* inscrutable, aren't we?" The Shang said, his voice dancing with sarcasm. "It's as simple as the budding of a field flower. *I* wish Oregon to remain autonomous. Consequently, I offer you an alliance—including military."

Corcoran looked at the ceiling, blew a blue smoke ring or two, then asked, "And what's in it for you? Besides the joys of international relations, I mean? Nobody these days offers an alliance out of the sheer goodness of his heart."

The Shang laughed loudly, as though Corcoran had told the best joke of the year.

"No, no, no!" he said, "You have my word that tawdry *principles* are not involved! I propose no high and noble moralities to eventually be broken and consequently disappoint all parties. No, President Corcoran, this is pure pragmatism. Pure short-range interest, the kind you Americans have been so good at inconsistently pursuing ever since your nation's birth. Our interest is a trade."

"Trade? But you've got that for free. We've already said we're open for business to all—"

"Not trade. A trade, Mr. President."

Corcoran frowned, "Okay, shoot. I'm listening."

"As you know, we are working toward the, well, the *proper* historical incorporation of Taiwan into Greater China."

"I didn't think they wanted any part of you."

"Nevertheless," The Shang said sharply, "the time for incorporation is finally at hand! We tried in the Clinton years and failed. The matter has come full circle again. The trade I offer you is this. For our unlimited commitment to aid your independence, you must cut off all trade with Taiwan."

"I can't quite wrap my ol' cortex around that, Emperor. Say again?"

The Shang sighed, "Is it so hard to perceive my intentions? Really, I had expected better from an American!"

"Oh, I'll do my best to stumble along with you."

"Let me be more specific. I am beginning the process of fully isolating that province," the Chinese leader said impatiently. "When it is weak enough, it will walk through our gate, like a sheep desperately seeking water and feed. Japan, Korea, Singapore, and several other Asian nations will soon make public their cooperation with the will of The Shang on this matter, so it would help to have an American st— er, republic, cooperate as well. Now do you understand?"

Corcoran frowned and said, "Well, tell me, sir, just between two relatively new heads of state, what kind of incentive did you use to convince the Japanese, Koreans, and Singaporans to go along with you?"

Without warning, an implacable iciness coated the Shang's quiet voice, "Why, the same incentive I shall offer you if you refuse our alliance and its terms, Corcoran."

He let the words hang in the air. After ten seconds, Corcoran finally asked, "And that would be?"

"We will, as a great Chinese diplomat once said, make it impossible for you to continue your present form of existence. Good-bye, President Corcoran. It may be a good evening to pray to your ancestors."

After a moment, the line went dead.

Corcoran slowly replaced the receiver. It was not the threat that gave Corcoran goosebumps. During his war experience and his life in public office, he'd been threatened more ways than a monkey could tease. No, it was the sound The Shang had made right before he hung up. It had been a light, eerie giggle. It didn't sound quite human. Or entirely sane.

Chapter 24

"The Pinch"

Think the Shang's bluffing?" Secretary of State J.B. Washington asked. He and Corky's other advisors had heard everything from another room. The president wanted their first-impression opinions.

"If he isn't," said Ben Colby, "he's got us in a remarkable predicament. If we appeal for help to Uncle Sam—well, Sam's going to demand a price, too."

"Uh-huh," J.B. said, stroking his full beard, thinking of an incident from childhood with a cousin who was now the U.S. President.

"And the price will surely be that we rescind our secession declaration—either join up, or die," Colby said, clenching a fist, then making a cutting motion across his throat.

"Overdramatic," Corcoran said, pulling a piece of stray tobacco leaf off his cigar.

"Maybe not," J.B. said.

"Sounds to me like it could be the same option The Shang is offering us," Sparky Katz offered, eyes sizzling with frustration. "Some choice."

Katz had thought that part of Oregon's grand strategy was to avert a war with the U.S. But now the new republic was facing a completely different kind of threat from a powerful, opportunistic foreign nation—the one that had squelched the entire, rejuvenated Russian empire. Americans could be counted on to pay attention to body bags on the nightly news. But based on their bloody actions in suppressing rebellions in Russia, word of which had only recently begun to leak out in detail, The Shang's armies probably couldn't care less about dead North Americans—on TV or not. Including dead Oregonians. She shook her head, sat back, and began nervously tapping her nails on the arm of her chair. She wished that she and Corky could talk about all this between themselves, quietly, with a glass of wine and time to really *consider* things.

"So what does our illustrious new defense secretary have to say about it?" Colby asked, turning to the jeans-clad man to whom he'd relinquished one of his two titles. Colby retained the duties of the national security advisor and there was plenty of work for him in that position. He himself had pushed to have Erik Hochman aboard as defense secretary, although he'd at first toyed with the idea of letting him have the security position. Both jobs together were too much for Colby, and the president didn't have time to take on any more, either. Hochman was quick, imaginative, had combat experience, was schooled in the history of strategy and political theory, and was unafraid to offer his opinions to a strong-willed Corcoran. Corcoran liked him, and his ideas, better than any of several retired veteran U.S. generals.

Corcoran studied Hochman's appearance. He was almost as big as he was. Blond and blue-eyed, with a rounded, heavy jaw and neatly trimmed red-brown beard. Also slightly overweight, but it didn't seem to bother him.

Hochman smiled with his eyes and shook his head, as he often did before talking. Life was fun, if endlessly ironic.

"I think we ought to act as though it's a full-blown conspiracy," he said.

"Whoa!" Corcoran said, stopping a match halfway to a fresh cigar he'd peeled from its wrapper. "Well, okay, lay it out," he said, seeing the suddenly serious look from Hochman.

The new defense secretary crossed his legs and said, almost professorally, "Let's consider the opportunity costs and profits. Look at the situation from their perspective. If it's a conspiracy, if it's the Sam and Shang Show, we'd be better off treating it that way— wouldn't we?"

Corcoran got the cigar lit, then said, "Convince me."

"Otherwise they could easily outflank us. If we assume no conspiracy, yet there is one, we're wide open to a strategic pinch—Sam on one prong and Shang on the other. If not, well, we're not out anything and we'll have prepared for the worst and experienced benefits from it."

"Such as?"

"It'll make us jack ourselves up enough to devise some things we wouldn't otherwise consider for defense. For one thing, I believe that we're banking too much on weaponry. A lot of what we've inherited looks better on paper than it does in fact. I wouldn't count on more than a quarter of it being functional—and that's only if we can use the other stuff to cannibalize for spare parts."

"Oh, man," Corcoran said, "that's a punch in the gut."

"Well, there's another fist coming," Hochman said. "I've toured as many of the troops as I can, and while morale is fairly high, so is strategic confusion, especially since The Shang's guys landed on the beach. The Regular and the militia grapevines have been buzzing about that. One of the worst things in the world is to sit around for ages and not know whom you'll be fighting, or even worse, fearing that your leaders don't really know."

"Well, *do* we know?" J.B. asked.

"That's not the point," Hochman said. "You've got to give the men clear enemies. I suggest spreading the word that the U.S. and China *are* working together against us. Makes 'em both bigger rats."

"I'm no expert on these things," Katz put in tentatively, "but don't you risk overwhelming the men with the thought of double enemies like that?"

"No," Hochman said, "quite the opposite. Especially if we brag about our victories."

"What?" Colby asked. "You mean the beach insurgency?"

"I mean exactly that, and any other encounters we might run into. Let's turn them — and anything related that we can think of — into hero tales. Get them simplified and romanticized. There's nothing like success stories to build confidence. And when you've got forces as small as ours, you've got to do all the confidence building you can. I'd also recommend bragging about other, more general victories. Such as yours," he said, turning his eyes to the commerce secretary.

"Mine?" Katz said, her hand to her throat.

"That's right," Hochman said. "You think the men wouldn't appreciate how, for instance, you got most of the big media to base themselves in this state? Heck, that's one of the best grand strategic maneuvers I've ever seen. What American president in his right mind would want to blow away the press? It's a pretty big briar patch. Or how about the way you got our Asian foreign friends' businesses set up here, providing trade and jobs for our adjacent states, helping them pull out of their economic downturn?"

"But those weren't strategic, just common sense."

"The hell they're not strategic," Hochman said, leaning forward intensely. "War is politics by massive force. But you're better off doing as much as you can without going that far. To the rational grand strategist, war is a last resort. The deadliness of war means that you should do all you can to think of other, lesser ideas, because they're not *actually* lesser. They're the ultimate application of Hart's indirect approach. The most indirect approach to war is to avoid it — while achieving your main goal. I hope we can do that. If we're smart, I think we can do it."

"So basically," Corcoran said, "with both your conspiracy idea and this emphasis on 'earlier options,' as you call them, you're saying we need to insure for the extremes."

"Pardon me, sir, but you've only got half of it," Hochman said. "I'm saying that we need to do all we can to make sure the extremes are unnecessary, while simultaneously acting as though they will be critical."

Sparky Katz nodded. This was new territory for her, but

she was catching on. In fact, she found it quite intriguing.

"Prepare for the worst, but do your best with your least," she said.

"Exactly. I call it the strategic high wire walk," Hochman said lightly.

"If you do it right, you move across your chasm of troubles in one piece?"

Hochman nodded and glanced appraisingly at Katz. At first, she hadn't liked the man. She didn't know exactly why. But she was starting to admire his sharp mind, and had even found her thoughts wandering— She suddenly blushed, but no one was watching her. Hochman had already shifted his gaze to Corcoran, who, like everyone else, was listening to the new defense secretary. Katz crossed her legs and sat up straight, taking a deep breath. Things were always happening to her that she didn't expect. Well, she reminded herself, there's no such thing as an evil thought. If you can't think it, you can't evaluate it. She forced her attention back to Hochman.

"So these concepts prop each other up," Hochman said, "The Shang's already done us a favor by pointing out the vulnerability of our beaches. That's caused us to beef up our sand bug brigades. Think of his wider threat as another unguarded beach. Look how it's got us discussing new outlooks and different options!"

"All right, I think you've nailed down your point," Corcoran said, pouring himself coffee from a decanter.

J.B. Washington said, "Erik's pointed out some blinders. Big ones. We've not only assumed that we'd be dealing with a single enemy, but have been pretty inflexible about whom that enemy might be. Sure, we've contemplated whether the Californians or some other states might send some of their guard boys in after us. But that's all part and parcel of the U.S. threat, as far as we were concerned. This conspiracy thing's especially worth examining. For instance, what if the U.S. decides to let The Shang *have* us?"

"What!" Katz yelped, bouncing half out of her chair.

"Interesting theory," Corcoran said, "but Sam'd never

stand for it. You of all people oughta know that, J.B. Let's be completely serious."

"Well, hold on, sir. There's a sense in which J.B. could be on target," Hochman said. "There's evidence in history to support his view."

"I don't remember that chapter," Corcoran said, a touch irked at being contradicted. He repressed it; an old man's tendency, he thought. He sipped his coffee and sat with his elbows on his desk blotter, another cigar burning itself into oblivion in his ugly beartrap ashtray. He looked expectantly at Hochman.

"I'm thinking of how the Russians waited for the Japanese to pacify Manchuria," Hochman recalled. "As soon as the Japanese were weak enough—and that took several years of World War II pounding by the U.S.—Malinovsky's forces moved along a 5,000 kilometer front, conquering 60 miles a day. In about a week, they'd taken Manchuria. The point is, Stalin hadn't been crazy about the Japanese being on the Asian mainland, but he was smart enough to roll with the punches and bide his time."

"So," Corcoran asked, "the President of the United States is going to let China stomp us, bide his time, then come in and pick up the pieces?"

"Could be," Colby said, two fingers on his chin, "could very well be. Makes sense."

Corcoran shook his head doubtfully and said, "A parallel out of history isn't going to convince me that Sam Washington would have anything to do with such a nefarious plan. He may be my enemy, but he's no mass murderer."

"That's the beauty," Hochman said. "*He* wouldn't be. Not as far as the PR goes. It's perfect. He could blame it all on the Chinese. Instead of having to suffer like he did with that massacre of our militia down south, he could turn the press against the Chinese. Then Sam could move the U.S. Army in and 'liberate' us, see? The Chinese pretend to panic and back out— with some sort of face-saving negotiated agreement, of course. They don't lose anything. Sam forces us back into the Union.

Click, click. Like a fine-tuned clock."

"Machiavellian," Colby said.

"I'll say," Corcoran said.

"However," Colby said in his deep voice, almost pomp-ously, "let us not forget that thousands of honorable men have throughout history proven capable of doing devious things in brutal times."

He glanced at J.B., wondering if he'd spring to his famous cousin's defense.

Instead, J.B. told a story reinforcing Hochman's views.

"I remember when Sam and I were playing Monopoly once — we were about, oh, eight or nine — I was creaming him. He was almost out of properties and money. Then he landed on one of my big, built-up pieces — Park Place, I think it was. Hotel there; the rent would've broken him. He showed his dis-appointment on his face, and I felt sorry for him. So I offered him a loan. It was totally against the rules, and he could barely believe I would do it. But he took it. As I handed him the money, do you know what he said to me? He said, 'J.B., if I take this, I'll come back at you. I'll come back, and I'll get you down. And when you're down, I won't have mercy.' Well, I didn't believe him. My cousin was too nice a guy, so like an idiot I lent him the money."

"Yes?" Colby said after a moment. "So did he?"

"What, win? Oh, yeah. And the stinker didn't bail me out, either. No equal opportunity lender, that guy. When I ranted and bawled about how unfair it was, he just looked at me for a few seconds. Then he said in a nine-year-old voice already as hard as mahogany, 'I told you so, J.B. You were warned.' His tone, his words, the look on his face — they scared me. From that moment, I always tried to keep Sam on my side. I know that part of Sam Washington is still in him. From what I've seen over the years, it's grown stronger and he *enjoys* it. If he believes that the Union is jeopardized, if he thinks our se-cession will hobble his ultimate ability to defend the United States — oh, yeah, Sam'd make a deal with Satan himself."

Into the resulting silence, Hochman said, "Maybe he already has for all we know."

Corcoran looked sharply at him, but Hochman didn't catch it. Then Corcoran sighed inside, realizing Hochman had no way of suspecting what Corcoran, for an instant, had thought he might suspect.

"Let's recall something else, guys," Hochman said. "Even if Uncle Sam intended to somehow stop things short of a bloodbath, war has a tendency to get out of hand. Damage inevitably occurs in ways, places, or times that you don't expect. I think we'd be wise to plan for a two-opponent war. At least."

Corcoran said abruptly, "Okay. Sold."

He drained his coffee and set the cup down carefully. "Let's operate that way from now on. Go ahead with that romantic hero stuff, too. I'm sure Colby's propaganda boys can help you out on it."

"It should be no problem," Colby said. "As a matter of fact, I've already retained a couple of local fiction writers who ought to be perfect for it."

"What about this Candor business?" Sparky Katz asked, switching subjects. "That bothers me a lot. The idea of a troublemaker inside the highest levels of our government, eating away at everything we've accomplished—"

"You're not the only one," Corcoran said. "Candor's not getting his ears sweetened by anymore of these high-level sessions, and that's only for starters."

"But I mean," Katz pressed, "do you believe The Shang when he says that Candor is planning a counter-rebellion?"

Corcoran caught Colby's eye, then nodded. "Tell, her Ben. I filled Erik in earlier today. He says Sparky's our grand strategist, even if she doesn't know it. So I guess she has a right to the inside dope on Candor."

Katz looked bewildered.

Colby cleared his throat and turned to Katz and said, "Sparky, you've only been in on these full military situation briefings for a bit over a week. The fact is, we've known about Candor's secession group for awhile. Not everything, but enough, we think. We've got a good man inside his organization. We've known that Candor's been getting weapons from somewhere, although we figured it was from the U.S., mostly light arms, grenade launchers, a few mortars. But Candor's movement is weak. He's got a tight crowd of good ol' boys from the south coast around Coquille, Coos Bay, Charleston. Old coon-huntin' country, they used to call it. They stomp around and cheer his speeches. Other than them, though, there aren't as many sympathizers as Candor thinks. The south Coast isn't the racist hotbed it was decades ago. His boys enjoy his parties and beer, and tolerate his talk. It's true that there are a few young legislators leaning toward his racism and xenophobia. But we're slipping the word to them. If they want their political careers to last longer than a single term in this new nation, then they'd darned well better start distancing themselves from Candor."

He paused, glanced at Corcoran, who crushed out his fading cigar, and picked up the conversation, "The really good part, Sparky, is that Candor is being arrested for treason soon. We plan to wait until he gets back up here from his latest foray south, then grab him in full view of reporters. That'll discredit him and wipe out his group. That way—"

"Er, excuse me," Hochman said, shaking his head. "Sir, I've been thinking. Maybe we oughta ice that idea."

"Huh? Why? Look, I'm not letting him stir up more trouble. That bag of lizard parts is going to pay for all the trouble that he's putting us through."

"Sure, sir, I agree," Hochman said, nodding. "But what's the rush? After all, as Ben's pointed out, the guy is practically impotent politically."

"You don't know him like I do, Erik, so don't ever underestimate him," Corcoran said sternly. "Too many have who ought to know better. That's how he got to be Yapper of the House, you know."

"Okay, then why not let Candor *think* he's doing something monumental?" Katz interjected, grinning slowly, starting to get the hang of this strategy stuff. "It'll keep him occupied for awhile and he'll draw into the open any other lowbrows that we don't know about who could create serious problems down the road."

"I like it," Hochman said. "A grouser like Candor could be useful to us, and if we played it right he'd never know it."

Colby drummed his ample stomach with his fingers, smiled, and said, "Right, right." He raised an index finger and added, "When we get this new country rolling on the wide and breezy, we tell Candor what we did, how we played the line to him, how he was thoroughly, mercilessly exploited. *Then* we put the lintball away for a hundred years and let him do nothing but think about how badly he was had!"

Corcoran was grinning like a shark now.

So was Katz, who had come to hate Candor.

"Oooh! When the time comes," she asked, "may I be the one to tell him?"

"That I promise, Sparky, but I get to watch," Corcoran said, winking.

She blushed and thought, I really *do* love this man.

"That settled," Hochman said with inspiration, "how about using a variant of the same ploy against The Shang and Washington both?"

"Huh?" almost everyone said at once.

"Sure. Tell The Shang we agree to his terms. Then tell Washington that we've agreed, but were forced to. See how the U.S. reacts. It'll set things boiling and if we're observant, it should tell us whether Sam and The Shang are hooked up or not. It's a way of verifying, or disproving, the conspiracy theory. If nothing else, there's a good chance we'll be able to make a fresh deal with Washington."

"But, as you say, what if it's not a bluff? And what if Sam Washington *is* in on it?" Katz asked.

Hochman was about to answer, but to his surprise, president Corcoran suddenly cut things off with, "Folks, it's getting late and I'm hungry. Got to draw a line somewhere. I think we've milked enough out of the conspiracy cow for one evening. See you all tomorrow morning, barring The Shang's marching on the old governor's mansion."

Hochman watched Corcoran closely as the president shook hands with the other three people. After they filed out, Hochman slowly stood and took Corcoran's hand, too. He held it a moment and looked into his new commander-in-chief's hawk-hooded eyes and said, "Sorry for saying so, sir, but I've got a powerful feeling that there's something big you're not telling me."

Corcoran held the gaze, then smiled and said, "Yep. And you'll find that any president, sooner or later, will do that to everyone who works with him. Chief's prerogative."

"Yes, sir," Hochman said after a couple beats. He flashed an uncertain smile and left the room.

"Sorry, son," Corcoran said softly to himself, shaking his head, "but you would've had to have been there. Even a man of your breadth of thinking probably wouldn't understand. I just can't take the chance. Even defense secretaries can't be allowed to know certain things."

Chapter 25

"Nowhere Meeting"

Duke Majorin, C. "Cease" Ilandres, Raylee Dixon, and Santini Androtti shifted nervously in their seats. They were dressed in casual Western clothes—jeans, boots, long-sleeved shirts, cowboy hats. It was not the normal public attire of state governors, not even in the Far West. The four were gathered around a rough, wooden table at a small restaurant in the tiny town of Post, Oregon. Post was nestled in the high desert above the Prineville Reservoir on the Crooked River. To city people from the East, the place would be called "the middle of nowhere." For practical purposes, it was. The governors were there for three main reasons. First, it was out of view and earshot of the media. Second, it was a relatively convenient distance from their respective states, California, Idaho, Washington, and Nevada. Third, the President of the Republic of Oregon had asked them to come. These days, given how much the four neighbors owed to their booming ex-brother, one did not lightly turn down such an invitation.

"Any idea what this shindig's about?" Ilandres asked the other three.

Majorin squinted at the faded menu, decided he wasn't hungry, and said, "Well, he called me at home a couple days ago. Said it was 'the trip of the year.' Told me I couldn't afford to miss it. I took the hint that it had something to do with Uncle

Sam, but I'm not sure what."

Androtti said admiringly, "Everything old Corky does nowadays ticks off Sam."

The other three governors chuckled. Irritating the federal government was a tradition as old as the West. It was normally thought of as a sporting activity, somewhat like shooting speed limit signs.

"I surmised that it concerned taxes," Dixon said, pushing her new Stetson back off her forehead. She scratched a patch of reddened skin on her brow. Unlike Androtti, she seldom wore hats. "But considering how ubiquitous taxes are, I suppose that could mean almost anything, too."

"Hmmmm," Androtti said, looking at her from under his long, black Italian eyebrows. He shrugged. "And here I had a hankerin' that it'd be a trade pact revision."

"You're partly right, all of you," a rangy man with a heavy brown mustache said. He wore a faded sheepskin coat and a gray, wide-brimmed hat that had seen a few years in the weather. As he spoke, he rose from a cracked red vinyl stool at the cafe's breakfast bar. He'd been there, only a few feet away, eating and smoking, when the governors had wandered in a half-hour earlier. Nobody'd paid him the slightest bit of attention. A bit taller than normal, he otherwise looked like a thousand other people in this part of the West. He momentarily lifted his hat to reveal his full face, winked, and slipped into a vacant seat next to the governors.

"Well, if I'm not desert dizzy!" Androtti said beneath his breath. "It's the Ree-public of Oregon's Prez hisself!"

Despite his Italian ancestry, Androtti had a thick Western drawl. He reached out and shook hands, as did the others.

"Excuse me if I leave the face fur on," Corcoran told them, keeping his voice low. He touched his thick, false mustache. "I flew in this morning on my Rutan one-seater to a buddy's spread down the river a bit. He six-wheeled me in. I don't mean to sound paranoid, but I'd just as soon nobody else knew who I was at the moment."

Androtti glanced at the lone waitress in the place and

shrugged. The girl, plain and somewhat tired-looking, was busy reading a Hollywood gossip magazine while doing her nails in two shades of bright red and pink. Except for once refilling their coffee mugs, she'd ignored their table.

"Wouldn't worry if I were you," the Nevada governor said. "I'd hazard a bet that she's interested in other kinds of celebrities."

Raylee snickered. "Oh, I don't know," she teased, "she might make an occasional exception for a handsome radical like Corky, here."

She poked Corcoran in the ribs with a chubby fist.

Corcoran flipped Dixon a slow bird and the Washington governor guffawed. They were old, good friends. The waitress glanced up, made a sour face, and flipped on a TV over the milkshake mixer, instantly absorbed in a soap opera.

After a few minutes of political gossip and personal pleasantries, Majorin checked his watch and came to the point, "Pretty mysterious stuff, this get-together, Corky. What's the dope, huh?"

Corcoran hit them with both barrels: "How'd you all like to jump the U.S. rustbucket and join a real ship like Oregon?"

Majorin's mouth hung open, then he said, "You mean secede like you did?"

Corcoran nodded. "With all the benefits we got."

Majorin rubbed his chin and developed a small furrow on his brow. "I don't know. We'd have all the problems, too."

Corcoran shrugged. "Yep."

Androtti cocked his head and said, "Aw, Duke, c'mon! Wet your snout in a trough that's half full, for Pete's sake."

"Well, I don't know—"

Ilandres's eyes crinkled and he began whistling an obscure old southern tune with a double meaning, "When We Blow Those Blues Away."

Majorin, whose family had originally come from Alabama, began a slow, broad grin.

Dixon punched Corcoran on the shoulder and demanded, "Hell, what took you so damned long to ask us?"

Chapter 26

"First Crack"

U.S. President Sam Washington threw his bear claw pastry across the table, narrowly missing a vase of yellow and orange chrysanthemums. Secretary of State Craig Goldstein had never seen the president let fly like that. He'd seen him angry, of course, but not throwing mad. Nevertheless, Goldstein's eyes widened only slightly. He sipped his coffee, giving Washington a moment to compose himself. Goldstein had been raised in a large, rambunctious family. Hurling handy objects had been considered a part of the normal, emotional leading indicators.

Washington huffed and then thumped his morning intelligence briefing with his forefinger. He rumbled at Goldstein, "Four states want to bail out and join Oregon? Why didn't someone wake me up last night to tell me about this?"

"Well, they haven't actually decided—"

"I could've been working on this for hours already!"

"Perhaps someone was afraid you'd throw your nightstand instead of a bearclaw."

Washington squinted at Goldstein and said, "Sorry about that. But we've been here for a good ten minutes and you didn't even drop a hint."

Goldstein nodded and said, "Correct. That way I was able to observe your full reaction more objectively. Not to mention a lot more safely."

"I'm really not in a laughing or a guessing mood this morning, Craig."

Goldstein held up a hand. "Sam, take it easy. I merely meant that the messenger of bad news often finds it tougher to keep his head about him."

"Hrmph!" Washington groused. He contemplated the lucky flower vase, then gave the secretary a brief, lopsided grin. "Guess you had the guts to be here. Now, what did Corky offer those governors to get them to consider secession? Surely they can't be serious?"

That's what you believed about Oregon, too, Goldstein thought. But what he said aloud to the president was, "It's easy. He'll give them what they want, what Oregon already has. Low taxes, nearly completely free trade, almost no regulation, full immigration of talented outsiders, and all the West Coast ports, which do nearly as much volume as the East, Gulf, and Lake ports put together these days."

"Etcetera."

"It's what Vice President Leininger's been telling us for months could happen."

"Well, at least he's implied it," Washington muttered, moving his coffee cup in small, contemplative circles.

"Let's not forget that this whole thing is still in the air," Annette Washington said from her chair to the president's right. "The four governors are almost all convinced, right?"

"Majorin is said to be the weak link, which would be to our benefit, *if* true," Goldstein said, nodding at the First Lady.

"I'm not so sure it is," Annette said. "But no matter how solid the governors are on seceding, they have to run the idea through their legislators. Governors aren't dictators anymore than presidents are."

"Right," Goldstein said. "There will be some opposition and maybe we can exploit it."

The president stroked his beard and nodded and asked, "Like what?"

"Like a lot of Southern California people lap at the federal trough and don't want to change," his wife said. "The Hollywood Subsidy Act of 2005, for example, ought to help. A lot of big studios now get federal grants to compete against overseas outfits. To counter that sort of thing, Corky's undoubtedly decorated the whole radical capitalism cake and thrown in free plates."

"I don't get the plates bit," Sam said.

"Ah, well, I heard he's willing to lend them his hot-shot commerce secretary to jack their economies up fast, like she did Oregon's," Goldstein said. "She could do it, too. Tailor-make stuff for them."

"She that good?"

"A fireball. What's her name? Something feline. Kitty?"

"Katz. Sparky Katz," the First Lady said.

The president snapped his fingers and said, "I remember her now. Good woman, according to the spy dope. Never ran into her myself. She's pretty young, isn't she?"

"And pretty," Annette said.

"Yeah, I caught glimpses of her on the news. God spare us competent lookers! Present company excepted," Washington said quickly, winking at his wife.

"What next?" Goldstein asked.

Washington stopped circling his cup and instead began tapping a rhythm on its edge with a fingernail. He slid deeper into thought, simultaneously scootching down a notch in his chair. He kneaded the bridge of his nose with a thumb and forefinger for a couple minutes, letting things fall into place.

Goldstein let him think. Meanwhile, he saw no reason to miss breakfast, such as it was. He took a maple bar off a hand-painted ceramic White House serving plate.

"You don't seem particularly taken aback by the event," Washington said abruptly.

"Eh?" Goldstein asked, chewing.

"This could complicate the Chinese thing."

"Oh." Goldstein wiped frosting from the corners of his mouth, sipped his coffee, and considered his reply carefully. "No, I suppose I'm not shocked, Sam. Since Corky personally burned our noses, mine in particular, I've been looking at the whole shamus afresh. From Oregon's perspective, I mean."

"Know the enemy?"

"For me, the bottom line is a lot easier to write than it once was."

The First Lady asked, "Which is what, Craig?"

"The ideals of the U.S. union, as practiced, not as preached, would pale compared to the real benefits of confederation with Oregon, as both preached and practiced."

"Very philosophical," the president said sarcastically, instantly regretting his festering grumpiness.

"No doubt that's what California and the others are also thinking," Goldstein said, ignoring Washington's irritation. "It's a clear picture, easy to grasp. A lot easier than wading through our forty miles of federal regulations, taxes, restrictions, and monopolies. Leininger's been more accurate on the impact of that than we initially realized. The salient fact is, it's the picture we've got in this political frame. And we've got it whether or not we like it."

"Well, I don't like it," Washington burst out, his apparent frustration surging like a dose of amphetamines. "And it's going to stop one way or another. Corky's sticking too many tree branches in the spokes of my wheels."

His face was red. Goldstein looked speculatively at the flower vase. At least the bear claws are gone, he thought.

The telephone buzzed at the president's elbow. Ignoring both the voice activation and the viewscreen, he grabbed the receiver and shouted, "Yeah, what? Oh, Ella. Sorry. No, just having my usual weekly chat with Craig and Netty. Who? Corky! That son of a sailor wants to talk to me? Why, the gall of the— What? Right now? Ella, you tell him to shove it— Huh? Oh. Oh. Yeah, well, in that case. You don't think so, huh? Okay, all right then. Put him on—closed line. But give me ten seconds to bale my mental hay, will you?"

Washington reached for his water glass and took a sip, wetting his mouth. Closing his eyes, he cleared his throat, took a breath, then said, "Okay, Ella, put the upstart on."

"Corky," he said, "I see you're trying to hijack some more of my boys. What? Do I like it? No, I wouldn't say that's a terribly accurate description of my mood. But later on that subject, okay? What's this hooey about The Shang? Ella says that's why you called. Says you said that he's threatening you. Yeah? He did, huh? Oh, you do, huh? Badly, huh? Well, well, well, well. I'd have to meditate on that a spell, Cork, ol' buddy. But I know this right now. There'd be a price for our help. A stiff one. What? Oh, give me a break! Take a wild guess. Yeah, that sinks the dime right in the old carnival jug. Uh-huh, that's right; you'd have to rejoin the U. S. of A. and talk your four friendly neighboring governors out of their wild idea of confederating with you. One Civil War was enough for this nation. Huh? Oh, I imagine it does stick in your craw. Tough! That's the deal! Think it over hard. What? No, no, I've never spoken to the little demigod. But if The Shang's serious, from what the CIA and DIA tell us, he's got the power to crunch you—especially considering that you don't have our defense umbrella anymore. Hey, don't whine to me about it. That's the way you wanted things, remember? Goes with the territory. That's right. If you'd like to rethink your position, I'll be here. But make it snappy, Corky, because I've heard The Shang doesn't like to be kept waiting. Besides, McDouglas and his forces will need plenty of lead time to consolidate defenses against The Shang. Yeah, I suppose it's kind of hard-hearted, boxing you in like this. But you weren't exactly a nice Little Miss Muffet when you threw your curds and whey in my face. No, sorry. Absolutely no compromise on this one. It's the best deal you're going to get. Yeah, you, too. Nice talkin' at you."

Washington punched off the line with a vicious stab. Then he took a deep breath, looked at Goldstein, and winked. "How'd I do?"

Goldstein smiled. "Sounded good."

Annette Washington nodded.

"It better have," the president said.

Three thousand miles away, Corcoran punched off at his end and replaced the receiver in its cradle. He looked at J.B.

Washington, Ben Colby, Erik Hochman, and Sparky Katz, his own regular group of advisors. They'd all listened to the conversation on the speaker.

"I'm forced to surmise that we have our confirmation," Colby said. "He didn't sound at all surprised that The Shang had threatened us. They're working together."

"I wouldn't have believed it!" Corcoran said.

Katz looked at Hochman. Hochman spread his hands.

"I'm still not so sure," J.B. Washington said. "My cousin's lack of surprise bothers me. It's not like Sam to be a poor actor. If it were really a conspiracy between Sam and The Shang, wouldn't he have tried to act more outraged for the record? I would have. After all, it's his home state that The Shang's threatening."

"Sometimes, " Sparky Katz said slowly, "we can be hardest on our own family members—especially if they turn on us or embarrass us."

"Or both, in this case," Colby added.

"Well, maybe you're right," J.B. said. He scratched the crown of his head.

Corcoran watched him a moment, then pursed his lips and turned to his defense secretary. "We can't let this kind of thing go unanswered, not under my administration. It's decision time. Here it is. Erik, you tell whomever you need to get moving on operation Snowjob. Hit the whole target list. You sure you've got enough equipment to make it work?"

"Yes, sir," Hochman said. "More than enough. And we should be able to coordinate the timing almost to the minute."

Corcoran faced his state and commerce secretaries, pointing at each in turn.

"Colby, you have your eyes ready to help placate and grab Majorin when his collar turns red at the feds. Make your stuff look good. He's really the only one on the line. And Sparky, you spin your golden threads and have 'em ready for Colby and me to pick up. We're going to need the best you've got when the time comes."

Colby nodded.

Katz said, "I'm on it."

"I don't think Sam's going to want to have me bark in his ear for awhile, so you'll have to do it."

Washington gave a thumbs up.

"And me," Corcoran said, "I'll be getting ready for another series of secret conferences with soon to be ex-governors!" He clapped his hands sharply. "Okay, confederates! Let's rack 'em, whack 'em, and sack 'em!"

PART TWO:

"A More Perfect Union"

Chapter 27

"Snowjob"

The fifteen-foot stealth cruise missile was painted deep black. On its nose was a golden dragon, breathing red fire. The golden dragon was the official symbol of the Shang Empire. Skimming close to the earth at just under 600 miles per hour, the missile had been in the air for over two hours, undetected by radar. As it approached the outskirts of Grand Island, Nebraska, it automatically veered to the right around the town. The missile's terrain sensing computer and GPS sensors kept it a mere thirty feet above the tops of a line of trees along the Platte River. The missile had several more minutes to go. Its final target was Omaha, largest city of the state, home of several U.S. military command installations, some known, some completely secret.

The missile had flown in from the West. Its actual launch point would remain unknown for years. But logical deduction would assign a highly probable origin, somewhere in the Pacific off the coast of Northern California, from a submarine. At that moment, twenty-one other missiles like it were homing in on their targets: Seattle, Portland, Los Angeles, Boise, Las Vegas, Phoenix, Salt Lake, Great Falls, Cheyenne, Denver, Albuquerque, Houston, Tulsa, Wichita, Pierre, Bismarck, Minneapolis, Des Moines, St. Louis, Little Rock, and New Orleans—one city in every state west of the Mississippi.

As the missile skimmed over the farthest flung suburbs of Omaha, it suddenly angled up into the night sky. It topped at three thousand feet and released its payload. The missile flew on, circling left across the city, finally diving into a large pasture outside the town of Fremont a few miles to the northwest. A small explosive charge made sure that fragments of the missile were scattered for several hundred yards. One of the fragments contained an easily discernible portion of the national dragon symbol.

Back over Omaha, thousands of tiny objects began descending, fluttering like confetti through the moonlight. As they descended, it became obvious that they were not confetti — they were too big.

A bent old man stopped and gazed upwards. "Leaflets," he explained to the dog he'd been taking for a midnight walk. "It looks like leaflets. Like they dropped in Europe way back in World War II."

The dog looked at the falling pieces of paper and let out a quick bark, then began a low, continuous growl.

"Oh, shut up," the man snapped. "You bark at anything you don't understand."

The dog wagged its tail.

One of the leaflets landed near the man. He shuffled over and painfully bent to pick it up, first letting his dog sniff it. The old man's sight was better than his bones and he could clearly read the message. He scanned it twice, shook his head, then read it again, silently mouthing the words. He crinkled his nose, crumpled up the paper, threw it in the gutter. He urged the dog along and continued his walk.

Under his breath he muttered, "Stupid joke."

But the authorities of Nebraska and twenty-one other states did not take it as a joke. Nor did the President of the United States, who officially first heard about the incident while catching an early morning broadcast on *Fox News*. It would take his intelligence experts hours to catch up; their initial reports would uncover little more than the networks had. It often seemed to happen like that, Washington thought. It was an age when reporters had more freedom to roam and ask questions than government agents did.

Washington had arisen early, unable to sleep, events resting on his shoulders like a load of brick. His wife, Annette, was busy taking a shower. As he began spooning coffee into the brew filter, he flipped on the news to catch the five o'clock headlines.

"—rning, I'm Lyndsy Salvador," the announcer had just begun. The president noticed that she had more worry lines on her face than usual and was glassy-eyed. Maybe she hadn't slept any better than he had.

"*Fox* has learned that during the night," Salvador began, "leaflets were dropped over several cities of the Western U.S. Incredibly, the leaflets contained a military threat."

Washington turned on the coffee maker, and leaned closer to the kitchen bar TV. The First Lady padded out in pink slippers and bathrobe, her hair up in a white towel.

She noticed the intensity of her husband and asked, "What's going on, Sam?"

Raising an eyebrow, Washington indicated the TV. She joined him, leaning a hip against him, resting one hand on his shoulder. He smiled inside and covered her fingers with his. Concerns about the outside world had not been the only thing contributing to his lack of sleep.

"I have one of the leaflets here in the studio," the reporter was saying. She held the paper toward the camera, which zoomed in for a moment.

"That's the symbol of the Shang Empire at the bottom of the page!" Annette Washington exclaimed.

"Sure is," her husband said. "Imagine that."

"I quote directly," Salvador reported, her face growing pale. "'To the people and authorities of the Western United States of America, be warned. This is not a prank, a hoax, or a publicity stunt. This message was dropped by a sophisticated stealth cruise missile of the Empire of The Shang. The missile is undetectable by pitifully outdated American technology. But there is no need for alarm. The missile, and others like it, carried only paper. However, they could easily have carried atomic, biological, or chemical weapons. You are completely vulnerable to our power. Nevertheless, we do not wish to harm you. The Shang wishes only peaceful co-existence and mutual co-operation. To achieve it, the entire Western United States, all states West of the Mississippi River, are hereby ordered to enter a benevolent association with the Shang Empire. The association will be total. You will become a part of the Empire. There is no other choice. If your governments refuse, if your people resist, our unstoppable missiles will, one by one, begin to destroy your cities. Do not be foolish, Americans! Unify with the Empire voluntarily and avoid bloodshed and agony! Become part of what will be the first, true, world civilization! Join the Empire peacefully, and together you can participate in the sublime rejuvenation of the planet under the guidance, grace, and eternal wisdom of The Shang. Refuse, and you will join your ancestors! Your state governments have one week to make up their minds. Any state that does not cooperate by then will feel the Sword of The Shang. The sword will not be merciful."'

Salvador's voice quavered slightly as she finished. She looked into the camera and added, "*Fox News* has also received reports that local authorities are finding what are tentatively identified as pieces of the aforementioned cruise missiles. The missiles reportedly bear markings of the Shang Empire. As to the— Wait just a moment, I'm receiving an update."

She glanced down at her desk's computer screen.

"We have some new numbers for you. Authoritative sources have told us that twenty-one—I repeat, twenty-one— Shang cruise missiles, apparently one for each Western state, did indeed drop copies of the leaflet we just read to you."

She looked off camera and nodded to someone.

"Wait a minute," Annette Washington said, "aren't there twenty-two states west of the Mississippi?"

"Yeah," the president said. "Unless she's not counting Louisiana, which straddles the Big Muddy."

"Oh, true."

"This is interesting," Lyndsy Salvador said, pausing and looking inward, apparently receiving another update through her headset, which she touched with a finger. "Yes, I've been informed that the Republic of Oregon was able to detect and shoot down a Shang cruise missile as it approached the City of Portland. In fact, I understand that we have the President of Oregon on the video line, live, with us now."

The screen split and Corcoran's image popped onto the right half.

"He looks remarkably fresh," Annette Washington observed drily.

"Sure does, and as smug as the squirrel who just found the world's biggest walnut," Sam Washington replied, stifling a yawn even as adrenaline sparked his nerve endings.

"Can you hear me, President Corcoran?" Salvador asked.

"Just fine, Lyndsy!" Corcoran boomed. "Good morning!"

"Er . . . good morning, sir. We've heard that your defense forces destroyed a Chinese cruise missile last night. Can you confirm that rather alarming statement?"

"Indeed, I can. And 'alarming' is, I believe, an understatement. Defense Secretary Hochman informs me that the missile was detected by our new airborne infrared radar and other unique technical means. The missile was well seaward when we spotted it."

"I see. And how far out to sea was that, Mr. President?"

"Oh, I'd say about fifty miles or so, off the south coast. Give or take. We figure it was launched off a sub. The missile was a lot like one of the U.S. Navy's Tomahawk-5's."

"Are you accusing the U.S. of—"

"No, no! But the U.S. secretly sold basic cruise technology to China years ago, before Big Three. The Shang's apparently modified it considerably, with a number of semi-clever stealth innovations. This was undoubtedly a Shang weapon. We've found the parts, as I understand several other states have. Nope, there's no second-guessing about who lit these firecrackers!"

"I see. Mr. President, the leaflet claims that the Shang missile cannot be detected by U.S. technology."

"Well, as you know, I'm not given access to U.S. government military secrets these days. But I'd say it's probably true. The U.S. didn't have any detection devices like that when we dehooked ourselves. The Brits had a modified Cimbaline system they might have loaned— But never mind. The point is, we are not the U.S., Lyndsy. You know that. Your whole operation is based here, too. If I'm not mistaken, some of it's in Portland, a high probability Shang target."

"Er, yes, Sir." Lyndsy gulped visibly. "Are you saying, then, that Oregon's technology can actually stop The Shang's cruise missiles? I mean, if he were to launch more?"

"Oh, sure." Corcoran smiled and let out his best cracker-barrel chuckle. "You see, a small, vulnerable nation like Oregon has a great incentive to invent new defense systems fast. Don't forget the Israeli developments of years past. It's especially important for us to have superior detection and anti-aircraft/anti-missile systems."

"Well," Lindsay said, "thank you for—"

"Incidentally," Corcoran said sharply, making sure Salvador didn't cut him off. "I want to stress that we had no problem shooting down that missile. Zero. We got it with one swing of the flyswatter. As a matter of fact, that's what we've named our new anti-missile, 'The Flyswatter.'"

"Yes, er—well, are you—" Lyndsy began, then started over. "I guess my follow-up question is: Are you saying Oregon feels safe? I mean, despite The Shang's threats?"

"I repeat. We can swat down whatever he sends." Corcoran waved a hand casually, as though brushing aside a mosquito. "Of course, I wouldn't want to live in any *other* area of North America. They're definitely vulnerable. And by the way, I don't think The Shang's bluffing. I think he really will attack the Western states if they don't knuckle under. Too bad they don't have a place under our defense umbrella."

By the end of the day, the California, Idaho, Washington, and Nevada legislatures had voted to join the Republic of Oregon—on the condition that Oregon would use its Flyswatter missile to defend them against The Shang. Commerce Secretary Sparky Katz was dispatched to help integrate the states' economies into the Republic of Oregon's. Defense Secretary Erik Hochman began explaining how the states' national guards should secure their independence from U.S. domination. Secretary of State J.B. Washington showed them how to stop U.S. federal operations within their territories, based on the plan Oregon had used.

The White House issued a stern, but vague warning to the four states to avoid "needless physical confrontation," but no federal troops moved off federal bases to stop the secessions.

Seventeen other Western governors, and two Eastern ones, privately inquired about the terms of confederacy.

Chapter 28

"Poker Face"

I tell you, we did not attack you!" the Shang hissed. President Corcoran gazed impassively at the diminutive man shown on his video screen. The Shang had called within minutes of Corcoran's appearance on the media, but for three days Corcoran had told his secretary to refuse the calls. The Chinese leader had already denied guilt—publicly and in private faxes and e-mails to the twenty-one Western governors and in a call to President Washington. However, contrary to The Shang's expectation, the more he denied involvement, the more the American public and politicians distrusted him.

Corcoran studied The Shang's angry features. The Emperor certainly didn't look very god-like. To the contrary, he appeared lividly human. Corcoran wished that he'd put him on video during their previous phone talk, when they'd discussed Lieutenant Li and the mini-sub incident. Normally, Corcoran preferred the old-fashioned audio-only phone mode. But it was fun watching The Shang perform, so he made sure he was recording everything. This was going to be too good not to spread around.

"It was a trick of the United States!" The Shang shrieked.

"I'll bet that's not what you told President Washington."

"Are you blind, Corcoran? The evil Sam Washington is trying to turn you against the peace-loving Shang Empire. Why

196 ☆ E. G. ROSS

do you not see that? It is so incredibly obvious. He has opposed your glorious bid for independence all along. It is him you should be accusing. *Him*, not me."

"Well," Corcoran drawled, holding out his cigar and looking at it as though assessing its quality, "seems to me that the evidence shows the opposite—that it's you doing the tricking. After all, the missiles had Shang markings. Every last one of them. And so did those grimy leaflets. Very sloppy printing job, by the way."

"Forgeries! Fakes! Lies! An American plot!"

Yep, Corcoran thought, legends of The Shang's divine nature were definitely overdone. He looked more like a tin tea kettle about to pop its seams.

Corcoran put an edge to his voice, leaned closer to the pick-up camera, and said, "Look, Emperor. I know you pride yourself on being quite an operator. Maybe over there in that medieval backwater, you are."

"We are an advanced culture!"

"Uh-huh, sure. Your inflated social opinions aside, I'm telling you this: when you start messing with the honey in these trees, you'd better cover your bare ass or its gonna get stung. Now, the fact is, we spotted one of your birds skimming the water fifty miles off our south coast. There were no U.S. Navy vessels in the area at the time, or boats, or planes, or anything of any other country capable of letting loose with that kind of weaponry. That makes you look about as guilty as a snake that swallowed a bowling ball."

"Corrupt fantasy and—"

Corcoran shook his head and said, "Nope, don't think so. I'm only glad we developed the radars and anti-missiles we needed to stop you from spreading your bird-cage paper all over our towns like you did over the Western U.S. states. Oregon has a long tradition against litter, you know."

The Shang's lips compressed into a small, fleshy dot. Corcoran thought they looked like a rat's butt.

"Now," Corcoran said before the Chinese leader could find his voice, "you keep your greedy mitts off my country.

And I don't just mean Oregon. I include our new confederates, Washington, California, Idaho, and Nevada — and anybody else who might join up, as I expect quite a few will in the
days ahead. So don't be hasty."

The Shang calmed himself slightly and tried a fresh plea:
"I assure you, Mr. President, that the Shang Empire is not your
enemy. We want only good relations — "

"Oh? oh?" Corcoran interrupted, poking his cigar at the
screen. "Then what was that intimidation you tossed at me
the other day? What were those threats all about? Didn't you
tell me, personally, that I'd better hop aboard your little anti-
Taiwan terror-train?"

The Shang stammered, gritted his teeth, glared, and then
said, "You have not heard the last of me."

He severed the connection.

Corcoran leaned back and slowly blew a couple of smoke
rings at the ceiling. For the benefit of his advisors who'd been
in the room and watched the entire exchange off-camera on a
wall monitor, he said, "I don't doubt it, you creepy little Napo-
leonic replica."

"It's The Shang's *next* move that worries me," Colby said.
"We can fake a Shang missile attack, but we haven't got a real
Flyswatter to shoot down actual missiles, right?"

"Right," Hochman said, his face dark. "We haven't been
able to get the old Patriots up and running and most of the rest
of the stuff, it turns out, might as well be sitting on a junkyard
shelf. The more we go through the inventory of what we inherited from the U.S., the worse it looks. There are a few things,
such as the micro-Rattlers and Wasps, but — "

"What about from overseas?" Colby interrupted, still on
his own train of thought. "Anything useful we can buy from
the Israelis, or, for that matter, the Taiwanese or our other
Oriental friends?"

"Not really. Their stuff isn't as advanced as we'd hoped —
or for reasons of their own, they're choosing to sit on it. Most
of it seems to be older generation U.S.-based hardware. We're
trying to get our old Israeli tactical lasers going — the *Davids,*

they're called now, based on a U.S. design called the *Nautilus* from back in the 1980s. There's a possibility of adapting them to an anti-cruise missile mode. But so far, the Israelis are withholding technical help, especially on the detection end. We suspect that they can penetrate the Chinese stealth technology, but they are denying it. It's my impression that they don't want to offend Uncle Sam."

"Didn't stop 'em from helping the Chinese years ago in a variety of ways."

"Well, sir, Bill Clinton was in office back then, and he was sloppier than usual toward the Chinese. It's certainly a different world today."

"What if The Shang guesses that we bluffed?" Katz asked. "What if he tests us with a real attack?"

Hochman grimaced. He knew the alternative, but Corcoran said it for him: "Then we'll probably have to pay Sam's price, Sparky. Tell 'em, J.B. You're the only one of us who Sam'll talk to these days."

"Sam says the U.S. *can* swat Shang cruise missiles, so-called stealth or not. A new nanosecond pulse radar attached to a thing called The Plate. He wasn't terribly forthcoming on the details. I've heard rumors, something about a gravitronic drive, whatever that is. Its use was apparently considered during the Engels Extension conflict, but never authorized."

"Then why didn't he knock 'em out?" Hochman asked. "I mean, why'd Sam let our fake Shang missiles through if he didn't have to? Makes no sense."

"Sam's secret weapon was undergoing maintenance. We caught him by surprise, I think. Pure luck. Or so he claims."

Hochman nodded, looking only half convinced.

Corcoran walked his cigar between fingers and said, "Uh, look, let's not spook ourselves into a corner. Sure, things could go wrong. But all bets are off for Sam and The Shang if our bluff proves out. Speaking as a ruthless old poker stud, my feel of the board says that it *will* work."

He puffed and smiled, holding the cigar in his teeth.

His advisors watched him. They knew Corcoran well. He

looked like he believed what he said. Trouble was, none of them could figure out why. This was the biggest chance Oregon had taken since declaring its intent to secede. If it backfired, they could lose a lot more than what they'd gained. If The Shang lashed out for real in his now-obvious state of anger and insult, and Oregon turned to the U.S. for protection, but the U.S. for some reason couldn't make the grade defensively, then the price might be millions of lost lives—not just in Oregon, but elsewhere. In the face of that prospect, Corcoran's cabinet people had to wonder what could account for their new president's confidence. All of them felt increasingly uneasy, as if they'd turned down a road that had looked right at first, but was growing less and less recognizable.

Except for one of them.

From deep inside, a flash of insight went off like a battle-field flare. He suddenly raised his estimate of his new president by a thousand percent.

"What are you grinning about?" J.B. Washington asked Erik Hochman.

"Oh, nothing," Hochman said, shaking his head, "nothing at all."

Chapter 29

"Not His Backside"

PRESIDENT FACES IMPEACHMENT (AP/DOW, Washington)—A group of U.S. Senators and Representatives of the Eastern Seaboard states today initiated the process to impeach President Sam Washington. The move constitutes the first serious impeachment talk since the days of Clinton.

According to the primary authors of the move, Senators Biden Troughwart (D-NY) and Representative Ron Cravenpull (R-VT), the rationale for the impeachment effort was what they termed the president's "flagrant sloth and ineptitude in failing to prevent the disintegration of the United States of America."

Cravenpull admitted that he did not necessarily expect the impeachment to "go all the way."

"Speaking from Republican history, if we can get Sam Washington to realize that he has to resign for the good of the country—just as Nixon realized he had to—then we'll have accomplished our goal," the Vermont representative said.

Troughwart said the nation needs "a strong new leader who for once will show some political backbone, not his political backside."

"My God," the New York Democrat told reporters on the steps of the Capitol, "this country is like a pair of thin pants. Oregon tricked us into bending over and now everything's coming apart at the seams."

Troughwart would not offer an estimate of how many Eastern states would support the impeachment move, but it's not expected that a single Western state will. That's raising constitutional questions.

Bork Robertson, a writer on constitutional history at Harvard University, said that "because the Western states, except Oregon, have not actually declared themselves separate from the U.S., and are claiming that their so-called confederation with Oregon is purely in the nature of a trade association, there is real doubt that even if all of the Eastern states voted for impeachment there would be a sufficient majority. As to the original legality of Oregon's secession, well, let me remind you that its action has already made the question a moot point. In *practice*, Oregon is no longer under U.S. law, no matter what the U.S. may think about it."

The situation has been further complicated by the fact that Oregon President Alf Corcoran, appearing last evening on *ABC*'s "Nightline," said the Western states were free to remain part of the U.S. if they wished.

"We never asked anybody to give up dual citizenship," he said. "We let the Taiwanese, the Japanese, and the Koreans keep their citizenship, so why not U.S. citizens? We're not looking to establish some sort of exclusive market in civics."

The statement by Corcoran surprised many observers who had believed that Corcoran wanted a complete political split between the Western and Eastern half of the U.S. Corcoran squelched that theory when he told *ABC*, "If that were true, then I wouldn't be trying to talk Eastern governors into joining us, would I? I'm not talking split, I'm talking unity—rational unity, not the old coercive kind that the U.S. drifted into."

White House Press Secretary Tom Rosco said that White House Counsel was "studying" the impeachment threat as well as the citizenship issue. The executive branch's lack of action—coming from the man who so decisively led the nation through World War Three—is deeply puzzling to many long-time Beltway observers.

CONFED FEEDS FRENZY

(BISnet, New York) — Financial markets soared today on news that all states west of the Mississippi have now formally requested confederation with the Republic of Oregon.

Seventeen state governors held a joint news conference in the lobby of the New York Stock Exchange (NYSE) to announce their move. The governors apparently took special pains to stress that their states would be deregulating markets, lowering taxes, and taking other privatization measures similar to those which have allowed the Oregon economy to grow so remarkably in the months since its secession.

Texas Governor Ewing J. Bushnell, speaking for the "Group of Seventeen," emphasized that while the states sought confederation with Oregon, they had decided not to secede from the union "at this time."

However, Bushnell said that if the federal government made any move to stop the group's association with the Republic of Oregon, full secession would be considered.

"As Texans, we do know a bit about secession," Bushnell said. "After all, we've been an independent nation before — just like Oregon was once back in the decade of the 1840s. If Oregon can be a republic again, so can we — if we have to. Of course, I hope it doesn't come to that."

The president of the NYSE, Jay "Primerate" Morganthump, accompanied the governors. He said that he wished to underscore that this was not a mass secession, but that "a mass secession, if it comes, will not necessarily be bad for business."

"In fact," said Morganthump, "I'd say quite the opposite. Oregon has been growing phenomenally in the last year or so. That's a great can-do example. I see no reason why the rest of the West could not follow in its footsteps, economically. Politically, too, for that matter, if things went that way."

Presidents of the NASDAQ and other exchanges, including representatives of those in Tokyo, Bonn, London, Kiev, and Singapore, echoed Morganthump's feelings. One NYSE official said the extraordinary unanimity was a deliberate effort to calm market jitters.

The DOW Jones Industrial Average of 30 blue chip stocks closed the day at 60,095, up 9,031 points, a gain of almost 18%, one of the biggest percentage jumps in the history of the exchange. The dollar rose against foreign currencies, confounding many currency traders' early expectations.

"After the initial shock, traders apparently felt that America was not in any serious economic trouble," Ernst Schmidt of the Geneva-based Swiss Credit Corporation said. "Short term political trouble? Well, the financial gnomes have seen, and they have smiled. No one—not even Oregon—has made a move to challenge the U.S. dollar. Everybody's still using it. My guess is that everyone will keep using it. We in Europe don't view the rebellion as a big deal. After all, America was born in rebellion."

A financial analyst for several credit houses said the mass move by the seventeen states of the Western U.S. has offset the war fears brought on by the Shang threat last week—a threat that has not been renewed and outright denied by the Chinese government.

Bear-Stearns senior economist Thomas Pechervick said today's markets were downplaying any major intervention by the U.S. Government to stop the confederation's spread.

"We just don't see it," Pechervick said. "What's Washington going to do—stomp on its own toes and drive the rest of the country into even deeper recession—and then outright secession? I don't think so."

Rukeyser/Blanston's company spokesman Jim Crawford agreed. "These are new times. You don't pull people together with artificial, heavy-handed national ideals and appeals to sacrifice anymore. Open markets are the glue. It's the old politicians who haven't caught on. Except for Corky of Oregon, of course. He's a hero to us here on the Street."

Boone Associates analyst Robert Heilbrander expressed similar sentiments. "If you've got unified, free markets, the political leadership doesn't matter much—and that's what Oregon is proving. People cross state and national lines all the

204 ☆ E. G. ROSS

time anyway, right? So what's the big deal about what you call a particular piece of political real estate? The U.S., the Republic of Oregon, the New West Confederacy, or some mixture? I mean, who cares? If things are free, business is business, right?"

However, not all the sentiment was favorable. Aubrey Landstrom & Company senior economist Jeffrey Archbow took a contrarian view. Archbow said that some analysts were not sure Washington could afford to ignore the secession in the long run.

"Maybe the Oregon Rebellion isn't officially spreading beyond Oregon, but it sure is in fact. It was one thing when it was Oregon alone. Or maybe even the West Coast states. But now that it's catching fire all the way to the Mississippi, the White House can't let the country fall apart as an economic entity. If that happened, it would be chaos for markets. I don't care what Corcoran claims, Oregon's too small to provide a defense shield for the whole continent. Markets need to feel secure. This is causing great uncertainty."

Archbow downplayed the fact that Oregon's defense forces were apparently the only ones able to detect and destroy The Shang's cruise missiles.

"He may or may not have secret weapons that can do that," he said. "There is strong doubt in the U.S. defense community. Without Uncle Sam, this continent would be open to all kinds of intimidation. We'd be divided and in turmoil. Opportunists move into chaos like that. Study your history."

"It's not chaos," NYSE's Morganthump rebutted when asked for his views on Archbow's remarks. "It's order. It's natural market order that's at stake. Oregon's providing it. Washington D.C. is not. Simple as that. I'd say the D.C. boys and all our pork-licking, old-thinking members of Congress had better wake up to the fact."

NEW REPUBLIC PACKS SURPRISING PUNCH
(JANE'S Defense Wire, R. of Oregon) — A spokesman for a private defense think tank said today that the new confed-

eracy forming around the Republic of Oregon could become militarily stronger than most analysts believe — and may already be. Ben Liddell, founder of the Strategic Military Affairs Research Tank, or SMART, as it's commonly known, pointed out that the larger states, such as California and Texas, have some of the biggest military facilities in the nation. Additionally, he said test facilities in Nevada, Arizona, and New Mexico "might become available."

Asked what "might become available" meant, Liddell said that the Oregon confederacy could make use of the facilities if it could acquire them.

"That's the stickler," Liddell said. "It all depends on whether the U.S. government will let them go. Technically, they are Uncle Sam's property. We used to think that it was hard to take from Uncle what he really wanted to keep. On the other hand, it wasn't too tough for Oregon to acquire the IRS offices and all the federal lands within its boundaries. The other confederacy states might use similar tactics against military assets."

Liddell said that if the Oregon confederacy managed to secure federal military facilities west of the Mississippi, it would become the second most powerful geographic entity in the world overnight.

"Then, if Washington decided to make trouble, it would have a true fight on its hands. Our guess here at SMART is that Washington will have to move quickly if it is to retain the high ground. Logically, it ought to try soon. If the White House waits much longer, I'm afraid the conflict between the Eastern U.S. and the Western U.S. will make the original North/South Civil War look like a Tupperware party."

A few days later...

OREGON MAKES UNCLE SAM SAY "UNCLE" ON TAXES

(BISnet, Denver) — One week after joining a trade confederation with the Republic of Oregon, the Western states of the

U.S. agreed among themselves to suspend payment of all federal taxes.

The White House called the move "an outrage" and vowed to fight the action in federal courts.

The president's political opponents immediately labeled his approach "anemic" and "bewildering."

"Take us to court, huh? That ought to be interesting," said Governor Ewing J. Bushnell of Texas. "We've decided that federal courts don't have jurisdiction in the West anymore. You see, we know how to pass laws and run courts all by our lonesome out here. We don't expect federal judges will have much to do this side of Big Muddy from now on. Of course, none of this means we're actually seceding from the U.S. No, sir. Not unless the White House and its Eastern buddies get snotty."

Simultaneously, the confederation of East Asian free nations issued a statement of "total support" for Bushnell's position, which the Texas governor admitted had been "pre-coordinated" with the East Asian Confederation head, Don Wan Too of Korea.

Bushnell said the decision to suspend federal tax payments became "mandatory" after a fresh review of the West's economic prospects. He said the suspension would turn economic recovery from a "hang-dog possibility to a chili-poppin' certainty."

In the first two hours of trading following Bushnell's announcement, the DOW average soared over 5,000 points.

POLL: PUBLIC LIKES NEW FEDERATION

(AP/DOW, New York)—A new national poll conducted by the Gallup organization shows that an overwhelming number of citizens in the Western states supports the decision to join the new federation with the Republic of Oregon.

Among middle class respondents, the chief reason given was the prospect of drastic tax reductions. Among most businessmen, the likelihood of lower regulations was nearly as compelling.

Simultaneously, and somewhat surprisingly, 90% of those

polled answered "yes" to the question, "Do you continue to view yourself as a loyal citizen of the United States?"

The White House called that answer, "encouraging."

A spokesman for the Organization to Impeach the President (OIP), now made up entirely of Eastern and Southern Congressmen, called the White House response "frustrating, inadequate, indecisive, and a clear indication that this president is no longer fit for office."

However, the impeachment movement itself is apparently in serious trouble. Three Eastern and two Southern state Congressional delegations announced that they were pulling out of OIP. The five states—New Hampshire, Michigan, Ohio, Virginia, and South Carolina—are rumored to be considering also joining the Oregon coalition.

Chapter 30

"The Burner Boys, II"

The tall man poured himself a whiskey, straight up. "Any one else?" he asked, gesturing at his two companions with a bottle of Jack Black. "Maybe with ice?"

"No. Coffee's fine with me," the young man said, stirring in cream and too much sugar. He had a headache.

The old man frowned impatiently and said, "Let's get down to it, okay? I've got only a couple of hours this time — otherwise I'll be missed. You know how much premium my profession places on punctuality."

"Fine," the first one said. He seated his big-boned frame with a grunt, sipped his drink, then looked at the other two. "Well? Who's first? You?"

The old man cleared his throat. He fidgeted with his glasses a moment, then began cleaning the lenses with a white handkerchief as he said, "Look, the U.S. has been mobilizing boys for months now: 90th Airborne, the secret C-units, of course, and others. Trouble is, the troops are getting antsy. They're suspicious that it's mostly smoke and mirrors, that they aren't ever going anywhere."

"Well, they aren't," the young man said, staring into his coffee and kneading his aching temples. "I didn't think they were supposed to, either. Except for that notable foray into southern Oregon."

"Hey, wasn't that a doozy?" the tall man said, chuckling. Unlike the other two, he was in fine spirits. "It worked so well it almost went overboard."

"A pertinent point," the old man said. "For now, the mobilizations have gone too far. We need to do something. They're nearing overboard status."

The young man kneaded his temples and asked, "How do you figure?"

"Pushing the troops from one training spot and base to another is making everything seem war-alert urgent."

"So? Isn't it supposed to?"

"But you can't keep it up. It's too draining, and after awhile, unconvincing. Whole lot of hoopla, no action. That kind of stuff starts making people ask questions."

"Troops are used to that kind of thing. I mean, hurry and wait isn't just a Navy motto," the tall man said. He swished the liquid in his glass, then sipped and smacked his lips.

The old man shook his head and said, "That's not my main concern. Word's going to reach the press. Count on it."

"The ever-evil media eye. Poke a stick in it, I say."

"Oh, now, don't take the media lightly. Some of them — including that grief-maker Ernest Pomp of the AP/DOW — are already getting fire up their foghorns. Remember, our idea was to make the media and Congress think that a *firm* military response would be forthcoming from the U.S. at any time. Too much delay and, well, it's already backfiring. That's my point. Otherwise the stupid impeachment thing wouldn't have gotten started."

"He's right," the younger man said, pinching the bridge of his nose, then sipping coffee and burning his tongue. "Don't forget that the massacre was a designed operation. As expected, it dampened the man-in-the-street's enthusiasm for a military solution to the secession. Wasn't that the whole point?"

"Well, certainly, but — "

"Seems to be working okay. At least that's what Zogby and the other pollsters say."

"Our confidants in both camps agree," the old man said.

"But you're missing the gist of things. It's not the public we ought to worry about now. They *always* take the underdog's side. It's an American tradition. The media, however, are another matter. They could blow it. They very well could be grit in the bearings."

"Could be," the tall man said, "but don't forget that most of them have shifted their headquarters to Oregon. That's a big one in our favor."

"Not all of them," the youngest said. "There are some holdouts. There's a lot of stuffy East coast culture built into some of them."

"Well, okay," the tall man said, "our analysis may have overestimated the impact. The big movers and shakers—the senior reporters and editors—most of their hearts are still on the East Coast. That's their heritage and constituency, granted. They are the ones blowing air on the impeachment coals."

"Yes, but that's not going anywhere," the old man said. "We've got the reins. So what's really bothering you?" He shifted irritably and rubbed his eyes with his knuckles. He felt like someone trying to write a letter through a film of grease. Things were too messy and not making the impact he wanted on the tall man. "Give me a little credit. I haven't had a stroke. But let's keep this moving the right way. That's what I'm trying to hammer home."

The tall man lowered his voice and said, "Take it easy. We're on the same side. What do you suggest—in practical terms, I mean?"

"That's more like it. Practically speaking, we need to lose."

"*Lose?*" the other two said simultaneously. A fourth man, who'd been listening by video phone finally said something.

"Yeah, I like it!" he exclaimed, stroking his beard.

"And also win."

"Stop talking in riddles," the tall one said. "It's not like you guys."

It was the old man's turn to chuckle and say, "You know, maybe I'll have that whiskey, now."

The tall man shrugged and poured him one.

"If I see the frog on the log, he's thought up a way to solve two big problems at once for us," the video participant said.

Despite his headache, the younger man grinned and said, "He's got another job for the Chameleon Unit."

"Yep," the old man said, accepting the whiskey and raising the glass to his boss.

Chapter 31

"Shifting Sands"

Corporal Bill Branner squinted at the shimmering, flat desert. Outside the hut—to his left and right, forward and back, as far as he could see—stretched a nearly featureless hardpan desert. In the late afternoon sun, the surface seemed to undulate, like the skin of some fantastic silvery monster. The skin was divided in quarters by a giant cross consisting of a fence and a road. The razorwire-topped, galvanized cyclone fence, into which the gatehouse was built, ran directly north and south. A blacktop road passed through the gate in the fence, stretching straight to the eastern and western horizons. Like the fence, the road disappeared into a haze of heat mirages, making the true horizon impossible to define.

Branner spat on the road. His saliva sizzled. Tar bubbled in cracks on the asphalt. He cursed. Born and raised near rainy coastal Astoria, Oregon, this was not his kind of place. He glanced at the thermometer under the eaves of the hut: 117 degrees. Branner shook his head. He knew that the surface of the heat-absorbing pavement was far above that. Stretching his long legs, he paced on the packed sand of the road's shoulder. The silvery silica didn't hold heat as well and tended to be bearable. If he stood still on the road itself for more than a minute, even regulation Air Force boots would not keep his feet from burning.

Once, on a day much like this a year earlier, in order to break the boredom and test an old rumor, he'd brought a raw egg with him in a sandwich cooler. In mid-afternoon, he'd cracked the egg and spilled the contents onto the road. They'd fried. It had amused him. Anything that broke routine was memorable.

He lit a cigarette and looked at the hut as he had hundreds of times before. It was painted white and blue. A gate sign, consisting of black and red lettering said, "Restricted Area: U.S. Air Force, Silver Sands Test Range." Smaller print warned against trespassing and instructed authorized personnel to present credentials.

Branner snorted. This corner of the gigantic Nevada base was seldom visited by anything other than sidewinders, road runners, lizards, and a few insects. A fly-over by a vulture was considered a major event. Other than the twice-per-shift humvee-hugging guard patrols, only one vehicle had passed through the checkpoint in the past week. It had consisted of a sober-faced maintenance crew, uneager to make small talk, gung-ho to finish some unspecified job and get out of the incessant, baking rays of the planet's home star.

Luckily, Branner's post was double-manned. Of course, he knew it wasn't really luck. Even the Air Force realized that a person could go nuts by himself on duty as isolated and desolate as this. Besides, there were safety regs involved. Every month or so, Branner was paired with a new companion, usually twenty years younger than himself. It helped. It made things tolerable. Branner himself had lost hope of getting anything better out of his superiors. Not that he expected it. He could stick things out. In only seven months, he'd have his twenty years and a decent pension.

He wiped his cracked lips with the back of his hand and flipped the cigarette away. He watched a thin trail of smoke die in the sand. He worked his tongue along the inside of his mouth. He craved a drink. A *drink* drink. Of course, that was impossible here. He'd have to wait 'til his shift was over. Angrily, he tapped out another cigarette and inhaled deeply, letting the hot smoke singe away the craving.

"Chuck it all," he said bitterly.

He grimaced, his weather-beaten features reflecting unbidden memories of his career's nose dive. It had all happened in less than three years. First his wife, who'd never loved Air Force life, had taken off with some engineer from Seattle. Then Branner had been busted. First he'd fallen from lieutenant to sergeant. That was embarrassing enough. His pay had dropped, too, but luckily his wife had wanted a clean break and demanded no alimony. Then, eighteen months ago, he'd been demoted again. There wasn't much lower to go. The problem wasn't his wife, of course. Never had been. Branner didn't believe in blaming other people for his misfortunes. He knew his trouble was older than his marriage of ten years. His trouble was as old as fermentation. He tended to get drunk too often, and when he did, he also tended to insult his wife, his friends, and his superior officers—not necessarily in any discernibly rational pattern.

The Air Force had put up with it for awhile. However, it finally decided that Branner was too much of a problem to keep in positions of profile—but not enough of a problem to kick entirely out of the service. After all, until his divorce, he'd performed well, restricting his drinking to occasional bouts that the service could more or less overlook. But post-marriage, his binges had become frequent. Simple jobs, away from liquor and superiors, were all he could handle, profile-wise. After he'd stubbornly refused gentle hints to quit, the Air Force finally shrugged and assigned him to guardpost 844, out on the far western edge of Silver Sands.

That's where he'd spent his days for the last sixty-two weeks. In a way, he thought it was a fair deal. Branner wasn't vindictive, not even toward the Air Force. He knew that he wasn't, by any serious assessment, much use to the service. He was intelligent and honest enough to admit that alcohol gave him courage when he least needed it and was most apt to endanger or interfere with others—others who could keep their heads together and get responsible work done. Someday he'd have to do something about his booze addiction. Sure. Someday. But not yet. Certainly not until he was out on pension with this hole from hell behind him. Then, well, maybe he'd try the Alcoholics Anonymous route. He shivered and dragged on his cigarette. He didn't know how he'd put up with the religious indoctrination of AA meetings. If that was still part of them. He flashed on his childhood. Branner's dad had been a flaming religious zealot. Branner had come to disdain anything to do with religion. He grinned to himself, suntanned eyes crinkling in deep folds. That attitude hadn't done his Air Force career any favors. The flyboys were the most religious of all the service branches. Touching the face of God and all that. Prudent to be on the good side of the Big Pilot.

He studied the stub of his cigarette, sucked one last burning drag out of it, exhaled heavily, ground the stub underfoot, then stomped back to guardpost 844.

"How's St. Peter?" he kidded the youngster in the hut, flicking the back of his hand toward the guy's crotch.

"Hey, watch it!" his partner yelped, jerking back. "I'm planning a family someday, you know!"

"Aw, take it easy, Farington," Branner growled, pulling out another cigarette. "Save your harassment suits for guys with money."

"Well," Farington said primly, "that's kid's stuff. Most of us left it in the seventh grade. Give it up, all right?"

"Yeah, that's me, a 40-year-old kid. Whatcha reading, Far?" he asked, noticing the open book on the work table.

"Uh, basic fluid dynamics," Farington mumbled.

"Yeah. I grant you."

"Huh? Grant me what?" Farington asked suspiciously.

"Why, I grant that you need to know the subject if you're gonna start a clan. Here's a hint. Your main fluid line is always located directly behind your zipper. How dynamic it is, I couldn't actually say."

"You've got a filthy, one-track brain, Branner," the younger man snapped.

Branner knew that Farington was a devout, conservative

Baptist. He loved to irritate him.

"Son, if you hadn't had a taste of squeezebox since your wife had left you, you'd be just like me."

"I know I'll never convert you to the ways of the Lord, but do you have to be so crude?"

Branner frowned and rubbed his chin thoughtfully, as though considering a major cosmological problem, then said, "Yep, reckon I do. It makes me feel better. You oughta try it sometime, Far. It's a kind of a cleansing process. A roto-rootering of the soul. Can Jesus do that for you?"

Farington wrinkled his nose and changed the subject with, "By the way, do you mind not smoking?"

"I mind a lot. It's one of the few miserable pleasures I've got left in life, Far. I'm not giving it up for you, the Lord, or the Air Force."

"But—"

"Kid, it's air conditioned in here. The guy who designed those things was probably a smoker himself. Doesn't that tell you anything?"

Farington sniffed and glowered.

Branner leaned closer and breathed a blue cloud out through his nose.

"If you don't like my fumes, there's a foolproof solution."

"And what's that?" Farington asked, waving smoke away from his eyes.

"Take a walk. I swear, you young no-smoking fanatics must think your lungs are made of flower petals. A little harmless exhaust gas and you believe your bellows will wilt. Or something will."

"At least we've still *got* lungs."

"Okay, okay," Branner said, realizing that he was leaning too hard on the younger man. Toward the end of the day, when Branner hadn't touched a bottle for eight or ten hours, he had a tendency to tease Farington unmercifully.

Booze, Branner thought, is like a woman; I can't live with it and can't live without it. Being like this, dry inside as well as out, teasing was one of the only ways he could let out the frustration of deprivation without risking the retaliation of a superior. When you got right down to it, Farington was all right. The kid never complained to higher-ups. Branner slid open the window and flicked out his cigarette. Farington raised his eyebrows at the concession and Branner winked at him. Farington blushed slightly.

"Don't get any ideas," Branner said, snorting, "cause I'm not *that* desperate."

Farington turned as red as a tomato and began rapidly flipping pages in his book.

Abruptly, the room grew too quiet. Both men looked around, trying to figure it out.

"Great," Branner said, "the air conditioner just quit!"

"Huh? Oh, *no!*"

Branner took two steps to the machine and rapped its casing twice with his fist. He checked the plug. He whacked the machine again.

"Nothing," he said. "Well, I'd better pull it down right now and have a look or we're gonna be two baked beans by this time tomorrow."

"Can I help?" Farington asked.

"Naw. This is fine. It's something to do."

Farington nodded and resumed studying his text on fluid dynamics.

By chance, Branner glanced off to the west, out the front window of the hut toward the descending sun. He blinked, leaned forward, and squinted into the haze over the road. He stared for several seconds.

He touched Farington's shoulder and said, "Hey, kid. Mark the page. We've got companionship rollin' this way."

Farington folded his book shut, shielded his eyes with his hand, and looked where Branner pointed.

From out of the distorting heat waves, two olive green humvees appeared, traveling side by side.

Farington said, "I don't remember anything at all scheduled for today."

"No, neither do I. Guess that's why they call us guards.

We're supposed to be able to deal with the unexpected."
Unconsciously, Branner rubbed the holster of the .45 pistol strapped to his side. It was a sleek new Smith & Wesson model, adopted by the service only two years ago. Except in practice, he'd never used a pistol in action. In his brief few weeks during the Arabian Wars, he'd always used a standard M-16 rifle.

In a moment, several troop transporters, twice as tall as the humvees, popped out of the shimmer of the road air.

"Well strangle Aunt Lizzy's rooster," Branner said, rubbing the scratchy stubble of his weathered cheek, "those things look *Army*. What business would olive-pickers have at an Air Force base?"

"Perhaps a joint exercise? Could be. They hold them here now and then."

"Hmmm. Maybe. I haven't heard of one for this time of year, though. Buddy, juice up our computer terminal. See what the brass have on tap for us out here in Buttsville. Maybe we went brain dead and missed an important gig."

Farington hurriedly flipped up the screen of the laptop-sized terminal next to him. He punched a couple keys and said, "Hey, this thing isn't working."

Branner frowned, "Has it got power?"

Farington peered under the table, wiggled the power cord. "Should have. It's plugged in. Both power and data cords look okay to me."

Branner pursed his lips and flipped the light switch several times. The lights were dead, too.

"Uh-oh," he muttered.

He jerked open the small cabinet in which two spare M-16s were kept. He pushed one at Farington. "Check your load, son. Do it now."

His partner's face went white. "But—"

"Your butt, your toes, your brain. They're all the same to me. Just do it!"

Branner made sure his rifle had a full clip. He pulled out a pair of binoculars from the drawer built into the work table and took a closer scan of the approaching vehicles. "Man, those guys are moving," he said. "Hey, wait a minute. This doesn't make sense. If they're Army, why would they be driving rigs without desert cam? Doesn't look like exercise stuff to me. Not out here where there's nothing green except sick lizards."

He adjusted the glasses. After a moment, he said, "What the—? There are no exercise markings on those rigs, Far. Not of any kind. Sure doesn't look like a drill."

He thought a moment, then said, "Okay, this has gotta be some kind of giant glitch in procedure. You take 'em through their ID's, Far. I'm scuttlin' out back of this shack, just in case."

"Uh, in case of what?" Farington asked.

His hands were shaking, holding the rifle.

Branner reached out and steadied the gun. Farington looked down stupidly at Branner's hand.

"In case? If I knew, Far, I'd probably have some Einstein-style idea, right? I just don't like the feel of it. These guys seem *wrong* to me. I think one of us has to be in back-up position."

Farington gulped, nodded, and moved out of the hut. Branner followed, quickly edging behind the small structure, letting the other man screen him from the on-coming vehicles.

Farington walked forward and stood in the center of the road. He raised his right hand as the first of the vehicles rapidly slowed and stopped before the gate.

Branner swore silently. Over a dozen troop transporters had halted in succession behind the lead humvee. Worse, on the horizon he caught sight of what looked like several M1A3 tanks moving out of the haze. Where did *they* come from? He could feel the grinding of their treads through the hard desert ground. Goose bumps rose on his arms. He watched the action with one eye peering low from around the hut corner. As he shifted his sight from the tanks to Farington, Branner saw his partner approach the driver's window of the first humvee. He said a few words, then unexpectedly grunted and slumped to the ground. His rifle clattered unused on the pavement. Branner heard no sound. Whatever they'd used, it hadn't been a gun.

"Now what, bright boy?" Branner muttered to himself, sweat poring off his forehead, burning his eyes. "You gonna fight a whole armored battalion with a pea-shooter and a .45?"

He wished he had a drink. He wished he had a whole liquor store. He squeezed between the hut's two trash cans, making himself invisible.

Chapter 32

"The Nothing"

His eyes hooded like a half-sleeping toad, the old Maoist was thinking furiously as he watched the young Shang.

For an hour, The Shang had been smiling, smoking cigarettes, and listening quietly to heated arguments among his advisors. They were still debating what to do about the "double insolence" of the United States and the rebellious confederacy led by Oregon. It was not actually a subject that interested their leader anymore. As he had explained to his advisors, he had succeeded in planting a false image of weakness in the minds of their enemies in America. That image would sooner or later be exploitable. In his own mind, he had come to terms with the matter. For his advisors, though, it remained a current topic. Just as well. The Shang encouraged debates about national policy. Not only did useful ideas emerge now and then, but it was a marvelous opportunity, a perfect time for The Shang to observe how the members of his inner circle thought — and how the political breezes bent and swayed them. More than once, someone had turned the wrong way, exposing unwise ambitions, and was snapped by the wind of The Shang. In newspaper terms, several top officials had gone to their esteemed ancestors by accidentally breathing the depths of the Great Canal.

Although the others seemed shamefully gullible, to the

Maoist it was obvious how important it was to remain on the Emperor's good side. The Shang had a reputation for divine justice. But the Maoist was no fool. The new justice was simply old ruthlessness in fresh clothes. He could work the political abacus better than anyone—except, perhaps, The Shang himself. Even there, the Maoist was no longer sure. His confidence in himself was returning. It was old experience against young brilliance. It was a classic battle, one of which he was more than worthy; perhaps the *only* man who was worthy in the breadth of the entire Empire.

The Maoist reminded himself that he had come through the fierce purges of Communism unscathed. He had clawed and hidden and clawed again. Somehow he had made it from the depths of the 1949 revolt against the nationalists to the fall of Mao. Then he had ascended from the rubble through the days of Deng and his unpredictable line of lesser successors in the eighties and nineties. Finally, he had witnessed the final fall of Chinese communism itself in the early 21st century. Suddenly he was at the right hand of The Shang. Yes, he admitted it: he had watched in awe as the tiny youth had quietly taken over China on the inside while the old Communists were preoccupied taking over Russia on the outside. It had not been hard for the Maoist to pick his new course in life. But while awe was one thing, worship was something else. He would not allow himself that indulgence. This nonsense about The Shang being partially divine was grist for fools. The Shang *was* peculiar, the Maoist acknowledged. On the other hand, many men were. The Shang was far from the first Chinese ruler to invoke popular delusions of divinity. The Shang was simply exceptionally adept at exploiting the foolish assumptions and emotionalism of his admirers. Objectively, there was nothing divine about it.

So, the old Maoist thought, here we are.

He had survived the terrible turmoil of almost two-thirds of a century. He had done it because of a powerful ability to perform political calculus. In this strange new regime, his cunning had finally settled down. It had begun to produce intriguing conclusions and speculations. For one thing, the Maoist saw that contrary to The Shang's carefully cultivated reputation for mercy, he was an extremely vindictive little man. He was clever at concealing it, true. But not perfect. The Chinese press said otherwise, but The Shang had been unable to convert or eliminate all the Communists. There were other survivors, although none so high as the old Maoist. There weren't many left, but the ones who remained were Darwinian; they were the fit who had survived. They were very, very good. The Maoist had slowly reestablished contacts with, and control over, this underground of deposed Reds. He had created a network of resistance and information. His comrades verified for him the hushed stories about "canal breathing" and other horrors. They provided the proof he needed about The Shang's falsely benevolent character. It paid to know the width of a shark's jaws, especially of the biggest or fastest shark around.

As though sensing these thoughts, The Shang glanced sideways at the Maoist. When their eyes met, The Shang winked mischievously.

The old man shivered inside. Outwardly, though, he managed to show nothing. He nodded respectfully and covered his true emotions by lighting a cigarette. In a few seconds, the irrational fear subsided, replaced by a deep, seething furor that The Shang could have such an effect on him. He soothed himself with the thought that the effect had diminished with acquaintance and practice. The rumored inhuman mind-reading ability of the Emperor had been a problem at first. But the Maoist had concluded that it was a simple, quite human trick. Yes, it was a good one. It worked five times better than it should have. But it had a down-to-earth explanation—namely, that one simply did not expect such manipulative cleverness from a virtual child.

The Chinese overly respected age. They made the mistake of equating age with wisdom. Generally, there was truth to the equation. But when an extremely young man rose to a mighty position rapidly, his accomplishments carried an extra kick: he was assumed to have nearly godly proportions of wisdom. Once one accounted for the fact that The Shang, although extraordinarily young, was also a genius—well, then one could conquer his little trick and resist its esteem-eroding effect. The essence of the trick was an affectation. The Shang had a knack—and it was probably no more than a gift at reading faces—for sensing when others were contemplating him. He would then draw sudden attention to it, startling his victim with the impression that his thoughts had been read. To bolster this impression, his assistants regularly, quietly spread the mind-reading rumor. To resist the trick, the Maoist found that it helped to pretend The Shang was an old man who wore a mask. It reminded him that the Emperor was only a man—although an exceptionally clever one.

Nor did the Maoist buy The Shang's claim that he'd shown deliberate weakness to Corcoran and Sam Washington. The old Red knew weakness when he saw it; he could feel it in his bones, like a radar antenna. The Shang *had* lost himself to his anger. It was the Americans, not The Shang, who had shown true strength and confidence in their positions. The Shang's effort to cover up his own weakness may have worked with his other advisors, but not with the Maoist.

The Shang had the intellectual capacity of a man, but deep within him lurked the temper of a child. He had lost it with the Americans. The Maoist concluded that he had identified a serious weakness in the Emperor. The only remaining questions were how and when to exploit it.

Chapter 33

"Frozen Flyboys"

B ill Branner watched the last of the Army-green troop carriers rumble off toward the interior of Silver Sands. He could hardly believe that no one had seen him. He'd scrunched in a heap behind the guard hut, with only trashcans for cover. But the Army—or whoever it was—had been single-minded. After Farington had fallen, two men had scooped him up and loaded him into one of the vehicles. Then Branner had heard someone fiddle around for a moment inside the hut. The gate was fully opened—how, he didn't know, since the power was cut—and the ensemble had roared through, off on some crazy mission in the interior of the big Air Force base. He'd counted fifteen of the new 16-wheel, Schwartzkopf troop transporters. The carriers had only recently come on line and they were monsters. Each could hold a hundred men. The vehicles were affectionately nicknamed "blackheads," the literal translation of the old Gulf War general's German name.

Branner had also noted eight tanks, five humvees, an assortment of self-propelled artillery, small missile launchers, engineering vehicles of several kinds, and what looked like a couple of mobile command posts complete with phased array radars and big, wide-spectrum digital satellite links.

He estimated that nearly two-thousand heavily armed men had penetrated his post in under fifteen minutes. It had been like a boulder rolling over a dollhouse. He stood, sighed, and quietly wiped the sweat from his eyes and stretched his cramped knees. His mouth felt like someone had stuck a hairdryer in it. But for once, the drink he craved was ordinary water. Reconsidering his position, he groaned softly, crouched, and crept on hands and knees around to the door to peek inside. No one. He checked all sides of the hut, but the invasion force had apparently left not a single man to guard the small post.

"Well," he muttered, "they're either awfully confident or just plain stupid."

He rummaged through the lockers and cabinets. The weapons had been taken, but they'd left the two guards' lunchpails. The insulated water jug, changed with each shift, had not been touched. He drew a pint and gulped it. Then he remembered the old two-way radio kept in the hut for emergencies. In the entire time he'd been at the post, the radio had not been used. There'd been no need. The computer link with its built-in two-way, optical fiber audio/visual line had never failed. He snapped open the panel to the right under the built-in desk and felt for the radio. Gone. On this score, the invaders were no slouches.

Branner glanced at his watch. It was nearly two hours before his shift would end. That was probably the soonest he could expect relief. The sun was low. It would be down in less than twenty minutes. Once it set, he knew the desert would grow cold quickly. Well, there was no point freezing his buns. At a reasonable pace, it was just an hour's walk north to the next post along the fence. The walking would keep him warm. It was much farther than that to anything inside the base. Silver Sands was huge. There were places where one could walk in a straight line for fifty, maybe sixty miles without seeing a sign of civilization. He pulled on his lightweight jacket and was about to start off when he frowned and thought, hell, why take chances?

He stuffed an orange and a candy bar from Farington's lunchpail, and an apple from his own, into his pockets. Then he filled Farington's empty thermos with water. Before trudging down the fence line, he checked the clip of his forty-five. He grinned and shrugged at the same time. It was probably silly to think he'd need food, let alone a weapon. One way or another, he'd catch a ride back to the barracks from the next hut. Whatever this nonsense invasion was about, it didn't concern him. He'd never experienced one, but he'd heard of surprise base penetration exercises run by one service against another. Now that he mulled it over, maybe they did it without vehicle markings. He couldn't recall for sure. But it would fit. The idea was to test perimeters, alertness, probe for weaknesses.

Ultimately, it made some hotshot brass get an erection. He pursed his lips and shook his head. No, he thought, that's just my own embarrassment talking. Let's face it. We blew it big-time. We were caught with our asses jammed in the can by exactly the thing we were supposed to be able to spot and report in time.

He smiled ironically.

"Forget it," he said to a tan lizard that scurried frantically from his feet, "there's not much they can demote me from here, so let's enjoy the walk."

Guardpost 845 was dark, but not deserted. The two men on duty were Smith and Franklin, whom Branner knew well enough through off-hour "attitude adjustment sessions." When Branner came striding up on the inside of the fence, he spotted Smith, a large blond fellow with a face so ruddy that it looked black in the moonlight. Smith kept his hand on his gun until Branner shouted a greeting from a couple hundred feet away.

Smith squinted into the darkness, then dropped his hand and asked jeeringly, "What happened, tough guy? That skinny Baptist crusader finally wave one too many pages of the Good Book at ya?"

"I got waved, all right," Banner said. "As in tidal wave."

After he'd sketched in the story, Franklin, a medium-built half-Korean, shook his head and said, "That explains why we lost power about an hour or so ago. We thought it was some damned maintenance kids with their over-educated thumbs caught in their alligator clips."

"Now what're we s'posed to do?" Smith asked, gesturing with his flashlight at the night sky.

Branner asked, "You guys should have a battery two-way under your table? They took mine."

Franklin snapped his fingers, smiled, and said, "Hey, I'd forgotten all about that old clunker."

He dug it out from the panel, flipped the unit on, and shouted, "Say, this is 845 to Silver Daddy."

He repeated the message.

"Forget it," Banner said, reaching over and touching the battery indicator light. "Look. You got less juice than a squashed bug."

He shivered under his thin jacket and looked out at the near-featureless desert. A light breeze had picked up, dropping the apparent temperature another fifteen degrees.

"Ladies, it's gonna get as cold as a penguin's pecker pretty soon," he said. "Either of you remember how to build a fire out of sand and rocks?"

Smith spat and swore, "Brass exercises pain my butt."

"Your precious butt's gonna be frozen painless if we don't figure something out before morning," Branner said.

"Stupid exercises," Smith repeated.

"Give us a break," Franklin snorted. "It's probably the only one anyone's ever sprung on you."

"Well, I think it's one too many from this Air Force," Smith said sullenly.

It wasn't until six the following morning that the three men—all grumpy and shaking from the cold—realized how accurate that statement was. Two humvees filled with four armed men rolled up on the guardhouse from the direction of the base's interior.

"Hey!" Smith shouted at the driver of the first vehicle, "It's the Silver Daddy rescue squad! It's about ti—"

Then he noticed the insignia on the man's helmet.

"Hey, you're not U.S. Air Force!"

"I sure hope not," the driver said laconically, raising his

gun. "You might say we're your new life insurance policy. We're a piece of the ROC."

"Piece of the —? Whoa!" Smith exclaimed, noticing that the driver's three buddies had quietly descended, fanned out, and raised their guns, too.

"What're you guys talking about?"

"ROC," the driver repeated. "Republic of Oregon Confederation armed forces. You pathetic frozen flyboys are now officially my POWs."

"Huh?" Smith and Franklin said simultaneously.

But Branner understood and he was smirking new lines into his face.

"Boys, we've been emancipated!" he said.

Chapter 34

"Aftermath Dispatches"

REBELS GRAB BASE
BULLETIN ** (Associated Internet, R. of Ore.) — One of the largest U.S. domestic air bases was captured last night in a surprise armed attack by Republic of Oregon Confederation (ROC) forces.

The attack, accomplished nearly without bloodshed, started around sunset. ROC soldiers on air and land established control over the huge Nevada Silver Sands facility in less than two hours. Consolidation operations continued through the night.

Word of the attack leaked out only a few minutes ago. The massive operation was apparently kept under wraps by somehow faking normal communications in and out of the base.

Ironically, the takeover was accomplished under cover of a military exercise designed to test the base's ability to defend itself against a surprise assault.

There is no official reaction yet from either the White House or from the Republic of Oregon.

PREZ ZAPS BASE TAKEOVER
FLASH ** (AP/DOW, Washington) — The White House press office says president Washington is "highly dismayed" by last night's "sneak attack" on Silver Sands Air Force Base in

Nevada. Press secretary Tom Rosco said Washington will hold a news conference within the hour to discuss the issue.

OREGON CHIEF CONFIRMS BASE GRAB

FLASH ** (AP/DOW, R. of Ore.) — President Corcoran of the Republic of Oregon has confirmed that his forces overpowered the big U.S. Silver Sands Air Force Base during the night. He said the attack was carried out on his direct orders and "with coordination of other friendly forces." Corcoran said that the takeover was "necessary for the protection of our new friends in the Confederation."

Corcoran said Silver Sands was crucial to the defense of the Western States because of its critical research and development facilities and a heretofore secret force of 200 fifteen-warhead intercontinental nuclear missiles.

"With our Flyswatter anti-cruise-missile, we're the only ones capable of protecting Silver Sands from the explicit, and we believe, still quite real threats of the Shang Empire," said Corcoran.

The Oregon president also said the move, through secret consultations, had gained the quick approval of the Western Governors. The governor of Nevada, Santini Androtti, was "crucially instrumental," according to Corcoran.

He said ROC forces "are on station and in control of all of Silver Sands' diverse departments."

"If The Shang thought the Oregon rebellion was going to give him an opportunity to intimidate America, he was wrong," Corcoran said.

OREGON RAIDS ICBM SITES IN THREE STATES

BULLETIN ** (Associated Internet, R. of Ore.) — The Associated Internet has learned that U.S. ICBM bases in Montana, Wyoming, and Kansas are in control of forces of the Republic of Oregon. The bases — the oldest in the U.S. — were apparently overrun simultaneously with the attack on Silver Sands Air Force Base last night.

President Corcoran of Oregon confirmed that the missile

232 ☆ E. G. ROSS

bases are now "safely in ROC-solid hands" and "protected from the fangs of The Shang."

"America is safe again," Corcoran said.

The White House had no immediate reaction to the latest report, except to say that it sounded "unlikely."

U.S. "PUZZLED" BY SILO SNATCH

FLASH ** (UPI On-line, Washington, D.C.) — The U.S. Secretary of Defense Grieve McDouglas has confirmed that ROC forces have, indeed, taken complete control of U.S. ICBM bases in Montana, Wyoming, and Kansas, as first reported by Associated Internet.

"We are puzzled. We don't know how it was accomplished," McDouglas said, "but we'll find out soon. On the other hand, the bases appear to be in no danger, nor is the United States."

McDouglas said he was "sure" that Oregon had no intention of redirecting the missiles at any target in the U.S. He cited unnamed "highly reliable" sources for his confidence.

"We'll work this out," McDouglas told reporters. "The nation is safe."

MORE STATES HIT OREGON TRAIL

FLASH ** (UPI On-line, R. of Ore.) — Ten governors of states east of the Mississippi have petitioned for entry into the new Republic of Oregon Confederation, or ROC.

Oregon president Corcoran said the petition will be granted "immediate, favorable consideration."

Over three-fifths of the states of the U.S. have now joined or asked to join the Oregon confederation.

Simultaneously, the Republic of Taiwan has petitioned for confederation status "equal to that of any present or former state of the U.S.A."

Corcoran said Taiwan's petition would "be taken seriously" but required "careful study."

There has been no immediate comment from The Shang, known to favor incorporation of Taiwan into the Empire.

PRESIDENT NIXES NEWS TALK

BULLETIN ** (AP/DOW,Washington, D.C.) — President Washington of the United States has canceled a regularly scheduled news conference. Press Secretary Tom Rosco said the president was in "urgent consultation" with President Corcoran of the Republic of Oregon.

CONGRESSMEN STUNNED BY OREGON OFFENSIVE

(AP/DOW, Washington, D.C.) — An AP/DOW spot survey of key U.S. government officials indicates that reaction to the sudden takeover of key U.S. nuclear bases last night is one of stunned confusion.

"It was a body blow," Democratic Sen. Biden Troughwart told reporters, expressing a common sentiment among Eastern members of Congress. "For the first time in the nuclear age, this country no longer retains control of its main sources of land-based deterrent missile power. The White House was simply asleep at the switch."

"Incredible," said Republican Representative Ron Cravenpull, considered the most powerful conservative voice in Congress. "This is absolutely inexcusable. There's no way we can tolerate this. No way. The president is going to have to answer for this. I won't be surprised if it costs him his office."

Troughwart said he expected majority leaders of both houses of Congress to call a special session to consider whether "a state of war" with the Republic of Oregon exists.

However, a telephone poll by this news service found that only two senators and four congressmen from among the 32 rebel states are apparently willing to agree to such a session. It is therefore highly unlikely that a quorum can be formed. A quorum is the minimum number of members of Congress needed to legally conduct business. At least on this issue, it appears that the U.S. no longer has a functioning Congress.

PUBLIC YAWNS AT BASE GRAB

(AP/DOW, Atlanta) — A demographically controlled spot survey of 3,000 U.S. residents east of the Mississippi shows surprisingly little concern over Oregon's takeover of key U.S. military bases yesterday. Nearly 42% of those surveyed said the actions worried them "slightly" or "not at all."

Another 31% said they were "moderately" worried and 20% expressed no opinion.

Seven percent said they were "extremely" or "very" worried. Asked for reactions to the survey, top members of Congress and the administration expressed strong skepticism about the results. However, similar surveys by *CBS/New York Times*, *CNN/Today*, *Zogby/UA*, and *Gallup/Roper* showed nearly identical results. All four surveys have sampling errors of plus or minus 3%.

Chapter 35

"The Logistics Argue"

U.S. BASE TAKEOVERS
RAISE ISSUE OF TREASON;
Did ROC Forces Have Inside Help?
Special to the *Wall Street Journal*
by Ben Liddell

The surprise conquest of several key U.S. military bases by forces of, or assisting, the Republic of Oregon could not have been accomplished without the aid of individuals high in the U.S. government itself. That's the consensus from interviews with dozens of defense experts both in and out of public service.

The experts also believe it's probable that a group of military commanders, working with one or more persons deep in the administration, has committed treason.

Such implications are not the product of wild speculations or half-baked conspiracy theories. Rather, they are based on the facts about how U.S. military installations are guarded and what is necessary to breach them.

A wide range of defenses and warning systems is involved. The systems range from satellite and airplane radars all the way down to armed patrols and electric fences on the ground. Everything from fighter jets, to artillery, to anti-aircraft missiles, to unmanned drones, to various secure communications systems, to hundreds of ordinary telephone lines, to entry/exit codes, to mobile mini-radars and robotic surveillance devices — all of these provide both warning and deterrence. All would have to be neutralized or side-stepped in order for an alert not to be sounded and defenses to be defeated.

The experts say that the problem is actually bigger than that. A large number of such systems would have to be dealt with simultaneously at four major installations in Nevada, Wyoming, Montana, and Kansas. That is considered next to impossible.

As one ex-defense intelligence commander put it, "It would be like taking over a city and not having anyone notice — or at least not have anyone talk about it to anyone outside the city for several hours. The logistics argue that it would take divine intervention."

Short of the divine, the experts say that there is only one other possibility: that key defenders themselves participated intimately in the takeover, or were tricked into doing so. Only they would have had the ability to massively misdirect, turn off, and fake the normal defensive alert net.

It couldn't be done for long. Apparently it wasn't — and didn't have to be.

Jason G. Dickinson, a base defensive tactician and former official of both Army intelligence and the National Security Council, agreed.

"If the attacking forces themselves were disguised and in place, all you'd need would be a few minutes to an hour," Dickinson said. "If an insider, or a group of them, could stand down the major warning devices and divert or somehow get people to ignore the less serious ones for awhile, then a successful attack would at least theoretically be possible. Even so, it would require an absolutely extreme level of precision and timing."

That leads to what is perhaps the biggest question of all about the takeover. How could an inside job of such treacherous proportions be planned without anyone finding out?

One analyst says there might have been several ways of doing it: "For instance, it could have been a small gang of military leaders. To start with, that is. The heads of all four bases would certainly be candidates for suspicion."

However, he admits that such a group would find it "rather difficult" to by-pass their own commanders, which "necessarily implies" that those commanders were involved.

"Certain codes and access requirements can only be authorized with great difficulty," says a Pentagon officer who deals with such matters almost full time. "For instance, you can't just waltz into a missile base, point a gun at a couple guys, and grab control of a nuclear arsenal. A whole stack of clearances and checks and balances have to be circumvented before you can reach that point."

Who could grant this "ultimate" authorization? Not even the head of the Joint Chiefs of Staff, the experts agree. In peacetime, their consensus is that there are only two serious possibilities: the secretary of defense or the president.

Erik Hochman dropped a copy of the *Journal* on President Corcoran's desk.

"Yeah, I read it. So what?" Corcoran asked, chewing on the stub of a cigar.

"He's right," Hochman said. "Something else, too."

"Oh?"

Corcoran gazed blankly at his young secretary of defense for a moment. Then he abruptly rose, walked to the door of his office, stuck his head out and said to his appointments secretary, "Let my three o'clock come in as soon as he gets here, Sarah. Yeah, the old guy. That's him."

He closed the door and returned to his desk, pulling a cigar out of his humidifier. As he sniffed it, he looked at Hochman and asked, "Well? What else?"

"I think you and President Washington cooked up this entire takeover thing, sir."

"Stiff charge," Corcoran said mildly.

Too mildly, Hochman felt. It wasn't the reaction he'd expected to hear from his president.

Corcoran looked him up and down and asked, "You sure your nose isn't just bent out of joint because I passed you by on this operation, Erik? Sorry about that. But you're new and it was conceived long before you came aboard. It was a matter of planning security, that's all. I figured on tellin' you about it soon enough, if that's the itch in your ear."

"It's one of them."

"Well, then, if you've got more than a theory, you'd better explain yourself," Corcoran said, glancing at his finger watch. "Make it fast. As you heard, I've got a visitor in a few minutes. I can't keep him dangling. Now sit down and let's hear it."

Hochman took a deep breath. He edged onto a chair and began ticking points off on his fingers.

"First, the writer Liddell was right about the difficulty of busting through big base defenses with massive force. To do it properly, you'd have to have the help of high civvies. Second, those so-called ROC forces weren't ours."

Corcoran snorted. "How do you figure?"

"Because unless you've got some Greek-god giant units stashed away somewhere, they'd have to be ones you could move across several states without anyone seeing. That'd be like leading a herd of elephants through the livingroom. I don't buy it. So my guess is that they were units provided by the U.S. government, but dolled up to look like ours."

"Far-fetched."

"It could work, especially if they looked like something that appeared relatively innocent to the base defenders. That way no ROC markings would be necessary. However, that couldn't be done by a few military commanders on their own."

Corcoran fingered a cigar, but didn't light it. He nodded and said, "You've still got my ear. Go on."

"They'd have to have authorization from the U.S. Secretary of Defense, or from his boss, in order to assemble and train units in secret on what would be a fairly massive scale. Then the units would have to somehow be inserted near the bases, probably on the pretext of special training maneuvers of some

kind, or perhaps as rotating defensive units for the bases themselves. And that would take months of — "

"Okay, okay," Corcoran said, a small smile tweaking one
corner of his mouth. "I see the frog on your log. You've made
your point. What do you want me to tell you?"

"I think before he falls on his face, you'd better tell him
everything," said an oddly familiar, rather rough voice from
the door.

Hochman snapped his head around. He hadn't heard the
door open. The man was tall, stooped, heavy-set, white-
bearded. His skin looked red and weather-beaten. He wore a
gray London Fog trenchcoat and a matching fedora. He moved
into the room slowly, as though he might have arthritis. He
glanced at Corcoran and flashed a quick, ironic grin. Hochman
noted that Corcoran's face showed respect and almost . . . def-
erence, something the Oregon President seldom showed anyone. Hochman hadn't the foggiest notion who the old guy was.

Chapter 36

"Tattlers"

Authorities don't know the cause of the blaze, which killed four children and was not brought under control until after midnight."

For a moment, *Fox*'s Lyndsy Scarlett pretended to look down at her paper copy, even though she, like all network announcers, read 99% of her copy directly from an electronic prompter screen.

"In news overseas, there was . . . Excuse me, I've just received word that both houses of Congress have apparently tried but failed to raise a quorum for a vote on the missile base takeover controversy. Let's go to our Capitol Hill correspondent, Peter Schoenbildt."

The "Just In" animated satellite logo faded and the handsome, wide face of Schoenbildt came on. He was standing with the Capitol Building picturesquely placed over his left shoulder. A breeze was catching his blond hair and whipping it around his face.

"That's correct, Lyndsy," he said. "Not more than ten minutes ago both House Speaker Sunderleaf and Vice-President Leininger, acting in his capacity as Senate President, attempted to round up enough members to consider the issue. However, despite sending the sergeant-at-arms out and about, not nearly enough members could be found to form a quorum.

In fact, it was much worse than anticipated. In the Senate, only 20 members were brought to the floor—half of them under protest—and in the House, only 100 or so could be collared. Some of them were, to put it mildly, dragging their feet, even though they were more than willing to show up to deal with other issues. As I heard one of them yell to Sunderleaf, 'Bake, you'll get a quorum for almost anything but this.'"

"Peter, did either Sunderleaf or Leininger say whether he would try again tomorrow?"

Schoenbildt gave a boy-next-door grin, brushed back a lock of hair, and shook his head. "No. In fact, when I tried to talk to Sunderleaf later, he literally shoved me and two other reporters aside as he rushed out. We heard him mumble something about not appreciating getting his ears stuffed with cotton by the president. We don't know for sure what he was referring to, but I should mention that rumors on the Hill have it that Sunderleaf—always close to President Wash-ington—has had a falling out with him behind the scenes over the president's handling of the entire Oregon rebellion. My sources tell me that Sunderleaf believes the president has been misleading not only the public, but key congressional leaders. I've heard that members of the president's so-called core group, or inner circle of advisors, have for quite some time suffered the same deception."

"Peter, can you elaborate in any detail?"

"Well, I really can't, Lyndsy, not without getting into a lot of unverified speculation. A reporter hates to admit his ignorance," he said, flashing an aw-shucks grin, "but in this case, I'm quite as much in the dark as my media colleagues here in Washington D.C."

"Can you at least—"

"Excuse me, Lyndsy. I wanted to say that I spoke with Senate Majority Leader Biden Troughwort a couple hours ago. He said that a White House source has told him the president will make an announcement on the entire situation sometime tomorrow."

"I'm sorry, Peter. What situation is that? His spat with

242 ☆ E. G. ROSS

Congress or the missile issue?"

"That wasn't clear. Both, I expect. Troughwort said he would demand to be fully briefed before then, as he put it. However, I have to say he didn't express the sentiment with a lot of confidence."

"Er, thanks, Peter. Right now, I'm told we have Bob Lonsdorf standing by in Sacramento. Bob's been diligently digging into that strange story about the massacre of troops by U.S. forces in Southern Oregon awhile back. Bob, that situation with the South Mountain Contingent was never satisfactorily explained, was it?"

"No, Lyndsy, it certainly wasn't. In fact, the entire incident seemed extremely odd to those of us who were grudgingly allowed on the scene on that cold, gray day several weeks ago, a day very much different from the weather here in Sacramento, as you can see."

Behind him, the sun shone in a bright blue sky.

"As you may recall, three soldiers of the Oregon militia, which suffered heavy casualties, were captured and held by U.S. forces. The government called them medical detainees, even though at a later news conference two of them explicitly stated that they considered themselves to be prisoners of war. I have just learned that one of those men, Granvey Lopez, has been missing for over ten days. While the U.S. government claimed that he was never a prisoner, they are now calling him an escapee. Go figure. My sources in the Army tell me that the escape was deliberately kept from the press. Officials hoped they could catch Lopez on their own, quietly. They obviously failed and are now asking the California public, and the public in surrounding states, and in the Republic of Oregon, to assist in his capture. They are calling Lopez dangerous and possibly armed, although they admit there is no evidence that he is carrying weapons. Apparently he was not armed when he escaped and officials are refusing to say how he did it."

"Bob, isn't it likely that he simply slipped back into Oregon, his homeland?" Scarlett asked, voicing the obvious question for her viewers.

"You would think so, but officials with whom I spoke don't believe it. As a veteran war correspondent, I've had a lot of years judging service double-talk. It's my hit that they are telling the truth this time. For some reason which they are not divulging they honestly believe Lopez is still in the California vicinity."

"But Bob, California—and for that matter, all of the Western States—are part of the Oregon Confederation."

"Yes."

"How is it, then, that the United States Army still holds any sway there?"

"For the simple reason that no one in California has taken the drastic steps that Oregon did, yet. For one thing, the various U.S. armed forces branches are much larger here in California than in Oregon. So the U.S. Army and other services are, in effect, islands of the American government in the middle of enemy territory, figuratively speaking."

"Figuratively, Bob?" Scarlett cocked an eyebrow.

"Well, I know it sounds strange, but most people here still consider themselves loyal U.S. citizens, even though they are members of the Oregon Confederation. They are not hostile to U.S. troops here. In fact, it's been pretty much business as usual between them and the California community. The rank and file U.S. troops whom I've interviewed swear that they remain dedicated to defending the U.S. But at the same time, they refuse to condemn Oregon as their enemy. It's a little known fact, but many of the boys serving at California facilities are Oregonians. They were trapped here—metaphorically, anyway—when the Oregon Rebellion happened."

"Uh, Bob, getting back to the Lopez story, is there any chance that he might surface on his own? As I recall, he was fairly outspoken when they put him on display. Is it possible he might make his way to the media somehow?"

Londsdorf grinned. "Well, if he does, he should know that *Fox News* is willing and able."

Scarlett chuckled. Both of them knew that such lucky breaks happened about once every ten years.

Now off-camera, Lonsdorf sighed and unclipped his lapel microphone and handed it to his cameraman's assistant. The young man took the mike, gestured with his thumb toward the mobile news van and said, "There's someone over there who wants to talk to you, Bob. Said you know him from way back."

"Yeah, I bet," Lonsdorf said sarcastically. It was probably another news groupie looking for an autograph or handshake. It was weird. Many viewers thought newsmen were in the same category as movie and rock stars. He wandered over to the far side of the van and found a man with his back turned. He was dressed rather seedily in an old blue plaid flannel shirt, jeans, and a pair of scuffed brown shoes. He was shuffling from foot to foot, fidgeting. Lonsdorf tapped him on the shoulder. As the man turned around, Lonsdorf jumped back almost two feet.

"You!" he shrieked.

"I know you're in the broadcast business, but could you hold down the hollering until you hide me somewhere?" the man said dryly.

Lonsdorf recovered quickly. He jerked open the van rear door, pointed, and said, "Get in. The inner sanctum of the road press. The safest place in the world."

Geez, not in a million years, Lonsdorf thought.

Lopez the escapee flashed a broad smile and climbed into the *Fox News* truck.

Chapter 37

"Chameleons"

Lonsdorf looked at the man sitting across from him in the small, sidestreet cafe three blocks off Old Town in Sacramento. Lopez had refused to say anything until Lonsdorf assured him of a meal and a safe place to stay for a few nights. Lonsdorf agreed to buy him lunch and to let him crash at his tiny hotel room in the east suburbs. Before heading out to eat, they'd stopped to let Lopez shower and change clothes. He'd kept his beard, claiming that the ten-day growth would make him less conspicuous. He'd also borrowed a baseball cap and he kept the brim pulled low. Lonsdorf had thought Lopez was crazy to want to go out to a public restaurant, but admitted that the shower and fresh clothes had made the man almost unrecognizable. The danger of being spotted was probably slim as long as no one asked to see his I.D., which they probably wouldn't if Lopez simply stayed out of trouble. Lonsdorf intended to make sure of it. This escapee was a big fish that wasn't getting away.

Lopez had insisted that Lonsdorf tell no one else at the network about him, at least not until he was satisfied that he could trust the veteran newsman.

"If that were a problem," Lonsdorf asked, "why did you come to me?"

Lopez wolfed a giant mouthful of German sausage omelet and washed it down with hot coffee. He smacked his lips, then said, "Man, this is sure better than scrounging in garbage cans or copping plates at the mission."

"Eat up," Lonsdorf said. "It's on my boss's expense account. Again, why me?"

"Saw some of your reports."

"So? Other guys did 'em, too."

"Yeah, but after awhile, everybody else quit digging. You acted hungrier. Besides, you're an old guy. Old guys are calmer. They tend to listen better."

"So I'm listening," Lonsdorf snapped, wincing at the remark about his age. He was only 54, although prematurely white-haired. He snicked a Camel out of a hardpack, lit up, and asked, "How'd you get out, Lopez?"

"That doesn't matter," Lopez said, shoveling into a mound of greasy hash browns. "Man, this is the first decent meal I've had in—what?—three days, I guess."

"What *does* matter?" Lonsdorf said, pulling out a small notepad. "Besides your breakfast, I mean."

Lopez frowned and slipped snake-quick out of his seat and into the booth on Londsdorf's side.

When Lonsdorf looked alarmed, Lopez said, "Don't worry. I'm not making a pass at you."

He did a sit-down frisk of the reporter and said, "Just making sure you don't have any recording junk. Guess not. Okay. Sorry. Your profession isn't known for high ethical standards in interviews."

He grinned at Londsdorf's ruffled look.

"As I said, I'm listening." Lonsdorf blew smoke at the table as he glared up at Lopez and clicked a ball-point pen open. "Okay if I take notes? Or is that going to endanger your sense of fair play, too?"

Ignoring the caustic question, Lopez said, "First, I'm not an Oregon militia man."

"Huh? I didn't get that."

"Yeah, you did. But that's all you get to hear at the moment, I'm afraid."

"What are you trying—?"

Lopez shook his head. He waved at the waitress and ordered a second meal, cupped a refilled coffee in his hands, and sipped it silently.

He looked at Lonsdorf and said, "Gimme a cigarette."

Lonsdorf grunted and handed him the pack and his lighter. He watched Lopez fire the weed, closing his eyes as he inhaled. The reporter was baffled and irritable. He didn't like anyone, not even a potentially valuable source, to jack him around. Maybe he *was* an old guy. He was certainly too old to take this kind of game in easy stride. Or was he? He could try.

"What kind of angle are you running, Lopez?" he asked, making himself smile. "And what do you mean, that's all at the moment? You're showing me candy and then slapping my hands when I reach for it."

"Boy, you media geeks are touchy, aren't you? I've heard you were. Well, forget it. Inside, I'm a lot touchier than you could ever think about being. Peel yourself off the ceiling, okay?" he asked, seeing Londsdorf's tight grip on his pen. "We're waiting for someone. When he gets here, I'll talk. I want a witness."

"So much for gaining your trust."

"It's the best way to do it. Remember the old Reagan saying? Trust but verify."

"It was actually Russian, sure. But tell me now, who is this mystery guest that—"

"Me," said a raspy voice. The man who owned it sat down next to Lopez. He was trim, blond, crewcut, and probably no more than twenty-five or thirty years old, maybe five years younger than Lopez.

"Corporal B.J. Erikson of the 90th Airborne. B.J., this is Bob. You've probably seen his mug on the tube."

Lonsdorf shrugged and said, "Sorry, Erikson. Your name doesn't ring a bell. U.S. Army, huh? Don't you know your guys are looking for Lopez here?"

Both men laughed loudly.

"He knows," Lopez said, glancing around and bringing

his mirth under control.

"Well, Bob, in the first instance, I'm not really a corporal," Erikson said. "In the second instance, old Granvey here actually—we call him Granny, but he probably hasn't told you that—Granny isn't with the Oregon militia. And I'm not really with the 90th. We're both part of a U.S. outfit called the Chameleon Unit. It's more than one, really, but that's the name for the guys doing our kind of stuff."

"And what kind's that?" Lonsdorf asked, cocking his head skeptically.

"My group was among the ones that took over all the ICBM bases, as well as Silver Sands."

Lonsdorf half-laughed, but Lopez picked it up and rolled on, explaining, "We're the ones who set up that sham about a firefight with the South Mountain Contingent in Oregon."

"Sham? Did you say sham?"

"Read my lips, old guy. There was no firefight."

"Hey, I was there," Landsdorf said. "I saw bodies and blood and—"

"No. You were there when we wanted you there. Not before. You saw faked bodies, staged carnage. Don't be so arrogant, Bobby boy. You news sniffers weren't allowed in until everything was set up. It was like a tour of a movie studio. All an act. Nobody was even hurt, except for a few guys who caught colds in the awful weather."

"This is nuts," Lonsdorf said under his breath, tapping his pen on his pad, wondering whether he should just get up and leave.

"Ain't it, though?" Erikson said, sending a grim glance at Lopez. "Now we're getting somewhere. Maybe you're not so dim after all, old guy."

Lopez nodded back, his face reflecting his friend's emotions. Lonsdorf frowned, reading their expressions. In a half second, the atmosphere of the conversation had completely changed. The levity had disappeared as if an elephant had stepped on the only clown in town.

"Tell him, Granny," Erikson barked. "If we're still heading where we said, let's get on with it."

Lopez's black eyebrows lowered and his voice almost hissed, "Look, Lonsdorf, we're here because we swore to uphold and defend the Constitution of the United States—and our government tricked us into tracking dog-doo on it."

"I thought that happened all the time in government," Lonsdorf said cynically. "What makes this case different? You guys some kinda patriotic whistleblowers or something?"

"Yeah, I guess we are," Erikson said, leaning into Londsdorf's face. "You got a problem with patriotism?"

"Uh, no, not at all," Lonsdorf added hastily. He was for patriotism, when real.

"Look," Lopez said, "it's not something that takes an Einstein to understand. We don't like what's going on."

"Right," Erikson said. "And we want to do something quick to stop it."

"We want to cut the arm off this beast before it whacks anymore good people," Lopez said. "Because it will, you know. It's going to end up smacking so much stuff that there won't *be* a Constitution in a few more weeks."

"Or a country," Erikson added.

"Or a country," Lopez repeated softly. He looked directly into Londsdorf's eyes for a few seconds. "It's pretty simple, old guy. At this moment in history, you're the one person in the whole world who's got the power to stop Uncle Sam from blowing himself right out of existence."

Chapter 38

"Burners Out"

Oregon Defense Secretary Hochman looked at the old man in President Corcoran's office. At first, the stranger hadn't activated any memory cells. But now, something about him seemed familiar. Hochman scratched his head contemplatively, trying to figure it out.

"Forget the guessing, Erik," Corcoran said with a chuckle while nodding at the old man. "Go ahead, peel."

The newcomer's "arthritis" vanished as he straightened. He was taller than Hochman had thought. The man took off his coat, then his hat, revealing a fairly youthful head of reddish hair, touched with white only at the temples where the hat hadn't covered it. He reached up and pulled off an excellent false white beard. Beneath it was a much shorter, red one. The "old" man had instantly shed thirty years. He tilted his head sideways and gave Hochman a questioning look. He was, of course, the President of the United States.

"Oh, God," Hochman said, feeling the blood drain from his cheeks.

"Nope. I've certainly been called Satan, though," Sam Washington said, smiling.

Corcoran laughed at the look on his defense secretary's hang-dog face.

Hochman tried to mutter something, found his mouth too

dry, swallowed twice, then said, "I'm surprised and not surprised at the same time."

"You've hooked the haddock," Corcoran said. He glanced at his watch. "But now, it looks like it's about time for a real old man to arrive."

Almost as soon as he'd said it, his secretary buzzed to confirm. In a moment, Grieve McDouglas, Hochman's counterpart in the U.S., entered. The U.S. Secretary of Defense's only disguise was a set of street clothes and a baseball cap. For a man whom Washington D.C. hadn't witnessed outside either a suit or uniform in forty years, it was enough.

Hochman, stunned, shook hands with both Washington and McDouglas, then said, "Corky, without meaning to push the situation, what's going on?"

Corcoran pointed at him and said, "Keep your powder dry, son. You'll get an explanation in a minute. Let me get our guests settled."

The Oregon President poured coffee all around and then led them to chairs at the side of the room.

"Well shucks, who wants to start?" he asked, looking from Washington to McDouglas. "Better snap to it. In about ten minutes, I'm informing the media that Sam and I are nearly ready to hold a joint national press conference."

"It was your idea, Corky," President Washington said, winking. "Seems like you ought to do the honors. Grieve and I are purely along for the ride. But let's hurry it up. That presidential double sitting in for me back in D.C. isn't exactly the best of actors."

Corcoran snorted. "Well, *nobody's* just along for the ride on an operation like this."

Washington shrugged. McDouglas scratched his ear and twisted in his chair; he felt uncomfortable out of uniform.

"Fine, then I'll explain," Corcoran said, reaching for a cigar. "Erik, you're looking at three of several guys who call themselves the Burner Boys. That comes from the idea that if we didn't pull this off, a buncha butts were gonna burn. Mainly ours. They still might. Quite a few months ago, after Ben Colby propaned everyone's wicks with the idea of taking Oregon solo out of the Union—"

Corcoran was interrupted by his intercom. Instead of answering it, he took two steps out of his chair, opened the door, and shouted, "Yeah, what? Don't you know I'm—"

The men inside heard his end of an exchange with his secretary:

"Oh? Hmmm. Right. Were, huh? Well, that's good. Thanks. Oh, sure, go ahead and set up that national news conference. Give us about an hour. Yeah, call 'em all—electronic, print, slime-scrapers, the works. Tell 'em it'll be both me and Sam. Right, together."

Corcoran closed the door, stepped back to his desk, plopped down again in his chair, lit his cigar, and between puffs explained the interruption.

"Erikson and Lopez—we just took 'em into custody in Sacramento," he said. "The muscle-tails we had on 'em said they were ready to spill to that *Fox* reporter, Lonsdorf. Well, one of 'em was. We got the reporter, too. He screamed, but there wasn't another choice."

"Uh-oh. Their boss is gonna yowl about one of his employees in the clink," President Washington said.

"We won't keep him long. Anyhow, there's no damage they can do after you and I bark the media dogs into a howl. Besides, Londsdorf's been a fairly straight putter over the years. He'll figure out things after he's cooled a spell."

"Good thing Lopez was loyal to us and snagged Erikson," McDouglas said. "It's not easy to turn a pal in."

"Exigencies of conflict," Corcoran said. "Erikson was ready to blab to the press with his suspicions days ago. Lopez saw that Erikson was capable of becoming sand in our bearings."

"I don't follow," Hochman interjected.

McDouglas twisted in his chair to look directly at the young Oregon defense chief. "Erikson had convinced himself that it was all a plot to wreck the U.S."

"Uh, well, wasn't it?"

"Oh, sure, but only in a sense. Erikson was set to spread

around a bad version of the real story. Lopez was in deep with us from early on; an ex-DIA man who handled heavy stuff for us. Helluva an actor, too. He knew the wider picture and tipped us. Then he pretended to side with Erikson, and finally got him to put things off for a meeting with Lonsdorf. It could have been with anyone, but Lonsdorf was convenient. The point was just to sidetrack Erikson as long as necessary."

"Great move by Lopez," Washington said, looking remarkably relaxed as he sipped coffee. "Deserves a medal. But one question before Corky gets back to briefing Mr. Hochman here. What motivated Erikson to try to blow it all?"

McDouglas shrugged and said, "He tasted a few raw ingredients and guessed the wrong recipe. He was trying to do the patriotic thing. I can't blame him. It isn't easy to suddenly believe that you're treading treason's line. Better men than him have bolted, afraid for their country. Anyway, let's get on with this thing, okay?"

"Yeah, fill him in, Corky," Washington said. "Time's wasting. We've got a new nation to answer to. And an old one."

Corcoran nodded and tapped ash off his cigar and continued, "Okay, here's the black and white. You can see the colorized version when we show it to the nation, Erik. Basically, the U.S. was going downhill fast. Taxes and regulations were soaring and nobody knew how to stop 'em. Everyone — well, except for a few ex-Soviet-style dinosaurs — understood that it was out of control. But our so-called leaders of Congress couldn't shake out of their pork habits long enough to set a new course. The senators beholden to the grain subsidy lobbies were afraid of losing the farm vote. Those beholden to teachers unions were afraid of seeing them bolt. Those who owed favors to the entrenched, government-protected old-line industries didn't dare buck them. Everyone was afraid of offending *some* block of voters. They were triple-locked into their special-interest dens. In the abstract everyone wanted something better — deep inside themselves, they did — but they all preferred someone else to take the first step. The two views were irreconcilable. It was political gridlock. Our 'honorable' policymakers

254 ☆ E. G. ROSS

were collectively too stubborn, cowardly, or vindictive to get off the federal dime. Even the governors and the presidency were stuck."

"I sure was," Washington said. "Vice President Leininger tried to turn me, but I thought he was too radical. Too radical! And look what I ended up supporting!"

"Okay, we were all to blame to some degree," Corcoran went on, shaking his head. "Nobody claims it was a pretty picture. The country was caught in its own headlights—frozen in place and running over itself at the same time."

Washington winced at Corcoran's bag of mixed metaphors, but said, "Then something completely unexpected happened, something from outside D.C.—Oregon seceded. A whole state simply said, 'Go to hell!' Nobody'd expected that. Nobody'd thought of it. It wasn't in anyone's wildest dreams. An absolute non-option."

"Yet all of a sudden," Corcoran said, "Sam and I recognized an opportunity that had been placed in front of us like a chest of lost crown jewels. The answer'd been there in the Declaration of Independence all along. But people had concluded that it was quaint, outdated, and irrelevant. It was something that didn't, that *couldn't*, apply to the modern age."

"Oregon showed us, in undeniable Technicolor reality, that it did apply and could be done," McDouglas said quietly. He raised his eyes to the ceiling, reciting from memory, "In the course of human events, it becomes necessary for one people to dissolve the political bands which have connected them with another." He glanced at the others and said softy, "Those are the words, slightly paraphrased, written well over two centuries ago. Gentlemen, in the light of recent events, I finally see how far ahead of their times the U.S. Founders were."

Corcoran checked his watch, blew gray smoke at the ceiling, leaned forward, both elbows on knees, and said to Hochman, "The more Sam and I kicked it around—at first by encrypted video phone calls—the more we started to realize that this half-baked Oregon Rebellion could be used to remake the whole U.S. of A. However, the trick would be to encourage the rebellion's peaceful spread until more of the country was inside the rebel circle than out. Otherwise it would all come apart like a straw shack in a hurricane."

Hochman nodded. "So the main function of President Washington was to keep things calm until that happened?"

"Oh, more than that," Corcoran said. "Sam had to neutralize the U.S. armed forces using every trick in the book. That was clear from the get-go. That's when we took Grieve in, who, by the way, had come up with the same idea on his own."

McDouglas raised an eyebrow and said, "Well, close enough. I knew there were powerful commanders who felt as disgusted as I'd become about the course of the country. We talked. The upshot was, we kept the plot wrapped tight, limited to no more than a dozen people. That was almost too many. Everyone else who did our bidding never knew enough to blow a whistle. That's the deal with a good conspiracy. Sharply limited knowledge.

"Except this guy Erikson," Hochman noted.

"Erikson suspected enough to cause trouble, but not in time. Inconvenient small fish. You always face such possibilities. But we'd planned for it. We had people watching for the signs. Bill Brighton of CIA was in early. He did a lot of watchdogging and logistics. The kid's really come along since Big Three. He'll do fine."

"Okay, so now what?" Hochman asked, pulling out and lighting a cigarette. He needed something to do with his sweating hands.

"Now," Corcoran said, "we explain to the country — to the U.S. — that it can no longer function without the consent of the Oregon Confederation. We give the U.S. a choice. It accepts the conditions of the ROC — all the new freedoms, lower taxes and regulations, and the rest — or keeps going down the tubes. Most of the states have already joined us."

"Precisely," McDouglas said, grinning. "Exactly as it had to be. Now, it's mainly a matter of pointing out the obvious choice to a few dissenting states."

"I don't understand what happens to Oregon, though.

Does it rejoin the U.S. as a state. If the U.S. accepts ROC conditions, I mean?" Hochman asked.

Sam Washington had a mischievous smirk on his big face when he said, "All states will be free to join either ROC or the U.S., or both. Who knows? Maybe the U.S. and ROC will join each other!"

Hochman slowly started to smile.

"Now you're getting it, son," Corcoran said. "Just set aside all your preconceived civics class notions for a minute and think. If one government gets out of hand, the other will straighten it out. In effect, it's a new level of the old checks-and-balances system. The U.S. has always in fact had three governments. We just called them branches: judiciary, executive, legislative. More than that, really. Each state was partly autonomous and also had its divisions and subdivisions, jurisdictions, so forth, all the way down to local school boards. Including their own state armies."

"Look," Washington picked it up, "having both ROC and U.S. national governments will be like having a choice of two stores to shop in. If one starts raising prices unreasonably—in this case, the price of government—then the people can ignore it and shop at the other. Pretty simple."

Hochman put both hands to his eyes and asked, "What if war breaks out between the two?"

"Do people let Wal-Mart go to war with Sears?"

"Well, that's true, but department stores don't have nuclear arsenals."

"No, but they've got armed security forces. They don't attack each other. Anyway, was there a real war between ROC and the U.S.? Did the people show signs of supporting one?"

"Oregonians were sure willing to fight!"

"But the rest of the nation didn't see any point to attacking them, did they? There was no rational self-interest to be had. So, the U.S. states coasted along, watching the ROC states free themselves one after another, thinking about it, gradually seeing the advantages of joining Oregon's maximum liberty system. The people weren't idiots. Like people throughout history, they just wanted to be left alone as much as possible. Oregon was showing them how to get there and we pushed the process along behind the scenes."

"There was a bloody civil war once in the U.S. What about that? Weren't you worried?"

"Look," Corcoran said. "The worst is always *possible*. We're trying to set up a system that simply makes it less *likely*. We're not talking utopia. Yeah, a civil war could happen. But it could have happened at anytime in the last hundred-fifty years. However, consider this. Is a civil war more likely if people have less freedom of choice about their government—or if they have more choice? Which way gives people a more peaceful alternative? Which way gives an extra incentive to avoid shooting? Which do you suppose is riskier—a wider array of liberty, or a smaller array?"

"The way with more choice," Hochman said before he could think of a counter-argument.

"Right!" Washington said, slapping his hands on his thighs and rising. "Corky, we've gotta cut this short. It's almost time to tell the country—or should I say countries?—about what's been going on."

Corcoran raised his coffee in a toast: "To them both. May they keep each other free."

McDouglas and Washington raised their cups and looked pointedly at Hochman. After a moment, he smiled and did the same, joining the toast.

Later that night, Corcoran and Sparky Katz were sharing a private dinner in her studio. A full moon shone through the skylights. Two candles on the table provided the only other illumination. She had made the dinner. They had dressed formally—at his request.

"You've been grinning from ear to ear all evening," Katz said, sipping her red Zinfandel, a Secret House vintage from Veneta, Oregon.

He nodded and placed a small box on the table. It was wrapped in white paper and a green bow. Green was Katz's favorite color.

Katz put down her wine. Her face grew somber.

"Is that what I think it is?" she asked.

"One way to find out," Corcoran said, his eyes dancing.

"Be careful what you ask for," she whispered, reaching for the package.

She tore off the ribbon and paper and held up a small, leather-covered black snap box.

She took a deep breath, glanced at Corcoran, and slowly lifted the lid.

A gold ring with two small emeralds nestled cozily in the black velvet.

She closed her eyes for a moment.

"Will you?" he asked.

"Yes," she said, looking into his eyes.

"Thought so," he said, holding up his wine glass

"And your clue was what?" she asked, clinking his glass with hers.

Two perfect tears ran down her face.

Corcoran couldn't stop grinning.

"Now we can stop skulking around like the guilty people we aren't," he said.

"And never were," she said.

Chapter 39

"Dragon Slayer"

Two weeks before the Burner Boys revealed their existence to Hochman and the nation, a radically different sort of revelation had taken place in the bowels of the Shang Empire.

In his secret war against The Shang, the old Maoist had long sought to penetrate what was known in the Chinese press as the "Holy Journal." This was the Shang's daily diary of state, dictated nightly to a loyal crew of human transcribers. Such a method, The Shang felt, better suited his exalted status than crudely typing or speaking into lowly transcription computers. There was more satisfaction issuing orders to people than to machines. The Shang had often told the Chinese press how he "hoped" the Holy Journal would one day be published as a book, a kind of Bible of statecraft. In that way, future leaders would be able to rule with at least a faded imitation of The Shang's eternal wisdom.

However, the diaries contained more than what was admitted, more than general theories of politics. As the Maoist discovered, they also detailed many of The Shang's plans for the nation, his estimates of key personnel, his thoughts on crucial foreign intelligence issues, and his recollections of deals with other heads of state. The old man thought these inclusions in the journal—where determined eyes could eventually pry—showed incredible arrogance and carelessness by The

Shang. The action exposed The Shang's lack of experience and fueled the Maoist's belief that much of the Emperor's rise was due to the good fortune of unique circumstances. Sometimes history spat out very young leaders this way. A few, such as Alexander the Great, went on to rare glory. The Maoist was determined to make sure that The Shang did not.

That The Shang found it necessary to write things down was proof that he was far from omniscient or immortal; not that the Maoist had ever believed either. But many did, and the time would come to expose the fraud. Another indication was the implication that the "eternal" Shang would himself someday die—otherwise, why speak of "future leaders"? Surely The Shang would not abdicate the throne!

The Maoist had pursued various means to get a glimpse of the Holy Journal. Among his approaches was to find a willing tongue in The Shang's executive office complex. All empires, no matter how divine they allegedly are, require a hive of workers to gather, collate, and file—workers who must be trusted with the highest of state secrets. Like workers everywhere, no matter how carefully screened, some are always weaker than others. The Maoist had looked for a man of vulnerable character who also had at least partial access to the Holy Journal.

He found what he was looking for in the form of a young transcriber. Not only did the youth have regular and astonishingly specific access to the journal, but he had a monumental vice, one which was among the oldest and simplest in China: addiction to opium. Much of his meager monthly salary went toward the drug. Eschewing the more modern pleasures of the Wire and genetically engineered pleasure drugs, he smoked opium religiously—but only after work. He thus preserved a reasonably clear head for his time on the job and prevented his vice from easily being discovered. Were it found out, he would surely be fired; probably executed.

The Maoist's uncovering of this highly placed addict was not accidental. He had agents among the opium dealers who regularly followed likely looking prospects after they made buys, prying into their backgrounds, setting up possible blackmail opportunities. The agents found that the transcriber's income had recently fallen well below his level of addiction. Or rather, his addiction had risen beyond his means. The Maoist concluded that the man was not only a weak individual, but an increasingly desperate one. Opium was speaking louder than fear of the boy-god Emperor.

Under the circumstances, it had been a simple thing to make a deal with the addict. It was good that the Maoist had. It turned out that the transcriber had a memory for detail as profuse as the old man's underground sources of opium — sources which he and his Communist comrades had long used to pad their private Geneva and Singapore bank accounts and to effect various forms of bribery and blackmail.

A particularly intriguing detail from the holy diary was that The Shang had, throughout the rebellion of Oregon, been in clandestine contact with both the President of the United States and the President of the Republic of Oregon. Both Americans had gone to extraordinary lengths to make matters appear otherwise, of course. They had deceived not only their populace, but some of their highest staff members. The Shang for his part had played the enemy, going so far as to permit the "unauthorized" ferrying of small amounts of military equipment to a dissident group on the south coast of Oregon, allowing the Oregonians to use Shang markings for their mock cruise missile attack, and then acting unconvincingly outraged at both incidents. This made the danger of a Shang threat look more real to the two presidents' advisors and the American people.

The Shang had also successfully hinted that he might use military force to reincorporate the Republic of Taiwan. This he had no intention of doing, for the prosperous republic was worth far more in trade than as booty. But the ruse had further supported Corcoran's carefully painted picture — to some of his own advisors — of The Shang as a ruthless intimidator. Among other things, it had given the Oregon president an excuse to be a Samaritan by suggesting Taiwan might join the Oregon federation — the real point of which was to secure billions of investment dollars from the island nation's overflowing savings accounts.

In exchange for this and other cooperation, the Americans had promised The Shang only one thing: for a period of twenty years, they would not initiate any sort of attack on the Shang Empire—as long as the Shang refrained equally from attacking America. If the Shang broke the agreement, the Americans promised that their war technology would make him the first to die. Reading between the lines of what the transcriber related, it was clear to the old Maoist that the "cowboys" had somehow proven this point to The Shang. The proof had involved something called the Plate. The transcriber said that The Shang had barely mentioned it, and what exactly it meant was unknown. But to the Maoist, that wasn't the issue. The specific nature of the proof was obviously so shocking or embarrassing to The Shang that he had left it out of his journal. It was The Shang's psychological response that intrigued the old man.

He had laughed deeply. The Shang seriously feared the Americans. It was quite the opposite of the unflappable, ultraconfident image the Emperor so successfully projected to the world and even to his inner circle. Looking back, it made sense. The Shang was constantly talking about the Americans, perfecting their game of poker, examining their culture, their military encounters, their heritage—in short, studying the enemy.

How utterly boyish, the Maoist had thought, to be frightened of those one looks up to, yet never admit it.

The Maoist felt there was virtually no chance that the Americans would attack China. They were sobered by China's huge nuclear arsenal—as well as the antimatter guns it had presumably taken over in conquering Russia. The Americans were forever worried about being swallowed by the "yellow hordes." Hadn't their own President Truman, not known for cowardice, feared becoming mired in China, even firing his best general to avoid it during the Korean War? And what had the Americans done to prevent China from swallowing Russia at the end of the Third World War? Exactly nothing.

After a long evening spent with the transcriber, the Maoist's confidence had soared, like a spring trickle turning to a flood. He hadn't felt such a surge of sureness in himself for decades. There was no doubt about it; he had enough to bring down The Shang. But first he would have to create chaos in China. Chaos was the ice on which he would skate to power. It would be easy. He would trick the Americans into believing they'd been *really* attacked by The Shang. It could be done in a way that would also allow China to deny it, just in case the Americans entertained any sudden silliness about massive retaliation. The trick would have to be severe enough to provoke them into killing The Shang, if they actually had the means. But no matter. That wasn't crucial. The crucial point was that The Shang would *believe* they had such means. His fear would be enough to bring him down—with a well-timed shove from the Maoist and his friends.

Chapter 40

"Crazy Cruise"

Three days before the ROC and U.S. Presidents' joint press conference, another would-be future president was entering a well-lit warehouse on the southern coast of Oregon. Weeks before, Bard Candor had decided that the Oregon Confederation had gone too far. There were many things to which he objected, but most of all he hated seeing his beloved state sold off to foreigners. Particularly repulsive to him were those "little yeller fellers." He could see, even if Oregon's leaders could not, that beneath their politeness lurked sinister hearts and minds. Of course, Candor also felt that there were too many Latinos, blacks, and other un-Oregon-types with suitcases full of money and no understanding that his land was never meant for them.

Candor didn't regard himself as a racist. He had been genuinely shocked when Corcoran had made the accusation. Other races were fine. No problem—as long as they stayed out of Oregon's destiny. The fact that people of many races had been involved in the settlement of Oregon almost from the beginning did not count, for Candor thought of himself as a selective preservationist. He was a man dedicated to preserving the heritage bestowed by those original settlers of Oregon of whom Candor himself personally approved. Not the Indians (he refused to call them Native Americans); in his mind they were merely another gang of stumbling primitives. Never mind that the Father of Oregon's wife was Marguerite Wadin McKay McLoughlin, an Indian *and* an outsider from the vicinity of Lake Superior. One could always find exceptions to any rule. Candor meant — and there was no other way to say it — the better *white* men and women who had braved the Oregon trail and made this beautiful land into something fit for civilized living. He also thought that this naturally excluded most Californians. After all, although they were mainly Caucasians, had they been able to read the signs directing them north, they'd never have turned off the Oregon Trail south to California, would they? In his mind, the Californians obviously derived from stock of inferior mentality.

Now, in the name of unbridled economics and quick prosperity, Oregon's leaders had lost sight of their hallowed history. In Candor's view, Oregon would soon not be Oregon anymore. Oregon's leaders had betrayed the state's unique heritage of ethnic underpinnings.

Unfortunately, what was happening was beyond rational control. Candor knew it, as any perceptive leader should. And when the rational was not possible, then the irrational must be tried — at least, the irrational as men of smaller vision would see things. Candor knew that he was a man of broad and clear vision, a man with the outlook that only the pursuit of noble leadership could evoke. He was not bound by common conceptions. He was "a big picture" man.

As he entered the warehouse to the cheers of his followers, he was flanked by loyal friends. He had been told by a source in Salem that Corcoran had a spy in his midst. Who knew what such a man might do to disrupt Candor's plans? It could not be allowed. So he had hand-picked his guards and closest advisors. Naturally, he'd been forced to cull out several men on hunches alone. They were royally angry, and he almost sympathized with them. After all, he'd known some of them a long time. But on the trail to glory, one couldn't take chances. There had been black marks about each of those men. One had a wife who looked suspiciously Oriental. Probably a good man at heart, but clearly weak in his appetites. Another's daughter had married into a Mexican family in San Diego. Ties like that could stain a fellow's judgment if push came to shove. Then there was the fellow whose son several years ago had protested U.S. Selective Service registration at that nest of perverts and turncoats in Eugene, the University of Oregon. Who knew what corruption unknowingly seeped back into a father from a son like that?

As he mounted the podium and raised his hands to the applause, he knew that he'd been right. Stalin had said it best: you can't make omelets without breaking eggs. The first eggs to break were often those closest to the frying pan. True leaders, if they were to fulfill their destiny, must be unafraid of harsh steps to preserve their purity of purpose in its many forms—some of which only they, by their naturally superior insight, were qualified to grasp.

He scanned the crowd, nodding and smiling to the whistles and stomps and friendly hoots. These were his people, his kind. Good old boys; hard workers; men who knew who belonged and who didn't belong. He knew that they were not unique to the Oregon Coast. In every town and city he'd be able to find them. His allies were everywhere, only waiting for his enlightened leadership to bring them out of their slumber and reclaim what was theirs.

"My friends!" he shouted. "My friends!"

The noise grew louder. Candor grinned, basking in it for a few moments. Then he waved for silence and when he got it said, "Tonight is a great night. Tonight I speak to you of a counter-revolution to take Oregon back for Oregonians!"

The crowd roared.

Candor saw signs in the crowd.

One read, "We shoot slant-eyes!"

Another, "Stick a Spic for Oregon!"

And another, "I love coon hunts!"

Crude, of course, but Candor knew that the common people must have their outlets. Their strong passions were valuable. He could channel their emotions into useful endeavors. He'd spent years doing it already. It was the only reason the warehouse was full this night. He conservatively guessed that he had many thousands of loyal followers in the state. It was plenty. Hadn't the Bolsheviks taken over the Russian government with only a few *hundred* men? And old Russia had been a far bigger country than Oregon, yes siree!

He motioned for quiet again and said, "Folks, I've promised you a lot. And so far, I haven't been able to deliver much."

Vehement disagreement arose from the crowd.

"No, no, it's true," Candor insisted, almost in a confessing tone, shaking his head. Lowering his voice to a near whisper, he said into the microphone, "But no more. No more. The Oregon-for-Oregonians movement has a new and formidable weapon. I've asked you here tonight so that you can see it for yourself. I direct your attention to the platform behind me."

Someone flipped on a row of lights and illuminated a heretofore obscure object covered by a sheet of black canvas. Under the sheet lay what looked like a fifteen-foot length of large sewer pipe. The crowd shifted uncertainly.

Candor strode proudly to the object, grabbed the canvas by a corner and jerked it to the floor in a single motion. The crowd gasped.

"Oh, yes!" Candor said. "It's exactly what it looks like. This, my loyal friends, is a genuine, fly-up-their-pants cruise missile! And unless they come around to our way of thinking, we're gonna fly it right at those thieves in Salem who are stealing our state!"

His audience screamed in glee.

"You bet! You bet!" Candor shouted. "But it's more than that. Because it's also equipped with a living, breathing, five-kiloton atomic warhead. This baby has enough nuclear oomph to wipe out Corcoran and his little band of traitors for good. And when it's done, we'll run the state like it should be run — by the right people, the people who now have *might* on their side. My friends, we're takin' Oregon back!"

The audience bellowed agreement. After calming them, Candor said, "Now I don't know when we'll have to use this little device. Let's hope the mere threat will make Corcoran see sense. We don't want to hurt more innocent people in Salem than we have to."

Leveling his eyes at his followers he added urgently, "But if we have to, we will! It's them or us!"

This time he let the stomping and cheering continue as he wandered into the crowd. While he shook hands and let people slap him on the back, a crew of grim men silently covered the missile, hitched its six-wheeled firing ramp to a pick-up truck, and moved it out of the warehouse under heavy guard. To the few in the crowd who noticed the activity, Candor simply told them that the missile was being taken to a "safer location."

The most difficult spy to detect is the one who converts himself. He has all the advantages, chief among them, a long history with the people against whom he turns. He knows them and they think they know him. There is no reason to suspect him and that gives him tremendous leeway.

Carlton Campeneau was such a man.

He'd lived in Coos Bay all his life, working mainly in the timber industry and later as a longshoreman loading the logs that he'd once helped cut. When fewer Oregon mills could afford world market prices, many of the logs went overseas through the Port of Coos Bay. It had kept the worst of the recession from Campeneau's door. He could see, with his own eyes, that were it not for "the little yeller fellers" who purchased Oregon's logs, his longshoreman's job would have long ago been shoreless. He'd raised five kids and put three of them through college. He had a nice house and garden, his wife was becoming a successful artist, and they had two fairly new cars and a small, used, deep-sea fishing boat. It was a good life, far better than his immigrant father had had before moving his family from Louisiana to Oregon's coast decades earlier.

Campeneau had attended several of Candor's rallies, mostly out of curiosity. Candor had, all in all, been a good man in Salem. Campeneau had voted for him six times. But the man's latest rantings didn't cut it. Campeneau could not bring himself to hate the foreigners who had helped make his life. Nor could he find it in himself to hate President Corcoran.

Campeneau's conditions had improved with Corcoran's lower taxes and less restrictive trade policies. More logs than ever were being shipped through the port. He'd gotten two raises in the last three months alone. Campeneau had been astonished by Candor's unveiling of the cruise missile. Up until then, he'd regarded Candor's xenophobic ravings as harmless smoke-blowing by a politician whom time was passing by. After all, until this night, Candor's rallies had tended to be little more than barbecue and beer parties preceded by a short sermon from Candor. A small price to pay for a good time. Many of Campeneau's buddies went to the monthly warehouse meetings. He figured that he didn't have to particularly like Candor to enjoy food and drink with friends. But when he watched Candor casually talking of nuking fellow Oregonians, including the man who'd almost single-handedly pulled Oregon and the U.S. out of deep recession, Campeneau had felt both fright and fury. Maybe no one else saw it—or if they did, wouldn't say so—but it was clear to him that Candor was off his rocker. Campeneau thought the man was quite capable of carrying out his threats. The smoke-blowing was about to turn into genuine fire-breathing.

Campeneau hoped the cruise missile was merely a joke, some kind of mock-up stunt. But out of the corner of his eye, he'd watched the way Candor's men had removed it. They'd been constantly wary, extremely careful—and fully armed. It didn't look like a joke. Campeneau decided there was no point in taking chances. The stakes were too high for a reasonable citizen to remain silent. From his home later that night, the longshoreman dialed an old fishing buddy up in Springfield.

Chapter 41

"The Wider Imperatives"

The trick," Candor told his small group of advisors, "will be to find the best target at the best moment."

As they nodded, Candor turned to the Oriental man sitting slightly apart from the others. A taciturn representative of The Shang, the man was an expert at operating the missile which the Empire had so generously and unexpectedly provided Candor and his rebels. Candor's boys clearly didn't appreciate the contradiction of having to depend on a slant-eye. He was the sort of person they wanted to keep out. But they had behaved themselves after Candor sternly pointed out that in order to fight devils, one often had to make short-term, pragmatic deals with them.

"Mr. Xiao," Candor said—pronouncing the name "shoe" instead of "zhow"—"how quickly can you input the coordinates into that thing after we pick a target?"

Xiao shrugged. His English was perfect, although with a stiff British accent.

"Under an hour; perhaps a good deal less," he said. "It's rather a primitive model and a bit of a chore to calibrate both the target location and—"

"Yeah, yeah, okay," Candor said, moving a hand sharply through the air, cutting off the Oriental. "That's all I need to know." Candor forced himself to smile. "I'm sure you know your work as well as I know mine. I don't have time to learn missiles and you don't have time to learn politics."

Xiao grunted and inclined his head slightly. He had been ordered to cooperate with this filthy fish at all costs. As far as Xiao knew, he was carrying out the wishes of The Shang. But unknown to Xiao, his boss, an Imperial submarine commander, was a loyal friend of the Maoist. This was purely their mission, not The Shang's. The commander had transferred the ground-launchable missile from a submarine to an isolated beach south of Coos Bay a few nights earlier. He had ordered Xiao to stay with Candor and follow his orders concerning the missile—including arming and firing it. Xiao was uncomfortable with Candor, but not with his mission. He was true to the boy-god and if the Emperor wanted this, there was doubtless a reason which mere mortals could not fathom.

Candor turned back to his men and said, "Now naturally there's no *if* about torching this baby off." He pointed at the sinister form parked in the corner of the deserted seafood cannery. "It's only a question of when. First, in order to get the missile at all, we had to promise The Shang crowd that it would be used. For some reason, the Empire wants everyone to know that it supplied this firepower—after the fact, naturally. I don't know the ins and outs of The Shang's thinking, but then, we don't have to. He's got his problems, we've got ours."

A skinny man with scraggly hair asked, "How's anybody gonna know it was a Shang missile? Not exactly gonna read the serial number after it blows to atoms!"

Xiao snapped an answer without being asked. Candor frowned, but let him speak.

"The blast is a special shaped charge which only the Shang Empire builds," Xiao explained. "American intelligence will recognize its characteristics, I assure you."

"By the way, more about that shaped charge stuff later," Candor said. "As to the second reason why we have to fire the missile, all of us here know that Corky isn't going to go down on mere threats. My yak about issuing a warning to him was pretzels for the beer heads in the warehouse—bless their hard-working little white hearts."

Several of his inner group chuckled.

Xiao looked away contemptuously. He would be glad when he could return to a civilized land where one did not have to gaze at the pasty skin of these American worms. Candor smiled to himself and thought that the sooner he was done with that Oriental slit-peeper, the better.

Aloud, he continued, "Their motives are in the right place, but our common followers don't have the means to see the wider imperatives of the situation. That's why we're leaders and they aren't. Whatever else we think of the S.O.B., Corky's the fighting type. So he has to be taken out. Hopefully, we can wipe up most of the low-brains close to him, too. That's the tricky part. Corky's advisors are like bees these days, in an out of the hive all the time, meddling in everything."

Candor lit a cigarette and checked a small notepad.

"Now, logistics," he said, exhaling smoke in the general direction of Xiao. "The missile covers ten miles a minute. That means once it's targeted, it'll take about ten minutes to get from here to Salem; not even twice that to Portland. If Mr. Xiao can get it targeted in, say, thirty-five or forty minutes, then we can respond to opportunity, from decision to blast, in an hour."

One man whistled and asked, "That's not bad, but how do we know when to start?"

"Taken care of," Candor answered briskly. He was feeling good, invigorated, alive. So this was what it meant to be a leader with real power!

Candor ticked points off on his fingers: "As you know, we've got several of our younger representatives serving in the new government. They're going to keep an eye on executive schedules and try to give us everything they can. However, I'm not a guy who believes in waiting around forever. I want to get on with it. Oregon's careening down the river too fast. If we can grab the helm quickly, there's a fine chance that we can steer the whole U.S.A. away from all this laissez-faire crap. Cut off the head and the body falls into our lap. So to speak."

He grinned. His men dutifully did the same.

"And then *we're* the head," a burly fellow said.

"You got it. For days, we've been infiltrating armed men into both Salem and Portland. Those are the two burgs where most government business is done. I'd guess that there's a 90% chance that one of them will be where we can get the whole corrupt Corcoran court at once."

"You guess?" someone said. "Hell, it's a *nuke!*"

Candor shook his head and explained, "Actually, the serious blast damage will be limited to about 100 square blocks around the capital complex; about ten blocks to a side. It's called a pure fusion bomb, a new type. Very small and efficient and controllable. Even so, quite a few people might survive near ground zero, because the capital complex is crisscrossed with underground passages between buildings. That means we'll have to move our men in on the ground to mop up any important people who shouldn't have survived—and secure the city. We'll set up our own temporary government, probably to the west in some of the downtown commercial office buildings. The prevailing winds this time of year tend to be from the west. They'll keep the little bit of fallout—and there's virtually none from one of these new bombs—from our headquarters area. Same deal for Portland, if that should be the target. But if the winds shift, we'll adjust accordingly."

He paused to grin reassuringly. "Don't worry, fellas, we've got contingency plans for this whole operation."

"Uh, what about ground radiation in the mop-up area under the blast?" the skinny man asked. "And how about ROC armed forces? You haven't mentioned them."

"As I said, not enough radiation to worry about with a pure fusion bomb. Anyway, given how fast we plan to be in and out of the central target we wouldn't pick up many rads even if the radiation was pretty hot. As to ROC forces, they'll be too stunned to organize in time. We'll be in control before they know what hit 'em. It's going to be a surprise attack that goes down in history—and we'll all be a part of it. We'll all be in the schoolbooks, fellas!"

"I would've thought a five kiloton warhead would do

more damage than what you've mentioned," a sallow man with a thin mustache said.

Xiao snorted softly.

Candor frowned but ignored him and said, "Although the missile itself isn't the latest technology, the bomb is. As I said before, it's a special shaped charge. It'll be ignited from about 2,000 feet and spray most of its energy in a cone downward toward the target. Little damage outside that cone. A ground blast would be too limited and an ordinary air blast would spread the effects wider than we want. We want to rule, not ruin. With the shaped charge, useless damage will be minimal, but enough for the job. I got that about right, Xiao?"

The Chinaman nodded stoically.

"So now we wait," Candor said, stubbing out his cigarette and grinding it with his heel. "That's the game. But knowing how things work in Corky's circle, we'll get our opportunity at anytime. The first decent chance, we'll move the missile out the back door and light the fuse. But we're not moving it before then because keeping it here lets Mr. Xiao line up more of his magic launch tricks beforehand. Otherwise, I guess, it would take a lot longer." He glanced at The Shang's man for confirmation.

Xiao nodded curtly. Technical illiterates, he thought. It's no wonder The Shang will soon rule the world.

"Okay," Candor said. "Security's good here, so we should be fine in the meantime. We've got fifty men in and around this old cannery and it's out of the way enough that nobody's likely to come snooping. Besides, it'd take a small army to bust through in time to stop us."

He paused a moment. "You all with me? Anybody getting yellow feet?"

Xiao winced.

Several of the men snickered at the missile expert's pained expression. Candor smirked, raised his right fist and held it over his head and boomed, "Oregon for Oregonians!"

His men raised their fists and repeated the slogan.

Chapter 42

"Second Thoughts"

Carlton Campeneau hung up and cursed. It was the third time in two days that he'd called, leaving messages. Once again his friend Larry Rigg hadn't answered. Campeneau sighed. Well, it wasn't easy getting hold of Larry lately. His job heading the Springfield Independent Militia took a lot of time. He was constantly traveling. He could be almost anywhere in the state, or even out of state. The SIM had gone on joint exercises with militias of northern California, Southern Washington, Idaho, Montana, perhaps others of which Campeneau wasn't aware.

The volunteer militia concept had become increasingly popular with surrounding states, both as a way of raising preparedness and of cutting state defense budgets. Whereas they used to be regarded as right wing gun-nut clubs, now everybody wanted to know how militias worked. Rigg, as head of one of the older ones, was training fledgling outfits. The SIM had become a model unit and it supported itself by contracting out services whenever it was unobligated to work for the Republic of Oregon. It did so largely by charging consulting fees on a wide range of aspects of training: gun safety; tactical maneuvers; discipline; organization; survival; even the business end of things, including how to manage mailing lists, prepare field manuals, keep books, and so on. All this ran through

Campeneau's head, but assuredly did not help him with his present problem.

He left his workshop garage where he'd been puttering and went into the house for a beer. It was seven in the evening. His wife was shopping and the two remaining children, both in high school, were off with dates. He had the place to himself. He took his fresh beer back to the garage and plopped into the worn-out recliner that his wife refused to let him keep in the house. He called it his "thinking chair." As far as he was concerned, if his faithful, favorite chair was exiled to the garage, then so was serious thinking.

He took a long swig of brew and then went over his present problem one more time. The crux of the matter was that he didn't know whom to call *except* Larry Rigg. Campeneau's longshoreman's work hadn't given him many opportunities to get to know important people. Thus, although he'd thought about calling the president's office, he was sure he'd be brushed off as some kind of vegetable patty from the boondocks. After all, who was going to believe a log loader who claimed that the former State of Oregon House Speaker was planning to nuke the capitol of his own country?

That was his first problem. There was something else. The more he thought about Candor's supposed missile, the more he wondered if it really was one. This doubt had put a damper on his desire to drive up to Salem yelling for everyone to duck because a tiny Oregon town was suddenly a hostile power about to belch atoms at thousands of people. He chuckled to himself and swallowed more beer. It sounded sillier all the time.

What had spurred his new doubt was the fact that Candor had so openly advertised—to several hundred people in the warehouse—that he possessed the missile. Candor shouldn't be that stupid. Couldn't be. Silly, a blowhard, kooky, maybe even dangerous in some ways, okay. But not an idiot. Not a mass murderer.

Anyway, even if Candor had slipped a wheel bearing, surely others at the beer bash had entertained reservations about the missile idea. Surely somebody would say something about the missile and word would reach Corcoran's people. On the other hand, there may not have been any doubters or worriers like Campeneau. Candor didn't exactly draw the critical intellectual types to his side. Second, if anyone else felt as Campeneau, he could be just as alone and unsure what to do, especially if he had enough brains to realize that the story sounded so nutty that it would be like trying to convince the government that a full-blown flying saucer was about to land on the capitol lawn.

He looked at the wall phone above his workbench. Still . . . Then, vividly, he remembered the looks on the faces of those grim men who'd moved the missile. Maybe the missile was a prop or ploy or joke. But those good ol' boys sure hadn't acted like it was. They'd acted like men assigned the job of detaching a hornet's nest from a post with their bare hands.

He reached for the phone again.

"Yeah?" came a tired voice on the third ring.

Campeneau let out a long sigh and asked, "Larry, thank God! It's Carlton, over at the bay."

"Hey! How's the fishing these days?"

"Don't know. Haven't been out for a couple weeks. Listen, I've got a wild-ass story to pass on. It might sound as loony as a flyin' hippo, but I've gotta get it off my chest."

"You're no loon, buddy. I'm all ears. Shoot."

After he told Rigg about the missile, the militia man said nothing for several seconds.

"Well," Campeneau asked, "how many hands short of a clock am I?"

"I don't take it that way. Between you and me, the scuttlebutt is that Candor is under watch—on presidential orders. Don't forget that my second-in-command is the defense chief's brother. I hear things. Candor's a truck without brakes rolling downhill. He could end up almost anywhere. He probably *is* as screwy as you thought he was in the warehouse that night. Where's this thing he calls a missile? Where's he got it parked?"

"Don't know. Could be anywhere. Up in the woods, in an abandoned building, hidden along the beach somewhere.

Shoot, it's small enough, it could be in someone's garage. Might not even be in town anymore."

"Is Candor?"

"Yeah, I think so. Sticking close to home."

"Then the missile is probably there, too. From what Hochman says about Candor, my guess is that he'd probably want to put the match to that firecracker himself. He'd get off on it. Does the bastard own any property?"

Campeneau chuckled. "*Does* he? Man, the guy's a walking real estate office. Houses, commercial buildings, land. According to what a pal of mine in the biz says, his specialty is buying run-down places and fixing them up or waiting for growth of the city to run up their values. With a little help from his friends on the zoning boards. Or so the rumors say."

"Think your pal could get a list of what Candor owns?"

"Probably. But it might take a day or so."

"Get it sooner," Rigg said, easing off the couch where he'd intended to catch a couple hours sleep. "It's likely that Candor's using a place he owns to hide the sucker. He's a controller, and he'd feel most in control on his own property."

"Will do."

"Good. Meanwhile, I'm putting a few of our SIM men into motion on my own authority. I've got a lot of leeway to move my militia around the state. Fortunately, we're not engaged anywhere at the moment. I'll pass word to Hochman's office that we're taking SIM down your way, although I'm going to hold off saying exactly why. I'd be in deep dung if I panicked the capital on this without checking it out. Candor could be running a fancy political bluff to try to embarrass the Oregon government. I could just see him faking a missile, letting Salem get all worked up, then denying the whole thing and exposing Corky as a paranoid. From what I hear, it'd be his style. Besides, Corky's got enough on his mind. He just told everybody he's getting married. Damned if I'm going to be the man to spoil the president's honeymoon."

Campeneau chuckled. "Yeah, he might remember you awhile for that."

"Okay, I'll probably bring about fifty troops."

"I thought your outfit was up to nearly 300 these days."

"It is, but too big a posse raises too much dust. I'll say it's for recon exercises. We do a lot of those on the coast these days. Don't want to alarm anyone by prematurely screaming about nukes. Not 'til we're sure. Anyway, even if Candor has a real missile, it's unlikely that he's got a nuke aboard."

"Well, he said he did, Larry."

"I know, but he's a practiced liar. A guy like him has to be. Doesn't necessarily mean anything. It might be a paper mock-up. Or if it's real, he might have something else mated to that thing."

"But I thought—"

"What? That all cruise missiles carry nukes? Most don't."

"Been reading too many comic books, I guess," Campeneau said sheepishly.

"If he's got anything, it's more likely some kind of conventional warhead, or at worse, a chemical weapon, a so-called 'poor man's nuke.'"

"Hmph. All this time I just assumed he'd told the whole truth, that he had an atomic stinger on that friggin' wasp."

"Well, maybe it's best you did think so. Otherwise maybe you wouldn't have felt compelled to call. At the very least, it's worth checking out."

Campeneau thought about it a second and said, "I would've called anyway. He was talking about killing some darned fine people."

"Right. I'll be bringing the boys over starting tomorrow morning over a period of several hours. Make it look like we're coming to fish. I've got guys who could sneak into the Queen of England's bedroom and steal her toilet lid. Got some interesting new equipment I've been itching to try out, too. We'll check out Candor's property from your list. Probably have to wait until dark tomorrow to do it, though. Safer."

"Uh, Larry?"

"Yeah?"

"What if that missile isn't here and *does* have a nuke on

it? Then what do we do?"

"That'd be worrisome. But one step at a time, okay? See you tomorrow."

Campeneau hung up and immediately dialed his friend in real estate. He was luckier than he'd been with Rigg. His friend was home. Campeneau gave what he thought was a rather lame excuse about helping a reporter who was investigating Candor's financial dealings. The friend agreed to provide the list. He was an honest agent and had heard lots of stories about Candor getting special official consideration on the sly. Maybe it was true, maybe not, but the real estate agent had ample experience with Candor's xenophobia and disliked the man intensely. Bad for local business. If he could help a reporter get the goods on Candor's illicit connections, he was all for it.

Chapter 43

"Seen This Puddle Before"

It was almost midnight and Corporal Karl Hochman looked disgustedly toward the beach and shivered, although it was not cold. Ocean waves were washing ashore gently in the soft moonlight. To most people, it would have been a beautiful evening. He spat into the sand at his feet and let go of a few, choice swearwords.

"Seems I've seen this puddle before," he muttered to Sergeant Larry Rigg.

Both men were partially hidden behind salal brush on a remote rise overlooking the sea not far outside Coos Bay.

Rigg raised the corner of his mouth in a half-smile as he peered to the south through night-vision glasses. He was focusing across a quarter-mile of driftwood-littered beach toward a rambling, modern split-level home. The home's stats said it contained at least four-thousand square feet. It was currently unoccupied. It was owned by Bard Candor. Its dimensions made it a good candidate for hiding a cruise missile.

"Well?" Hochman asked impatiently, wishing he could light a cigarette but knowing it might be seen if he did.

"Not a thing," Rigg said. "If it's stored there, surely there'd be some guard activity. At least perimeter patrols. Something. But it's deader than I-5 roadkill."

"Maybe that's what he'd *think* we'd think. Maybe he's

left it there by its lonesome to throw snoopers off."

Rigg asked, "If it were your missile, would *you* leave it unguarded?"

Hochman kicked a root in the sand and said, "Naw. Prob'ly not."

Rigg lowered the glasses and let them hang by the strap around his neck. He scratched at the itchy stubble on his chin as he thought.

"Well," he said, "let's check it out anyway. But to me it looks like we underestimated Candor. I'm thinking that he knows it would be too obvious to store the missile on anything he owned."

Rigg glanced at his watch. "Corporal, get on the horn and touch bases with the other teams."

Karl Hochman did so. They'd found nothing. This location was the last on the list. None of the dozen or so properties suggested by Campeneau's friend had contained a missile or anything remotely suspicious. Rigg was frustrated. He had brought forty-nine SIM men, dividing them into seven teams of seven. The teams were small enough to be mobile, yet big enough to handle a fair amount of trouble if they couldn't avoid it. He and Karl were in Team One.

Rigg spoke into the ultrawideband radio that all his men were now equipped with. Tiny and utterly untappable with a respectable range, the radios were a unique product of one of Oregon's own small firms that once did special work for the U.S. Defense Department. Rigg considered the high-tech jobs a significant advance for SIM's tactical capabilities. The radios were digitally encrypted, of course. That let each team use a simple code. Team One, code one; Team Two, code two; etc. The codes would jump frequencies at random intervals. Their coordinated computers kept track of everything automatically. Rigg didn't understand it except in principle, but the upshot was that interception was thought to be possible only to God.

Rigg ordered the other five members of Team One into action. They'd surrounded the house thirty minutes earlier. They now slipped in for a closer look.

Watching through their glasses, Rigg and Hochman spotted only brief movements of shadow. An ordinary observer would've seen nothing of Team One, even if he'd known what to look for. The men were the best, a big change from some of the bumbling recruits of not so long ago. The months had been crammed with action for Rigg's militia, speeding by like telephone poles at two-hundred miles per hour. Paradoxically, the months also seemed like years. So much had happened.

In less than ten minutes, Team One entered the house and swept it. Abandoned. No missile. Rigg ordered the men to rejoin him and Hochman. Hochman finally got to light a cigarette. Four others lit up, too. With the advent of Smoke-Bloc, CigSafe, and other genetically engineered lung protectants, smoking was on the rise again.

"Now what?" the corporal asked, exhaling.

Rigg shook his head. "Well, now we— Oops, hold on a sec." He touched his earpiece. "It's Campeneau."

Rigg had given Campeneau a radio, too, assigning him code eight. In a general way, Campeneau knew the area and the people. Because of his friendship, Rigg had thought of bringing him along, but decided against it. It was bad policy to take amateurs on real missions. Because of their lack of training, they could be dangerous, as more than one platoon had discovered about tag-along reporters in Vietnam, Somalia, Kosovo, and elsewhere. By giving Campeneau a UWB, if he thought of anything useful beyond what Rigg had already pumped from him, he could say so pronto but never be in the way. Hochman and the other men switched to code eight to listen in.

To Campeneau, Rigg said, "Hey, fisherman, not a nibble on anything here. Checked all the lines, too. Zilch. We're on smoke break, then heading home."

"Maybe you won't want to cut bait quite yet," Campeneau replied. "Appears the Candor list wasn't big enough."

"Oh? How so?" Rigg replied, catching Hochman's eyes.

"My pal the real estate agent provided you a rundown of sole ownerships by Candor. He got to thinking that maybe we'd be interested in the joint deals the Bard's hooked into."

284 ☆ E. G. ROSS

"What've you got?"

"Five of 'em. Three are private homes, one is five acres of timber up in the coast woods a few miles."

"And the fifth one?"

Campeneau chuckled and said, "You might check this one out first, Larry. It's an abandoned fish cannery. Big enough to hide a small army. It's a couple miles or so back up the beach from where you are. Don't know why I didn't think of this joint ownership angle before. Sorry, man,"

"Everything in its time. You did good. Something else?"

"A longshoreman friend of mine on another dock, a night owl, called a few minutes ago. We talked a bit and he mentioned that Candor's got at least forty men who act as his personal guard. My pal knows several. What's interesting is that none of 'em have shown up for work for a couple days now. Could be Candor's got his best boys standing watch over that missile. Some of those guys are mighty good with guns, pal, so watch yourself."

"Appreciate the heads up," Rigg said.

He asked Campeneau for precise directions to the five pieces of property, thanked him, and signed off.

He turned to Karl Hochman and the other members of Team One. "Okay, guys, you and I have got at least one more place to check."

It was late and his men were tired, but no one complained. They knew how serious the mission was. Besides, it was a hell of a lot more exciting than showing kid recruits which end of a gun to stick against their shoulders.

As his men hoisted their equipment, Rigg said, "This one's in spitting distance and it's the best prospect yet. As you heard, if it's for real, there could be heavy opposition. If it proves out, we'll get the lay of the land, then wait and pull in the other teams. Let's look and see."

As Team One began the two-mile hike down the beach, Rigg gave swift orders for teams four through seven to recon the three houses and woodland property. There was no sense wasting time in case the cannery was a dud. Rigg thought that parcel up in the woods was also a fair candidate. He passed on the addresses, warning the teams not to try to take on heavy opposition.

"Wait for backup, boys. Let's be heroes, but smart heroes," he said.

Chapter 44

"Bingo Night"

Man oh man," Corporal Hochman whispered, staring at the gray, weathered sides of the cannery, "if that was a henhouse and I was a fox, I wouldn't try to grab a chicken unless I had about ten friends with me."

Rigg agreed. "I've spotted at least a dozen men in the last few minutes. If this is Candor's private army, he's probably got half of it patrolling the grounds. Is Stan Crothers doing anything?

"No. He's heading one of the idle squads, Team Two. I checked on 'em while we were hiking in. They were going off to hog snacks while they could."

"Tell 'em to drop 'n' hop. Crothers and Jamie Simpson are our two best infiltrators. Get his team and Team Three over here. Have 'em come up low in the beach scrub paralleling our entry. We don't want to take chances advertising ourselves. While we're waiting, we'll do a more detailed perimeter search and rough-map what we can."

Hochman nodded and shivered at the cool, south wind that had been picking up for several minutes. It seemed to be growing stiffer. A few gray clouds were scuttling across the sky and he could smell moisture. Looked like a squall was moving up the coast.

"How far do you want Crothers and Simpson to go in?"

he asked, scanning the area.

"As far as they can in order to safely use the snakes and the bees."

"Why not play it safe and send the bees in from here? They can fly, can't they?"

"The wind. It's a problem. Not enough power in those little bugs. Crothers has been experimenting with them back in Springfield."

"The specs said wind shouldn't bother 'em."

"I'll trust Crothers' experimentation over a spec book writer's opinion any day of the week."

Hochman shook his head and said, "Well, I sure hope that techno-crap works. 'Cause if it doesn't, I don't trust Simpson's skills yet and I'm not even sure Crothers is *that* good. Not with Candor's dogs snufflin' all around that fish barn."

Rigg nodded and said, "If anyone can, Crothers can. And don't underestimate Simpson, Karl. Little Lycra pants has come a *long* way since we first recruited her."

"I think she's trouble," Hochman griped.

Rigg was well aware of Hochman's other doubts. He knew his second in command didn't like Crothers and Simpson serving in the same team. If Stan and Jamie weren't lovers, they were sure moving in the general direction. In Hochman's view, love and war didn't mix. Ever. Besides, he also had severe misgivings about women of small stature being in combat. On principle, as he'd often told Rigg, there was a physical limit to what they could handle. He was of the old school. He believed the odds would one day catch up to Simpson—and endanger her team in the process. Rigg knew there was some truth to it, but SIM had been short-handed from the start. You made do. That's how it was.

"Karl, we've *got* to know if that missile's there. Simpson is part of the package—like it or not. Anyway, maybe we'll luck out. This could be a hunt club party. A bunch of guys toting guns doesn't tell us much in itself."

"After midnight? Running patrols? You don't believe that for a minute, Larry."

"Maybe not. But it's not a matter of belief. There are laws in Oregon about unwarranted intrusions on private property. For all I know, we're in violation right now. I don't know how far Candor and Company's property lines extend around this broken-down piece of fish mortuary. I didn't ask. We might be trespassing."

Hochman snorted. "Big deal. This is war. Or could be. I know that Candor's got a mean disposition if crossed, Sarge. But given what's at stake, if he's got a missile in there with a bad-ass warhead, I'm inclined to keep legal technicalities to myself for awhile. I've always believed hindsight was nine-tenths of morality."

"You should've been a lawyer, Corporal."

"Yes, sir. The day I sell my balls for hamburger."

"Get Crothers and Simpson. Tell 'em to bring their high-tech gadgets."

"Right."

While Hochman ordered the two idle platoons to join them, Rigg talked to Campeneau.

"Might be bingo night at the old ladies home," Rigg said. "Can your real estate buddy get me a floor plan of this dump? And if not that, how about an aerial map?"

"See what I can do," Campeneau replied. "Might be tough this late at night."

"Try. We need fins for upstream swimming."

"I'm paddling already."

"Call me soon."

"Crothers will be here in about an hour," Hochman said, after flicking off his radio. "By the way, if it *is* the missile site, are you planning to take 'em tonight?"

Rigg glanced at the threatening sky. He shook his head and pursed his lips sourly.

"Must not be more than three hours 'til daylight," he replied. "I'd prefer a night operation. This storm moving in will help hide us, but this joint sprawls across a promontory. That means three sides are water-bound and relatively open."

Hochman made a quiet raspberry sound at the sky, then

raised and focused his infrared goggles for a few seconds. "That promontory must be a third of a mile across, landward," he said. "Still, it's rough terrain, so there should be some wiggle room for Stan and Jamie."

"Not much, though," Rigg acknowledged. "Too easy for Candor's goons to patrol. From all the troops he's got, it looks like he has no intention of being caught napping. None of those guys down there looks sleepy to me."

"Me either. Pretty sure I've seen at least two guard dogs," Hochman observed.

He flinched and cursed at a seagull that had hovered for a moment, squawked, and dropped a load in the sand nearby.

Rigg scratched his forehead and said, "We don't want to rush this. If it is a big boomeroo that he's got, it's going to take some planning to take it."

"Yeah, but if Candor torches that sucker—"

"If he's actually got one, we don't have the slightest idea of his agenda. We don't know that he'll torch it, period, Karl. If he does, it could be weeks. Anyway, I'd probably need your brother's authorization to raid the place. Maybe even Corky's."

Hochman looked surprised. "Why?"

Rigg reminded him that Corcoran was supposed to have a spy close to Candor. While Rigg wasn't actually entitled to that knowledge, with a second-in-command whose brother was defense chief, it was hard not to learn of such things.

"I'd forgotten," Karl said. "Yeah, okay, I see. If we rush in then we risk blowing an existing operation. That'd get us fried, salted, and sliced."

"We'd risk killing a good man, too, whoever he is." Rigg waved his hand, as though brushing away the subject. "But all that's ahead of us."

"Sure is a lot we don't know down here in gruntland. Whatever happened to that all-digital, top-to-bottom flow of complete military knowledge that was supposed to be the rule this century."

"Well, we're just a snotty little militia. I don't think the Joint Chiefs ever meant to include us in the process. Tonight

I've got just one concern: to find out if that missile's in there."
Rigg checked his watch and said, "We've got awhile, let's pull some weeds and coffee."

He and Karl scooted into the hollow of a dune to light cigarettes and pour coffee from their thermoses. They continued talking quietly while waiting for their own team to finish doing what could be done to fill in more details of the area.

Ten minutes before Crothers and the rest showed up, Campeneau called.

"You guys got a video loader there, right?" he asked. "I can feed you pictures."

"Yeah," Rigg said. "You got a layout for me?"

"More. My pal decided that I was such a pest that he'd stay in his office late in case I called again. He hates Candor, so it's worth it to him. Anyhow, he pulled the junk and fed it into the little laptop you lent me. Got both aerial and county maps as well as a floor plan. The floor plan's old, though; may not be reliable. That cannery was remodeled a gillion times over the years. But it'll be a start."

"We'll make do," Rigg said, taking the team's own two-pound, ruggedized laptop from his pack. He fished out an auxiliary cable and plugged one end into the machine. The other end he plugged into a jack on his UWB headset. He booted the computer and opened a graphics file.

"Okay," he said, "ready to import. Fire away."

In seconds Rigg had the data. He quickly double-checked the files, calling them up to the high definition nine-inch screen.

"Looks good, Camp," he said. "Anything else?"

"Yeah. Frank—that's my real estate pal's name—says there used to be two or three big sewer pipes under the plant. He thinks they empty into the surf from the cannery. That cannery was designed back before the days of coastal pollution controls. I didn't check, but he says at least two pipes are shown on the floor plan. They might give you a backdoor."

"We'll check it out."

As Rigg finished with Campeneau, Crothers and crew showed up. Explaining what was wanted, Rigg and Hochman huddled with them over the cannery graphics.

"Not many differences on the outside," Crothers said, pulling his lower lip thoughtfully. "But it may not mean much. Scramble a man's insides and he still wears the same skin. Your guys see anybody on the roof?"

Hochman shook his head.

Rigg said, "Nevertheless, they might be there, laying low to avoid attracting attention. The cannery's probably visible from some houses and a short stretch of this county road." Rigg pointed to the overhead shot in three places. "People might start asking questions if they spot armed men parading around in the middle of the night atop what's supposed to be an abandoned building."

Crothers said, "Yeah. Got ya, Sarge."

The young man was still taciturn, but he'd refined his heavy drawl and twang since joining the SIM. He'd once told Rigg, blushing, that he didn't want his men to think he was a country hick. Unknown to Crothers, Rigg had privately talked with Jamie Simpson. She'd agree to help Crothers in that department. Rigg thought that Crothers was going places someday. He was quick, honest, kept his promises, and daily became a more independent thinker. He was becoming quite the whiz with computers. He had a natural knack for grasping technology. Looking back, Rigg realized that Crothers, not quite seventeen, had already left his boyhood behind somewhere in the mist of his militia service.

"Think I'll try that sewer pipe on the right first," Crothers said, gesturing toward the map. "If it doesn't work, I'll do my best to improvise."

Hochman looked around. "Where's Lycra-butt?"

"Don't call her that, sir," Crothers said hotly. "She didn't come with us. She's sicker'n a dog. Something she ate, I guess. Got the heavy heaves and a belly-ache. Anyway, she couldn't get her snakes workin' — some glitch in the firmware for the steering interfaces — so she's gonna try to fix 'em between trips to the ivory throne."

The snakes were technically known as Rattlers. They didn't

look at all like snakes, more like phone-sized eight-wheeled toy trucks. In fact, they were mini-reconnaissance robots. Versions of them had been in service since the 1990s with the Army and Marines. SIM had inherited several, and Jamie Simpson was their "mother."

"The Corporal didn't mean to insult Jamie, son," Rigg said. "He's just scared to death of water, whatever its form. Makes him say stupid stuff."

Crothers' heat dissipated almost instantly. He grinned up at Hochman. He'd forgotten about the big man's notorious skittishness about the sea.

"All right," Rigg said to the teenager. "We'll see you when you get back. Make sure it's before daylight, otherwise you might have to hole up for quite awhile without food or water."

But Crothers was back in less than an hour, dripping wet and shivering.

"What happened to you?" Rigg asked, looking over the private's condition.

"Had to swim through about thirty feet of seawater in the pipe," Crothers explained, his teeth chattering.

Hochman turned nearly white and snapped out a fresh cigarette. His hands shook as he lit it. He'd go into a place like that on the day he fried his socks for breakfast.

"It's dark as the devil's tail in there, too, and the pipe is a kind of a half-rock, half-concrete tunnel that's sunk in the middle about fifty yards inside," Crothers explained. "Seawater washes in from the side through a break in the tunnel. Old cave-in, looks like."

He pulled a blanket around him that one of the men draped over his wet shoulders.

Rigg checked the time and gazed out to sea, then said, "Looks like high tide now. The pipe might be clear at low."

"Yes, sir, that's what I thought. Anyway, past the water, the tunnel rises for about a hundred yards nice 'n' easy. It curves a few times, but more to the right than the left, winding toward the back of the building. It comes up into about a three-foot-deep open trench inside, right behind a couple of old, rusty boilers. Dark. Nobody there. A bunch of little trenches empty into the big one, all built into the concrete floor. Some of them are covered with steel walkway grating. It's a kind of open sewer. They used the same system in one of the fruit canneries I worked for in Eugene a year ago. Anyway, I found the cruise missile."

"WHAT!?" both Hochman and Rigg said simultaneously.

"Why didn't you tell us?" Hochman snapped.

Crothers looked at him steadily and said, "I'm telling you now, sir—in as logical an order as I can."

"Where is it?"

"In the back in a big room with a couple of sliding doors," Crothers said. "The doors face onto asphalt. Looks like it was a truck loading area once. An old rail line is there, too. The rail and a road curve parallel around the south side and come out about here."

He pointed to a wide gate shown on the aerial shot.

"Yeah," Rigg said, "we spotted the gate. Padlocked; two guards. A cyclone fence runs across to the north. We scouted the length of it. No breaks. What else, Crothers?"

Crothers accepted a mug of thermos coffee from Hochman. He took a long swallow and his shivering seemed to diminish.

"Well, uh, let's see . . . couldn't get the bees to work. The seawater got 'em, maybe. Don't know for sure. They got awful wet, but I'll dry 'em and check 'em out later. There was a lot I couldn't see, Sarge. The bees could have helped if they'd have actually worked."

"I *knew* that high-tech stuff would crap out on us," Hochman said.

"I'll get it working," Crothers said, "don't worry."

"What else *did* you see?" Rigg asked.

"Beyond the doors maybe twenty or thirty yards is a concrete dock against the water. I think there was once a wooden extension, but it's gone now. Just a few posts in the surf. They might've brought in some of the fish there from the smaller boats. Not sure. Most of the bigger ones were probably unloaded closer in, on the northerly side. It's longer there and better protected by both a jetty and the building. The pipe I went up is close, off to the east, almost halfway to the steel fence. Didn't see any other pipes. The fence is partly ripped away where it dips toward the water. Even at high tide you can get at the pipe by wading. No guards down there. Probably think they can see everything from upstairs. They're wrong. It's a deceptive angle and there's plenty of cover among the rocks, if you're careful. You could move everybody in, Sarge."

"What else?" Rigg asked.

Crothers sipped more coffee and went on, "Well, the water in back, behind the two doors and the dock beyond them, looks deep. Saw the remains of a conveyor belt on stilts right at the edge." He pointed at the old floor plan. "I think there used to be a roof covering a lot of the dock. That's all gone. Open to the weather. Just a buncha rotting struts. There's kind of a raised area to the north side, next to the right-hand door. Some old machinery there; couple of little electric Allis-Chalmers forklifts and a big gas Hyster scoop shovel. Rusting away in the weather."

He pulled the blanket tighter around his shoulders and looked expectantly at Rigg.

"Looks to me like all they've gotta do is roll the missile through the dock door and kick it in the pants out to sea," Rigg said. "Sweet. If we *do* have to move, timing could be critical to us. They can't know we're there for anymore than a few minutes. To the last second would be even better."

"Uh, Sarge, there are a couple other things," Crothers said.

"Yeah?"

"That missile had The Shang's very own dragon painted on the side."

"Whoa," Hochman said softly, inhaling his cigarette and hissing the smoke out between his teeth. "What on earth *are* we gettin' into?"

"And the other thing?" Rigg asked, controlling his emotions with effort.

"There was a radiation symbol on the warhead."

"So much for your poor man's nuke," Hochman said to

Rigg. "Looks like this is the real thing after all."

"Or Candor wants us to think it is," Rigg said, immediately shaking his head. "Doesn't matter. In either case, from now on we treat it *as* a puke nuke."

Chapter 45

"Get Pictures!"

"The trouble is, none of us here has ever seen a true nuke before," Rigg muttered later, as he ate a sandwich.

He and Hochman were off to one side from their men, sharing a wee hours breakfast. The moon was down and it was more than an hour before dawn. The silvery sheen of the sea had given way to black and rough churn. The wind had grown stronger and the clouds were a heavy, dark gray mass, moving fast toward the north.

Hochman shrugged. "Well, we've seen one now."

"Have we? Who's gonna trust what we're saying? Even your brother is going to want some hard evidence. So far, we've got an eyewitness report of a teenager."

Hochman thought a moment, then nodded sourly. "See what you mean. That's how it would look. And so far, we're the only people aware of the situation."

"If we're going to convince others, I'm thinking we'd better send Crothers in to get pictures."

"Right now?"

"You bet. He can get in while it's still dark and get pictures when he finds an opportunity at dawn. Otherwise, he'll have to hole up and wait until evening and use a night lens. Tough, but I don't see another way. We've got a couple light-enhancing attachments for our digital cameras. Give him the one with the 36 million pixel resolution. If he can get daylight shots or snap a few under the interior lights, so much the better for us."

"Right."

"Wonder if Erik and Corky already know," Rigg said. "You ask me, it's an awfully quirky situation unfolding."

"Huh?"

"Their spy. That bothers me."

"I don't get you," Hochman said, wadding up the plastic wrap to the sandwich he'd finished eating and stuffing it in his pack. He hated litterbugs.

Rigg took another bite out of his own sandwich, turned his head into the wind and squinted sideways at the dark sea.

He said, "Think about it. Something's off here. How come no one's already taken this Shang bird out? If your brother's spy-guy is operating inside Candor's top circle, why didn't he tip anyone *days* ago?"

"Maybe he did. From what Erik's let drop, my guess is that SIM's too low on the totem pole to be notified about strategic issues. Remember, even though we're a lead militia, we pushed our own noses under this tent. We're still secondary to the Regulars. That's rubbed off on Erik a bit, I think."

"I don't buy it, Karl. If Corky or Erik knew, that nuke would be history by now. I'm thinking that Corky's peeker has been watched too closely himself—or taken out or compromised. Or maybe there's some plan we don't know about. It could be anything. It smells bad."

"Well, you said it yourself. We can't roll in like a herd of mad rhinos."

"I know. If Corky's man is alive, then he could have a timetable and a cover, neither of which we want to puncture."

"On the other hand, if he's somehow been neutralized then it won't matter."

"Right. That's my next point. In that case, it's even more urgent that we get the evidence on our own. Keeps coming back to the same thing. We've got to send Crothers in again."

Hochman asked, "Okay, when we get the photos, then

what? This little UWB set-up we've got is a closed loop. We can send and receive pics among ourselves, our own compatible laptops, but not zap to anyone else. I guess the U.S. Army's got the capacity to access satellites, the Internet, phones, whatever—but we scavenged these babies and they're purely local tactical, closed loop. More secure, but limited for this mission."

"Well, maybe Campeneau's real estate buddy could help out. Might be able to hand-scan the info frame by frame right off the UWB laptop screen into his office machine. Probably lose some resolution, but it would get it out of the loop and up to Salem. It would make our point. Never mind that for now. If I have to, I'll drive the pictures. Go talk to Crothers. Get him moving before we waste any more of his dark."

Crothers had just finished drying out another, special type of micro-robotics. He packed the gear in a waterproof duffel from one of the men's "fishing" gear and headed out.

Rigg ordered all of SIM except his own squad to disperse and resume their visitor guises for the coming daylight hours. Most of them simply headed for their campers or to local motels to catch up on sleep. It had been a long and busy night and adrenaline had a way of wearing men out. Rigg told them to sleep light.

A hard, chilly rain began to fall across the beach. Team One spread around more coffee and cigarettes, then moved into the scrub to keep an eye on the cannery. One of them found a rise off to the south from where he could see the back dock. That was where the missile would probably be rolled out—if Candor suddenly decided to go nutso. Rigg hoped not. After the other five members of the team were gone, Hochman and Rigg remained together, watching the front of the cannery and keeping a lookout for stray hikers who might stumble onto their base.

"In this muck?" Hochman asked incredulously. "Whose gonna go tramping around in weather like this?"

"You don't fancy water. Some people do. My dad used to love to hike in the night during storms."

Hochman didn't argue. People could be weird.

Just before daylight, Crothers called. He whispered that he was through the pipe and inside the building.

"I'm up on a kind of mezzanine overlooking the room with the bird. Problem, though," he said.

"What?"

"The missile's covered up. It's sitting on a kind of boat trailer with a hitch. I must've been lucky to see the bird exposed before."

"Well, anyway, they've got at least six guys hanging around. Four are playing poker at a little table not more'n twenty feet from the missile. I couldn't talk like this except they're makin' more noise than a flock of jays. Two more guys are yakkin' and smokin' on the other side. Three or four others have come in and out, including through the back door. No way I'm gonna get a look at the thing for awhile."

"What about your mechanical bugs? Can *they* get us the pictures we need?"

"I don't know. I think they could get under the tarp on the missile, but it might be too close and they might not have enough light."

"I don't want might, I want try. Now."

"Yes, sir."

Rigg called the man on the rise who could see the back door from the outside. The man confirmed that one of the big sliding doors had periodically been cracked open enough for people to slip through.

"Seen Candor around?" he asked Crothers.

"Uh, well, sir, I'm not sure what he'd look like. I've never seen him to know him."

Rigg swore at himself. He should've provided a picture of Candor for Crothers. It had totally slipped his mind.

"I did see one interesting guy when I first got up here, sir," Crothers said. "Chinaman, I think. He lifted a corner of the tarp and fiddled around with something on the missile. He's dressed a little differently than the others. Pretty much keeps to himself."

Rigg nodded and said, "Looks like Candor might have his

own expert, probably loaned from The Shang. If there's a way, Crothers, have your bugs get a picture of him. Close-up, if you possibly can."

"Yes, sir. You got it."

Crothers unsealed the duffel bag and pulled out a container about the size of a shoebox. He punched in a code on the ten-digit keypad and flipped open the lid in two sections. One became a video screen, the other a small keyboard. He quietly fed in another code and punched "enter." From out of the box, a dozen bumblebees arose, humming softly. They hovered just a few inches above the box, turning this way and that, orienting. They weren't really bees, of course. That's just what Crothers' called them. They were technically known as micro-Wasps. They were a product of SORDAT, a U.S. armed forces research department dedicated to developing unusual technical systems for Special Operations Forces. Oregon had inherited the micro-Wasps because they were on loan to the Guard when the state seceded. Somehow this particular "box of bugs" had found its way to the SIM.

Crothers loved it. The micro-Wasps were almost silent, not much louder than a dragonfly. They were painted to look like real wasps, and from a distance they could fool anyone. Powered by tiny, nano-engineered motors, they had a flight-time of not quite 30 minutes. They flew exactly like wasps, using tiny graphite wings. The science of insect flight had been coming together for decades and was now mature. Married to high performance microscopic computers—each bug had the power of a 10-gigahertz chip—the Wasps could actually run circles around real insects, and defend themselves if need be. Each bug had a microscopic ceramic cannon that shot an extremely toxic acid for self-defense—or offense in certain cases. Rumor had it that a swarm of the bugs had blinded a certain Third World dictator, precipitating a coup in his island nation.

Crothers watched the micro-Wasps rise a little higher to scan their surroundings with their miniaturized video sensors. For a second, the video screen showed a jumble of broken images. Then the merge program in the main computer built into the bottom of the shoebox pulled the bugs' different images into a coherent, 360-degree view of the cannery's interior.

Crothers used the heat-sensitive mouse pad to zero in on the image of the tarped-over missile. He highlighted the missile with a red box, then clicked the F2 "seek" key. Immediately, the twelve micro-Wasps sped away, spreading out to approach the missile from all angles.

Within seconds, completely unnoticed by the men, the bugs had worked under the tarp wherever there was an opening. In some places, there was not enough light to get decent pictures. These particular bugs didn't have night-vision capabilities. But in other places, including the underside of the rocket and the rear, engine-area, they did. Crothers' flicked his monitor images from bug to bug, snagging snapshots out of the continuous video stream. It could all be done later, of course, much more carefully, but if he couldn't get out, it might be too late for that. Sometimes dirty was the only quick a guy had.

In under five minutes, he had the best he thought he could get, and ordered the bugs back. The micro-Wasps returned, one by one, and settled into the niches built into the sides of the shoebox. On the computer screen, a blinking light indicated that each was refueling its miniature engine. Crothers didn't know what their fuel was. The manual for the device said it was a sealed system and classified. Once the box was out of fuel, the bugs were dead until SORDAT restored it. Any attempt to break into the box to analyze the fuel—or into a bug to do the same—resulted in a miniature explosion that ruined everything. Some Oregon scientists had tried. One had suffered severe eye damage and the other was nursing a badly burned hand.

Crothers closed the box and patted it tenderly.

"Good job, boys," he said. "Someday I'm gonna adopt you little guys. No tellin' what you could tell me about Jamie!"

The rain redoubled as daylight came. The men of Team One were stoic about it, but Rigg knew their spirits weren't all they could be. They'd been up for too many hours on intense alert and were getting drenched to the skin. Two of them were sneezing. He didn't want them moving around more than necessary in daylight. That would greatly increase the chance they'd be discovered. If Candor got so much as a hint that his game had been spotted by a ROC militia, Rigg didn't know what he'd do. More than once, Rigg felt that his self-initiated investigation was a mistake. If inadvertently tipped by SIM, Candor could decide to fire the bird for that reason alone. Use it or lose it. Yeah, from what he'd heard, Candor had that kind of mentality. A bad move by SIM could precipitate a small nuclear holocaust and jeopardize the future of a fledgling nation. Despite the cold rain, Rigg was sweating. He'd never have guessed that so many lives could be riding on his shoulders. He was not afraid of the responsibility, but he fully felt its weight. Now you know why generals ache, he thought.

Chapter 46

"Bird Kill"

By early afternoon of the day that the presidents of the U.S. and the Republic of Oregon planned their surprise announcement to the media, Crothers had been holed up in the fish cannery for nearly nine hours. His joints throbbed from the chill and the hard metal floor of the mezzanine. His muscles were cramped from his inability to risk much movement. Although his youth provided resiliency and he remained alert the whole time, it was frustrating.

No opportunity arose to adequately photograph the entire missile. Nor would it have done him much good at the time. For some reason he couldn't fathom, the UWB system wasn't accepting the shots that the micro-Wasps had taken. That meant that his own unit's video channel was almost certainly on the blink. He should have double-checked it before he left. Crothers felt frustration burning the back of his throat. The guards had never left the missile. The Shang's man had lifted a corner of the black tarp several times to fiddle with something, apparently tapping at a keypad. Unfortunately, he'd always worked on the side opposite Crothers' vantage and only for seconds. There'd been no time to send the bees in. Crothers got shots of the Chinaman in action, good facial close-ups, but never more than a glimpse of the missile showing part of the jet exhaust. Knowing little about cruise missiles, Crothers wasn't satisfied. He had no idea if such a skimpy revelation would constitute proof. He doubted it. The best shot would be a full view, especially one catching The Shang and the radiation symbols.

When things finally began to change, they did so with a rush. A husky, rather short, balding fellow with a gray fringe above his ears strode in with the cockiness of a banty rooster. He was dressed smartly in a severe, dark business suit. One of the card players dropped his hand and shouted in surprise, "General Candor!"

"Snap to, boys," Candor barked.

General Candor? Crothers thought. Since when?

At least he finally knew what Bard Candor looked like. Almost twenty individuals, armed with hunting rifles and pistols, followed Candor in, chatting among themselves. Incredibly, Candor went straight to the missile and quickly flipped off the tarp.

Crothers sent his micro-Wasps in and got several very clear shots of the "general" and the exposed missile together. He held his breath, hardly able to believe how swiftly his luck had shifted for the better.

Candor swatted idly at one of the flying robots, as though brushing a mosquito aside. It easily avoided his hand and, using an erratic, highly insect-like course, returned to the shoebox.

Candor spun on his heels and raised his hands for silence. The room quieted quickly.

"Okay, boys," he said. "Z-hour is here. Just got word from our people in upstate." He paused for effect. "Corky and—get this—and that gutless President of the United States, Sam Washington, will be holding a joint media conference within an hour—in Salem! Looks like virtually every egghead of the Republic is going to be there, too.

Candor drew a finger across his throat in a cutting motion and grinned. His followers laughed. Candor shouted, "This is it, boys. Once we wipe away the capital scum, it's going to be Oregon for Oregonians!"

He raised his fist as he shouted the last three words. The

armed men echoed his salute.

The scene reminded Crothers of footage he'd seen of Adolph Hitler and his minions. Christ, he thought, this creep's one lobe short of a brain.

Candor looked at his watch and announced, "We launch in less than an hour. The target is the capitol building itself. Mr. Xiao, get it ready to go. Boys, hitch the bird, get those doors open, and sweep the launch deck. We've got an entire state to steal back!"

"Oh crap!" Crothers whispered to himself as a clammy chill ran down the middle of his back. His legs felt weak and his heart raced. He consciously slowed his breathing and tried to swallow several times.

Candor pointed a finger at the Chinaman, who nodded curtly. He moved toward a panel in the missile and began tapping in information. Candor watched him narrowly for a moment, as though not completely trusting him. Four men moved to open the big rear doors of the cannery. As they did, rain blew in and Crothers could see the large paved dock covered with puddles.

Crothers silently flicked on his radio.

"What the hell's going on, Crothers?" Rigg's voice crackled into his earpiece, just as Crothers was about to speak. "My boy on the hill says both doors are swingin' wide."

"Yes, sir, you better get moving, because they're lighting the nuke any minute!" Crothers said, his voice squeaky with tension. "Candor says he's gonna blast the capitol. We've gotta stop this sucker *now*, Sarge!"

"Okay, son, take it easy," Rigg said calmly. "Sounds like picture-taking time is over. Did you bring a gun in with you?"

"Yes, sir. Never without it."

"Get it and put the bees away in a safe place. We'll have use for your evidence later. I assume you got some decent looksees in the last few minutes?"

"Plenty! Enough to grill Candor like a bad steak!"

"Okay. Lay low and stay where you are. We'll need your overhead firepower when we get there. Some of us are following your path in. Others will be advancing from outside. When we start shooting, you do, too. Not 'til then, all right?"

"Gotcha, sir!"

"Waiting's over," Rigg snapped to Hochman. "Team One's going in now, on the double."

Hochman looked confused. Rigg gave him a rapid-fire summary of the situation. "I'll take care of it. You call the other teams, Corporal. Tell them to get here as soon as they can. Looks like this is one of those times when they're going to have to run without a full-bore battle plan. We will be engaged when they get here."

"Er, sir, shouldn't we notify Salem to evacuate?" Hochman rubbed the growth of beard on his cheek. "I mean, if we don't destroy the missile, we can't let those innocent people get fried."

"Corporal, think about it. It would take too much time to convince Corky and Company—if we could get 'em to believe us at all. Even if we did, an evacuation would barely get started by the time the missile slammed. I don't know much about nukes, but I do know they're 95% blast. So with people panicking for their cars, there'd probably be a lot more casualties than if they stayed in their buildings."

"Hell, vaporization is vaporization."

"No. Just for those directly under the blast. A little ways out, there'll be lots of survivors. But only if they're sheltered and those capitol buildings are heavy concrete. Out in the open, their chances are a lot slimmer."

"But the tunnels underneath—"

"Yeah, if there were time. Nuclear civil defense has been dead for decades in America. Citizens have no idea what to do and we sure don't have time to teach 'em in sixty minutes. People up there are more likely to head for the parking lot to make it home to momma than sit tight in a tunnel and wait for the big boomeroo. Anyway, most of 'em probably think like you—get out or say bye-bye to their backsides. Corporal, they wouldn't know where to scramble or how to ramble, so—"

"Yeah, so it's up to us. Period. Gotcha, sir."

Rigg nodded, hoisted a pack to his shoulders.

As he checked his gun he said, "We stop it here, or it happens, Karl. Simple as that. Now tell the other teams to get moving. They'll have to improvise on conditions as they arise. You pick the man to lead them, probably that old duffer, I forget his name. You know, the one who's the crack shot next to Crothers. He seems to have a natural head for tactics."

"And us?"

"The seven of us in Team One will try to knock out the missile from the inside."

"Pretty skinny assault force. I don't like it."

"Well, I'd say wait for the others, but for all I know Candor could get lucky and launch in twenty minutes."

"I thought we had more time that."

"Maybe we do, maybe not. I'm not risking thousands of lives on a maybe—not if we have a half-decent chance of stopping it ourselves."

"I'm not sure how decent it is. Bad tactics."

Rigg looked at his second-in-command, and said, "Karl, I just don't think the rest of our boys can get here soon enough and slick enough to avoid tipping Candor. He's bound to have the lookouts to spot a force of over forty men. We can't risk it. Team One is small enough to get in unseen. The more I think about it, the more I think this may be our best shot at the mission, despite the force ratios. That puke nuke bird's gotta be killed at all costs. We're gonna make the first payment. Let's hope it'll be enough by itself."

Hochman straightened up, beating down his doubts, though they were there and they were strong. Rigg had never disappointed him.

"You got it, Sarge," he said, holding gazes with his friend for a moment, suddenly wondering if this was their final hour of life. Well, if it is, he thought, I'm going to go out with the best. An almost identical thought ran through Rigg's brain, but like Hochman, it wasn't necessary to verbalize it. Simultaneously, they reached out and shook hands.

"Good luck, Corporal," Rigg said.

"You, too, Sarge," Hochman said. "Let's pluck that bird

'til it screams."

Rigg had decided on a simple pincer approach for Team One. Hochman would take three men down the scrub-strewn rise from the south overlooking the back dock. Rigg would lead the remaining two men through the pipe the way Crothers had gone in. One of Hochman's men would put down grazing fire with the team's M-60 machine gun, covering the advance of the other three if they were spotted and fired upon. But their advance would be done in silence and stealth to the last possible moment. The gunner had orders to avoid hitting the missile if possible. This was because Rigg didn't know the wisdom of piercing a nuclear warhead with bullets. He didn't want to somehow contaminate half of Coos Bay. He wished that he'd paid more attention to the subject of nuclear physics in school. Only if the missile were ignited was the gunner to aim for it as a last-ditch effort to squelch its launch. As thin as our ranks are, Rigg thought, plunging through the tunnel with his tiny two-man squad, it may come to that.

The tide was half out, so the sunken section of the ancient sewer pipe was not fully filled with seawater. They nevertheless had to swim several yards before the angle rose sufficiently to clear the liquid. Wading out of the water in the dank pipe, gasping for air, their clothes were heavy, sticking to their legs, making them feel like they were carrying an extra thirty pounds. The water in the pipe also smelled bad, resembling a combination of rotting fish and feces.

"My girlfriend ain't gonna lay her hot bod against me for weeks after this," one of the men muttered.

"Amen," the other said.

Rigg was the only one with night goggles—SIM didn't have enough for everyone—so the other two followed his sounds. As they got deeper under the cannery, light began to break through cracks in the old pipe from above, apparently finding its way down through breaks in the ancient concrete floor. Rigg put the goggles away and halted their advance for a few moments to allow their eyes to adjust to the gloom.

As they resumed their progress, the squad's boots made

squashing sounds and water dripped from their clothes, splashing in high-frequency echoes along the tunnel. The noise worried them, unconsciously slowing their pace. Rigg halted the advance. They could hear voices shouting and footsteps thudding somewhere above. It was hard to tell how far away the noise originated. He pointed upwards, then made a "perfect" sign with his fingers.

"Their sounds will mask ours," was all he needed to whisper. Reassured, the men resumed forward faster. They instantly frightened several rats out of a black fissure in the pipe. One of the men spat an obscenity as he banged his head on the low ceiling. They listened to the scratching and screeching of the rats; the animals scampered away up the tunnel.

A couple of minutes along, the squad encountered a cave-in which three-quarters-filled the passageway.

"What the—?" Rigg said under his breath, "Crothers never mentioned this."

Single file, they crawled over the stinking mud, rock, and broken cement pile on their stomachs. Something black and shiny slithered away from Rigg's face, but he never saw what it was. Maybe a snake.

They took a minute to breathe. Rigg noticed that the air was slightly cleaner. The stench of the lower parts of the pipe was fading. A glow of slightly brighter light showed at a sharp elbow ahead. Advancing through it, they found themselves under the boiler room.

"This is it," Rigg mouthed quietly.

The tunnel had ended about eight feet below a manhole-sized opening with several small trenches running into it at different angles.

Rigg smiled at his men and gave them a thumbs up. They grinned through dark, mud-caked faces. Anything seemed better than that hellish sewer pipe.

Rigg climbed four steel rungs and slowly raised his head to scan the cannery floor. There was no one in the immediate area. Before getting out, he looked around and overhead, noting cover and alternate routes, alert for patrols.

The boiler room was not actually a room, but a large nook. The corroding boilers shielded him from a large open area littered with broken conveyors, wooden pallets, rotten nets, stained shipping cans, wrecked electrical processing machinery, clumps of oily canvas, and decaying cardboard boxes. Beyond that, toward the back, perhaps a tenth of a mile on, lay a brightly lit open space. From inside, the cannery seemed gargantuan, much larger than it had from outside.

In the far distance, Rigg could see the silhouettes of men running back and forth and he could hear their shouts, echoing unintelligibly.

Apparently our advance took us under part of that area earlier, he thought. That must have been where all the noise had come from.

He shook his head. Well, maybe not. In the dark, he'd lost track of their course. Perhaps they'd passed beneath a different part of the complex where other men were gathered, men who might easily surprise them from behind.

He frowned and looked around again, also worried about dogs or lone guards who might be moving in the shadows out of sight. Candor would have been smart to post such patrols. Rigg would have done so.

After three or four minutes of listening and watching, he silently wormed out of the pipe on his belly to get a better view, ordering the others to remain below and wait for his hand signal. He crawled forward to peek around the front of one of the boilers. At the far side of the brightly lit room were the two broad doors, now standing open to the storm. Etched starkly against the gray daylight was the deadly, slender form of the cruise missile atop its launch trailer. Several men were milling about, looking as keyed up as cats on coffee.

Rigg took another precious two minutes to plot possibilities for advance, looking for areas of reasonable cover. Finally he had what he wanted fixed in his mind and motioned his two men out. As they drew next to him, he pointed, indicating the target.

"I imagine our best bet," he said in a low voice, "is to

disable the thing by ruining its controls or it engines. Don't shoot or touch the warhead. I'm scared of what we'd spread around or set off if we did."

They nodded vigorously.

"The thing can't be that sturdy," Rigg said. "A cruise missile's basically a fast, light jet airplane. If we can damage the rear section, that should do the trick. I'm going to take the high road." He indicated a network of catwalks and maintenance platforms almost fifty feet above the floor. "I'll begin the action. When I do, you follow. I'm going to try to take out anyone who seems to be working on the bird. I don't know why that didn't occur to me earlier. If we can knock out the human brains of the thing, it might be as good as junking the computer brain. That Chinaman's probably the best bet. Seems to be Candor's technical expert."

"Manley," he said to the taller of the two men, "you slip along the back wall there." He pointed. Skinny, bearded, and black-haired, Manley nodded and moved out, his face tight with strain. He moved like a lanky cougar, silent and sinewy.

"Now Carter," he said to the other, "you go down the other side." Red-haired and thick-armed, the shorter man headed where Rigg had indicated. Also quiet, Carter shambled like a badger.

Rigg found a ladder next to the larger of the two boilers and began to climb.

Okay, Candor, you moronic barbarian, he thought, here comes civilization.

Chapter 47

"Plucking Session"

"Crothers?" Rigg whispered into his UWB.

"Yeah, Sarge. Where are you?"

"Don't jump, but I'm up high, about twenty-five feet above you and sixty to your left. In toward the center of the room."

Startled, Crothers looked around wildly before focusing where he should. Rigg was crouched on a catwalk only a couple yards beneath the open-beamed ceiling. He was next to, but slightly higher than a hanging light. The catwalk was made of plate steel, so the sergeant was hidden from Candor's scurrying men below and relatively well-protected.

"Jeez, Sarge!" Crothers said softly into his radio, "I didn't even know you were there."

"You're not the only one who knows how to sneak up on people, son. Hold on a second. Manley, Carter? You boys in position yet?"

"Been gettin' sore waitin' for you, Sarge," came Manley's soft voice. "I'm up on a stack of old tote boxes about twenty yards from the bird."

"Just got here," came Carter's breathless voice. "Behind some oil drums way over to the right of the doors, but back in a corner. Not nearly as close as Manley. I don't have a line of fire. Too much junk between the bird and my position. But I have clear sight of the doors. If they try to move that thing through, I'll have something to say about it."

"Okay, hold there while I check with the Corporal."

"We're stuck," Hochman said, his voice filled with frustration. "Cooper slipped his leg into a hole halfway down the hill. Compound fracture and bleedin' like a cut radiator hose. I'm holdin' a tourniquet to him now. Smith's up high with the M-60. That only leaves Zach, and I don't know where he is."

Out of the corner of his eye, Rigg saw the Chinaman raise up from the missile and give an okay sign to someone below whom Rigg couldn't see.

He heard a yell that could only be Candor's, "Push the bird out, boys, and put fire to its tail! Let's barbecue!"

Several men cheered and six of them began to physically shove the trailer with the missile toward the open doors and the storm beyond. Rigg hadn't expected that; he'd assumed they'd have to hitch it to a truck or some kind of powered rig.

He swore. Practically nothing was going their way.

He nervously pulled his lower lip, then said urgently into his radio, "Corporal, Candor's launching. They're rolling it out. Is Zach there yet?"

"Yeah."

"Okay, leave him to tend Coop as best he can. Tell Smith to stay at his big gun and be ready to give us whatever fire we ask for. You sneak down as fast as you can. Any help is better than none at this point."

At that instant something crashed to the floor directly beneath Crothers. The room went utterly silent for five seconds. All eyes below turned toward the sound under the mezzanine. Everyone listened.

Candor's voice boomed out, "What was that?"

Most of Candor's men had guns up and ready. Rigg and his squad made themselves flat in their varied positions. Every man held his breath.

"Just an old bucket!" someone snarled, holding it up.

"Sorry, Sarge," Crothers whispered. "It was behind me. Didn't see it."

"Hey, someone's up there!" another rifleman yelled, pointing in Crothers' general direction.

"Sanders, Alston, Baker—get up there and find him," Candor snapped. "And keep moving that missile. Nothing's to stop it, do you hear? *Nothing!*"

The noise level rose again and Crothers' voice came over the UWB, "Sarge, I kicked it over the edge when I shifted positions. I didn't mean—"

Rigg looked down at Crothers and shook his head. The best antidote for guilt was action.

He said, "Past blast. Forget it. Focus on now. Looks like those guys are trying to find a way up to your position from my side or behind you. Stay cool. I'll cover you. I can see every move any of 'em make. Think you can hit that bird's daddy with your rifle?"

"Sir?"

"The Chinaman. He's followin' the missile toward the door. I imagine he's its programmer. Its brains. Can you hit him from there?"

"Uh, yeah, sure, Sarge."

"Do it."

Rigg watched Crothers aim and fire a three-round burst in a single, easy motion. The shots echoed hugely in the big room. The head of Shang's man snapped sideways spraying blood, shredded tissue and bone.

Most of Candor's men hit the floor or dodged for cover, enraging their leader.

"Get up, you filthy little cowards!" Candor's voiced boomed. "Stay at your posts! We've already got men going after the shooter."

Four of his men looked at him, shook their heads, and backed away, looking scared. Killing thousands of people over a hundred miles away by using a missile was one thing. Getting killed here, today, individually—well, that was suddenly something else. They turned and ran out the huge doors. Several others followed.

Candor bellowed in outrage.

"Good shooting, Private," Rigg said. "Got a bead on that

loudmouth Candor?"

"Nope. I think he's hidin', actually," Crothers' voice was controlled, but shaky. "Believe he's over to your left behind some old green metal trash bins."

"Sarge, maybe I can get him," came Manley's voice.

"He's yours."

Rigg heard two shots. One bullet pinged and whanged through the room, glancing off the catwalk not four feet away.

"What the *devil*?" Candor squeaked.

"Aw, crap," Manley whispered, "he moved just as I fired. Uh, oh. They're lookin' this way."

"They're all around us!" someone on the floor shouted in panic. "They're *everywhere*!"

Three more men, including two who had been advancing on Crothers, abandoned their positions—if they had any—and ran out the doors into the rain. Although Candor yelled at someone to follow and kill the deserters, no one tried to stop them; too many friendships were involved.

But the men pushing the missile forward did not panic. Neither did a dozen others who suddenly appeared in a fast march through a door to the far left behind Rigg's perch.

Where's he been keeping this bunch? Rigg wondered.

Candor's new boys muscled their less disciplined fellows aside and quickly formed a tight ring around the missile. They were no weekend can-plinkers. They were carrying M-16s, not hunting rifles, and clearly had undergone training.

Part of Candor's praetorian guard, Rigg thought.

The missile moved slowly on, doggedly pushed by six bruisers. The special guards stayed with it and began firing systematically upwards. They swept in all directions, taking no chances on where overhead shots might come from next, trying to force possible snipers to keep their heads down. Bullets buzzed through the cannery like supersonic wasps.

The nose of the missile reached the front door and kept on moving through.

"Faster, you loafers!" Candor yelled. "I've got a country to conquer!"

One man yelled back, "Not with *my* help, you don't!"

He shouldered his rifle and headed for the doors. With hardly a blink, one of the praetorian guards raised his gun and shot him dead on the spot.

"Anybody else wanna leave?" Candor sneered.

There were no more desertions.

None of Candor's boys had Rigg's position nailed, so he figured he'd have the best chance of hitting the missile's tail. He didn't know what else to go for now. Even though the Chinaman was dead, it appeared Candor was confident he could launch the weapon. So much for my lop-off-the-human-brains theory, Rigg thought. He wondered if perhaps all one had to do was push a button, the Chinaman having programmed in everything else prior to being killed. If so, any one of the dozen-and-a-half men around the bird could send it flying with its awful cargo. Given Rigg's skimpy knowledge of modern cruise missiles, it sounded like a prudent assumption. No way could he and Crothers alone take Candor's hotshot guards out. They might get a few, but not before the missile was outside and out of their line of fire. Team One would have to aim at the missile itself.

In his peripheral vision, Rigg saw Crothers working at his bug box. Dozens of the tiny micro-Wasps rose up and headed down toward the missile. Just as they disappeared from view, Rigg saw a man edge his head and shoulders up over the top of a thin metal ladder directly behind Crothers. The private had his attention elsewhere. Candor's man grinned wickedly and raised a pistol. Rigg fired. His shot caught the man in the middle of the back. He groaned and toppled, hitting the cement floor with a heavy thud. His pistol clattered loudly across the floor.

Rigg had saved Crothers' life, but the shot had now exposed his own position. A hailstorm of lead came his way from the alert guards. All Rigg could do was squeeze flat against the steel catwalk plating. The firing didn't stop. They knew where he was and didn't intend to let him get in any easy shots at them or the missile until it was out of range.

"I'm pinned," he said into his UWB. "Somebody draw their fire!"

Crothers shot three times. Two of the guards and one of the missile-pushers went down, the latter screaming and holding his stomach. But a return shot creased Crothers' temple and he slumped, limp on the floor of the mezzanine.

Without warning, Carter made a zigzag dash into the open toward the missile, firing as he ran. Caught by surprise, two more of the guards fell. Then Carter yelped, grabbed his face, and fell flat. Blood rapidly formed a large, dark pool around his head. He would never raise it again.

For a brief few seconds, the firing turned away from Rigg. He sneaked a quick peek, then sent three bursts at the missile, unable to tell if he'd hit anything. He thought he'd winged one of the pushers, though. The man started limping, but kept to his position. Bullets whined and snapped against the metal plating beneath him. This time, Rigg scooted rapidly backwards. Unable to see this maneuver, the guards kept up steady fire against the empty location. Within thirty seconds, Rigg had backed over a hundred feet away, but he saw at least five men moving below him. They were carefully scanning upwards, perhaps anticipating his actions, but unsure how far he'd gone. Three of them found ladders and began ascending. Rigg glanced at the missile; it was halfway outside and still moving.

He wished his squad had come equipped with grenades, but SIM generally did not carry them on recon missions. Rigg held to the school that too much firepower bred carelessness and clumsiness and thereby hindered stealth. He vowed to re-examine that policy in the future—if he had a future.

"Manley, you still there?" he whispered into his radio.

"Yeah. Don't know why they didn't spot me, but th—"

"Manley? Manley?" Rigg shouted.

After several seconds another voice came on and said, "Who the hell *is* this, anyway?"

Rigg recognized the pompous tone. It was Candor. Apparently Manley was down and Candor had his radio.

"Answer me!" Candor yelled. "Aw, it's too late for 'em,

anyway. Junk this stupid—"

Manley's UWB went silent. According to the tiny digital indicator on Rigg's own receiver, it had been shut off, or perhaps smashed.

"Corporal, you read me?" he called to Karl Hochman.

"Yeah," Hochman said. "I see the bird coming outside. I'm back of some brush about fifty yards from it, maybe less, but there's a steep gully between it and me. Aw, no! Where'd that come from?"

"Karl, what's happened?"

"I'm hit, Larry. Sniper 'round the side of the building. Didn't see the sneaky sumbitch."

"Bad?" Rigg asked his friend.

"Leg. Gotta go. He's comin' for me. But he ain't' gettin' me easy. Whack the bird, Sarge. Make it worth—"

Hochman's transmitter stopped sending.

"Smith?" Rigg asked, trying to reach the M-60 gunner on the hill. He received no answer. He could no longer see Crothers; a series of ventilation fans blocked his view. But the last time he'd looked, the private hadn't moved and there had been some blood on the mezzanine next to his face.

Looking back toward the doors, to Rigg's horror the missile was all the way outside. Still in sight, but out in the rain. However, that also meant that its guards, who had moved with it, were unable to see his position as well. He rushed forward up the catwalk, hoping to get a fresh shot at the rear of the missile. His feet made the metal plates ring as he ran. He drew some scattered, half-hearted fire from Candor's regulars below. One man suddenly reared up a ladder in front of him, trying to bring his M-16 to bear. Rigg shot him in the face and ran on. Gaining position a few yards beyond where he'd been before being spotted the first time, he flattened out and sighted at the tail of the missile. He got off two bursts, then felt a sharp burn in his left shoulder. It was followed by another in the back of his right leg.

"Damn, not *now!*" he cursed.

He staggered halfway up to one knee, twisting, trying to

see. A man had gained a catwalk about fifty feet away and was firing a pistol. Rigg cut him down, then collapsed clumsily onto his butt with a thump. He rolled over onto his stomach again and raised his gun toward the missile. Grimacing against the pain in his shoulder, he pulled the trigger. Nothing happened. Empty. As he watched helplessly, the missile rolled completely out of sight.

Teeth clenched in pain, he tried calling Smith, Hochman, and Zach. None of them responded. He looked over at Crothers' vantage. As his vision began to blur, to his great surprise, he saw that the private was no longer there.

A few seconds earlier, while Rigg was running, Crothers had snapped back to consciousness with a start.

His head felt like someone had hit it with a two-by-four. There was caked blood on his temple. He blinked his eyes and got his bearings. He was still where he'd slumped forward on the mezzanine. He looked down. The missile was almost through the doors. He caught only a glimpse of the tail and the end of the trailer. He scanned over at where Rigg had been, but didn't find him. He thumbed his radio. It wasn't working. He was on his own and there was only one thing to be done. Somehow it had come down to him, and him alone, to prevent the launch of the missile. He turned for the micro-Wasp control box. He didn't find it. Looking down, he saw it smashed on the floor below. He must have knocked it off when he'd been shot. Once the bees ran out of fuel, they'd die. Sorry li'l buddies, he thought.

He scrambled toward the rear of the mezzanine. There was a rotten wooden door in the far wall. He'd spotted it during his first recon almost eleven hours earlier. He gave two jerks and it practically crumbled in his hand. He shoved splintered boards aside and rain stung the left side of his face. Thirty feet up, he was looking down at the north wall of the building, out of sight of the back dock. A rickety steel ladder clung precariously to the side of the old cannery. There was no one in sight. Only a hundred-forty pounds and muscular as a monkey, Crothers glided down it, hit the concrete, and tip-toed over to the corner of the building. Dropping down on his belly, he sneaked a scan of the storm-washed dock.

He was behind the raised area with the old machinery. The ancient scoop shovel was in front, facing the center of the dock. He heard two bursts of gunfire from inside, then silence. That had been Rigg taking fire, but Crothers didn't know it.

In a crouch, he worked his way between two wheelless forklifts and peered over the blade of the scoop. All three machines were parked near the top of a crumbling concrete incline. His position was no more than a hundred feet from the missile, which was now rolling to a stop. All gunfire had ceased, and although the guards were alert, they seemed less wary; they felt the battle had been won and their nuclear nightmare was going to succeed. Crothers slowly raised his gun and aimed at the missile. It was now or never. Nothing happened when he pulled the trigger. He examined the gun and discovered that it had jammed. He worked it, but couldn't get it to work.

He bit his lip and looked around.

Stay cool, he told himself, this ain't no worse than bein' cornered by a bear.

He noticed that the scoop shovel had intact tires. The two, four-foot-diameter main tires in front were blocked with wedges of wood. Crothers grinned. At least this one *had* tires. Sitting beside one wheel, he kicked the wedge loose. He scurried under the machine to the other wheel and did the same, although it took four tries. Then, when it appeared no one was looking his way, he slithered up into the seat of the shovel's cockpit. The windscreen was covered with years of grit and caked silica, making it practically impossible to see in from the outside. Crothers had run his share of farm equipment and the controls of the scoop were standard. He found the brake and released it, then took the machine out of gear. It began rolling forward, imperceptibly at first, but quickly gathering momentum as gravity drove it down the incline onto the main dock. He'd gone forty feet and was pushing twenty miles an hour when Candor's guards spotted him and began firing.

Crothers made sure the machine was heading for the missile, then dove out, rolling. As he sprinted for the rear of the building, he kept the scoop shovel between him and the shooters. Behind him he heard alarmed yells followed by a deep crunching sound. He glanced over his shoulder. The shovel had smashed into the missile trailer's side and lifted it up at a nearly forty-five degree angle. No one was watching Crothers now. All eyes were on the missile. The masses of the heavy steel trailer and the giant scoop fought each other for a moment, then the trailer settled back, pushing the shovel aside. The missile platform rocked on its shock absorbers for a half second, then was still. The missile was apparently intact. Jarred, but intact.

At that moment, Candor ran out waving his arms and shouting, "Fire it, you idiots! Fire it! What are you waitin' for?"

One of the guards nodded, but did a bizarre thing. He growled, spun on his heels, raised his gun, and shot point blank into the missile's rear section. Before he was cut down by his astonished fellow guards, he had pumped a dozen rounds into the bird. A small tendril of smoke or dust rose slowly from the bullet holes.

"No, *NO!*" Candor screamed. He rushed to the missile's far side and did something Crothers couldn't see. With a screech, the missile platform raised up on its hydraulics, lifting its cargo to a skyward angle of about fifty degrees. The bird's cold-launch rocket banged to life. Crothers felt the blood drain from his face as the missile launched itself. In less than a second it had cleared the dock. The disposable rocket engine fell away and the missile cut in its jet. Its nose swung back and forth twice, like a dog smelling a trail, then steadied. The nuclear cruise missile headed north over the ocean, gaining speed swiftly, heading hungrily for the capital of the Republic of Oregon.

Candor was literally jumping up and down in a puddle shouting, "Yes, yes, *yes!* Go you bastard! GO!"

Crothers felt sick. He closed his eyes in despair.

Meanwhile, deep inside the missile, a half-dozen micro-Wasps had survived. They were single-mindedly carrying out the mission that Crothers had given them several minutes earlier. They'd crawled into the missile through bullet holes and spread out—not to photograph, but to kill. Two of the bugs aimed their ceramic acid cannons at a bunch of wiring and emptied them. Two others shot at the missile's fuel tubing. The remaining two had located computer chips and began hitting them with their acid payloads.

From his position, Crothers heard Candor's gleeful tune change to, "Oh, no! No, no, *no!*"

Crothers looked out to sea. His sharp eyesight spotted the bird. Instead of angling northeast, toward Salem, it had turned south and was trying to fly almost straight up. The gunshots and micro-Wasps had finally taken their toll. With a sputter, a belch, and a cloud of smoke, the cruise missile's engine died. For a second, the missile remained poised in midair, its nose to the clouds. Then it slowly fell tailwards a hundred feet into the waves. Disappearing underwater for a few seconds, it bobbed back to the surface, tail high, deadly fusion bomb cargo aimed at the ocean depths. For a half-minute or so it rode the rough sea, sending a wisp of black smoke into the heavy, blowing rain. With one last gurgle, it sank. A lone seagull circled the spot, let out an insulting shriek, and flew off.

Chapter 48

"Don't Tread on Me!"

Rigg was dimly aware of moving. His shoulder felt like it had a railroad spike in it and his leg throbbed with a heavy, dull sensation. He had his right arm around someone and that person was saying something to him. Rigg vaguely knew that he nodded and agreed, but all he could focus on were his feet. They seemed to be carrying him somewhere but didn't appear to be under his direct control. Gradually he realized that he was being forced to stoop as he moved and that there was a horrible odor coming from somewhere.

"Wh— where is this?" he mumbled.

"We're in the tunnel, Sarge," a strong, young voice said.

Rigg squinted sideways. There was too little light.

"Crothers?"

"That's me," Crothers said. "Far as I can tell, just you and me are left. Manley and Carter didn't make it. Don't know about anybody else."

Rigg forced Crothers to stop, gripping his arm with his free hand, and demanding, "The bird? What happened to the cruise nuke?"

"Dead. I rammed it with a scoop shovel and then stung it with wasps."

"Huh?"

"Never mind, Sarge. You're losin' blood and they're after

us and in a minute you're gonna have to hold your breath while I swim us through the water in this stinkin' pipe, so—"

"Wait, I—"

"Sorry, Sarge," Crothers said, "no time for that."

They had reached the flooded section.

The shouts of angry men echoed behind them.

"Who are they?"

"More of Candor's men. Take a deep one," Crothers said, and before Rigg had time to object, Crothers had plunged them both under water. Rigg's vision was blurring from lack of oxygen by the time Crothers hauled him out the other side.

"Okay," the younger man said, giving them no time to catch their breath, "let's keep movin'. I don't know how good of swimmers they are."

A few dozen yards farther on, Crothers unhooked Rigg's arm and said, "Sit here a minute, Sarge. I've got a surprise to set up for our friends back there."

Crothers flicked on a small flashlight. Rigg watched dully as the teenager pried a crumbling piece of concrete from the wall. He reached in and pulled out three sticks of dynamite strapped together with a battery and timer.

"Where'd that come from?" Rigg asked, his mind clearer now from the swim through the cold water.

"Had a helper. I radioed Jamie Simpson. I told her to bring it in and stash it—even if she had to puke all the way. We borrowed it from a shed we inspected t'other side of town. Jamie, you here anywhere?"

Simpson stepped out from a dark crack in the tunnel and grinned, "Right, here, big boy. Give me the Sarge and you do your thing."

Rigg looked from Crothers to Simpson, "This ain't regulation SIM, Private," Rigg said weakly.

Crothers smiled and nodded. "Sure ain't, Sarge. And be glad of it. But I figured a back-up could never hurt."

He let Simpson steady Rigg as he set a timer and replaced the explosive in the hole in the wall. He and Simpson gathered up Rigg and double-timed onward.

"We got about thirty seconds, Sarge, so hoof it like you mean it," Simpson said.

Rigg did his best to run.

The blast knocked them onto their faces when they were about a hundred yards along and past two broad bends in the big drain pipe.

As he wiped grime from his face, Crothers chuckled, "Quite a wallop, huh? Guess that cooled their hot little heels."

"Hoped it cooked 'em, not cooled 'em," Simpson said, her eyes flashing.

"Figure it'd take Candor's boys at least a minute to decide whether they wanted to dive into that flooded muck. Took me three."

When they emerged from the pipe seaward, they heard the sounds of choppers. One had already descended into the front parking lot of the cannery. Republic of Oregon troops were jumping out and sprinting toward the building. To the northwest, at least five other helicopters were coming in.

Rigg and Crothers were spotted in less than a minute, held while their identification was checked, then taken away for first aid. As he was being led between two medics, Rigg felt the world spin and lost consciousness.

It seemed like only seconds, but when he awoke, he was in a hospital bed. To his left was a window, to his right was another patient, facing away from him.

Rigg painfully pushed himself up to a sitting position.

"Where the — ?" he asked the room, his voice no more than a gravelly mutter.

The man in the next bed slowly turned to face him.

"Hospital in Springfield. You're back home, Sarge," said Corporal Hochman.

"Hey, I thought you'd *bought* it!" Rigg barked, covering his relief. He tried to swing his legs aside, but felt nauseous.

"Easy, buddy," Hochman said. "They say you gave more blood than Dracula sucks in a good week."

"Yeah, guesso," Rigg said woozily, lying back, closing his eyes for a moment. "What's the story? How'd you make it?"

"Played possum and blew the bastard away when he kicked me, that's how."

"What about Coop and Smith and Zach?"

"Coop's okay, but he's gonna lose a leg." He shook his head. "Smith and Zach are gone. Don't exactly know how they got it."

He brightened up. "But hey, Sarge. Guess that little snot-nosed Crothers is the one who stopped the bird!"

"Yeah, I think he did."

"Not just me," Crothers said from the door. Standing next to him was the Oregon secretary of defense.

"How's the blood, bro?" Erik Hochman asked, nodding at his brother Karl.

"Thicker'n water, I guess," the Corporal answered.

"Heard they'd stuck you in this luxury hotel. Thought I'd come in and see how many concubines they let you keep."

"Afraid they went out with women's lib."

It turned out that Karl had already talked to his brother by phone several times. Rigg had been unconscious for a bit over two days.

Everyone shook hands, then Rigg asked, "Crothers what did you mean, not just you? Not you, what?"

The private blushed and said, "Guess I took credit too soon. One of Candor's own special guards blasted the missile in the tail. He did a lot of damage, although I shook a few things loose when I rammed it with the scoop shovel. Then there were my bees, of course."

"That turncoat guard was actually our man inside," the older Hochman explained. "The one whose cover I'm told you were so worried about blowing."

Rigg's face hardened and he said, "There wasn't any other way. We had to go in."

The defense secretary raised his hand and said, "Easy, Sarge. I know. We're glad you did, too. You provided enough distraction so our man could give us a call. I was muckin' it up with two presidents at the time and had to rush out like my mother'd just died."

"Huh? Presidents?"

"You'll get all this later," Hochman said, waving away the subject. "Candor had his men watching each other so closely—even sent 'em to the john in pairs—our boy wasn't able to get word to us until you guys stirred up the anthill. Can't tell you how he did it. Classified. But he had to have a couple minutes away from anyone to pull out some special equipment and make it work. Something about your operation must have given him the time he needed, because it gave us enough. We had Regular units on maneuver not far up the coast. It took about a half-hour to mop up Candor's men and capture the little Hitler himself. After the missile failed, his beer-gutted counter-revolutionaries didn't have a whole lot of fight left in 'em."

"Your man didn't make it, then?"

The elder Hochman looked down for a second and shook his head.

"No," he said. "But he knew it could end that way. We all do."

Rigg paused, then swallowed and asked, "How many of SIM are gone?"

"Your boys?"

Karl Hochman answered, "Those you know about from our own team and six others from teams three, six, and seven. Team Seven saved Coop, by the way. Got there after the missile fizzled, then kept Candor's guard's pinned down 'til the ROC boys could get in."

Rigg's face looked grim.

"Almost ten men," he said. "That's a hefty chunk out of a small outfit."

The defense chief nodded and said, "That it is. But they saved thousands. Don't forget that. You don't get much more on an investment."

"Yeah," Rigg said. It seemed to take a lot of energy to force a small smile. "Yeah, I guess they did at that."

The announcement in the *Beijing Times* was brief. While

playing poker one night, The Shang's aura of immortality was unexpectedly, but conclusively disproven. By means unknown, the boy-god, the old Maoist, and five other top Chinese leaders mysteriously fell dead. Autopsies revealed no cause of the multiple demise. Apparently one moment they were alive, the next, not.

There were rumors of strange noises and an odd, faint, plate-shaped light in the sky near the Emperor's palace that night. But the connection, if any, was too insubstantial to be mentioned in official accounts.

Unofficially, the stunned servants and guards who had discovered the dead also found something else: a flag. It was spread carefully across the poker table to cover the cards and chips and The Shang's dragon symbol. The flag was a simple design with a succinct theme: a coiled rattlesnake, and beneath it the words, "Don't tread on me!"

That was unofficial, of course. Never proven.

Bright afternoon sunlight and a balmy breeze swept the top of the hill. In the far distance, the snow-capped peaks of the Three Sisters glittered like white diamonds. The fir and pine woods of the lower Cascades contrasted starkly, providing a blanket of velvety deep green. Several blue-and-black Stellars jays, looking like executioners with hoods, screeched at a pair of interloping crows, which cawed back. A flock of two-dozen red-breasted robins hopped busily through the grass, intent on their worm hunting, oblivious to their noisy cousins. Brilliant orange California poppies swayed among the gravestones.

Virtually the entire leadership of the Republic of Oregon was gathered for a ceremony commemorating the members of SIM who had died to save the young nation.

President Alf Corcoran was flanked by Secretary of State J.B. Washington, Commerce Secretary Sparky Katz (soon to be Mrs. Corcoran), and Defense Secretary Erik Hochman. While President Sam Washington of the U.S. was unable to attend, in his stead were "Burner Boys Number Two and Three," U.S. Defense Secretary Grieve McDouglas and CIA chief Bill

Brighton. Several state governors made it, among them Duke Majorin of California, Raylee Dixon of Washington, Nevada's Santini Androtti, and Idaho's C. Ilandres—the first to join the Republic of Oregon.

There were hundreds of other people crowded around, too: friends, family, every member of SIM, and many, many strangers who had heard or read of the events and felt they must be there.

Sgt. Larry Rigg, leaning on a cane, stood between Corporal Karl Hochman and newly promoted Corporals Stan Crothers and Jamie Simpson, Robotics Specialists. The latter two stood arm in arm, new gold rings on their hands.

Rigg had asked Ben Colby to cap the ceremony with a short speech. It had been Colby, after all, who had begun what SIM's men had died for.

Colby looked at Rigg. Rigg nodded.

Colby stepped forward to the opposite side of ten open graves—nine for SIM members, one for Corky's spy. Colby rubbed his bald head and solemnly looked over the crowd which now nearly covered the southern and western sides of the little hill. More people were arriving as he looked. He noticed that everyone, from the oldest man to the smallest child, seemed to avoid trampling the wild poppies. He smiled. He liked the unspoken sentiment.

He cleared his throat and his bass voice carried across the countryside.

"Ladies and gentlemen, I won't talk for long. There are certain events which are so profound, that long orations detract from their value. I'm speaking of rare events, events which in the history of mankind are like towering mountains. They stand so tall that they can be seen forever from vast distances."

He paused to scan the crowd.

"Not so long ago, we conceived and saw the birth of a new nation. Not so long after that, these brave men, totally unknown to many of us here, stopped a nefarious attempt to smother an infant in its cradle. To them, we owe more than it is possible to pay. Often that is the case. But there is one thing we can do. We can live up to what we brought to life and what they suffered to protect. We can grasp and hold the new freedoms we have created and nurtured. We can vow to never let them go. We can remember why we did what we did, and why these men made the ultimate investment a human being can make. We can *live*. Let us do so."

He bowed his head quietly for a moment.

"Amens" rippled through the crowd.

Colby looked at Rigg.

Bracing himself on his cane, the head of SIM bent stiffly and took a handful of dirt and threw it into the first grave. He repeated it for the rest of them. He shuffled back to his place, raised his head, turned to face his troops, and shouted, "Attention! Ready—ARMS!"

Almost three-hundred men and women of the Springfield Independent Militia raised their rifles to the sky.

"Fire!" Rigg shouted.

The guns roared in a single, massive shot.

All was silent until a small bird began a tentative chirping nearly a minute later.

For a few more moments, it seemed that no one wanted to move. People stood without speaking, most with tears on their faces.

Then President Corcoran turned and said gruffly, "Okay, people. Let's do what the man said. Let's live this good life in this good land. That's what freedom's for."

He looked down at Sparky Katz and smiled. Impulsively, she reached up and brushed a tear from his eye, then took his hand and squeezed it a moment. The president squeezed her shoulder, nodded, then strode away. She watched him go, a tall, strong, but aging man whose burdens did not look any lighter. Making a nation was one thing. Building one was another. She was glad she'd be able to help him as his First Lady, but right now, he had business to attend, as did she. She wondered how many days of their future would be like that.

Slowly the hundreds of people wandered away, one by one, in pairs, in small groups. Their talk was subdued, respectful, in low voices and whispers.

The cemetery workmen filled the graves and left.

Finally, only the flowers and a warm wind were left to follow the sun into the summer evening.

Chapter 49

"One Year Later"

OREGON, U.S. ABSORB ONE ANOTHER (AP/DOW, Salem, R. of Oregon) — In an historic open air ceremony on the White House lawn today, the presidents of the United States and the Republic of Oregon signed treaties and other documents readmitting Oregon to the Union and simultaneously incorporating the entire United States into the Republic of Oregon.

The ceremony capped year-long, spirited negotiations among state governors, Congress and both the U.S. and Oregon executive branches. The result was essentially a formalization of economic changes which had already occurred in most states, sparked by those in Oregon's rebellion.

According to President Corcoran, the double-nation deal would act as "another check and balance system" in order to "keep freedom wary and sniffin' down the right trail."

According to President Washington, it would be "a new layer of armor against tyranny."

The consensus of political analysts seems to be that the compromise was essentially a face-saving measure. Both presidents denied this view.

Among the two reunified nations' more significant compromises were those pertaining to the armed forces.

First, private militias were relegalized nationwide "in order to assist in the national defense and to act as a check on oppressive tendencies by any future American governments."

Second, command of the regular U.S. armed services, including bases outside Oregon overrun by ROC forces, were to be rotated between the U.S. and the Republic of Oregon. The compromise was designed to prevent either nation from dominating the other, yet maintain forces sufficiently integrated to be able to swiftly deal with foreign threats.

"MINOR" CHINESE PROVINCE SECEDES

(*South China Morning News Wire*, Hong Kong) — Following a secret ballot, the little-known mountain province of Biangzhou announced today that it had seceded from China in order to escape "the heavy hands of the infamous inheritors of The Shang."

A spokesman for the Priests of the Holy Imperial Council in Beijing called the secession "a minor publicity stunt" that could not possibly be taken seriously "or ever affect the integrity of the mighty Chinese Imperium."

Afterword

I'm often asked by readers, "Is all that technological stuff you put in your novels real, or do you just invent it?" Actually, reality is far more fantastic than most people realize—and behind-the-scenes progress is greater than the average Joe Lunchbox or Karla Keyboard realizes. As a long-time professional reporter and columnist, who's specialized in covering national defense issues, I have a wide range of sources on military and scientific matters. I'm careful to provide every device, weapon, or invention with some clear basis in fact. Yes, there's a certain amount of extrapolation involved. After all, when you write slightly into the future, as I do, you must project the reality a bit ahead. But the core of the technology is fact-based.

For instance, take "The Plate," — a mysterious U.S. weapon that I mention first in my novel, *Engels Extension*. In *The Oregon Rebellion*, "The Plate" finally does something and I hint at its propulsion system, electrogravitics or just "gravitics." Electrogravitics is a real concept that, in lay language, loosely involves the manipulation of gravity. The U.S. has had secret experimental projects devoted to the field, and related physics, for half a century. I would not be surprised to discover if one day Uncle Sam admits that many reports of UFOs were actually experimental electrogravitics vehicles. Even the prestigious *Jane's Defense Review* weekly has covered the subject. As Dave Barry would say, "I'm not making this up!" This is only one example.

Take another. "The Wire"—the pleasure-inducing device to which millions are addicted in both *Engels Extension* and

Project BTB —has experimental counterparts in reality. Several laboratories, public and private, have worked on devices that create various mental states through magnetic induction. (One experiment consistently produces false memories of UFO abductions, complete with slanty-eyed little gray men!)

Then there are the "Bees" in *The Oregon Rebellion*. For many years, the U.S. military has had black projects aimed at building miniature, insect-like flying machines. Already, there are working models as small as large butterflies. The Pentagon envisions such machines as tiny spy planes, but also as micro sabotage robots.

And so it goes. When you read about technology in my novels, you're reading about things that are likely to show up in your morning newspaper or Internet news service. Maybe not tomorrow or next week. But soon.

About the Author

E.G. Ross lives in Western Oregon. A military, foreign affairs, and economics writer and editor for over three decades, Ross is currently editor of the worldwide Internet daily, *www.ObjectiveAmerican.com*. He produces the monthly print newsletter, *The Objective American* and is CEO of Enlightenment Enterprises, Inc. which provides publishing and telecommunications services. Ross also serves as chief writer for Understanding Defense Research, a think tank. In his spare time, he draws political cartoons and helps run a miniature-horse ranch.